Stars Awoken

An Apocalyptic LitRPG
Book 7 of the System Apocalypse

By

Tao Wong

Copyright

This is a work of fiction. Names, characters, businesses, places, events and incidents are either the products of the author's imagination or used in a fictitious manner. Any resemblance to actual persons, living or dead, or actual events is purely coincidental.

This book is licensed for your personal enjoyment only. This book may not be re-sold or given away to other people. If you would like to share this book with another person, please purchase an additional copy for each recipient. If you're reading this book and did not purchase it, or it was not purchased for your use only, then please return to your favorite book retailer and purchase your own copy. Thank you for respecting the hard work of this author.

Books in The System Apocalypse series

Main Storyline

Life in the North

Redeemer of the Dead

The Cost of Survival

Cities in Chains

Coast on Fire

World Unbound

Stars Awoken

Rebel Star

Stars Asunder

Anthologies

System Apocalypse Short Story Anthology Volume 1

Comic Series

The System Apocalypse (On-going)

Contents

What Has Gone Before

When the System arrived on Earth, it brought monsters, aliens, and glowing blue boxes that altered the reality of humanity. Gifted with Classes that must be Leveled and Skills that provide reality-altering powers, humanity struggled to survive when modern electronics failed under the flood of Mana. In a year, over ninety percent of humanity fell, leaving the remnants to pick up their lives.

John Lee is one such survivor, starting from the depths of the Yukon and traveling south to aid humanity in its struggle to stay free of their Galactic overlords. As a settlement owner in British Columbia, he joined forces with the remnant military forces of the United States on the West Coast and proceeded to wage a war to free the Canadian prairies and the US West Coast. Forced to take his Master Class Quest by the Erethran Honor Guard and the Erethran Champion, John returned from the Forbidden Zone planet he was portaled to with new powers and to a changed Earth.

Working together with his friends, many whom had changed and gotten on with their lives in the four years he had been exiled, John aided Earth in establishing a planetary government. Forced to fight both the Movanna and the Fist, John and his friends are betrayed by other humans at the very end. Even betrayed, Earth has managed to form the very first planetary government based on a Dungeon World. Now, John travels to Irvina with the Earth ambassador, in search of answers of what the System really is. And what, if any, place an ex-computer programmer turned warrior has in it.

Chapter 1

Watching the stars flash by on the observation deck is a strange experience. In hyperspace, they stop being a single point of light but instead become streaks that appear and disappear as we cross unimaginable distances in the blink of an eye. The journey to Praxis is about a week in, but I still haven't gotten enough of the sight. It reminds me, again and again, how small I am and how unimaginably vast the universe is.

Not that it's my first time out of Earth's solar system, but being Portaled directly across thousands of light years isn't the same thing at all. There's no sense of journey that way, no sense of growing wonder. This trip feels more real. More… momentous.

"John?"

Mikito's voice brings my head up to stare at the little Japanese woman. She has cut her hair again, turning it into a short bob. She's dressed in what I call adventurer chic—dark, armored jumpsuit with holstered beam pistol and knife on her hips made from monster parts and nano-modified thread. Her usual weapon, the naginata Hitoshi, is stored away at the request of the captain. Something about too-sharp weapons in his fragile ship.

"You're back. You win?" I say, raising an eyebrow as I lean up against the standing table.

Ever since Mikito found out that there's a virtual, holographic projector of the fighting arenas onboard, she's spent a good portion of the trip there. I tried it once, but the disparity of having your virtual life points deducted for blows you never felt was too much for me. Even if my life is like a game in some ways, playing a game in the game of my life is a little too meta for me.

"I did."

"Great." I acknowledge the notification that arrives a moment later that informs me my hundred-Credit bet on Mikito has paid out. A sizeable betting pool revolves around the virtual games. And a good bet is a good bet.

"John Lee and Mikito Sato." The cultured voice cuts off any further conversation as both of us turn. In front of us is a grizzled older man, curly hair speckled with grey and shorn tight against his scalp, highlighting his dark umber black-brown skin. The man wears a multi-pocketed vest and cargo pants while offering us a friendly smile. The British accent is familiar, though I struggle to place it. "And of course, the Spirit Ali."

Purely by instinct, I eye the rest of the viewing room. Set against an outer hull, the glass—or whatever clear material they use to create the viewing walls—provides an amazing view. A part of me wonders if it's even clear. They might just be very good screens reflecting what is outside. If so, it's an amazing illusion.

The illusion is so good that this and the other three viewing rooms on the observation deck are filled with the various Galactic guests of the merchant cruiser we are shipping with. Even if the merchant ship is mostly meant for cargo, it's large enough to carry slightly over two hundred passengers in its various cabins without impacting its main task. Though, I'm led to understand, some of the less-expensive cabins are no better than jail cells. Around us, the Galactics are a mixture of the exotic, the bizarre, and the familiar. Truinnar mix with Yerrick, Dwarves stand elbow to elbow with Akkorokamui squid humanoids in full-body water suits while Lilitu—avian-humanoids with bird legs—talk to Pooskeens. Galactic civilization at its finest.

Ali looks up from where he floats in his pint-size form at my shoulder and does a double-take. He flicks his hand slightly, dismissing System screens that no one else can see, as he stares at our new guest. "Oh wow. It's you! I mean, I knew you were onboard. But whoa!"

"You know him?" I say with a frown, tilting my head toward the starstruck Spirit.

"You don't?" Mikito says, shaking her head. She puts her hand out to shake the stranger's. "Good to see you, Harry."

Well, I got that part. I stare at the notification information above Harry then watch as Ali updates it further for my use. Oh. Oh…

Harry Prince, the Unfiltered Eye (War Correspondent Level 39)
HP: 520/520
MP: 1780/1780
Conditions: Reporter's Luck, Nose for Trouble, Just a Bystander

"Oh! You," I say, realizing who he is when I see the full details of his Status. I might be somewhat ignorant about those who made a name for themselves during my absence, but Harry is a special case. For one thing, I recall seeing him at various battle sites in the last year. Curious that I didn't remember him being at those sites till now.

"That'd be his Skill, boy-o." Ali sends to me telepathically, reading the slight changes in my facial expression with the ease of a long-time companion.

I swear, we're like an old couple sometimes, picking up on the unsaid. Except, you know, without the sex. Wait. Old people have sex, right? Actually, never mind. I'm glad for the distraction as Ali populates Harry's Skill information for me.

Skill: Just a Bystander
A rare non-Combat Skill that will allow non-combat personnel and observers to traverse through battlefields and other combat regions with greater safety. This Skill hides the User from casual observation as well as reduces the effect of indiscriminate attacks.

Effect: User sees a +500% increase in Stealth, Disguise, and Camouflage skill levels while this Skill is active. Untargeted attacks and spells have a 50% reduction in effect on User. Additionally, memory and area-of-effect mental manipulation Skills and spells must be specifically targeted at User. Lastly, memories of User will be obscured until active recollection or trigger event occurs.

"Yes, me," Harry says with a smile. "I was hoping to speak with you both."

"Why?" I ask suspiciously. If he had a tape recorder, I'd be giving it the stink-eye, but I'm willing to bet Harry's got an equivalent Skill for that. Who needs physical toys when the System works just as well? If not better.

"It seems like the rumors are true," Harry says, keeping that reassuring smile on his face. "But you need not worry. I'm not looking to make you the target of my reports. At least, not directly."

"Then what do you want?" I ask while Mikito stays silent, sipping on her newly delivered orange slushy cocktail, and watches the interplay.

"You know I'm part of the diplomatic press corp, right? Well, technically. But the fact is, there're a half-dozen reporters setting up to follow the ambassador around, covering all the politics," Harry said. "But the minutiae of politics, that's never been my thing."

"Blood and guts is yours. And you figure following Mikito and me will get you that," I say, my lips tightening.

"Some respect there, John! Harry Prince is more than a blood-and-guts reporter! He's an award-winning reporter who did amazing exposés about your pre-System world. The Unfiltered Eye has shot some of the best works for Earth since the System arrived. He's even been considered for an Ummi," Ali interrupts, waving. "An Ummi!"

"What exactly is an Ummi?" I say.

"Just a Galactic award," Harry says, waving to dismiss the topic. "I won't say the fact that you and Ms. Sato are known loci of violence is a detraction from your attractiveness, but I'm looking more to report on areas outside of the diplomatic scene. As your stated intentions are to break from the team immediately upon arrival…"

"You figure you'll shelter under our kind arms." I shake my head. "No thanks."

"Now, there's no need to be hasty. While I'm not a Combat Classer, I do have a number of—"

"No, thank you. We're not a tour group. In fact, you can—"

The remainder of my sentence gets interrupted by the ship's klaxon. Everything flashes purple while the discordant whine interrupts conversations everywhere. A moment later, we get a System notification from the ship's captain.

Ship-wide Alert!

We have encountered a pirate fleet. As per Galactic conventions, we are matching speeds with said pirates. All non-insured passengers, this is your prescribed warning.

"What? They're matching speeds with the pirates?" I frown in confusion. Still, it doesn't stop me from standing and dressing myself for trouble. Armored jumpsuit, protective vest, weapons belt, it all goes on, drawn from the System inventory.

"Galactic convention. Since pirates can buy ship routes from the System, it's hard to avoid them. Rather than actually fight the pirates, merchant ships take out insurance for such incidents. When the pirates dock, the System registers the fact that they've 'pirated' the ship and said insurance companies pay out the Credits. Makes it nice and easy for everyone," Ali says.

"*Honto baka dane!*" Mikito swears, and I can't help but agree. It really is idiotic.

"What about this part about uninsured passengers?" Katherine, my ex-secretary and now the designated representative for Earth, speaks up the moment she nears our table.

Trailing behind her is Peter Steele, the Planetary Diplomat, who is busy muttering over his commlink. At a guess, he's herding everyone together. The man is still a full tie and suit ensemble in space while waving his hands around as he harangues whoever is on the line.

"Well, that's the problem," Harry says, his eyes unfocused. "From what I can see, uninsured passengers include all of us from Earth."

"Why didn't we get insurance?" Mikito says with a frown.

Katherine glares at the little Japanese lady before she admits through gritted teeth, "I didn't realize it was needed."

"Wouldn't matter much anyway. Some of our members have quite a high bounty on them," Harry adds, looking at me before switching his gaze to Mikito.

"Damn."

That, sadly, is not news. Ali informed us of that unfortunate fact a while ago. In truth, all of us carry bounties—Katherine and Peter for their positions, and Mikito and myself for the trouble we caused on Earth. Of course, Katherine's and Peter's aren't high enough to send anyone with sense after them, especially considering Peter has his cheat Skill, Diplomatic Immunity. On the other hand, Mikito and I have done enough damage to enough people that our bounties are significant enough that Ali felt the need to warn us of potential problems.

Katherine frowns. "What should we do? Will they take us as hostages?"

"Well, normally they'd either do that or just have you transfer all your belongings and Credits to them," Ali says. "Or, you know, take you guys as slaves. But boy-o and Mikito make things a little more complicated."

"Because of our bounty sizes?" I say.

"That too. But mostly because I don't think you're going to pay them off," Ali says.

I chuckle ruefully as I finish buckling my belt. The damn Spirit knows me too well. Still leaves the question of what we should be doing. "We allowed to fight in the ship?"

"Allowed?" Katherine's jaw drops. "When do you ever ask?"

"We're not barbarians," I say with a sniff.

"Boy-o's worried he's going to have to pay for damages. And while the captain and pilot would prefer you didn't, they are covered under insurance," Ali says.

"Great." I grin, cracking my neck. "I've been missing a workout."

"Yeah, about that…" Harry says, his eyes refocusing on me for a time. "Understand that if I add anything more, my Shop Skill will stop working."

"You want protection."

"Yes."

"Done."

Harry nods. "There are three Master and twenty-one Advanced Classes in the pirate ship. They're armed and ready to deal with significant resistance on boarding."

"Three Master Classes! Thousand hells," I curse. "What are they doing out here?"

"Making money cheaply," Ali says. "Payouts from the System and insurance companies are based off an intricate calculation of force, Pilot Skills, and ship firepower. The higher the weight on the pirates' side, the higher the payout percentage. In this case, they're shooting for a full payout."

One of the strange aspects of interstellar travel that I'd learned was the way Skills made a difference. While the spaceships themselves could fly through space, hyperspace travel was a creation of the System—at least the way we did it. As such, the Skills of a Pilot made a huge difference, as did the captain's secondary support Skills. I'd even heard of one Legendary Pilot who disdained the concept of normal spaceships and flew around a fully habitable planet.

"Levels?" I finally say. If they're Level 1s or close to it…

"Eight, fourteen, and twenty-three."

"Damn. And how do you know all this?" I look at Ali. "And how is it you don't?"

"I'm buying the information from the Shop at a discounted rate," Harry says, smiling thinly. "One of my Skills—Background Research—gives me access to information for stories I might write. Another, War Correspondence, allows me to access certain aspects of the Shop anywhere. It lets me file my reports and buy information as needed."

"Nice," I say.

Ali sniffs at me, indicating he's affronted by my questioning of his ability. But I don't have time to deal with the Spirit, as the others are looking to me for a plan. Which, frankly, is worrying in many ways but something I've gotten used to. That hesitant web developer is gone, burned away in the fires of the apocalypse.

"All right. I'm assuming we don't have to worry about them destroying the ship?"

When Harry and Ali nod, I rub my chin. That's good. Still, my brain keeps stalling on the fact that three Masters are involved. There's really no way for me to win a fight against three Masters. Then again, I cast my memory back to the science fiction books and movies I've seen, and my eyes open wide.

"You thought of something, John?" Mikito says, perking up.

"I have. Maybe. Depends on a few things, but we're going to need help. Katherine, Peter, can you find out how many of the other passengers are uninsured and willing to fight?"

Katherine steps back as her eyes glaze over, her mouth moving as she silently contacts the passengers she's spoken to. Peter deals with the passengers on the observation deck, moving from group to group. His bodyguard trails after him.

"Now, Ali, Harry. Tell me, in detail, how pirate raids work. Step by step, as close as you can get it."

Chapter 2

Interstellar combat, if you disregard cheat scenario abilities like Star Trek teleporters, have to follow certain rules. Firstly, you've got to catch your prey. That's relatively easy to do when the System will give you details at the wave of a hand and the passing of a few Credits. Secondly, if you're actually looking to board and take the ships or its passengers, you need to get your people over. That requires you to either connect your big, lumbering ship to another big, lumbering ship or, and this is definitely the preferred method, send over a smaller, more disposable shuttle. Or shuttles, I guess.

That, of course, makes ambushing them as they arrive the go-to method. The shuttle bays are the obvious chokepoint. Of course, if I know it's an obvious chokepoint, the Galactics do too. There's no way we're going to out-maneuver these old hands if we play it safe. Even if they normally don't have to deal with foolhardy foes, I've got to contend with a level of institutional knowledge. All that means is that we need to get creative.

Luckily, the first rule about space combat plays into our hands here. Both ships need to drop out of hyperspace, slow down till the pair matches velocities, then the shuttles have to make their way over. To ensure the merchant ship we're on doesn't randomly open fire and destroy their original ship, the pirates are keeping a good distance from us, forcing the shuttle to make its way across the expanse on its underpowered engines.

"Katherine. We good?" I speak aloud so everyone present can listen in. Crammed as we are in this room, there's not much to divert people. Better for the volunteers to get some idea of what's happening than stew in their own thoughts.

"I'm at the bridge with the captain and Pilot," Katherine says. "They've reluctantly agreed to give me access to their sensors. Feed on the way."

"*Got it!*" Ali sends to me mentally.

A moment later, a new notification screen appears. This notification screen is set to public, allowing my fellow uninsured a three-dimensional view of space around the merchant ship. The merchant ship is a big, blocky hexagon with a cone tip, rather than the sleek vehicle we've come to expect from aerodynamic planes. Galactic technology has become so trusted, there's no need for windows anymore—beyond leisure requirements—so the bridge is situated in the center of the cone itself. The main thrusters are at the back of the ship, with smaller maneuvering thrusters dotted throughout the ship. While the ship can, and does, fly without the aid of the Pilot, his abilities make everything so much faster and more efficient.

In the distance, the pirate's ship is menacing, a more "traditional" and sleek vessel that has more room for thrusters and shielding than our blocky merchant cruiser. The front of the pirate ship contains the mounts for their beam weaponry as well as extra armoring and shielding. Not that our merchant vessel stands a chance in a stand-up fight. A fast-moving blip crosses the distance between us.

"So you're certain they won't blow up the ship if they lose a lot of their men?" I mutter to Harry as Ali focuses on adding more data to the screen.

"Likely not. Pirates exist on a calculus of cost and nuisance. They're a nuisance to interstellar trading, but so long as they aren't too costly, no one will throw out a large Quest to rid the galaxy of them. Destroying interstellar ships automatically puts them in the 'too costly to live' column, and the Merchants Alliance will put up a Quest," Harry reassures me softly. "It's a fascinating facet of Galactic society. The articles on this are really interesting reading. I bet that given time, crime on Earth will look very much like this."

"What, you mean it doesn't already?" I say with a snort. "Pretty sure some of the gangs in the USA, the Yakuza, and a bunch of local warlords in the Middle East have figured that one out already."

"True," Harry says, his fingers wiggling as if he's typing on an unseen keyboard. "I'll have to add that to the article. I wonder if there's a Class that could calculate exactly how much—"

With a slight roll of my eyes, I shift my gaze to the giant notification screen. Already I see lights popping up all over our now-wireframe ship as Ali adds known positions for all our people. Katherine, Peter, and a quarter of our fighting personnel are in the bridge, there to protect and safeguard the ambassador.

As I said, space fights like this have certain rules, if you exclude teleportation. Thankfully, most Class Skills that allow teleportation of some form, like my Blink Step or Portal ability, also have limitations. Most of which come down to knowing where you are teleporting to. There are, as I understand it, rare Skills and spells that let you teleport or Portal into unseen, unknown locations, but they come with a significant Mana cost and even larger risks. Since most merchant ships have anti-scrying wards built into them, it's hard to get a good look at where you're teleporting to. Add in the illusionists and other Classes whose entire grab bags include tricking people, and teleporting becomes a lot trickier. Teleporting into solid objects is generally fatal—to the teleportee, the teleporter, and everyone nearby. Still, if there's a time and place for a Skill like that, pirating other ships in space seems to fit the bill. Which is why Katherine and Peter have guards.

"We have any updates on the shuttle?" I say, eyeing the rapidly approaching dot.

"Nothing yet," Katherine says. "The sensors on this ship are less than stellar."

"Okay," I say.

I turn to look at Harry, who shakes his head. He isn't reading my mind of course. It's just that I've asked him before if he can purchase information about the shuttle occupants from the Shop. Unfortunately, his Skill has certain limitations—and details like that isn't considered "background" knowledge. It doesn't help that he's directly involved now, putting further limits on his Skills.

"Can we go over the plan again?" a hesitant voice, filled with a lot of sibilant hisses, asks. The speaker is speaking in Galactic, a language whose base is draconic but modified for humanoid voices and mixed with the various languages of the elder races. Unsurprisingly, every single human downloaded that language from the Shop before we left.

The volunteers are a mixed bunch, a large percentage of them coming from the human guards that are part of the diplomatic team. The rest are a mixture of Adventurers who were too poor or too stubborn to pay for proper insurance, individuals looking for some mayhem, and a few merchant guards. The actual merchants themselves are, of course, covered. The Adventurers are a wide range of races—everything from your standard fantasy fare to a half-cyborg creature that rolls around on wheels, a floating blob of green jello with tentacles, and something that looks like a cross between a cockroach and a slug.

"Simple enough. If there's only one Master Class in that shuttle, we hit them hard and roll them over. That's unlikely to happen. More likely there's at least two of them in there, potentially all three. In that case, we're going to beat them in detail." When the various human and non-human Adventurers stare at me, I shrug. "More details to arrive when we get more information. But Mikito has you split into various teams. When the Portal opens, you just need to go through on your turn and blast anything that isn't on our side."

There are a lot of uncomfortable looks at my words, but considering this entire group is a slapdash affair, more complicated plans are as likely to cause mayhem as anything. The American military have a saying—Keep It Simple Stupid (KISS), and frankly, my experience has been that that works. Then again, I'm no Rommel. I've just picked up a few things in my time.

"Remember what your roles are in your teams and concentrate on that. You've got your team leaders. They'll highlight your targets. Team leaders should know who to take out first, but Master Classes need to be contained while you take down the small fry," I say. "Beyond that, I'll be focusing on the Masters as much as possible, along with Mikito."

The bodyguards look relieved, the aliens a little more inscrutable. But I know, from what Peter said, the only reason they're agreeing to this is because I'm here. Otherwise, even serfdom is generally better than death.

"John, we have twenty-three and a half life-signs on the shuttle," Katherine's voice cuts in before I can dig the hole any deeper.

"A half?"

"Hold on. I'm getting clarification. Yes, Peter? Draugr? That's… well, okay." Katherine pauses before she speaks again. "John? Can you ask Ali?"

"Ali?"

"You need me now?" Ali says, shooting a look at Harry before smirking. But he doesn't hesitate long. "Draugr. Remember the little Richard problem we had? Yeah well, Draugr are another damn attempt to get around death." Behind the Spirit, a number of the Galactic Adventurers nod and twitch, confirming the Spirit's words. "They have a unique Class that makes them impervious to pain, have a visible level of regeneration, resistances against physical and magical attacks, and close combat Mana striking abilities."

"Sounds like great soldiers." Harry's lips compress as his eyes focus on a spot a few feet from his face.

"Sure, if you like your soldiers psychopathic, prone to violent outbursts, and cannibalistic," Ali says.

"Anything else we can get from the sensors?" I question Katherine.

You would think that shipboard sensors wouldn't be able to gather data like Classes and you'd be right—if we were talking normal science. But there's nothing normal about physics since the System came into play, especially not when Class Skills are in the equation. And the merchant ship, while not having the specialized roles of Sensor Technicians and their ilk like a warship might have, does have a captain and a helmsmen.

"One second." A tense moment later—one that has the shuttle slide within a few inches of our ship on the screen—and Katherine's speaking. "They're going for docking bay four. And we have confirmation that all three Master Classes are on board. One is showing extremely high Mana density in their body. The other two are registering average and low levels."

"Mage of some form then. And fighters," I say. "Thanks. Let me know if there's anything else."

"Of course," Katherine says. "Out."

I fall silent, staring at the shuttle as it approaches and merges with our ship. There's no sensation, no thunk or shift in the ship as the shuttle connects with the docking bay. The only real change is that Ali throws up a new screen, one showing the inside of the docking bay. Surprisingly, rather than the door cycling open like I'd expect, we get something coming right through the still-closed door. A ghostly crawling octopod exits the docking bay doors and surveys the surroundings. In moments, the ghost octopod is joined by another pair. The trio of ghosts split up and head down different exits.

"Sensor ghosts," Ali explains. "They're controlled by one of the Advanced Classes in there. Most of their kind have little in combat ability, but they're rather hard to deal with without using magic. Mana-based attacks are the most effective."

The docking bay doors finally cycle apart, both inner and outer hatches sliding open with a hiss that only happens in my head. While Force Shields are used as secondary and emergency stops, they're unreliable under high-stress situations. Better to rely on actual, high-tension metal alloys for everyday use.

The pirates pour out of the docking bay in waves, a quartet moving forward to set up mobile portable force shields as a reinforced strongpoint. Behind them, five more take station, watching over the room with beam rifles, wands, and bare hands. When they are certain things are clear, the remainder of the pirates swagger out. Immediately, Ali populates their Status information for everyone, even adding helpful little bracketed letters to indicate the Class stages. After all, with the sheer variety of Galactic Classes, it's impossible for me to know all of their relative stages at a glance.

My eyes are drawn to the trio that come out near the front, idly strolling forward with an air of supreme confidence. I don't even need the little M after their Classes to know they're the Master Classes. The sizes of their health and Mana bars are sufficient. The first to catch my eye is a round, tubby, furred creature with stubby hands and legs and beady little eyes.

Muk Muk, Shaper of Kumak, Winner of the Three hundredth and eight Suar, … (Woven Shapeshifter Level 14) (M)
HP: 4290/4290
MP: 1030/1030
Conditions: Altered Shape, Elastic Skin, Muscular Reconstruction

"He's a shapeshifter and he chose to look like that?" I say, shaking my head.

A quick review of the information Ali populates gives me a rough idea of what I'm dealing with. Melee fighter with the ability to shift forms to play tank or damage dealer, depending on the situation. His Skills buff either form, though unlike a specialized tank or damage dealer, he's not as good.

"He might be specialized for space combat, boy-o," Ali says. "So lots more tanking and damage dealing ability and fewer forms, especially big ass, pants-wetting ones."

"Right," I say, shifting my gaze to the next form and nearly missing him.

Klimaras, (Mercenary Commando Level 8) (M)

HP: 3100/3100

MP: 2783/3090

Conditions: Blind Spot, Sense Weakness, Shadow Friend, Force Shield

Stealth damage dealer. Pretty much an assassin rogue. The fact that the humanoid carries a series of knobbly rods is interesting. Also, even standing still, Klimaras seems to fade into the background, which speaks of some impressive stealth skills. And probably a few Skills thrown in on top of that. Keeping track of him will be important. Either block his first attack or die kind of thing.

The last figure is the most interesting. At first, I mistake the robotic body it manipulates—a bulbous monstrosity with a pair of rotating guns and liquid metal stalks for feet and arms—as the creature. But on closer inspection, I see a hand-sized humanoid sitting inside a clear-glass cockpit that bobs around inside a volume of gel, moving his hands in time to the movement of the robot. Pink hair, a pair of hands, and a single fin make up the Master Classer in the robot.

Yidma, Overgeared (Artifact Tinkerer Level 23) (M)

HP: 430/430

MP: 2893/3820

Conditions: Shielded, Armed and Armored, Artifact Connection * 7

"What's it doing?" I frown, staring as the robot works on setting up something on the floor.

The pirates don't look to be in any particular hurry, standing around and eyeing the doors leading to the docking bay while their sensor ghosts scout out the surroundings.

"Teleportation pad. Probably keyed to artifacts on the boarding team." This voice is squeaky and low.

I look sideways to stare at the Pooskeen Adventurer who answered me. I almost glare at him before I rein in my irritation. Just because his race tried to kill me doesn't mean he's going to. Or at least, I try to tell myself that.

"Tinkerers are more support Classes, replicating Spells and Skills via their gear," the Pooskeen says.

I offer my nod of thanks while turning my attention to the last pirate of interest.

Draugr U-129, Doom of the Waza, Cannibal (Advanced Draugr Level 18) (A)

HP: 3110/3110

MP: 150/150

Conditions: Draugr, Envenomed Claws, Paralyzing Bite, Undead Resistance

"Pretty damn low Mana," I say.

"The Draugr's condition uses a lot of Mana, reducing their total Mana Pool. It also affects their regeneration significantly," Ali says.

"Tough looking son of a bitch," Harry says, staring at the Draugr.

The creature is crouched, chewing on a piece of meat whose origin I don't want to consider. The creature is humanoid, with clawed fingers that are disproportionately long, hips that sit way too high on the body, and a grey-scaled, flaking body. The Draugr has no armor, clothing, or weapons, though the fanged teeth and claws are weapon enough.

After that, I let my eyes dance over the rest of the pirate crew, taking in details. A lot of individuals with beam weaponry, though almost all of them carry melee weapons of one form or another. Very few dedicated spellcasters, and of those, most are healers. A quick explanation by Ali reminds me to watch my own spells. No one wants to be shot out into space because some idiot spellcaster forgot to tone down his fireball.

With the information turning over in my mind, I settle on a plan as the nervous lizard-creature speaks up again. "Are we going to attack them? What are we going to do?"

"We're going to wait. Mostly," I say. "Katherine, send out team four and two. Put yourself on an intercept course with those sensor ghosts. I want them destroyed."

"Roger."

"Got it, John."

I watch as the teams head out, the dots on the wireframe shifting as Ali does his best to keep track of the sensor ghosts and our people. Thankfully, my Level increases have pushed up the little Spirit's ability to wield a much greater influence on the System. And, when things become necessary, he can enlarge his body and materialize to kick some ass. Surprisingly, the Spirit has gone back to staying in his smaller form for the most part, seeming to prefer being tiny, semi-translucent, and invisible to most.

"They're splitting up." Mikito says, bringing my attention back to the docking bay screen.

As she said, the three Master Classes are splitting up. Two groups leave, led by one Master Class each, in the direction of the cockpit and engines. The Tinkerer stays behind, working diligently to set up more fortifications and defenses, including a pair of large turrets.

Tinkerer-Modified Limi Flame Throwers

They're modified flame throwers, boy-o, supported as much by the Tinkerer's Skills as they are by actual working technology. Damage is going to be extremely high, so try not to get burnt.

Damage: ??/??

Rate of Fire: ??/??

Capacity: ??/??

Not particularly helpful, but it's clear that the longer the Tinkerer has to work, the more of his toys he'll be able to build. Still, I'm forced to wait till the pirate teams are a decent distance from each other. One advantage we have is that the merchant ship is huge.

"Team four here. Sensor ghost down."

"Good," I say, eyeing the suddenly fast-moving group nearest them. "Retreat to hold 4 − 3."

"Roger." Our team's dot moves fast. Which is good. Except…

"Oy, idiots. The other way," Ali speaks up before I do. He takes over giving them directions while muffled curses from the group erupt over the joint channel.

I ignore it all, eyeing the other sensor ghosts, who have slowed down and are darting through walls at a more regular pace. Unfortunately, our attacks mean that the pirate teams have sped up.

"Team two. Pull back." Their acknowledgement is ignored as I turn to the rest of the volunteers around me. "Get ready. We're going in."

I meet Mikito's eyes, knowing that the Samurai knows what I want. She gives me a half smile, her naginata in hand as she readies herself to dart through the Portal, casting Haste and other buffing spells on herself. All around us is the dim glow of various beneficial spells layering on the group, healing, mana, and defensive spells popping up one after the other. I take the time to layer my own Soul Shield on myself and Mikito before adding a third on Harry.

"Ready," Mikito says.

Activating the Class Skill takes a few seconds of concentration. The moment the pitch-black Portal opens, Mikito darts through. The other end of the Portal opens up right in front of the docking bay doors. It gives Mikito a fraction of a second of surprise—more than enough time for the Samurai to attack. Rather than going for any single individual, she darts forward, intent on destroying their teleportation portal.

The rest of the teams jump through, one after the other, firing weapons, casting single-target spells, and activating Skills in a rush of destruction. One team swerves left, the other right, focusing their fire on the flame throwers that have turned around. Unfortunately, hidden shielding keeps them in working order, the spells, bullets, and beams splashing harmlessly against them.

"Oooh, rats coming through the Portal. How annoying…" the Tinkerer says.

Even as the Tinkerer turns toward the teleportation portal, Mikito's Charge smashes apart the defensive shielding around it, tearing apart the contraption. As her naginata buries itself in the sensitive machinery, Hitoshi glows, Mana flooding the artifact.

"My pad! Damn you. That took months to build. How did you break the shielding? No. I'll just have to take that weapon of yours. I can see it's an artifact, oh yes." The beam weapons on Yidma's robotic form fires even while its legs patter over to the side, where new liquid-metal tendrils extend, patching together new machine parts that appear from its inventory.

"Move, people," I snarl at the teams bunched up around the Portal.

I've kept the size of the Portal big enough for two people to go through at a time so that stray attacks from the other side don't come bouncing back, but it also creates a bit of a chokepoint. Especially when the Adventurers and bodyguards hesitate about jumping through.

Heat washes through as the flame throwers kick in, burning a few unlucky, unshielded Adventurers. The teams on the other side are doing their best to take down the shields, but they're hampered by the dozens of tiny drones the Tinkerer is throwing out and still building. I watch as the health of one slick-furred creature drops as it's lit up in yellow and green flames. Hastily cast Healing spells extend its agony as the weapons chew through him.

"Boy-o, those shields are reforming based off his Mana. It's a Class Skill," Ali says. *"You're going to have to hit hard enough to pierce the active regeneration or take him out."*

Frack it.

"Move!" I tear past the group, in a couple of cases literally tossing my allies aside as I push forward. A moment's concentration and the Portal slides open wider, allowing me to dive straight into the inferno. Already, I see the integrity of my Soul Shield drop as the damage ticks up. "Portal closing. Wait for orders!"

That's about all the warning I have time to give as both pairs of flame throwers, a newly constructed beam cannon, and something that shoots metallic spikes focus fire on me. I swear mentally, wondering why I didn't just charge in myself first.

My Soul Shield shatters under the onslaught, flames washing over my body even as the first spike impales my raised left arm. I cut another aside as the beam scorches my side, then I see my target. Blink Step takes me right above him, my favorite position to unleash a multi-bladed Blade Strike. Each arc of solidified force and Mana-edged strikes cut toward Yidma, only to be stopped inches away by a solidified Mana Shield.

Yidma, Overgeared (Artifact Tinkerer Level 23) (M)

HP: 430/430

MP: 1278/3820

*Conditions: Shielded, Armed and Armored, Artifact Connection * 7*

Shield Integrity: 874/2037

"Oh, another Master Class. No wonder the rats have some guts," the Tinkerer says.

I land, my sword bouncing off its shield. The replica blades from Thousand Blades miss as the robot scurries backward. In his place, he drops a pair of four-legged drones with hammers for hands that swing at my knees. A portion of my mind splits, focusing on increasing both my Strength and Agility to root me in this reality more strongly. The action makes me the immovable object the drones pound on, throwing them off-balance. It's a fraction of a second, but that's more than enough for me to cut them apart with my conjured Soulbound sword.

"Boy-o, you're going to get incoming in about six minutes. Draugr is coming back, hell-bent on having a good tasting, and I've lost track of the Commando," Ali reports in.

"Other Master Classer?"

"Still on his way to the engine room."

"ETA?" I'm cutting through the swarm of drones that the Tinkerer keeps creating or pulling from the other Adventurers. He's entirely focused on me, which is great, except for the fact that I can't get to him.

"Three minutes. He's cutting through the doors like crazy."

Snarling, I throw up a Soul Shield and charge forward, putting everything I have into the direct attack. I throw on Vanguard of the Apocalypse and Thousand Steps, giving me a slight boost in speed and strength. The drones crash and spin off my Soul Shield, monofilament blades and Mana-charged beams failing to penetrate.

Then I'm at the damn Tinkerer and slamming into his shield with my sword. A second later, the remainder of the trailing swords from my Thousand Blades Skill smash into the shield, and together, we overload the Tinkerer's ability to stop the attack. Up close and personal, I grab hold of the bulbous body, charging an Enhanced Lightning Strike in that same hand even as I lift. A moment later, I've interposed the Tinkerer between his drones and me. Then I release the built-up charge of lightning in my hand.

Funny thing. Electricity set free in a metallic structure has a tendency to ground itself—fast. Even with a part of me guiding the flow of electricity using my Elemental Affinity, the vast majority of it floods right through the Tinkerer's robot's metallic legs into the floor, rather than jumping to the drones. And being the closest meatbag, I'm eating a ton of free electrons. It creates a feedback that has me clenching my teeth so hard they could shatter and causes smoke to peel off my skin. If I could scream, I would.

Artifact Tinkerer Slain

+249,381 Experience Gained

The experience notification flashes right in front of my eyes, along with a loud chime, clear enough that it cuts through the pain. I stop the channeling and sag to my feet, groaning as I shudder from the pain. Damn Tinkerer must have had a billion and one resistances in that bot to have survived so long. As it stands, my own health is down by nearly seven hundred points, never mind the rest of the damage I've taken from the Tinkerer's other toys.

John Lee (Level 23 Erethran Paladin)

HP: 2238/3470

MP: 1873/3220

"No kneeling on the job," Mikito cries out, dancing past me as she cuts apart a pair of drones. A wave of her polearm and an arc of flame and Mana explodes forward, catching a pair of Advanced pirates. Like living energy, the flames wrap around the three, holding them still for precious seconds as Mikito continues to dart through the docking bay, bringing aid and destruction as necessary.

"And where were you when I needed help?" I grumble as I stagger upward. But I know it's a bit silly of me to complain. I'm the Master Classer, and Mikito had her hands full with the rest of the pirates.

An explosion turns my attention to one of the two flame throwers, now a melted wreck. Surprisingly, the second isn't being attacked any longer, as the team focused on it turns their attention to a trio of pirates. Both groups are hunkered behind mobile barriers, trading spells and bullets while a still body lies between the two groups. As I raise my sword to cut down the flame thrower, it fires on a pirate, catching the half-hippo creature in the back with a concentrated blast of fire. All around, I realize that our side has the upper hand.

"Tick-tock. Two minutes till engineering falls," Ali says.

My eyes narrow, thoughts whizzing by at a thousand, a million, miles an hour. Even then, my hands move to pull and down a Mana potion and a Healing potion. A wash of green light sees my Health shoot up as one of the healers on our side finally gets around to helping.

"Mikito, you're in charge." I'm already forming the Portal to our holding room, ducking inside as I idly cut apart another drone.

No time to hear her answer, but I trust the Samurai has this. Hopefully she's got the Draugr.

Back in the holding room, I release the Portal and form the next one, barking orders out even as I do so. "The rest of you, we've got another Master Classer to kill. Ali, you're with me."

"John, do you need help?" Katherine's voice breaks in as the Portal forms and the Adventurers stream out.

A couple hold back, but I don't have time to deal with the cowards. Katherine's worried enough to even show up in video, so I'm treated to seeing my ex-secretary wearing my ex-mecha. Sabre looks good on her and, with all the upgrades, will help keep her alive longer. It pains me a little to have given it away, but at my Level, it's not that useful.

"Negative. Stay out of it. We'll handle them," I say.

Except that's a bit of a lie. I'm down a third of my Mana and health and we're only a third of the way done, the softest target down. Unfortunately, since we've lost sight of the third Master Class, I can't pull Katherine's people off her. I enter the Portal the moment it's clear then shut it, leaving behind the cowards as the teams set up the next hard point.

We don't even try hiding—there's no time and chances are it'd be of no use. There are so many ways for the wary to pick us out, there's no way we could hide all of us. Especially since they know we're fighting back. Too bad this area is pure metal or else I'd even throw up some Mud Walls. But I don't have a Metal Wall spell, so I make do with a couple of portable shield generators then pull out my latest toy.

Silversmith Jeupa VII Anti-Personnel Cannon (Modified & Upgraded)

This quad-barrelled anti-personnel weapon has been handcrafted by Advanced Weaponsmiths to provide the highest integration possible for an energy weapon. This particular weapon has been modified to include additional range-finding and sighting options and upgraded to increase short-term damage output at the cost of long-term durability. Barrels may be fired individually or linked.

Base Damage: 787 per barrel

Battery Capacity: 4 per barrel (16 total)
Recharge Rate: 0.25 per hour per GMU

The entire thing is nearly eight feet long, a pair of stabilizing tripods required to keep the beam rifle working. The moment I have the canon deployed, Ali flies over and patches directly into the weapon's auto-targeting software, feeding it all the information he can.

"Damn it, that's my toy," I say, stepping away and pulling a much smaller and less powerful rifle into my hands.

"Once you can read machine code and tap into the System, you can have it back."

Snorts of suppressed laughter erupt around me, everyone a little on edge. I ignore it all, watching the little dots in my minimap approach. Since I have the time—and knowing the kind of fight I'm expecting—I trigger all my Shield options, including the one in my ring, before continuing to drain my Mana battery. Constant low-level increases in my health come from healing spells cast on me and the System regeneration, pushing me up to nearly three quarters full.

"Incoming," Ali's voice cuts through my thoughts.

A moment later, the pirates turn the corner. A few hasty shots are snapped off, either blocked by shields or swatted aside on both sides.

"Hold your fire." I don't blame them—the Shapeshifter is a bit jaw-dropping. This must be its tank form, since the creature is armored in thick, overlapping plates of bone and metal on its six-footed, multi-eyed form. The damn thing looks like a pissed-off ankylosaur, and as it charges, glowing green streaks of light form all around it.

"Hold!"

Muk Muk covers a dozen yards in the time I take to speak. I watch out of the corner of my eyes how the power charges up in Ali's cannon, how spells and beam weaponry increase in their damage potential. And I weigh the options in my mind.

"Hold!"

Another dozen yards.

"Fire!"

Ali hoots as the anti-personnel cannon throws out green rays of death. Just the ancillary heat from the passing beam is enough to damage my Soul Shield. And the cannon is only the first weapon to fire. It's joined by dozens of other beam rifles, bullets, railguns, and yes, the occasional enchanted arrow. On top of that, targeted spells fly down range, as well as a few carefully controlled area effect spells. A pair of crouched humans weave a Grasping Hands spell, forming transparent, semi-solid limbs that grab and grip the pirates as they rush past, slowing down the entire group.

Into this storm of death, the pirates' erstwhile leader charges, his green light deflecting a portion of the damage. The rest of the attack break through his Skill and begins to cut through the remainder of his Force Shield defenses before they finally reach the Shapeshifter's armor. Immediately, the armor glows red from the heat, but rather than melting, it seems to disperse the damage.

Ali's already on his third charge, the anti-tank cannon never seeming to stop firing, and we've barely scratched the Master Class. Sheltered behind Muk Muk, the pirates push forward, only a few unlucky bastards caught in the fire.

Seeing the damn monster continue his charge, the team around me wavers. Rather than let them break, I decide to go for broke. The Aura of Chivalry flows out from me, covering the battleground and drawing the attention of our enemies. The moment my Aura hits the pirates is visible, even the Master Class stumbling in its track. That pause is enough for another group of hands to grab its legs, slowing it down further.

Aura of Chivalry (Level 1)

A Paladin's very presence can quail weak-hearted enemies and bolster the confidence of allies, whether on the battlefield or in court. The Aura of Chivalry is a double-edged sword, however, focusing attention on the Paladin—potentially to their detriment. Increases success rate of Perception checks against Paladin by 10% and reduces stealth and related skills by 10% while active. Reduces Mana Regeneration by 5 permanently.

Effect: All enemies must make a Willpower check against intimidation against user's Charisma. Failure to pass the check will cow enemies. All allies gain a 50% boost in morale for all Willpower checks and a 10% boost in confidence and probability of succeeding in relevant actions.

Note: Aura may be activated or left off at will.

All around me, I feel the group's resistance firm up while one unlucky or particularly weak-willed pirate actually turns around and runs. I drop my beam rifle back into my inventory and step around the shields, raising my hand and calling forth my sword.

"Time to end this," I say with a savage smile, swinging my sword down.

All around me, a dozen replica blades appear. The penultimate attack Skill of an Erethran Honor Guard triggers as the blades slice down, forming empowered blade strikes that slice through space and set fire to the very air and the shapeshifter. The monster might have defense and ablative armoring. It might be able to soak up hundreds of points of damage with its armor. But my own Class Skills are a hard counter, Penetration letting me rip through the armor and shielding.

Light fills the corridor, followed by thunder. Smoke from superheated metal and burned flesh hangs heavy in the corridor. As the smoke clears, it's obvious that not much of the corridor survived my attack.

Below, scraping sounds. I step forward, looking down to see the Master Class staggering back to its feet. My lips pull wide into a grin and I jump down, continuing our dance.

Chapter 3

"You destroyed three floors in that fight of yours!" The captain of the ship, an angular merman waving his flippered hand at me, is rather agitated. So much so that the rebreather apparatus stuck around his scaled gills is struggling to keep up.

"The Shifter was tough," I say with a shrug.

Even using Army of One, I only managed to lower the creature's health pool by half. That the attack had also torn apart the upper and lower levels was unfortunate. Since the majority of the pirates had managed to evade the collapse of the floor, I'd left to fight the Shifter on the lower decks while my strike team mopped up the separated pirates. With the anti-personnel cannon and Ali, it was a simple enough job.

Not that dealing with the Master Class was easy. Once he realized he was only fighting me, the son of a bitch had shifted forms to something smaller and faster, basically forcing me into a running battle through the ship corridors. It only ended when word came that all the "normal" pirates had been dealt with, including the Draugr.

Surprisingly, the Master Class Commando didn't make an appearance until the very end, when the pirates decided to call it a day. Rather than fight and destroy even more of the ship, we called a truce while I escorted the Shapeshifter back to the loading docks. From the cold looks the pair of surviving Master Class pirates shared as they exited through the docking doors, I had a feeling they'd have words on their ship.

"Tough or not, you tore up three floors and had a running battle through another floor. We had to delay for an entire day while my men patched the holes in the hull!" the captain complains. "Why, I should charge you for the damages."

"And double dip? I'm sure your insurance will pay for it. And if you try to come after me, I'll make sure everyone knows the kind of person you are. I wonder how many more passengers you'll get if they know you won't honor even the basic customs of the Galactic sphere?"

The captain's lips press thin before he stomps off. I chuckle softly, watching the merman flop away, before I turn to Katherine and Peter, who have been standing quietly to the side.

"Are you okay?" Katherine asks, her eyes roving over my body.

I'd taken the time to change clothing, so outside of some soot and blood, I look the same as always. Mass purchasing for the win!

"Fine." I grin. "Don't even have to regrow any limbs this time."

Katherine cocks an eyebrow. "We saw some of your battle with the Shapeshifter. When the cameras lasted at least. It looked violent."

"Eh, it wasn't so bad. He was a tad too fast to get a proper hit on in his agile form, but he was bouncing around too much to get in any real hits on me. Tore up my stuff real good, but it looked bloodier than it was dangerous."

"Those spinning swords of yours are rather interesting. Though they hampered your movements too," Peter says, pointing out one issue with my Thousand Blades Skill.

Once created, the swords follow the path of the original, but because I have a tendency to summon and unsummon the original sword, trajectories can get strange. While Intelligence increases don't necessarily translate to a "smarter" person in the way we think it should, the System seems to pick up on what we've done before and grow our abilities in that direction. Mostly. In my case, one of the side effects of my high Intelligence is the ability to recognize, understand, and manipulate the angles of my trailing swords. It still requires practice to do it consistently, since knowing and doing are two different things. Even so, there's no way I could fight the way I do without the Intelligence increases I've had.

It also comes in real handy when playing pool.

"Always a negative with Skills. You just have to figure them out," I say. "Though, I'll admit, most are easy. Too high Mana cost." I look directly at Peter, who grimaces, probably recalling his own ultimate ability, Diplomatic Immunity. Like my Sanctum, it protects against all attacks, but unlike mine, it only works on sentients. "Or a high level of side effects."

"Well, in either case, the pirates have left. I doubt we'll face another. It's bad form to attack a merchant ship more than once on a route. Never mind how unlucky we were to get hit anyway," Katherine says.

"You know, sometimes the Galactic System reminds me more of a third-world country than a developed nation." When I get puzzled looks back, I explain. "More corruption, more accepted corruption, than in Canada or the US. Well, surface-level corruption. I mean, pirates? Sects that run roughshod over everyone? And of course, the various empires that fight each other."

"It's because of all the empires and other interest groups vying with each other that pirates and their kind exist," Peter says, correcting me. "A good portion of those pirates are privateers in actual fact. Ships are forced to purchase insurance from multiple kingdoms if they decide to traverse between different principalities, increasing their costs and greasing even more palms. Those that refuse to do so... well, they might find their names discreetly handed over to a privateer. And it goes on, from criminal organizations to sects to corporations and even Guilds. If there's a way to game the System for their own good, sentients will find it."

I nod slowly. It's similar, I guess, to what I've been reading. As much as Galactic Society has accepted the fact that the System controls, well, everything, they also push its boundaries all the time. Guilds are meant to be non-political, non-aligned. It's why they're allowed to own land in multiple locations without being the actual settlement or land owner. Unlike, say, a kingdom, whose access and ownership of such a location would automatically make it part of their kingdom. To skip around that, they have to rely on individual ownership, which is a dangerous exploit. But there's nothing to stop a Guild from being staffed with people aligned with one empire or kingdom. And so, rules are bent. Or the way monarchies and their noble classes form, because that way, lines of fealty can be created which both work within the System and also bend its rules.

Speaking of kingdom-owned locations… "Did you work out how setting up the diplomatic mission is going to work?"

"Of course." Katherine sniffs. "Some of us read our correspondence."

"You're not still bitter about that, are you?" I grin. I admit, I had a tendency to avoid reading most of my mail after Katherine hired herself as my secretary. I only ever bothered to read items she highlighted as important and urgent.

Katherine scowls at me before relenting with a wave. "No. It was the right decision actually. Your skills were better used elsewhere."

"So. The mission?"

"Is relatively simple on the surface," Peter says. "We arrive at the Prax Solar System, dock at the main station, and transfer down to Irvina using the visas provided to us. Once we've provided the visas at the station, our diplomatic status is registered with the Galactic Council. We then have six months to locate a permanent residence in Irvina to set up the mission itself."

"And you're able to buy land for Earth?" I say, cocking my head to the side.

"Yes. Unfortunately, the city is huge and the locations we can purchase are limited, so we expect there to be significant issues," Peter says. "Once we arrive, Katherine will focus on finding us a long-term location while I reach out to our erstwhile allies for help."

"The Truinnar should be able to help with that, right?" I say.

"You would think so," Katherine says with a sniff. "But we're a small ally to them. Even if we've managed to do something no other Dungeon World has done, all it means in the Galactic sense is that they've got another vote. And a better deal for coming to Earth. For all that, they aren't bending over backward to help us. At least not on the Empire level. There's some hope with the Duchess, but we'll have to see about that in person."

I nod in acceptance of her words and figure they've got it mostly covered. I then take my leave before they drag me in any further. I've made my desire to leave, once we actually arrive at Irvina, clear. As Harry noted, Mikito and I have generated quite a bit of animosity with our actions. Being part of the official diplomatic mission would only cause trouble for them. As best as we can, I'd prefer for us to disassociate with the mission and Earth itself as much as possible.

Of course, that's harder than it seems because Mikito and I are backup security for the mission for now. While Katherine has her own security team, none of them are Master Classes. With the chaos happening on Earth after Bipasha's assassination, we need the few Master Classes we do have there. Until the Secret Service and their ilk Level up enough, Mikito and I are the closest things to heavy-hitters Katherine has to call upon. So we're going in under their diplomatic visas, no matter how much I'd prefer not to.

Not that I have much choice anyway. Irvina—and the whole planet of Prax—is a restricted area. Entering their solar system, never mind the capital itself, is heavily restricted due to the sheer number of interested parties. The only other way to do so is with sufficient Galactic Reputation. And for myself, well…

Galactic Reputation: 2
Galactic Fame: 2,308

That Galactic Fame number might seem high, but it mostly all comes from Earth. It's the sum total of the average fame level I have on Earth in each region, so while it looks high, it's only on the level of say, an international boy band before the System. Known enough by name, but damned if you could tell the difference between each singer. On a Galactic scale, I'm nothing.

As for my reputation, well, it's even more pitiful. While I made and completed a ton of deals during the run-up to the vote, when Bipasha was killed and the damn Senator refused to honor some of those deals, I lost a lot of reputation too. That Rob then proceeded to negotiate deals directly with the affected parties to pacify them gave me a new, unpleasant, and personal view of politics.

In any case, even with all that garbage, Galactic Reputation is difficult to generate. Moving the needle on the Galactic level requires a significant level of fame, positions, and deals.

Funnily enough, Mikito's numbers are much better.

Mikito Sato, Spear of Humanity, Blood Warden (Middle Samurai Level 46)

HP: 1990/1990

MP: 1400/1400

Conditions: Isoide, Jin, Rei, Meiyo, Ishiki, Ryoyo

Galactic Reputation: 8

Galactic Fame: 7,783

No surprise her fame is higher than mine. For one thing, she didn't spend four years stuck in a hellhole of a Forbidden Zone. Even if that act itself is particularly impressive, it's not particularly useful for increasing my Fame, and since I'm not out for glory, I've not been highlighting my little jaunt. Mikito, in my four-year absence, ran around the world doing good deeds, killing monsters, and clearing dungeons galore. Add the fact that she's managed to gain some

Fame in the Galactic Arenas and it's no surprise she's ticking higher than I am. Furthermore, without a bunch of bad deals pulling her down, her Reputation is pretty good too. For a newcomer Galactic at least.

"Why are you staring at me?" Mikito asks suspiciously.

"I'm not…" I pause then shake my head. "I'm looking at your Status. You picked up quite a few Levels since I got back."

Mikito grins. "You're not the only one who can cheat."

"Do I want to know?"

"Depends. Are you interested in entering the Arena again?"

"Ah," I say, shaking my head.

Of course. The experience and gold tithe. And now that the lady is tapping into a Galactic audience, her numbers are creeping up. Add in the numerous dungeons we've cleared and the battles we've fought for the vote, and well…

Not to be dissuaded, Mikito presses on. "Why were you checking out my Status?"

"Just thinking about our arrival. If we use our visas, we can get in. But that ties us to Earth."

"We have another option?" Mikito says.

"Not that I can think of."

"Then don't worry about it."

I grunt and head back to my room. She's right, but I can't help but think that there's got to be a better way. Or that opening up Earth to our problems is just asking for trouble.

***

Days later, the merchant ship finally exits hyperspace and begins the long trip through mundane space to the planet Prax. Technically, we're actually going to

Prax III, the largest and main space station that guards the planet's orbit. The station is so large, it could be considered a minor moon. Of course, Prax III isn't the only space station, with smaller stations set up equidistant in the pole positions around the planet. But Prax III is where entrance to Irvina is determined.

Prax III is constructed as a series of interconnected spokes around a cylindrical structure. Ships of differing sizes are housed along each spoke, docking at the stations and off-loading cargo and personnel as necessary. At the largest end are some of the in-system cargo ships, a couple of kilometers in length, while smaller, nimbler personal craft docks closer to the spokes.

As a mid-sized cargo vessel, we dock about a third of the way up one spoke. The rest of the passengers are requested to unload first, so us humans have a nice view of the cargo vessel unloading. Not surprisingly, the vast majority of the work is completed via robots, mostly controlled by a few Technomancer and Loader Classes. It's a beautiful ballet of movement, with multiple loader arms crawling across the hull of the ship. Unfortunately, what gets moved out are mostly containers, so I find myself bored with the process in minutes.

"What are they off-loading anyway?" I ask Katherine.

"The usual—monster drops, some of the higher-ranked crafted items from Earth, and some of the local delicacies. You probably know that one." Katherine points at a container that looks like every other. Seeing my puzzled look, the woman smirks. "Yukon gold."

"Ah, the beer!" I smile. One of my better investments actually.

For that matter, I take a moment to access my notification screens and check out my holdings. While I gave up the settlements, I still have a number of holdings in my name. Of course, most of them are under a management contract with Lana's investment company in the Yukon, but the random burnt-out buildings, residences, and stores that I purchased to have a good night's sleep in while traveling amount to a small fortune. Especially now that the towns and cities they're in aren't complete wrecks. Well, most of them.

I flick through the long, long list before I locate the information about the Yukon brewing company. As a direct shareholder and as a shareholder of the investment company, I have pretty much full access to their financials. My eyes widen when I see the details.

"How much?" I choke out in bewilderment when I see the gross revenue numbers.

"You finally bothered to check your holdings?" Katherine says with a slight smirk.

"The company's grown a little," I say weakly.

"A little. They are really quite thankful you've been willing to forego any return on your investments to allow them to continue investing in their production capacity. It seems that the 'Dungeon World Brew' has gained quite a following in Galactic markets," Katherine says teasingly.

"Right. I did say that, didn't I?" Explains why I've never seen a single Credit from that investment.

Hyper intelligence pulls the memory from my mind, a conversation held years ago, when I first gave the money to Lana. I told her to invest any returns, to build up the economy of Whitehorse, to give people jobs and a purpose when they had lost everything. So many years ago that I forgot all about it. It didn't seem to matter when we were fighting, and then... well. Forbidden Zone. After that, I had another big fight and the vote and it was just never something I thought about.

I guess that makes me a bad Chinese, not caring about Credits at all. My father is probably turning in his grave over the careless way I've treated funds. But somewhere along the way, between the apocalypse and the trail of bodies I've left behind, material goods have become insignificant. Illusionary even.

A small part of me, a guilty part, wonders if it's an unconscious way to punish myself. To serve penance. For all the innocents, all the lives, I could never save. For all the ills, all the destruction I failed to stop. A blade will kill a monster, but it cannot heal an injury. My blade could not give solace to those who survived or give direction to their broken lives.

"John?" Katherine's voice interrupts my gloomy musings.

"Sorry." I stare at the holding information for a second more before dismissing it. Not much use to me now. Not as if I can contact them to make any changes at the moment, and I don't really want to. If I die—no, when I die—at least some good will have come of my existence.

So.

What is, is.

"Looks like it's our turn," Peter interrupts my musings.

I offer the man a tight smile. Right. Onward and upward.

***

Are all Customs checkpoints the same? The same individual barriers, the same stern-faced officials who stare at you and their screens, acting as though they can see all your deepest, darkest, most perverted dreams? Sure, the Galactic Customs at Prax has the novelty of Galactics manning the station—meaning that there are numerous alien and fantasy races—but the set up itself is the same.

"John Lee. Redeemer of the Dead. Correct?" the Customs official says.

Staring at the giant, green, bug-eyed creature, I can see myself reflected hundreds of times in its compound eyes. That it can make even marginally understandable sounds from those mandibles is astounding. "Yes."

"You are attempting to enter Irvina via a secondary diplomatic visa issued to the newly created seat for Earth, correct?"

"Yes."

"Very well. You understand the limitations and expectations of your visa?" Bug-eye says.

"Not exactly."

"Then I recommend you read them in detail. However, in short, you are not allowed to vote in local elections. You only have non-citizen rights which means no access to local counsel, legal, and welfare services. You may only access the local dungeons after registering with an appropriate Adventurers Guild and receiving the necessary clearance. Doing so will require you to pay an initial access fee, then a portion of all your earnings will be taxed on the non-citizen tax rate. Breaches of the law will be charged under the secondary provisions for non-citizens, and felony charges will, at the minimum, see the banishment of offenders from Prax system."

I nod. One of the things that was required for us taking the ship at all was a download of all applicable Galactic and Irvina laws. In truth, once I'd paid for and downloaded the information, I'd felt extremely cheated. Galactic law is somewhat simplistic.

There's not a lot of it, since issues like public littering, graffiti, and defacement are non-issues due to the System dealing with those minor inconveniences. As for property ownership and retail, well, it's basically caveat emptor. A lot of the truly scummy predators are kept in check via the Reputation system. So while there's significant pressure to get the best deal possible, the products themselves are often sold truthfully. Just, perhaps, with a few issues that aren't mentioned.

The Galactic Council doesn't bother with issues like local welfare, leaving that to local systems and groups. If there's one advantage of the System, it's that it's hard for your "average" citizen to starve—food, Mana, and basic items are dirt cheap. That being said, hard isn't impossible. Of course, progressing above what is basic subsistence living is more difficult. Even so, to a human from the twentieth century, the "minimum" standard of living of a Galactic is sci-fi cool.

The vast majority of Galactic law revolves around felonies, specifically violence. Firstly, dueling is not only allowed but recognized. Considering the sheer volume and variety of violent Classes, it's no surprise that a violent solution to disagreements is acceptable. Since duels have to be acknowledged by both parties via the System, it is possible to turn down duels. Of course, that impacts one's fame in many cases, unless the degree of fame and reputation between the two parties is significant. After all, a Heroic Class individual isn't likely going to be bothered by being challenged by a Basic Class Artisan. And a Combat Classer challenging an Artisan of any sort is considered bad form and impacts both reputation and fame.

Outside of duels, murder is considered bad in the wider galaxy. Once you leave Dungeon Worlds, killing others has consequences. While self-defense is a valid defense, like our human systems, there are courts, jail time, and deductions to Reputation outside of specific circumstances. Like, you know, defending against piracy. If a Justicar, Tribunal, or other law enforcer ends up checking on the incident and rules against you, bounties can easily be placed. In such cases, the Justicar or other law enforcer may use a portion of the deceased's lost goods and Credits as collateral for the bounty. It's why higher Classed law enforcers are feared. They can even quadruple the bounty on an individual.

Outside of death, very few things are considered major crimes. On-going torture, certain kinds of sexual assault, body, mind, and soul-jacking are on that list. Short-term torture and harassment are considered fineable offenses, not even at the level of a full felony—unless it's an on-going harassment. And even then, punishment is only applicable if a properly designated law enforcement Class is around to act on it.

Prax law isn't much better. Oh, there are some details about welfare, training, employment laws, and the like, but it's mostly useless for someone like me who isn't a citizen. Caveat emptor covers the vast majority of what I need to know.

"That's fine. I don't intend to cause any trouble," I say.

Bug-eyes stares at me for a second before waving his hand over his screens. A second later, I get a notification informing me that my visa for Irvina has been approved. As I walk out of the customs lounge, I find myself bubbling with excitement.

Soon, very soon, I'll get to see my first real alien city.

Chapter 4

We travel down to Irvina via a beanstalk lift large enough to fit a couple of tour buses in it lengthwise. As we drop down through the bountiful clouds that cover the city, I'm grateful that the planet itself is close to Earth standard. About seven percent heavier, from what I recall, with a single sun like Earth and a sky that shades everything to a darker blue. Perhaps the biggest change is the massive moon that dominates the night and sometimes daytime sky. It's a bit of a shock, but Prax is a dry planet, with a series of smaller landlocked seas rather than our ocean-ridden planet.

Once we break through the clouds, the megacity of Irvina spreads out beneath us. The end of the beanstalk comes down near the center of the city, and the city stretches for untold kilometers on all sides. The city itself is strange, with lots of greenery and small squat buildings in the center before being bordered by giant skyscrapers that remind me of downtown Vancouver or New York. Those skyscrapers are so tall that they throw the streets into deep shadow. Walkways connect the silver-tinted buildings while gravtrains carry passengers around. In some ways, the city reminds me of a ball sitting in the middle of a spread silk scarf, a bowl of buildings ringing a single central hall and the stem of the beanstalk. Small moving dots that traverse the open air slowly resolve into flying cars and animals, moving with ordered precision along clearly marked air routes.

It's one part *Fifth Element*, one part *Shadowrun*, and one part medieval fantasy world. All that's missing is a steampunk blimp and we'd have a real hotpot of fantasy elements. In fact, as we get closer, I realize that there are even flying figures interspersed among the flying vehicles and creatures. The flying individuals are as varied in their modes of transportation as everything else, some sporting wings, others glowing with telekinetic power or a Skill, and of course, the usual array of weird tech.

"Do you think Earth will be like that one day?" Mikito says, gazing at the bustling metropolis with wide eyes.

"Nah. A bunch of harpies or drakes would eat them all," I say, pointing around. "Most Dungeon World cities try to keep flight to a minimum. Too many flying things with major territorial issues."

Mikito makes a face but ends up nodding. Harry's head swivels slowly while he holds up a hand as if he's recording with that hand too. He's not the only reporter doing so. The entire group is busy recording images for their next segment. Some are using Skills, others bobbing tech cameras, and a few even hold up crystals. Next to me, Katherine is muttering to Peter, pointing out various landmarks. I overhear a little.

"That's the diplomatic district ringing the main hall, borders the river on that side, and if you follow the river down, it sweeps up to meet the main road. I'll highlight it for you," Peter says to Katherine.

I listen in a little more as they discuss buildings and places, but I get bored fast. It doesn't help that I can't see what they're seeing in their notifications. Or the fact that I've never felt a desire to buy real estate. By the time I had enough, the Vancouver real estate market was well beyond my reach. And then, well, I moved up to Whitehorse and things went to hell. I guess I am a landowner now, but that's just because safe zones are important.

"Where's the library?"

"Highlighting now. You sure you want to go do something so damn boring?" Ali complains even as he lights up the library.

It's a huge building, even in comparison to the skyscrapers. It's a blocky rectangle without windows but a lot of designs along the edges, giving it a bit of a gothic look. Of course, the gargoyles littering the building are strange and scary, parodies of monsters and nightmares. And, on closer inspection, a few of those gargoyles seem to be lighting up in my Status window.

"I came all the way here to get some answers, no?" I smile grimly.

All that time on a Forbidden Zone planet has taught me a few things about the System Quest. For one thing, Mana is integral to the entire thing—it's the source, the fuel for the System. But it isn't the System, which is another thing itself. A set of rules, a set of regulations, an overarching Big Brother that manipulates and evolves us at its whim. The System is a mystery, even when it is everything for those of us in the System.

"You and a billion other Questors," Ali grumbles, arms crossed. *"If you end up spending more than a decade in that library, I'm killing the Contract no matter what kind of penalties I have to endure. Got it, boy-o?"*

"Loud and clear." I hide my smile, remembering how vehement Ali was against the entire thing on the second day. I guess we've all changed.

***

The rest of the trip down was quiet enough. Katherine arranged accommodations for all of us, and rather than attempt to find a place myself, I've gone ahead with it. At least in the short term, this plush hotel is more than adequate. It does say something about Galactic society that among the amenities offered is a fighting arena and personal combat trainers.

I look around the suite we've been given. It's a little extravagant—a separate living room, a set of three bedrooms, and even a mini-kitchen.

"Who'd you bribe to bunk with us?" I ask Harry as he comes out of his own room.

Mikito's taking her time in her own room, depositing a host of personal items. I don't bother since my Altered Space is more than large enough. Not as if I'm carrying monster parts right now.

"Katherine. I pointed out that if I'm following you around, I won't be following her," Harry says unashamedly. "So. What's our plan?"

"I'm going to look around the city." I glance at Mikito who walks out of her room, running a hand through her short hair. "You're welcome to join."

"Of course. Always good to know the layout," Mikito says.

"That's settled then. Ali, I'll want you to be perusing the System for places to rent," I say, rubbing my chin. "If we're here for a bit, I don't want to stay here longer than necessary."

"Sure. I'll go look for a derelict house."

"Funny," I say before pausing. "Exactly how much are we looking at anyway?"

"Buy or rent?"

After a moment's hesitation, I say, "Buy." Might as well get a feel for the place.

"Two-bedroom place in a respectable neighborhood—say in the third ring—we're looking at just over eighteen million Credits," Ali says.

"What?" My voice goes up a couple of notches. "I could buy a damn settlement on Earth for that!"

"It's Irvina. Largest populated Galactic city, longest-running capital. Most of the land here's owned by corporations, guilds, and the elder families," Ali says, shaking his head. "If it wasn't for the fact that the Council set a limit on how much property each corporation can own based off its size and revenue, there'd be nothing for anyone."

I guess that makes sense. Even in our world, the problem of corporations growing larger and larger, becoming too big to fail, is a regular occurrence. "Why would the corporations and guilds let them do that?"

"Do what?" Ali says then answers his own question. "You mean put the regulations in place?" When I nod, he snorts. "As if anyone's telling the Inner

Council what not to do." As we stare at Ali, he sighs. "The Inner Council's made up of nine council members, at least five of whom are Legendary Classes. The others are representatives of the major empires and factions. They're the real rulers, but luckily, they try to do as little work as possible.

"As for the main Galactic Council, they're the ones who make the big decisions like the System expansion and Dungeon Worlds. They also try to set up new laws, deal with inter Empire and Faction disputes, and organize expeditions. Also, whine. Really, they mostly whine a lot."

I guess it does make sense that even if you have corporations and guilds with members in the millions, a single Legendary Class can make a huge difference. It's not just the fact that they're individually incredibly powerful. It's also the numerous allies and debts owed to them. Add on the fact that it's really, really hard to lock down even Master Classes in a fight, and you can understand why Legendary Classes are so powerful, they can take out entire planets by themselves. Add Heroic or higher level fleeing Skills, and well, how are you going to deal with them? From what I understand, few Legendary Classes fall to anything but the Forbidden Zone or another Legendary. Even if the guild or corporation has a Legendary of their own, it's not as if that's going to stop the destruction.

"All right. So buying is out," I say, diverting the topic. Not as if I've got that many Credits on me. Even if I sold everything I own, including my investments, I'd probably fall short.

"Pretty much. You'll want to consider renting on the third or fourth ring," Ali says.

He waves, and a map of the city blooms before all of us. A quick adjustment and the "rings" that radiate from the Galactic Hall are highlighted. The first ring is the smallest by far, consisting of an area barely larger than downtown Vancouver—a couple of kilometers across at best. Each subsequent ring grows wider, with drops in security, cost, and amenities. These rings are mostly created from differences in architecture and System-enabled features, making them difficult to pick out by naked eye.

"And these are the dungeons?" Mikito says, tapping a gate symbol.

A moment later, the map highlights all the gate symbols—one gigantic, three large, and another nine smaller gates appear across the map. The gates themselves start at the third ring, which hosts the gigantic gate symbol and radiate outward, with the smallest gate symbols on the eighth—and last—ring.

"Yup. It's why I'd recommend the third or fourth ring," Ali says. "Adventurers and their guilds all congregate around the Prime Dungeon. Not surprisingly, a lot of accommodation there caters to you guys too. There are even rest houses with their own internal butchering yards and repair stations."

"Got it." I shrug. "Well, I guess we should start at the smallest ring and go out for our trip today."

There's a long silence, punctuated by Harry turning to Mikito and saying, "Is he serious?"

"Yes. John's not very good at reading the rules." Mikito's lips twitch slightly.

"What?" I say, irritated.

"The first ring is restricted so that even citizens of Irvina are not allowed in. The second ring is restricted to those with high Reputation and diplomatic statuses," Ali says. "The third ring is limited to Adventurers and their ilk of sufficient standing. Since you came in on a secondary diplomatic visa, that's where you can start. If not for your current standing, you wouldn't even be allowed in this hotel."

"Oh." I pause then decide to ask the question anyway. "And I'm assuming all that was in the document they sent us?"

"Yes," Harry says, disappointment tingeing his voice.

"What's with that tone?" I growl.

"Just sad when you learn your heroes have lead feet too," Harry says.

"Hero…" I sit there, stunned, while Harry stands.

His actions pull the entire group to the door. Shaking my head, I move to catch up with them, calling after them even as they ignore me.

"Hey! What do you mean by that?"

***

I never do get my answer, but it doesn't matter. Once we leave our hotel, the only public transportation we can access sends us directly from the second ring into the third. Only then does it click how annoying staying at that hotel will be for some of us. Of course, the vast majority of the people on Katherine's visa don't care. Whether it's setting up new business networks or talking to other diplomatic groups, they're going to be working closely with the lady. It's only a major issue to those of us who borrowed the visas for our own selfish ends.

High-rise buildings or not, the second ring at least has some greenery. By the time we hit the third ring, the buildings crowd around one another, leaving little space for anything but air. Only a few major roads run through the city itself, and many of those roads are covered by walkways or buildings that run over them.

"What's the ground like?" I ask Ali. While I can get occasional glimpses, it's too dark to make out anything.

"Varies a lot. From the dungeons to the main guilds, auction hall, and merchants' quarter, it's clear of everything but traffic. No one wants to drag a manticore body through a street crowded with beggars and impromptu food stalls. Outside of those areas, the streets get clogged up with enterprising merchants and your usual vagrants," says Ali. "There're a few parts, mostly in the fifth ring onward, which have been taken over by nocturnal and other dark-loving sentients. Bottom couple of floors are filled with low-rent shops normally, then you get more expensive—but still affordable—accommodation with the cheapest residence areas in the twentieth or so floors and above before you hit the connected floors.

"Anything low means you can and will use the public transportation on the ground. Or just, you know, run. Accommodation in the middle has the worst of both worlds—not connected to the gravtrain tubes but not in easy reach of the ground either. Even with hypertubes to move people around, you're still stuck waiting a lot. Add in vampires, driders, and other dark-loving sentients and well, you have a portion that's set-up in near permanent darkness."

"Right. So leave the ground alone unless necessary," I say.

The group falls silent as the little bubble car we're in floats along the grav tracks, swinging along the sides of buildings, swooping up and down and missing other cars and busses by inches at times. The first few times it happens, I brace for impact, but soon enough I stop worrying about the matter and just enjoy the ride. I took a look at the schematic details of the grav tracks and the bullet trains and individualized bubble cars when we arrived, and I have to admit, I'm completely lost. I can tell there's a lot of gravity and electromagnetic forces in play, but the how and why eludes me. There's a high chance a chunk of that is because much of this was built by Skills.

"Small windows," Mikito says, pointing at a series of tiny windows no taller than a pair of fingers put together. The sheer number along the side of the building is quite amazing.

"Ah, enclave of smalls. Not everyone wants to live in small town. And because of the way architecture works, these are cheaper," Ali says. When I raise an eyebrow, the Spirit sighs. "Right. Most Galactic cities have a few parts that are meant for non-standard humanoid races. How many and what size varies, but you've got small town, big town, semis, quadpedals, and noxes.

"Small town is where the tiny sentients live. You know the kind—sentient mice, sprites, and fairies, that kind of thing. Bigs are the giants and their kind, of course. Semis are the semi-corporeals who range from sentient elementals to ghosts and some types of spirits. Quad-pedals include any of those with non-standard bipedal figures, while noxes are non-oxygen breathers."

"How come we've not met many of them?" Harry says.

"Why would you?" Ali says, shaking his head. "Outside of the giants, who took over the Alps, most bigs can't fit into your standard dungeon configuration. Smalls can, but they struggle against standard monsters until they hit Advanced Classes. They've also got their own culture, including planets and the like. Semi-corporeals did turn up, but they're hanging out in places you guys don't care for. The middle of volcanoes, the deep ocean, the Mojave Desert, so on and so forth. As for noxes, well, you saw some. Hell, the captain who brought us in was one. But most prefer to stick to their own Dungeon Worlds or home worlds. Not a lot of fun choking to death because your respirator died."

Well, that makes some sense. Environmental factors might be of less concern once you head up in Levels, but that doesn't mean that we're comfortable in weird environments. It's like the various dungeons I've heard of that sit in the middle of some space lanes. They're just a lot less appealing to a ground-pounder like me. Still, if I ever get bored, running a dungeon while suited in a full-on spaceship mecha sounds kind of cool.

The next few hours has us watching the scenery pass us by. Soon enough, everyone grows a little too bored. You only view so many similar alien buildings before you're done, even if Ali does his best to point out the major landmarks and pepper his discussion with informative little tidbits. Rather than continue on the same old same old, Ali guides us to the merchant district. At that point, we split off, since everyone has their own little shop to visit. Harry hits the

Shop sphere while Mikito decides to do some window shopping in the physical shops. As for myself…

"There's a branch office?" I say, my eyebrow rising.

"Of course. It's Irvina. Where else would they have a physical shop if not here?" Ali says, waving me on. "It's been ages since I've visited it. But prices will be a little lower."

"Fine. I'm coming." I take off after him, the pair of us strolling through the cavernous innards of the building.

Pedestrian walkways, crawl ways, and roadways run alongside one another. Everyone's mostly following the laid-out routes, the occasional oblivious or arrogant rulebreaker receiving a violent reminder of why the rules are in place. It's kind of amusing how people just move around the burgeoning fights and occasional accidents with barely a glance.

Violence is, at worst, a fineable offense. After all, when everyone heals from broken bones and cuts within ten minutes, there's little concern about such acts. It does lead to certain circumstances of bullying, but it seems a Galactic norm to ignore all but the most egregious events. It's why guilds, associations, sects, and corporations are so popular—always good to have someone looking out for you.

By the time I make my way to the shop, I've had to break one set of legs and throw up my Aura to scare off the idiots. The shop itself is a simple affair— yellow trimmings on the outside with large double doors that are keyed to one's Status. I step forward and the doors slide open, allowing me in.

***

Once inside, I find myself in a beautiful yellow room with a simple counter to greet guests, a waiting and lounging area for those wanting to take their time perusing their wares, and a couple of doors. The layout is a copy of their main offices, so I know from previous experience that those doors lead to private rooms where a customer can browse the wares themselves.

The moment I enter, a svelte young thing comes up to me, all willowy form and transparent dress. That what she exhibits beneath the dress involve dozens of small mouths with hundreds of tiny teeth kind of mutes any allure the angular-faced, slit-eyed attendant might have.

"Redeemer Lee. It is a pleasure to meet you." The attendant bows, one hand over her right chest. "I am K'Senia Maroo. What may I do for you, Redeemer?"

"Got a bunch of things to sell," I say.

K'Senia nods and waves toward a private room. I follow the lady, idly eyeing the area. I kind of miss having actual physical products to browse, but considering the size of the room we're in, I'm assuming they just deliver it from whatever warehouse they use. Once inside, a gesture is all I need to dump my gathered items onto the floor. Loot from pirate corpses and their used gear makes up the majority of my merchandise this time around.

"Ah, I see you've had a busy trip," K'Senia says. "Do you intend to continue traveling without insurance?"

"Not really."

"A pity. I won't inform our proxies to be ready for more such material then," K'Senia says, deftly moving the loot around to sort and price everything.

"There're people who do that regularly?" I say.

"Of course. It's quite a popular pastime among certain Master Classes. And nearly all Heroics. Of course, most pirates leave Heroic Classes alone. Even a Heroic-level Artisan is a danger, especially when one considers most have significant influence in the galaxy," K'Senia says. "The optimal time for such activity is around Level 20 to 40 for combat Master Classes."

"I'll keep that in mind."

K'Senia finishes up with her work and sweeps everything into her storage before asking to be excused while she deposits everything away properly. I nod and turn back to my notification screens, restocking my usual assortment of grenades and disposable weaponry. It's frustrating how expensive everything keeps getting as I go up in Levels.

I hold up one of the many things I have to repurchase and glare at the rather expensive toy.

High Explosive Grenade (Tier II)

Hand-crafted from mithril and oxmallium alloys, the HEG II is a mainstay of Advanced and Master Class Adventurers, able to clear large numbers of low Level creatures.

Base Damage: 287

Area of effect: 5 meters radius

Cost: 1250 Credits

I have to buy a dozen of these just to be safe, not to mention buying incendiary grenades, flash grenades, Chaos grenades, and even portable shield generators. Sure, the effect is amazing and everything has to be handmade at these levels to do the kind of damage we're looking for, but it's still a ton of funds. And still not as good as a single strike from my sword. But it's an area effect attack that throws up a ton of fire and smoke, which is useful.

It's one of the major differences between the real Erethran Honor Guard and me. I'm a lone fighter, without the resources and funds that back the entire army. They can afford to purchase handcrafted mecha and repair them when they're inevitably damaged. If I tried the same, I'd be even poorer than I am right now. As much as I'd love to equip myself with the latest tech, it's not viable.

"Redeemer Lee, it seems we have an item awaiting your pickup," K'Senia says when she comes back. "Would you like to take ownership of it now?"

"Of course."

A moment later, K'Senia has twitched her hands and handed the knives to me. I blink at my old friends now firmly etched with runes and reinforced with stronger metals. Rough edges have been worked out, along with numerous minor adjustments. I pull out one, staring at the item's new status with awe.

Enchanted, Reinforced Toothy Throwing Knives (5)

First handcrafted from the rare drop of a Level 140 Awakened Beast by the Redeemer of the Dead, John Lee, these knives have been further processed by the Master Craftsmen I-24-988L and reinforced with orichalcum and fey-steel. The final blades have been further enchanted with Mana and a piercing Skill, as well as a return enchantment.
Base Damage: 238
Enchantments: Return, Mana Blade (+28 Damage), Pierce (-7% defense)

"Very nice," I say.

As I look around, K'Senia cannot help but smile a little and point down the room to the farthest corner. "Feel free to test out your knives. These rooms are rated to withstand even Tier I attacks."

I nod in thanks, pulling the knives from their sheaths and reviewing each weapon. There are minor differences in the base damage—probably due to various defects in the way I first crafted the knives. More importantly, the enchantments make these weapons deadlier than ever. These do nearly double the damage of my soulblade when I first received it. I could easily one-shot any low-level monster with these.

Once I've verified everything, I look at the simple baldric that's been enchanted as well, providing the return enchantment a focus. With a shrug, I toss the knives underhand at the far wall.

There's nothing special when I do—no explosions, flashing lights, or swell of music. The knives fly out of my hand with a smoothness that seems all too familiar, grouping themselves within millimeters of one another and sinking in nearly all the way to the hilt. K'Senia raises an eyebrow, appearing somewhat impressed.

Me? I'm more impressed when the knives flicker and suddenly reappear, one after the other, in the enchanted baldric. I test the weapons again, tossing them one after the other and counting off till they return. Just under three seconds.

"Hey, Ali, these won't randomly return if I throw them really far away, will they?"

"Maybe? Depends on how far. The runes have two triggers—time after impact and time after reaching throwing speeds. You can also forcefully return them by touching that rune." Ali highlights a rune on the baldric for me. *"Push your Mana into it and boom. Knives back in sheaths."*

"Thanks." I make mental note about that and the potential problems the enchantment might have.

These are a nice addition to my attacks, one that doesn't require me to use my sword. The biggest advantage of these weapons is that they give me a ranged option that isn't Mana intensive or as flashy as my Blade Strike.

I slip on the baldric before turning to K'Senia and pointing at the skill I was browsing while she was gone—Galactic Body Language. "So…"

"I see you've begun to face issues," K'Senia says. "I'm surprised this was not recommended to you earlier."

"Yeah, about that. I don't get why I was able to read most of the Galactics on Earth perfectly well, but now I'm getting conflicting feelings. It's rather frustrating when you Galactics go from happy to sad to outraged. At least, from your body language."

"Skill translation," K'Senia says. "You understand that the skills you purchase, language and otherwise, often are derived from individuals? Or in the System's case, a large number of said individuals?"

"I got that."

"Then you should be cognizant that such information comes with behavioral and body language knowledge as well. To make proper use of the correct body language, the System has to overwrite specific portions of one's body," K'Senia says. "In so doing, the original host's tics are overlaid."

"Wait. You're saying that because they learnt English from the System, they also got the body language from the individual the skill was taken from originally?" At her nod, I slowly rub my chin. "So when they spoke English, they were showcasing mostly human body language. Which is why I had no issue reading them." Except for one particular Truinnar. But I was never sure if that was because of his skills or because the man always set me on edge. In a good way. Mostly.

"Exactly. But most of us learn to speak Galactic while growing up. As such, there is no 'natural' body language to acquire, and so the Galactics you've met are all exhibiting their 'natural' body language," K'Senia says. "Most of us learn to read the major races quickly enough. Merchants like me then purchase ranks in the skill you are looking at. And in some cases, diplomats and others have Skills to ensure their meaning comes across, no matter which race it is.

"You, on the other hand, are relying on your human understanding of body language and movements. While some of that will, slowly, disappear, in the short term, you will be faced with significant misunderstandings."

I exhale, shaking my head, and swipe the skill over to my buy pile. Thinking about it, I chat with K'Senia about what else I should get. Soon enough, we've added a bunch of "generic" knowledge to the pile that I hadn't bothered purchasing or which Foxy, my normal attendant, had not recommended. Eyeing the large list and recalling the way the System likes to dump information directly into our bodies, I confirm the purchases for now. I've got dozens of other skills I want to purchase but taking this in batches is probably for the best. Even then, I'm sure not all of it will "settle" immediately.

Information floods into my mind and my eyes widen, flicking from side to side as my brain rushes to capture the information. My boosted Intelligence gets to work grabbing and sorting the flood of information, settling my mind down even as my body processes a series of micro-impulses.

Once that's done, I highlight a few new low-level spells. Mostly I add on to my control spells, layering some ice, metal, and air to the mud and fire walls I already have. I briefly consider adding a healing spell but discard it, happy enough with the one I have. Truth be told, my Mana is limited. Once again, I confirm the information and feel the rush as spell knowledge floods my mind.

It's painful to see more of my precious Credits flowing out, especially since my savings is limited. Unless I run more dungeons, what I have is what I have. Deciding against spending any more for now, I take a quick look at my Status Screen before heading back to the hotel.

Status Screen			
Name	John Lee	Class	Erethran Paladin
Race	Human (Male)	Level	24
Titles			
Monster's Bane, Redeemer of the Dead, Duelist, Explorer			
Health	3520	Stamina	3520
Mana	3330	Mana Regeneration	273 (+5) / minute

Attributes			
Strength	238	Agility	318
Constitution	352	Perception	178
Intelligence	333	Willpower	358
Charisma	116	Luck	72
Class Skills			
Mana Imbue	3*	Blade Strike*	3
Thousand Steps	1	Altered Space	2
Two are One	1	The Body's Resolve	3
Greater Detection	1	A Thousand Blades*	3
Soul Shield	2	Blink Step	2
Portal*	5	Army of One	2
Sanctum	2	Instantaneous Inventory*	1
Cleave*	2	Frenzy*	1
Elemental Strike*	1 (Ice)	Shrunken Footsteps*	1
Tech Link*	2	Penetration	3
Aura of Chivalry	1	Eyes of Insight	1
Analyze*	2	Harden*	2
Quantum Lock*	3	Elastic Skin*	3
Beacon of the Angels	1	Eye of the Storm	1
Vanguard of the Apocalypse	2	Society's Web	1

Combat Spells	
Improved Minor Healing (IV)	Greater Regeneration (II)
Greater Healing (II)	Mana Drip (II)
Improved Mana Missile (IV)	Enhanced Lightning Strike (III)
Elemental Storm (Fire, Ice, Lightning)	Polar Zone
Freezing Blade	Improved Inferno Strike (II)
Elemental Walls (Fire, Ice, Earth, etc.)	Ice Blast
Icestorm	Improved Invisibility
Improved Mana Cage	Improved Flight
Haste	

When we get back that night, we have a very short discussion about plans for the next day before we crash, our first day in an alien world somewhat underwhelming. No gun fights, no major altercations. Just a lot of sight-seeing and a little shopping.

Chapter 5

"Are you a member, an applicant, or a browser?" the weedy old man with a tuft of hair sticking out of his gigantic ears asks me.

I stare at the weird gnome-like fellow, eyeing his suspenders for a moment before I answer. "Applicant please."

The Questors' hall is in the fifth ring, which was a bit strange to me at first glance. Only when Ali pointed out that not only do the Questors require a significant amount of space to store all their collected knowledge but also have little to steal did it make sense. Then add the fact that everyone knows Questors don't have much in the way of Credits and have the backing of some truly powerful folk. It's kind of like libraries on pre-System Earth. Sure, you could steal the books, and some people did, but was it worth it? Mostly, not so much. Add that together and the building, as a whole, was left alone by local troublemakers. The halls' visitors aren't so fortunate, but localized teleportation nodes and a direct transportation stop for the gravline keeps most of the crime down.

Not that assaulting and stealing is considered more than a minor, fineable offense. Damnable Galactic law.

"Very well." When the silence grows between us, the attendant finally rolls his eyes. "Show me your System Quest notification. How else am I to verify your suitability?"

"Oh! Sorry," I say, flushing slightly. Of course that would be the easiest way to get this done. Still, I'm a little irritated. It's not as if he gave any indication.

While my embarrassment turns to anger, Ali makes my quest notification appear before my eyes before sharing the information with the attendant.

System Quest (On-Going)

Learn what the System is about, its applications, methods, and origins. Knowledge of the System will give you strength. True knowledge of the System will provide something even greater than strength.

Reward: Variable and progressive

Status: 23%

"What the hell. That isn't what it was before!"

"Well, you want in, right? I figured changing the Quest wording back to its original would be better," Ali sends to me.

I mentally sigh. The Spirit used to change all my notifications and withhold knowledge "for my good," but we had that talk ages ago. But in this case, I just never bothered to open the Quest screen again. There wasn't a point. The updates on progress were sufficient for me. And while I might never tell Ali this, I kind of like his original wording better.

"Twenty-three percent. Quite respectable for a Questor who has only been on the path for less than a decade," the gnome says, becoming friendlier. "It's always a pleasure to meet a fellow Questor. You may call me Ric."

"John Lee, Ric." I offer him my hand. Ric stares at my hand before clasping it on the outer edge and turning my arm upward. I blink, but Ric seems to consider his actions perfectly normal. "I was wondering, what is the normal percentage?"

"For a Questor or the general public?"

"Both."

"For most, their completion rates sit between five and fifteen percent, depending on age and circumstance. To be considered a Questor and receive acknowledgement among our ranks though, a minimum completion rate of twenty percent is required," Ric says. "That number is impossible to achieve without dedicated research."

"Thank you. So as a member, is there…?"

"Oh, how forgetful. One second." Ric waves his hand over me then toward his notification screen.

A moment later, I get a new notification.

Congratulations! You have gained membership with the elite order of System Questors.

Reputation +2 Galactic Reputation

Fame + 2000

Title Gained: Apprentice Questor

Renowned through the Galactic System, Questors search for the ultimate truth endlessly and fruitlessly. Perhaps, one day, they will learn the meaning of life. In the meantime, they continue their never-ending quest.

Effect: Gain +10% more experience from System Quest completion rates

"That's useful," I say, glancing at the Reputation increase. Getting Galactic reputation up is hard, since it mostly derives from Galactic-level Contracts or makes its way up from a bunch of local reputation points. Even if the Questors might be laughed at behind their backs, they're still a Galactic organization. "And the benefits?"

"Access to all Questor chapter houses. Access to our library of knowledge."

"Full access?"

"Of course," Ric says with a sniff. "What is the use of information that is locked away? Our goal is the betterment and progress of the Quest."

"Sorry." I pause before asking the question that has puzzled me. "What's the highest completion rate right now?"

"That would be Grandmaster K," Ric says. "He's at eighty-seven percent."

My jaw drops while even Ali whistles.

The Spirit asks the next, obvious, question. "So how come he hasn't written the encyclopedia of what he knows? If he did that, everyone would be at the same level."

"He did. And the results varied greatly," Ric says, shaking his head with a frustrated expression. "It seems that the only way to build your completion rate and come closer to the truth of the System is to understand and learn matters slowly. Even if the information is all provided, without a good grounding, it seems impossible for one to achieve the same heights."

"Oh, like learning math," I say. It'd be like showing someone Einstein's theory of relativity, e = mc2. Sure, it looks simple and everyone understands what it says, but they don't necessarily understand what it means or the proof behind it. Not unless they'd built the necessary knowledge beforehand. Though come to think of it, wasn't the entire thing physics more than math? But you proved it via math. And engineering.

"Yes, exactly! Once one has proven or understood the basic hypotheses and theories, then you can climb higher. It is hoped that more of the younger generation will join us in the search," Ric says. "Sadly, our work is dangerous, and too many promising youngsters fall too early."

"Dangerous?" I say, cocking my head. Thus far, I would call what I've done to get my twenty percent the opposite of dangerous.

"Extremely so. Just last week we lost Ium, a promising scholar, while he was attempting to disprove Waslter Kababa's theory of Mana flow and health regeneration. It seemed one of the monsters achieved a higher, unexpected rate of regeneration and bit off Ium's leg, hampering his escape from the dungeon."

"That's a whole new kind of field work," I say neutrally.

"Well, it matters not. At your stage, you should stick to the recommended leading list for now." Ric points behind him. "Go ahead then, young scholar. Do us proud!"

"And bore me to death," Ali complains as we leave.

Ric ignores Ali, an act for which I'm grateful enough.

***

The library itself is a bit, well, underwhelming. Don't get me wrong, there are miles upon miles of books stretching in all directions. The building has an open-air central column that allows those with flight abilities to travel with ease. Yet the total number of Questors within is small. I catch a glimpse of three people, and my minimap doesn't show many more. In the end, I walk ahead and touch the simple steel stand with my hand, allowing it to access my interface. A navigation menu blooms then flickers as Ali communicates with the system for me.

Completed reading list received

Quest updates received

Recommended reading list created. Map of book locations created.

A small map of the library flashes before my eyes, books highlighted. A large number are placed close to one another in front of me, but a number are scattered through the map in somewhat random locations. It only takes a few seconds to work out why. The cluster of books are the recommended reading materials, most of which I've already purchased. The rest are the books that detail random things I've either learned or considered and tested. Those are the areas where I've progressed above the "standard" level of a Questor.

"What's with the physical books anyway?" I ask.

"Copyright laws," Ali says. "The Questors have the rights to the works that stay in the library, but if someone wants to purchase them otherwise, they'd need to go through the Shop. Keeps the Credits flowing."

"And piracy?" I ask. Not that I intend to do so, what with standing in the middle of a giant library, but I'm curious.

Piracy of books and media was a major thing back on Earth before the System, what with the ease of access. Of course, everyone had their own excuses as to why it was acceptable, why they "had" to do it—inconvenience, difficulty in access, lack of funds, how it was a "victimless" crime. Hell, I'd done it too. But truth was, any excuse was just a lie to excuse our poor morality. Piracy was easy, because we didn't think we'd get caught and we didn't know who we were stealing from.

"Possible. It happens for sure. But few people do it in large quantities," Ali says. "A lot of these writers and publishers pay into the Copyright Bounty System. The CBS scans the System for broken copyrights and then adds the number and quantity to their bulletin, with the appropriate bounty. Bounty hunters stay connected to the Galactic bounty network, and well, it's often nice and easy money if they run into someone with a high enough bounty.

"There're even a few bounty hunters who spend all their free time running down people like that. They call the work relaxing. Seems like your average copyright pirate is a nice change from their normal marks. After all, the serfdom or Credit fine isn't worth the penalty of killing a bounty hunter."

"Huh," I say, rubbing my nose. The System would make something like that a lot easier. "What happens when they get caught?"

"Credit liens, fines, serfdom, the usual," Ali says. "All tracked through the System."

"Gotcha." Makes sense. I make further note not to break the law. Though… "What about all that human TV you watch? Isn't that copyrighted?"

"Pre-System," Ali says with a sniff. "Doesn't count."

I sigh, shaking my head. Of course it doesn't count. It's not as if the System is meant to be fair. I push that thought aside, deciding it's not my problem. Not right now. My problem is figuring out what to read first. After a time, I make my decision and head away from the cluster.

"You know, jumping ahead isn't always a good idea," Ali says as he floats alongside me.

"Whatever. I want to see how their recommendation engine works. And how good it is."

The walk through the stacks is serene, the atmosphere only slightly oppressive—like all libraries. At least there's no grey-haired harridan in a moldy wool sweater staring at me over thick lenses and scolding me when I make more noise than a mouse.

***

Hours later, I'm seated in one of the Questors' comfortable chairs, legs up and yawning slightly. Next to me are the books I've taken out and skimmed through for their details, providing me an understanding of the way the referencing software works.

Basically, most of the works recommended to me that aren't part of the basic reading list are what can be considered the next best thing to read after I've achieved a certain upgrade in my Quest. The tricky thing is, much of my success with the more advanced areas of the System Quest has been via fortuitous encounters. Like watching a dragon sleep, drawing in Mana. Or being dumped into a Forbidden Zone.

As such, my understanding of the reasoning behind the System and the way the System works is not necessarily detailed, just experiential. Which means that sometimes, the recommended books are too complex. In some cases, it's because the books are written by those who have come to the same understanding via experiments. In other cases, the books are written as a description of another individual's experience. In such cases, those experiential books are supposed to trigger quest updates for the next portion, rather than explain the point of those updates.

"This… is going to be complicated," I say, staring at the pile of work.

I can't exactly rely on the recommendations. And yet there's no point in sticking to the normal reading list either. I want—I need more of an understanding of the deeper intricacies of the System. If following the normal reading list was effective, then there would be more Questors with higher completion rates. Finding a balance between the two seems to be my big struggle for the next few weeks.

"You know, laughing by yourself like that makes you look rather insane," Ali points out as I break out chuckling to myself. "I mean, research makes me crack, but you've only been at it for, like, five hours."

"Nah, it's not the work." I chuckle again. "It's the idea that figuring out my best research method is going to be the big struggle of my life for the next little while. It's… nice."

"Boring!"

His opinion makes me chuckle further as I pull a chocolate from my inventory and get back to reading. Boring it is. I could do with boring.

***

"As can be seen from control group three, it is clear that Elemental Affinities are the most 'base' form of powers. The individuals who have Elemental Affinities have been gifted powers to wield forces directly, without the intervention of the System itself. As experiments in both the Forbidden Zone and outside System-activated locations have shown, there is no loss of Elemental Affinity abilities in both locations.

This result would further explain the Technocrats' obsession with such individuals and known criminal kidnapping, experimentation, and enslavement. Their actions in the Second Elemental War have resulted in the reduction of individuals with this power in the general sphere and the introduction of Spirits, Elementals, and other contracted eternal powers. (See Rum & Kol's Treatise on the Second Elemental War for further discussion)."

I pause for a second, putting a finger on the book, and look up. I stare at the floating Spirit. Ali never speaks about his past. About why he has a Contract with the System directly, or what that means. Of who, or what, he actually is. I know what he looks like, what he says, is drawn in many ways from my mind. Formed, as he said, when our Contract was formed. But it says nothing about what the man is. There are depths to the tiny Spirit that have yet to be explored.

When Ali looks up, a frown on his goateed face, I flash him a tight frown before turning back to my book. For now, all I need to know is that he's a friend.

'For our purposes, it is sufficient to understand that Elemental Affinities are the base. Spells are pre-System attempts at achieving the same affinities by those without the gift. Spells must use Mana as their catalyst in an attempt to replicate the actual functions an individual with Elemental Affinity is able to achieve by will alone.

However, it is clear that Spells are cumbersome and often, in the older variants, inefficient methods of replicating such effects. As an example, the original Flame Bolt spell requires triple the Mana cost of a Flame Bolt Skill and takes approximately two and a half times longer to cast. And, as we know, the Flame Bolt spell only requires a small number of calculations and formulae answers.

This leads us to the third variation on Elemental Affinities—Skills. Class Skills are, without doubt, System-generated aspects. There have been no records of Class Skills existing outside of the System. Furthermore, all Class Skills are not active in non-System-activated space, unlike manually studied spells. Even System-learned spells are useable outside of System space, though at increased cost (see W-12-A for 18888 Experiments in Mana use outside of System Space).

Skills are thus concluded to be the System's method of replicating Elemental Affinities. It is further believed by this research that…"

I exhale, shutting my eyes as my mind is barraged by a sudden deluge of Quest updates. I twitch, shutting them down as fast as they arrive, though a part of me wonders about the sudden increase. Interesting as Elemental Affinities are, and it is interesting, I'm not entirely sure why it's suddenly so important to the System.

But there's only one way to tell. I pick the book up again, focusing.

***

Days later, I walk into the hotel suite, moving around the armed and armored individuals in the room by instinct. I dodge the casual swipe of a polearm and snag a can of proverbial green juice and a sandwich as I head for my room. My increased Constitution might make sleeping a minor thing for me, but I've been up for days on end. Only the sudden thrust of the naginata's blade stops me, taking my attention away from the book I've still got open.

"What?" I say grouchily.

"It's been a week," Mikito says. "You haven't come back or answered your messages in the last few days. You obviously haven't even changed your clothing. You just left us to handle everything alone."

"Uh, everyone's alive, right?" I turn to stare at Mikito and my eyes narrow slightly, running over her combat-armored form, then move to the pair of armed humans in the suite. Their faces and names take a moment before they slot into place. Both are members of Katherine's security services. "Problem?"

"No," Joe, the short and bald fellow, says, his dusky skin mostly hidden under his armored jumpsuit. "We're hitting a dungeon today."

"Oh good. Have fun." At Mikito's growl, I raise an eyebrow.

"You didn't read Katherine's message, did you?" Mikito says accusingly.

"Message?"

"Aaargh! No wonder Lana told me…" Mikito mutters the last bit, but I hear it clearly. My eyes narrow, but the little Japanese woman glares right back at me. "Katherine told us we have to find a new place in ten days."

"Oh. I'll get right on that."

"The message was sent a week ago. When we arrived," Mikito says, stressing the last bit. "She forwarded it to me the next day when she realized you hadn't opened it."

"Oh. Ohh…" I blink, realizing we have less than three days left. Four if you include today. "Damn."

"Exactly." Mikito sighs. "I'm running a dungeon today. We need to increase the security personnel's Levels and earn some Credits. Harry's doing the research you were supposed to follow up on about finding us a place to rent. But all the places he can find require a one-year non-refundable deposit."

"One year!" I yelped. Recalling how much the rent was from what Ali mentioned, that amount is insane. "How are we going to make that much?"

"Dun. Geon," Ali intones then floats over to smack me on top of the head. "Like what you were supposed to be doing."

"Really?" I whine slightly and get another smack from Ali. It obviously doesn't hurt, which is why I'm allowing it for now, though I glare at the Spirit to warn him against trying again. "Fine. I'll… umm…"

"Figure out a guild to join today. After you rest," Mikito says, pointing her naginata at me. "Then do research on which dungeon we should hit and what quests we can get."

"Right, right." I bob my head in acknowledgement as the Samurai waves out her entourage.

The guards have great poker faces, barely letting anything escape. Too bad I've got my Eye of Insight so I can easily see their amusement and fear. Amusement at me. Fear of Mikito. Once they're gone, I sigh and scratch my head.

"I might have gotten a little carried away," I admit to Ali.

The Spirit snorts, and I down the green juice while walking into my room. Maybe I should regulate how much research I do. Even if I do enjoy the research and have a tendency to fall into the "zone" when doing it, getting out and killing things is good.

So. Guild. Quests. Dungeons. Death.

Right. Back to the usual grind then.

Chapter 6

A couple of hours, later after an entirely refreshing nap and even more refreshing shower, I'm wolfing down a large meal with Ali, though he mostly picks at the food and swills the alcohol.

"Are you sure we have to join a guild?" I say.

"Yes," Ali says. "Irvina regulations. It's how they control access, especially to the higher Level dungeons."

"Which are the ones we want to go to."

"Exactly," Ali says. "And there's nothing wrong with joining a guild. They do provide a ton of resources. And as a Master Class, you'd be highly valued."

"But there are cons too, right?"

"Well, sure. But I'll filter out the guilds with bad reputations," Ali says. "You don't have to worry about that."

"Not that kind of con. Pros and cons. Negatives."

"Oh. Right. Yeah, mostly around guild dues and occasional mandatory quests," Ali says. "And some guilds align themselves with various factions."

"I'd like to stay neutral." When the silence drags on, I finish chewing the piece of steak I'm eating and meet Ali's incredulous gaze. "What?"

"You literally just finished aligning your entire planet with the Edge. And pissed off the Fist and the Traditionalists," Ali says. "You are the most politically charged contractee I've ever had."

"Yeah, but that was politics," I say. "Not personal."

"You don't actually believe that, do you?"

"No. Not really." I sigh, my appetite gone. I push my plate aside, eyeing the feast left and pack it up to store in my inventory. While everything that goes in comes back out in roughly the same state, storing, say, a bowl of soup still needs care. Unless you want to accidentally pull it out the wrong way around. "Right. So we need to join a guild and it's likely one that'll be politically aligned. Unless there's another option? I mean, not everyone wants to join guilds, no?"

"There is one." Ali makes a face as he reluctantly admits the truth. "But it sucks. They take a good twenty-five percent of your take, compared to most others' ten. And with your status, we could probably get it down to five."

"Who?"

"The Non-Affiliated Guild of Adventurers—NAGA," Ali says slowly. "Not to be confused with the actual species. They offer certification, sale of goods to members, and guild quests. Membership with NAGA gives you access to affiliated guilds for use of their accommodations and other guild services, generally at a much higher price. Mostly, NAGA adventurers use that benefit in cities which don't have a NAGA branch, which is most of them."

I cock my head to the side. "That's it?"

"It's the crap choice of the undecided," Ali says. "Those who join it are either too scared to get involved with a proper guild, too weak to be accepted by anyone else, or too hesitant to reach for real power. Most of the time NAGA only gives you access to generic quests—the ones that are available for anyone. Material collection quests basically. Anything more specialized goes directly to proper guilds."

"But joining it means you aren't aligning yourself with any group, right?"

"Again, too late for that, boy-o."

I cross my arms, glowering at Ali. The Spirit returns my gaze, waiting for me to resolve myself to the inevitable. I hate the idea of getting even more involved in Galactic politics. I hate the idea that joining up with one group means I'll be forced to choose sides. The sides all have agendas and ideology that I might or might not agree with.

All I want to do now is research and work out why our world, my friends, my family had to die. All I want is an answer to the question of who put this damn farce of a System in place, why millions struggle to survive and millions more fight and bleed and die every day. Every year. Why billions have fallen and even more slowly fade away.

The System gives us Classes and experience, a guided way to grow. But it limits us too, forces us to use their Shop, their System. It encroaches on our privacy, demands that bodies be fed into the grinder of dungeons. It warps society to bend to its insane healing speed and Mana use, making things like violence an everyday occurrence. It creates tiers between society, offering those who were lucky enough to be born into a good family, a good guild, a leg up on Skills and Classes. Guidance on how to build yourself, on what Skills to purchase, what to focus on.

Never mind the tyrants and autocrats at the Heroic and Legendary Level. Stories abound of those who use and abuse their positions to rule over settlements, planets, or in some cases, empires. When someone hits that Level, it's hard to knock them down. A Master Class is powerful, but they can still be dealt with. Heroics require large forces to pin down and deal with. Large forces like guilds…

"If I do go with NAGA, what are the negatives? Beyond the obvious lack of help," I finally say, pushing aside my ambivalent feelings. Better to listen now than keep grumbling over something I can't change.

"Well, for one thing, you'll get pestered endlessly by all the guilds asking you to join them. Hiding away in the Questors' inner sanctum might save you a little, but once you actually go into the dungeons, they won't stop," Ali says. "Next, dungeons are similar to Dungeon Worlds. All those people you've angered? They can target you in there without risk. Most guilds set up times when their guild members enter the dungeons together, so they can aid each other if necessary—if it's viable for the dungeon obviously. Where that isn't possible, it's still safer to have a group around. Being with NAGA means you get none of that.

"On top of that, you'll be paying more at various stores and the like. There's no Reputation bonus with NAGA, so any quests you find and complete won't be as effective. With some of the bigger guilds, they're big enough that some of your enemies will back off. At least from open confrontations."

I nod. Thus far, no one has come to deal with us. Not directly. Though I'm wondering about the attack by the pirates. It'd be easy enough to pass word down to mess with us, and someone like the Fist or the Traditionalists had good reason to want to stop us from arriving at Prax. As for the Thirteen Moon Sects or the Zarrie, they'll likely come along to deal with us. Our only advantage right now is that with our Levels, they face the same issue as when they first faced us—finding enough people of appropriate strength. And in Irvina at least, they'll have to do it in a way that won't come back to bite them in the ass.

Still, the fact that I'm basically locking myself in a room means that I'm making myself a sitting target. Sooner or later, they'll come.

"You can stop grinning now. It's creepy." Ali pops a grape-like object in his mouth and chews. "Then there's all the stuff that a good guild will give you. Also, you might want to consider the fact that Mikito and the rest of your people are joining up."

"Mikito's joined a guild?" I say, then realize how stupid a question that is. Of course she joined one. Otherwise how could she get into the dungeon? "Which one?"

"Eh, there's an official and hard-to-pronounce name, but most call it Tig's Guild," Ali says. "Tig, the Guild Master, is a late-Level Heroic Class."

"What Class?"

"War Oracle. Very, very high Agility, haste, and other speed spells, combined with the ability to foretell the future and create buffs for those he's with. He's also got a variety of conditional high-attack damage-dealing Skills. Stuff like 'if X person moves here after three steps and if Y person is in this location and the moon is waxing' kind of thing." My jaw drops, and Ali shrugs. "Conditional Skills and Spells give more bang for the buck in terms of Mana output. Like three to four times."

"Damn."

"Lots of people have tried to replicate his success. A few have gotten decent results, but no one's made it to Heroic levels yet," Ali says. "Rumors are, he's also specced for very high levels of Luck."

"I can see how that'd work." I drum my fingers on the table. "All right. Fine. Tig's Guild might be viable. But tell me of some others."

"Right. Next, we've got the Tex-98s. They're aligned to the Technocrats. Not particularly an issue for you, but the reason I'm talking about them is that the Technocrats are sort-of aligned with the Questors too. Add the fact that we've got our Elemental Affinities and they'll be slavering over us joining them. Now, their Guild Leader…"

I lean forward and pay attention, resigning myself to some study about these matters. Whether I like it or not, I'll have a lot of options and I'll have to make a decision at some point. Best to make the decision while the ball is in my court.

***

Once we'd discussed and thrown around names and ideas, in the end, we came up with a short list of guilds. I stuck NAGA on that list because, well, I'm still drawn to the idea of being neutral. Even if I know I'm not seen as that. Probing my thought processes a little more, I must admit I'm a bit pissed with both the Traditionalists and the Fist for setting up Earth the way they did. So maybe I'm not as neutral as I'd like to think I am.

Once the list was decided upon, it was time to actually visit the guilds. While I'd seen the buildings that hosted the various Adventurer guilds, we hadn't stopped at them. Interestingly enough, the majority of guilds ringed Irvina's Arena, rather than the Prime Dungeon as I'd expected. It seemed that the dungeon had initially been set up some distance out of town, but years of development had enveloped it. Rather than the guilds, what grew up around the dungeon itself were the butchers, harvesters, and other shops that dealt with the produce of the dungeon. Instead, the guilds clustered around the Arena, a place to test and train their people while showcasing their strength.

"The Verdant Green Waters," I read, staring at the sign right above the double doors leading into the guild. The building appears relatively quiet, but that's no surprise considering it's the middle of the day. Most people would come in during the morning and evening. Only those who finish their quests early or are in to relax or socialize would wander in during the middle of the day. "A bit pretentious, no?"

"It's better in our native tongue," the short yellow creature with red cheeks says to me.

My ears twitch slightly as I glare at the fellow who managed to sneak up. It's particularly impressive considering I have the ability to see through most Stealth Skills and tech.

Peemoracha 'Pi' Kyaka (Level 38 Shadow Master) (M)
HP: 1780/1780
MP: 4530/4530
Conditions: Shadow Servant (x3), Linked Form, Shadow Clone

"Your native tongue?" I say.

"The founder was part of my clan," Pi says with a slight smile. "We get tons of our members from my clan. Even if we are small. Our clan, that is. Not the guild."

"Don't let him fool you. His 'clan' spans four solar systems and has a combined population over twenty billion."

"Right." I look at him with Society's Web for a second. Ever since leaving Earth, I've found little use for the Skill. After all, I'm trying as hard as I can to avoid politics. But the myriad webs, both small and big, that lead from him clue me in. "You're the Guild Master, aren't you?"

"Yes," Pi admits. "I sensed you outside. Your shadow's heavy. Thought it'd be time to deepen the shadows. Talk."

"Trying to convince me to join you?"

"Of course," Pi admits. "Inside?"

I sigh and follow the yellow man, grumbling quietly to myself. Still, this is a Tier II guild, like the rest on my short list. We decided to join Tier II guilds rather than a Tier I, not because we couldn't but because of the hassle involved. Better to be a big fish in a smaller pond than a big fish in a big pond. Since I don't want to be saddled with too many obligations, I can probably make my case this way. At least, that's what I try to explain to Pi.

But after my explanation, the alien sighs. "Not sure this works. We're about loyalty. Brothers in shadows."

I can't help but nod to acknowledge his point. The loyalty that the guild is known to share with its members was the main selling point and the reason I'm here. If I have to join a guild, joining one known to back its people seems a good trade.

"But loyalty has to be earned. You want loyalty from us. But only want to offer a little. Not a fair trade, no?"

I offer Pi a wry smile even as I admit he's right. After all, I'm basically asking him to give me full rights to do what I want while enjoying the protection of their guild and their services. In turn, I promise to only occasionally help them. And of course, pay my dues.

"Not going to work, Redeemer. You not want to change offer?" When I shake my head, Pi nods. "Not worth it then."

I grimace but stand, almost offering my hand before Ali's hiss and a note on Galactic customs makes me freeze. Right. Shaking hands is not exactly considered good manners in the galaxy. "No hard feelings."

"Good," Pi says with a flattening of his ears.

I follow the man out, sighing. Well, one done. On to the next.

***

"We at Enkrago pride ourselves on our connections throughout the Galaxy. We're always one of the first guilds to a developing world, ensuring that we develop strong connections with the natives," Joffrey says, the Enkrago's Vice-Guild Master. He is, amusingly, a bookish Hakarta with a pair of bladed whips strapped to his thighs. "Of course, in the case of Earth, we have established six guild halls in your 'Africa.'"

Well, that explains why I don't recall them. My time in Africa was cut short, mostly due to a rather unfortunate death while I was visiting. That kind of leaves a bit of a taint in other people's mouths. So I rarely visited, just popping in to deal with problems when they occurred.

"If you join Enkrago, we can guarantee you some of the best paid and most exclusive quests in the System. Our connections give us amazing opportunities that cannot be rivaled. If you're looking to join an expedition, get paid to hunt dangerous beasts, conquer settlements, or just explore new dungeons, we've got it all," Joffrey continues, almost bouncing in his seat in excitement. "I can tell you, a Combat Classer of your Level would attract a significant number of new, personal requests.

"On top of that, if I may be so bold, I can help you fill out your current party roster. Once we put out the word that the Redeemer of the Dead is looking for new members, we'll be flooded."

I raise my hand, but Joffrey continues to blither on for a few minutes. I have to switch on my Aura to drag his attention to me before I can speak. "That's great and all, but you didn't listen. I don't want to take on too many quests. Or find new party members. Or be bugged about new things to do. I have my own plans."

"Well, of course you do! And we'd do our best to meet them," Joffrey says, nodding firmly as his huge nostrils flare. "We will only send the most important quests your way. We can even set up a minimum deposit requirement."

"That's not what I'm saying. I'm saying I doubt I'll take on any quests at all," I say.

"Oh, of course. Most of our Master Classers don't. Just meeting with our patrons and taking one Class B or higher quest every six months should be more than sufficient," Joffrey says.

"Class B?" I open my mouth to question him then shut it, holding up a hand to stop Joffrey's blithering. "You know what, never mind. I think I've heard enough."

"Really? Perfect. I'll get the paperwork ready—"

"No, no. I still need to look into some other things. Don't worry, I'll call you if I decide to go with the Enkrago."

"Of course. You have my contact information, right? Well, here it is again," Joffrey says, though some of his enthusiasm has wavered.

I head out of the private office. Beside me, Ali is laughing silently and invisibly, a giant bag of popcorn in hand.

***

"That's it?" I say, eyeing the NAGA guild.

"Yup."

"That can't be it."

"It is."

"That's…" I look up and down the stall. It's literally a stall installed into the side of the building, large enough to fit the bored-looking grey creature with big eyes and nothing else. "Underwhelming. I thought you said there was a guild branch here."

"It is a guild branch. That's the guild master," Ali crows, savoring his triumph as I struggle to hide my disappointment. I mean, I like to think I'm not hugely influenced by glitz and glam, but seeing the difference between the large and ostentatious guild branches that I've visited and this…

"Maybe we'll come back later?" I say hesitantly.

Somehow, this physical example of how little the guild offers has hit more than all the talking we did beforehand. While the part of me that doesn't want to get involved still refuses to back down, the more rational part is telling it to shut up. Compromise is something I can do. The gods know I did more than enough of that while getting Earth on the Council.

***

Guild after guild, I pop in to talk to them. Some are obsequious and slimy, desperate to get me involved. Others are accommodating, willing to work with my requests so long as I am willing to compromise on my own requests. And others are more hesitant, wishing to work with me but wanting to explore our relationship on a temporary basis. It's not entirely the red-carpet treatment Ali had painted. Eventually, I find myself in Tig's Guild, Mikito's choice.

"Redeemer." Draco, the Vice-Guild Master of the Irvina branch, sits before me, legs crossed. That he has two that he crosses and two—and a tail—that he uses to balance himself makes the snake/dragon hybrid a sight to behold. After seeing his weird number of limbs, his beautiful purple and green scales and his long, lizard-like face aren't that shocking.

Draco min Tish, Vice-Guild Master, The Silent Killer, Nightwarden, Monster Slayer, Duellist, more... (Level 43 Inked Mage) (M)
HP: 1570/1570
MP: 9890/9890
Conditions: Flame Friend, Reinforced Scales, Ink Armor, Layered Power, Mana Battery (B), Health Battery (A)

"Before you ask, an Inked Mage is normally someone who uses tattoos to fight. Though with Draco's scales, I have a feeling that he's altered the way he uses his Class slightly."

"Vice-Guild Master," I say respectfully. His titles, if not his Level, would have me be respectful. As for his Levels… well, that's more than enough to make me somewhat wary. "Thank you for seeing me."

"As if I would not speak with a potential Master recruit. The Spear mentioned that you would likely arrive," Draco says. "I did warn the Spear that your acceptance to our guild would be dependent upon your own accomplishments."

"Oh?" I raise an eyebrow, curious. This is the first time one of the guilds has been so blunt. Especially when someone like Mikito has already vouched for me. I wonder if it's my Reputation. Or something else.

"You come with a degree of infamy. While we are—somewhat—aligned with the Expansionists, a significant portion of our members are also members of the Fist faction. That your actions have caused one of the Dungeon Worlds to become less welcoming to members of that faction is difficult," Draco says. "And while your combat ability is without doubt, it seems you have some reservations about joining a guild fully."

"I do." I consider how to say the rest. "Firstly, I'm always going to put humanity first. Guild or no guild, if there's a conflict—"

"A non-issue. Species-upon-species conflicts is a common exception."

"Good. I also don't want to accept quests willy-nilly. Frankly, I'm here at Irvina to study at the Questors' hall."

"Yes. The Spear mentioned that." Draco makes a face. "While we do not have any objections to Questors, we've found many of them to be either extremely foolhardy in their attempts to test new hypotheses or entirely too reluctant to join expeditions."

"Well, I'm not planning on running any tests that will endanger others." I pause before adding, "And I'm going to need a lot of funds very soon. So running the dungeons is a non-issue."

"Until you acquire sufficient funds," Draco says. "At which point you'll disappear and shelter yourself under our guild's name."

I shrug slightly, not denying his words.

"You are very straightforward."

"Is there a point lying?" I ask.

"No."

"I'm also not looking to get assigned any special duties or do any of the paperwork," I continue, figuring I might as well finish my spiel.

"That is a non-issue. Few Combat Classers are suited for desk work."

"Well, that'd be about it then." Really, my wants and needs weren't much. Just don't bother me and let me do my thing. But...

"I'm currently failing to see what we would gain from having you in our Guild, Redeemer," Draco says.

"Truth be told, so am I."

"Oy!" Ali exclaims, rolling his eyes as he floats over. "That's a horrible bargaining statement. And you know boy-o brings a ton. While he might not want to do quests, if you've got any bleeding heart quests out there, if you waved it in front of his face, he'd probably go help. Not too often of course, 'cause I'd get pissed."

"Bleeding heart?"

"Mana siphon quests," Ali says.

Draco nods, looking me up and down consideringly. "Ah. One of those. Rare at the Master level."

"He's all kind of rare," Ali says. "Add the fact that you haven't seen him and Mikito get to work. Your people might be good, but those two are another thing altogether."

"I've seen the Spear's returns," Draco says. "Impressive, considering her level and lack of knowledge of the local dungeons."

"Going in cold is kind of our thing," I say, stepping in. "In fact, if you guys ever have new dungeons—"

"Not a feature of our city dungeons," Draco says. "But the city does have kill and Mana thresholds for each guild. If you and the Spear are able to elevate our level…"

"No guarantees," I say.

"No problem," Ali says at the same time.

I glare at Ali, who opens up a notification window for me to look at. It's a ranking chart of the various guilds and their Mana dispersal contribution— a.k.a. kill points. As in, the Mana that gets dispersed when you kill a monster. And all it takes is a quick review to make me realize why Ali's willing to make the guarantee. The guild is close and getting them to the next level would only take a little bit of work. From what I recall of Vancouver's dungeon, the Mana points each monster provides increases as their levels increase. All I have to do is kill a bunch of high-Level monsters for a few days. Probably.

"You're confident, I'll give you that." Draco shrugs as he stands. "Well, let's see how well you do. You're a spellsword, correct?"

"Paladin of Erethra."

"I was speaking of your fighting style. Magic and sword, yes?" Draco says impatiently as he leads me out of the room.

I follow after agreeing, already having an inkling of where we're going. And while he hasn't agreed to us joining—and I haven't said I would—I have to admit, I'm curious to test myself out against his people.

He says, "Room three should be fine."

"Three?"

"We have four training rooms that can be used at any time. The first two are meant for Basic and Advanced Classes, the third for Master Classes. The last is set up for ranged combatants of all levels," Draco says. "You'll show us what you have in the third room."

When we arrive, I eye the training room. On first look, it seems to be a plain room filled with tall posts with arms sticking out of them. Those arms glow with enchantments—some sparkling with ice, others burning with fire, and even an occasional post cackling with lightning. The floor itself is dark sand while the ceiling is bare of any dangers. So. The moving posts are the greatest danger.

Well. That, and the six-foot-tall Amazon with flame-red hair that literally ripples as she stands there. I find myself staring at her chest, the disjointed look of her body throwing me off for a second before I shake my head. The galaxy is entirely too weird when basic symmetry is no longer an issue. On the other hand, the bow and arrows that my opponent carries is worrying, considering I also have an obstacle course to get through. Or would be if I couldn't Blink Step.

"Clear the room. Don't kill anyone," Draco says then steps backward.

I nod amiably, but the moment I take my eyes off the Amazon, she's drawn and fired her bow. The arrow shrieks through the air, and I barely dodge the attack, the arrow plucking at my hair as it flies past. A Soul Shield gets layered on within seconds, which is good because her follow-up arrow slams into my shield, the arrow head shattering into pieces and pelting my shield. I snarl, ducking low and hiding behind a post.

It's useless though. Her arrows arc over and around my cover as if she can see around it. I conjure swords and cut a pair of projectiles apart, but the second one explodes as I do so, wrapping me in flame. Which is exactly the kind of distraction I've been waiting for.

Ali's taken to the sky, hovering high above and observing the whole situation. He's high enough that I can use his gaze to Blink Step right behind the Amazon, throwing a cut as I spin around to catch her by surprise.

Funnily enough, I'm the one caught out. The ground surges up as the black sand parts, the sand elemental wrapping around my legs as it crawls along my body.

My cut still catches the Amazon high on her back, tearing apart her gleaming metallic armor. The attack isn't good enough to kill or disable though, as the Amazon throws herself into a roll to get away. In the meantime, the damn sand elemental glomps onto my arm and crawls up the rest of my body even as it constricts my movements.

Blink Step takes me high, but surprisingly, the elemental is still with me. I fall hard, since I can't actually splay or otherwise shift myself to take the impact. We land and crater the ground slightly even as I spot the Amazon raising her bow. A moment later, a sharp shock ripples through my side, a Mana-enhanced arrow landing in a tiny gap that the elemental created for the attack. It hurts, especially as the Mana arrows ignore my base defenses.

"You're annoying me," I growl. Flexing my arms, I find them pressed against my body as though steel bands were holding me down. Well, steel bands for my pre-System self. Pure strength seems to be out of the question. So… "Let it burn."

I call down the Beacon of the Angels right on top of the Amazon. The attack catches her by surprise, the beam of brilliant white light appearing from above with little warning as the woman focuses on my thrashing form. There's not enough time for the Amazon to dodge, though she tries. As for the sand elemental, there's nowhere for it to go. The beam splashes over both of us, sending the elemental screaming and rippling over my body. Even so, it continues to hold me down, unwilling to let go.

I growl softly, straining against the sandman and finding no give. By this point, I'm entirely entombed in the creature and it is attempting to infiltrate my orifices. Panic attempts to overtake me then, as claustrophobia asserts itself. Entombed, unable to move, my body slowly being invaded as oxygen runs out. It's a nightmare scenario of epic proportions.

But I've been in worse positions. Thousand hells, I threw myself down the gullet of a nightmare creature, choking on its bile just to win. And my mental resistances are better now. I no longer need to sheathe myself in anger. Instead I wrap myself in calm.

"Ali—polar zone."

I leave the Spirit to cast the spell for me, lowering the temperature and slowing down the Amazon and chilling the sand elemental. Then I cast Ice Blast, letting the attack out from my trapped hands into the elemental. Once, then again.

I feel it thrashing in pain. Without being asked, Ali continues to channel the Polar Zone while adding an Ice Storm above us. The temperature drops and drops, but I'm snug and warm in the elemental. The elemental is held together only by bonds of Mana and will, both of which are under attack. Its body hardens as it grows slightly wet from the ice and the spells restrict it. Already those questing tendrils that invade my nostrils have stopped moving. Even as my body coughs and jerks, attempting to free itself, my mind chants the spells and layers them again and again.

"Get out here, boy-o. Lady A is trying to pincushion me. And I'm too young to be an embroidery."

I'm too busy to even work out what the Spirit is trying to say. But as another Ice Blast smashes apart the elemental, I decide it's time. I throw my not-inconsiderable strength against the bonds holding me while drawing all the lent strength possible from the System, disregarding its other benefits. I feel my muscles bunch and twist and tendons tear, muscle fibers twisting and joints popping as my body, no longer held together by the System as I apply the full power of the Strength attribute, comes apart. Even as I tear myself apart, the System helps by healing me, stitching torn muscle and tendons together as fast as I tear them apart. I roar in muted agony as I strain, pushing against the elemental, blood flooding my mouth.

A crack, a snap. But this time, it's from the elemental as I shatter the sand cage of its body. It falls away and I roll aside as I Blink Step into mid-air, freeing myself of the foreign substances within me. This time around, the elemental doesn't come along, too damaged to try. Oxygen, blessed oxygen, floods my body. I find myself coughing and spluttering as blood and air mix in entirely inappropriate ways.

Gravity takes over and I fall, peppered by arrows. The first knocks me sideways, spinning me about, while the next two pierce my body and set up a circuit that runs between the arrows within my body.

"Aaaarggh!" High pain threshold or not, having your body cooked from the inside out is agonizing. I fall to the ground, scrambling to pull out the arrows. Another arrow sprouts in my shoulder, but I throw up a Spirit Shield to stop the next two while I toss the shock arrows aside. "You like lightning, do you?"

I raise my hand. Rage bubbles up in me as I watch the Amazon dash away and hide behind the spinning pillars. Even running away, dodging between the pillars, she's launching arrows at me. I layer the Soul Shield again, making sure it's all the way up before I release my attack.

Lightning darts from my hand, playing across the room. I don't bother trying to guide it, allowing the destructive power of free-flowing electrons to heat and shatter poles, to jump between enchanted arms to land on other extended arms. To ground itself in sand and flesh, to sear and cauterize, to melt and mangle. The lightning dances and I find myself grinning.

"Enough, Redeemer. I've seen enough." Draco's voice cuts into my fun, and I find myself sighing as I let the spell go.

About time. I'm down to the last thousand or so of my Mana. But as I survey the damage, I'm a little impressed with myself. The most damaged are the poles next to me, but there's a trail of smoking wreckage. On the ground about two-thirds of the way away from me are the Amazon and the elemental.

"How'd I do?" I say, strolling forward.

"A solid C."

"C?" I frown, the competitive Chinese in me rearing up. God knows how many times I've been beaten for getting a B, never mind a C.

"C. You took too long to deal with the sand elemental. And your coordination with your Spirit is lacking," Draco's voice is dispassionate as he continues. "You are able to deal a significant amount of damage, but your combat experience is still lacking. Your tactics are well-known and easy to predict. You react to danger instinctively by reaching for a larger, more powerful attack, rather than subtlety."

"It worked, didn't it?" I say defensively.

"It worked. For now. As you progress, more and better-trained opponents will appear," Draco says. "In the end, you're too used to fighting monsters. Until you apply yourself to fighting other sentients, until you gain the necessary experience, I cannot increase your rating."

I growl but clamp my mouth shut. He's right. The sand elemental and Amazon-girl are high Advanced Classes only. Even working together, they shouldn't have caused me so much trouble. They might have their own buffs, speed increases, and coordination, but I should have done better. Had to do better.

"Fine. You're right." I exhale forcefully. "But it's not as if I can just go around picking fights."

"But you can train. Here." Draco waves around the training room, which the System is already restoring. "The guild can provide a large number of training partners for you. Give you the variety and experience you lack."

"For?" I ask suspiciously.

"Well, you'll be training our people too. But I'll expect you to take up a guild-designated quest each month you train."

"I won't take just any quest."

"Agreed. But you will take one."

"Done."

"Then welcome to Tig's Guild," Draco says.

"You call it that too?" I say with a slight smile.

"I don't have the required number of vocal chords to pronounce it in the original language. Or the time to say its full name properly in Galactic," Draco says. "And the guild master has banned calling it anything but its proper name. As such, we've taken to calling it his guild."

I find myself nodding, accepting the fact that I'm now in Tig's guild. Even if it's not perfect, I like Draco. I like what he's selling, and since Mikito is part of the guild already, it'll make partying with her much easier. And frankly, of the groups I've seen, this seems to work for me. They might not be as close-knit as the Green Waters or as effective as the Enkrago, but a middle ground is good. A middle ground is balance.

***

I'm surprised when I finally get back to our hotel suite and find that I've got a visitor. Thankfully, the presence of familiar guards in front of the suite doors gave her presence away well before I walked in.

"How'd you get the key?" I say, flopping down in a chair opposite Katherine. Not that key is the right term, since it's more of a Status update and permission, but whatever.

"I am the one paying for these rooms," Katherine says. "Also, Mikito told me I could come in any time I wanted."

I grunt an affirmative, looking over the older woman carefully. For the first time in a long while, I actually look at my ex-secretary, taking in the changes the System had wrought upon her. There aren't a lot, but they're definitely there—a tightening in the skin on her face, the smoothing out of lines, and a little more luster in her hair. There's more definition in her arms and body, a slight filling out and slimming down as she grew healthier through the application of points. More interesting is the subtle pressure of presence that even I can notice, a significant increase from before. It makes Katherine stand out even when she's sitting still. Probably the manifestation of her Charisma points.

Katherine Ward, Ambassador for Earth (Level 11 Diplomat) (B)

_HP: 390/390_

_MP: 1820/1820_

Conditions: Condition linked (x4), Social Network, Shielded, Subtle Presence, Here be my Domain

Ever since she got the job as the ambassador, Katherine has branched and multi-classed. It's not the most effective way of getting new Classes, and I know at some point she might want to reset all her experience and points. The actual act of resetting Classes is something we've only recently learned is possible. Mostly due to a restriction being lifted by Rob as the new ruler of Earth.

Unfortunately, doing so comes with a huge cost. Resetting her experience points and Class Skills can only happen if an individual with the right Class is around, or via the System. But in doing so, you have to sacrifice a significant amount of experience points—somewhere along the lines of a third of everything gained. Not surprisingly, as with anything dealing with the System, there's a huge cost in terms of banked Mana and Credits, which is why most people dual Class, especially when they're low Basic Classes. In the short term, Katherine is going with the flow with her new Basic Class until things settle down. And it's not as if her other Classes don't have their own benefits.

"Right. So what are you doing here?" I say.

"Can't a woman talk to her ex-employer without there being an external reason?"

"She could. But you haven't."

"And here I thought we were friends." When I sit there in silence, not rising to her bait, Katherine grows serious. "We've met with a number of representatives in the city. And viewed a number of the available locations. In fact, we've viewed all the publicly available locations in the second ring. All twenty-three."

I frown, thinking back to the huge amount of space in those towers. "Why so few?"

"Most locations are held directly. Few are up for lease, even fewer are available publicly to those with our Reputation levels." Katherine pauses before adding, "And the few that are available are set at ridiculous prices."

"How ridiculous?"

"Three months of rent would use up our entire budget for the year."

"I guess we're going to the outer rings," I say, considering. "Probably third?"

"Fourth," Ali says, butting in. "Not worth staying in the third when it's dedicated to the Guilds. Those guys are even worse than the Empires at fighting over spaces. Though their leases change faster."

"Yes, fourth." Katherine inclines her head to Ali. "We've begun reviewing potential spaces. However, there is a disadvantage in doing so."

"Lack of prestige?" I ask. Not that it makes much sense to me. What does it matter if your IT company is in Seattle or Silicone Valley? In downtown Vancouver or Surrey? It's not as if travel between the two locations is that hard.

"Prestige and brand for potential investors for Earth is a concern. There are also security concerns. The fourth ring falls outside of the unofficial dentate of violent pressure tactics in the second ring," Katherine says. "Add the fact that it's easier to delay my arrival for important votes and it is less than satisfactory."

"Well, that sucks, but how does that affect me? Mikito's the one with the big Reputation points, thanks to her fights in the Arena. And she's not been screwed over at the last minute from bad deals." Yeah, maybe I'm still a little bitter about Rob.

"As you know, we've joined the Expansionist faction. Specifically, under the aegis of the Duchess of Kangana," Katherine says. "Her representative has indicated a desire to speak with you. In return, she will be willing to open up certain of her properties for our lease."

I twitch slightly before I still my reaction. That's not a name I expected to hear. Though I think that's mostly because I've been trying very hard not to think about her. Or a certain Weaponmaster who still wants my head on a block. "Speak? That's it?"

"There are probably more strings," Katherine admits readily, her expectant gaze weighing heavily on me.

My lips purse, tightening significantly, but I nod. "Set it up. I'll talk. No guarantees of anything else, but I'll talk."

"Thank you, John," Katherine says as she stands.

I raise an eyebrow at her abrupt departure but don't try to stop her. That elicits another mysterious smile from the woman, as if she can read my thoughts. This is fast becoming a bad habit, the way so many of my friends can read me. I mean, I've got that damn Subtlety Perk. Shouldn't I be harder to read? But maybe I'm not that sneaky.

The sofa molds to my body even more deeply as I slump, giving in to the sinful comfort. Every time you think you're out, they pull you right back in. I could even promise myself this is the last time, the very last, before I do something for myself but...

But I've long ago worn out that level of self-delusion. I am who I am, and a sucker for certain types of situations is one of them.

I sigh, letting my eyes drift closed as I discard worries about the Duchess, instead focusing on more immediate problems. Like the dungeon I've got to run tomorrow.

Chapter 7

The dungeon entrance we're waiting to enter is rather interesting. The dungeon itself is a giant biodome, one known to warp the space within to create an environment that is kilometers long. On top of that, there are multiple instances of the dungeon, allowing multiple groups to run the dungeon at any one time, which is one of its draws. Still, as we walk forward, I can't help but comment.

"Dungeon four-dash-three?" I say, shaking my head. "Couldn't they think of a better name?"

"It's practical," Ali says as he floats beside us. "When you've got multiple races, even with translation, it's easier to use numbers. Everyone uses numbers."

"Mathematics is universal," Mikito says agreeably. "And it's a good dungeon. Wide. Lots of quests to fulfill. Lots of monsters to kill."

"And patterned off a lost world, which makes it of cultural importance," Harry adds.

"Yeah, not interested in that last part. Though it's good training for the Forbidden Zone expeditions," Ali says, gesturing to a group of Master Classes and their late Advanced Class attendants standing around getting briefed.

I look over, eyeing their gear and set-up. There's no way to tell if this is a trial run for picking out members or just a training exercise, but in either case, the group looks suitably serious. Of course, the expedition group will get ported in deep, skipping the lower-Level regions right next to the entrance to get some proper training in. I wonder if they'll turn off all notifications too, just like in a Forbidden Zone.

"You don't speak much about the Forbidden Zone," Harry comments idly, clearly fishing.

"That's because there's not much to tell. Lots of monsters. Lots of violence." Lots of loss and pain. An abandoned civilization, a discarded species. And a single Paladin who refused to give up. Memories of suffering and injury, of good times and bad crowd my mind. Four years. The majority of my time in the System.

"There's more than that," Harry says but gets shushed by Mikito.

I shake off the thoughts as we join the line, adding only one sentence of caution for the reporter. "Don't even think about it. Until you're at least a Master Class, going there is a recipe for disaster. Even Combat Classed Advanced Classers can only hang around Master Classes for safety. Even then, they mostly die. Expeditions have a seventy-percent fatality rate, with the vast majority of losses among the Advanced Classes. And wipeouts from badly planned expeditions."

Harry nods dumbly, though from the interested looks he keeps sending after the expedition group, he's obviously still considering it. I dismiss the thought, knowing I can't stop him. Anyway, most expedition quests have minimum standards and a test for those who come along. In a place like the Forbidden Zone, hangers-on are just burdens.

"How about you, toots? Interested in joining an expedition?" Ali says to the characteristically silent Mikito.

"Maybe. As a Master Class," Mikito says, shifting her grip on her naginata. "We have something more important to focus on now."

"Good point," I say, cutting off Ali. "Anything I should know that isn't on the general description?"

Mikito seems to ponder the question. "Multiple monster types. Snakes, four-legs, simian-types. Mostly smaller, so hard to hit but with a lot of hit points. Tendency to attack in groups, using basic team tactics. Lots of herbs and other collecting quests. Variety drops as you get deeper in but value increases. Minerals too." I nod, even if most of that knowledge was already in the official information for the dungeon. "Maps are useless. Jungle moves, so you're constantly bushwhacking. Trees are alive. Lots of poison attacks. That's about it. What kind of quests did you get?"

I wave, sending over the information rather than speak. I doubt there's any difference, considering Mikito and I are part of the same guild. Harry joined a completely different guild, one that focused on support Classes like his. I know he's picked up a number of low-level quests for the area, but I also know he's mostly along for the ride here. Considering how old this particular dungeon is, there's little to be gained from reporting on it again.

"Same as mine," Mikito says disappointedly. "No special requests for the Master Class?"

I ignore her tone, knowing she's mostly teasing. "There were two escort requests for Advanced Classers into the more dangerous portions."

Unsaid is the fact that I turned them down. So all we've got are a bunch of collection quests for various loot drops from the dungeon. It's not particularly exciting, but considering how often this dungeon is farmed, it's not surprising.

As we talk, we finally reach the front of the line.

"Statuses," the robot intones, and we all flash the relevant part of our guild standings. The robot assesses the information before it speaks. "Please pick portal start location. Please take exit tokens. Store tokens carefully. Emergency teleportation exits will be fined as per dungeon rules 1.9.12.4.1."

We each grab one of the tokens that are deposited in the slot and put it in our inventory. Mikito takes charge of picking our teleportation location, choosing one that is two-thirds of the way in, close to but not in the main zone for Master Classes. Once the robot acknowledges the choice, the portal doorway changes color and we step through, entering our first alien dungeon together.

***

The first thing that gets my attention upon arriving is color. Trunks are a dark brown, nearly black, color. Instead of multiple shades of lush greenery, the leaves are all a sickly yellow and orange. Most of the leaves look like large ferns, branches spreading outward in expansive, sky-covering foliage. Occasionally, fruit and flowers can be seen, ranging in color from pus-yellow to garish pink. The whole ensemble makes the entire thing like a bad trip, or at least, what a bad trip looks like when Hollywood gets to work. I've never experienced one myself, and with my current resistances, it's something I never will.

Hallucinogenic poison resisted

Right. I tap my helmet, watching it extract from the banded metallic collar around my neck to cover my face completely. A second later, I'm breathing clean, clear air as the helmet filters out the slightly acrid, poisonous scent.

I turn toward Ali, who floats alongside. *"Poison?"*

"Eh. Humans don't handle the breakdown of the plant matter here well." The Spirit shrugs, looking perfectly at ease.

I try not to get annoyed. Mikito came in with her helmet on, as did Harry, so they probably never even realized I was unaware. Guild warnings probably missed the fact or ignored it, since it seems to be a human frailty. Eyeing the surroundings, I wait for the Japanese lady to lead the way. Right now, I'm just the muscle, since Mikito's been here a few times.

After a few awkward moments of no one moving, Harry speaks up. "I'm done with my videos if anyone was waiting for me."

"Great," I say. "Mikito?"

"I'm ready."

"Good."

Silence descends again, and still, no one moves. Awkwardly, I add, "You going?"

"Me?" Mikito tilts her head, meeting my gaze directly. "Aren't you leading?"

"Well, normally, but you've been here before."

"No, I haven't," Mikito says. "We've been a couple of locations back, working the edges of the Advanced Class region in here. I wanted to slowly work them in."

"Right, but you've been in the dungeon before."

"So?" Mikito says with a shrug. "It's not that hard."

I growl then throw up my hands, deciding to stop arguing. Fine. If she wants me to lead, I'll lead. It's not as if it's that big a problem. Since the deeper we go into the dungeon from the physical entrance, the more dangerous it is, I decide to cut parallel to the gate. This way we'll be able to stay in roughly the same level area, keeping us safe. At least till I have a better idea how dangerous this dungeon actually is.

Having decided on what I want to do, I communicate it to my friends. Ali flies ahead, taking over scouting. With his insubstantial body and ability to fly, the Spirit is a good scout. Especially after I make him go visible. His initial presence can and does elicit occasional attacks from dumb plants, fast teaching the rest of us which forms of vegetation to avoid.

There are giant flowers that spit acid or poison, vines that are so sticky a single touch binds you to them. After that, other vines drop from above, wrapping you around and slowly constricting. There's this set of fungi-looking biomatter that glows gently then explodes in bright light, blinding and flash-frying the area around them. Amazingly enough, the plants that exist next to the flash-shroom have grown to withstand these attacks. I spend a moment staring at the entire mini-ecosystem in fascination.

"The purple plants that look like rocket ships? The 'thrusters' get charged up by the explosions. When it's ready, the entire thing launches into the air, spreading the plant's seeds. Now, are you done?"

I grunt, accepting that Ali wants to keep moving. I admit, the alien ecosystem before us is absurd. Part of me wonders how much the System changed, how much has evolved because of the Mana density flooding the space, and how much was part of the original planet's biology. Unfortunately, academic musings are cut short by another threat, this time from a partly-sentient tree that expels its sap in a sticky, rubbery offense.

White Sap Tree (Level 67)

HP: 2138/2138

MP: 378/430 (Limited)

Conditions: Rooted

"Don't you dare say it," I say, snarling as the white gloop that covers my left arm pulls me closer to the tree. I conjure my other sword, sending a Blade Strike to cut apart the tree.

Mikito looks wide-eyed and innocent while Ali is too busy laughing.

"Anyone going to help?" I growl when I realize that it's not a single tree but a stand of them.

As I finish throwing a series of Blade Strikes at the now-spurting group, the cat-serpent creatures who've been stalking us launch their attacks. Of course Harry manages to avoid getting targeted and Ali's too high up, so it's Mikito and me who bear the brunt of the entire attack.

Mikito cuts one creature apart as her polearm spins, the Samurai dancing under the onslaught that flows around her. Since my off-hand is still gummed up, I take a different tack, conjuring additional blades with Thousand Swords and interspersing the blades between the monsters and me. As one bounces off a sword as claw and blade meet, I get a chance to assess our attacker.

Wild Clomix Type 4-3 (Level 89)

HP: 763/780

MP: 237/438

Condition: Camouflage, Soft Paws, Poison Claws, Shard Bite

I dance backward, moving outside of the ring of protective blades but giving myself some space to throw my Blade Strikes. The Clomix are fast, dodging my attacks with hops and jumps as they close in on me. Swooping down from his spot above us, Ali tackles one of the Clomix, smashing it into the earth as he solidifies himself. Then, straddling the creature, the little Spirit actually punches it, doing a good imitation of a ground-and-pound.

I admit, I'm distracted. The sight of a portly, olive-skinned, goateed Spirit straddling a writhing alien monster breaks my brain for a second for some reason. I cut and throw Blade Strikes on instinct, but the mechanical motions are easy enough for the remaining three Clomix to move around. Legs bunched, one jumps for my throat. Another goes for my lead leg, and the third prowls around to my side, ready for me to commit.

I block the first attack and pull my leg away from the second, but the third Clomix takes the opportunity to pounce, claws digging into and finding purchase on my Soul Shield. Then its mouth widens, distorting, before its teeth clamp onto my Shield and literally rip a hole in it. Surprisingly, the Shield is still present and attempting to close, but it's stopped by the Clomix's neck in the gap.

"What the hell?" I snarl, pommel-striking the creature's head again and again.

By my side, Mikito's extended her polearm again, using the weapon to cut apart the remaining stand of White Sap Trees as she ducks into their midst. The Clomix follow the woman, somehow avoiding being targeted by the fauna while they harass her.

Focusing on my own problem, I crush the monster's spine, watching as it flops onto the ground and out of my Soul Shield. The exhilaration of a job well done lasts only long enough for another monster to tear into my ankles, its poisonous claws sending foul liquid into my bloodstream. Stabbing it and its friend is entirely too satisfying, as is burning down the group of trees with a Firestorm once Mikito retreats. I'll admit, the Firestorm is probably going a little overboard, though the fire soon gutters out. Whatever these trees use for wood, it isn't half as flammable as Earth wood.

After that, I use one of the many dissolving potions that had been recommended and sold at the guild hall to get rid of the gunk on my arm. While I'm sorting myself out, Ali flits between bodies, looting and storing everything important.

"Well, that sucked," I say quietly, stretching my previously injured foot. I get nods from Mikito and Harry, who finally ended up getting hit by accident by one of the trees. The entire fight wasn't particularly successful even if it wasn't dangerous. More annoying. "Let's try to do better."

Mikito snorts. I offer a rueful half-smile. Yeah, it's my fault for getting distracted by the alien ecosystem. I give my brain a mental walloping, reminding myself that I'm not an academic but an Adventurer. Fight to survive, not stare at things while they bite off my face. Focused, we trek forward, looking for more trouble.

***

"Yellow mucous from the cobalt imola," I say, eyeing the dried glob Ali is levitating into a vial. "We need eight portions to meet the minimum delivery requirements."

"This should fit two-thirds of one vial," Mikito says, nose wrinkling. "Why do they need eight portions anyway? What if someone only finds six? Are they supposed to just carry the six around forever?"

"Of course not," Ali says patronizingly. "You either buy more from the hustlers outside the entrance or you sell to them yourself. No one likes carrying drops around with them forever. Well, unless they're a weird hoarder."

"I heard that!" I shout.

***

"Incoming!" Ali informs me, flashing a guidance arrow in the corner of my eyes.

I cut upward with my left hand while dropping, catching the striking snail-shark creature. Instead of side fins, it's got a slime-like bottom. Otherwise, the snail-shark's face, body, and the way it attacks is pure shark. My sword cuts into the monster's lunging face, bouncing off hard bone beneath its skull and forcing it backward.

"Thanks." I drop the sword and extend my arm, calling forth an Ice Blast that catches a pair of snail-sharks flanking Mikito.

The lady is dealing with her own attacker, trying to pry it off the shaft of her polearm so that she can finish it. A twist of her hips throws the snail-shark and the pole into another attacker behind her, finally freeing her weapon.

Harry is standing to the side, watching everything with both hands up and pointed at the two of us. From earlier conversations, I know it's his way of recording what is going on from two points-of-view. Even as I catch a glimpse of him, a snail-shark runs right past the reporter, ignoring Harry as it rushes toward me. Ali intercepts this one with a lightning bolt, sending it sprawling.

No more time to look. I refocus, flipping a conjured sword hand-over-hand at a monster while spinning around to attack with a third. Monsters. Monsters everywhere.

I wonder if their top fins taste good?

***

"Help!"

"Yeah. No," I say, grinning as I watch Harry spin around on the thread that holds him in the air.

I casually throw a Blade Strike at an encroaching spider, keeping the monster from draining Harry. It's not as if I want the man dead after all. But there is a certain amusement in watching the reporter spin about. At least the System doesn't share much of our combat experience with him, not unless he actively takes part. Probably the only reason Mikito is willing to suffer his presence.

"Mikito!" Harry calls.

"Busy here," Mikito says as she continues to raid the spider-bird nest.

Yes. Spider-bird. There's a real name for these creatures, but considering whoever named them had vocal chords that were nothing like humanity's, I'm going with spider-birds. On the other hand, their eggs are supposedly extremely tasty and in great demand at the local restaurants. The only problem is that they need to be carefully handled using a special type of glove and stored in a bag of the same material or else their flavor spoils.

"Ali, behind Harry," I warn the Spirit.

The little fellow laughs and swoops right through Harry, making the reporter let out a little shriek. It amuses me to watch Ali do a Superman fly-through, punching the juvenile spider-bird that was trying to sneak up on the dangling reporter.

After he completes one more revolution, Harry's face turns a little more green and his body arches as his mouth opens. I jump backward, dodging the explosion of vomit and snot that comes from the dangling reporter. He coughs and wheezes, the vomit and snot clogging up his breathing tract. At my nod, Ali flits back and burns off the threads, dropping the reporter.

Right onto his head. And his own discarded refuse.

What? He laughed at me first.

***

Down. Cut. Step. Knee in snout. Then extend foot and kick. Watch as cat-lizard creature goes flying into the thorny bush, impaling itself and dissolving on the acid and poison. Turn around, scan for threats, and realize there are none. All gone. Monsters dead. I exhale, shaking my head as I drop out of my fight mindset.

That's when Ali sends the notification.

Level Up!

You have reached Level 24 as an Erethran Paladin. Stat Points automatically distributed. You have 7 Free Attributes and 0 Class Skills to distribute.

One more Level. Sadly, it doesn't change the equation of power very much, though I know in many ways that I'm shooting up Levels at an astonishing rate. Gaining a Level as a Master Class in the middle range should be at least a year of dedicated work on a Dungeon Planet. Not, you know, wandering around a curated city dungeon.

Rather than slowing down, my Leveling speed seems to have increased. At least for the amount of work I'm actually putting in. There are a few reasons for this. Firstly, the banked experience from my time in the Forbidden Zone is making a big difference. It's one of the many reasons the Fist and other Master Classers like Forbidden Zones. Killing monsters in the Forbidden Zone is not only great for the higher amount of experience they offer but also allows the banked experience to be spread out over a period of time. Significant studies have been done to calculate the exact time-ratio benefits of time in Forbidden Zones to time in Dungeon Planets. A lot of those numbers even include details about the most common types of quests that Forbidden Zone entries provide.

The second reason is a matter of threats. I'm facing Master Level threats at times. At some point, I'll even get a Master Level Quest. As such, I'm jumping up in Levels because I'm getting the experience that a Master Classer should be getting while I'm still the equivalent of a late-stage Advanced Classer at most. Mikito is benefitting too, but of course, she really is an Advanced Classer. This dungeon run is a good example of the weird imbalance between Levels, our Classes, and the actual threat level we face. Dangerous to be here? Sure. But deadly? No.

I dismiss those thoughts for now, glancing over my stats and the free attribute points I have available. At my level, the actual amount I gain from having free attributes is pretty small, especially when you consider the high number of points they're meant to bolster. It's one thing to add three points when you've only got ten. Another when you already have three hundred.

It's why one of the leveling recommendations bantered around—mostly theoretically by a bunch of Advanced Classers, I'll admit—is to ignore high attributes and instead bolster lower ones. In my case, it would be either Charisma, Perception, or my lowest attribute, Luck. The theory is that since you're going to be so insanely out-classed in attributes by a Master Class who has already been focused on those high attributes—for example, a Mage in Intelligence, a fighter in Strength, a rifleman in Agility—it's better to upgrade lower attributes so that you have an advantage over them in other ways. So against a fighter whose focus is Strength, having more Luck might give you the edge. Or a higher Perception, allowing you to notice what the Mage is going to cast before he finishes.

It's an interesting Leveling strategy, countered by the point that given enough time, a Soldier who doesn't grow his Agility will likely be out-Agilitied by even an Advanced Fighter. Then again, there's the point that for most Master Classers, gaining Levels is difficult. So in many ways, the attributes they're looking at are the last attributes they can ever expect. If you knew you could never again change your build, what would you shore up?

An interesting theoretical discussion, but not for me. I know I'm going to Level up. By skipping the Basic Class entirely, my Leveling speed will continue to be high until I hit Heroic. At that point, I can expect things to slow down. On the other hand, I also know I am literally fifty Levels—the entirety of the Basic Class—underpowered compared to most Master Classes. The good news is that most Basic Classes only give a relatively small number of points per Level. Add the fact that I have my prestige Classes, and the gap in attributes at least isn't horrible. Except when facing a Master Classer who has managed to make his way up via prestige Classes.

In the end, the question for me is whether to double-down to catch up or reinforce for the surprise factor and target others' weaknesses? Put that way, it's pretty simple. I can't afford to fight my enemies head-on. I win—I've always won—by coming at things sideways.

So I dump the points into Charisma, Luck, and Perception and confirm the change. No Class Skills to allocate this time, though I'll have one next Level. Of course, I'd rather leave the Class Skill Point unallocated if circumstances allow. Being able to adjust my build to suit the situation, no matter how slightly, is kind of useful. But that strategy is getting dangerous as my enemies get more and more powerful.

Dismissing my Status screen, I turn toward my friends. "Shall we get going?"

***

Hours go by. After a while, we stopped heading parallel to the portal location and instead headed in deeper. As we do, the monster types we deal with grow bigger and larger. Some notable new monsters include a Cerberus-like lizard creature whose heads wield a variety of elemental powers. Occasionally those heads seem to conjure a particularly powerful combination, like the monster with wind, force, and fire heads that combined its attacks into plasma beams.

Then there are the various bear-like variants. Lizard-owlbears. Fish-bears. Snake-bear with triple heads. Of course, could you call something a bear if it was covered with scales, had paws but shot electricity off its gilled-and-snouted head?

That's the thing about trying to use human or human-mythological equivalents. Of course, some of those human mythologies or artwork came through via Mana bleed. But just as many don't have popular names. Or are just wrong.

On the other hand, I'm impressed by this latest monster. Very, very impressed by the giant, red-skinned-and-horned humanoid standing in front of us. Cloven feet, muscles that would make Conan cry, and a bladed whip held casually as smoke dribbles from its overly-large nostrils. It's lacking the wings of a balrog, and its horns curl up like a sheep's more than stick out like an elk's. I'll admit, I'm almost curious if the horns drop every year. How weird would that be, to be a demon that had to regrow your headpiece each year?

"John?" Mikito prods my side.

"Sorry. Just thinking," I say. "Think we can take it?"

Mikito's lips purse as she stares at the monster's status. I review it once again to remind me of the trouble we're looking at.

Greater Forest Demon (Level 103)

HP: 7183/7183

MP: 789/789

Conditions: Burning Aura, Vengeance, Demon Thralls, Pain to Blood, Heroic Regeneration

The Burning Aura would be a pain. Just looking at the scorched earth in the clearing the monster stood within gave an idea of what the aura did. Other than the vegetation that had grown to thrive in the extreme heat, there was nothing but churned earth and ash around the monster. I did wonder if he stayed in one location or if the Demon was nomadic. And if so, how did the vegetation survive? Then again, most of the vegetation around here was particularly resistant to being burnt down. Perhaps it could survive short-term contact with the Aura.

"Ali?"

"You're going to have hit him and keep hitting him. If you let the demon take a break, its Heroic Regeneration will fill in its health. Your Penetration Skills will be less useful too. Its Pain to Blood ability converts damage to health rather than stopping the damage entirely." Ali looks at Mikito's naginata before he asks hesitantly, "Neither one of you bought a regeneration block Skill, did you?"

"Poison," Mikito answers succinctly.

"Nope. I got Freezing Blade, which should be a little more effective here. I could hit it with a couple of Army of Ones." No matter how tough its regeneration is, I can guarantee a couple of my Class Skills would take it out. If I can make all my blades hit. Which isn't impossible.

"I'd be careful with that," Ali says, staring at a screen in front of him. "The Demon's got a Rage ability that'll allow it to ignore damage for a period. And another that will allow it to stop damage from any one Skill or spell source."

My jaw drops. "What? How the hell is that even fair?"

"It's a level 100+ monster," Ali says with a roll of his eyes. "They all have their own gimmicks."

"Can I buy a Skill neutralizer like that?" Mikito asks.

"Of course. Neutralizers are relatively cheap. You can even pick ones that target only a certain class of Skills," Ali says. "Oh, and Harry? You might want to back off a little. It's got a ton of area effect attacks."

"All right, if we're going to do this…" I review what I know.

The group inches closer together, and we plot out our plan of attack. It's almost a luxury, having the opportunity to plan a fight like this. It kind of makes me realize why some of the Galactics I've fought before seemed so slow at adapting. If this is their experience when dealing with monsters, then they really aren't used to sudden changes or surprise attacks.

***

Crouched in front of the monster, I find myself chuckling at the "plan" I put together. Really, it isn't that complicated—the vast majority of the time was spent discussing the various Skills the monster is known to use, their telltale signs if we had the knowledge, and our reactions. The actual tactic is a basic flanking attack that I'll start. Nothing like my insane plans to lure monsters into traps, stick myself into their gullets, or trap them in constantly teleporting Portals. This is a straight-up bash-and-mash. I'd feel guilty about it, but I've come to the realization that my tendency toward unconventional solutions mostly had to do with being significantly underpowered.

When you can bash-and-mash, why go through all that trouble?

"*Ready.*"

"*Eight more minutes and I'll be done with my latest episode. I really want to know if they got enough gold.*"

"Camera's set up."

Obviously, I ignore Ali and Harry's respectively inane and useless comments.

I call down the Beacon of the Angels, letting the entire thing start up high as it prefers to do. This has the added advantage of allowing the attack to come from outside the Demon's visual range.

Which is why the first the Demon knows it's under attack is a beam of solid white-blue light slamming into it and its surroundings, destroying vegetation and burning skin and muscle. Damage piles up, but I can see its health recovering immediately. I jump out of hiding, crossing the ground to it even as I call up my next attack.

Army of One creates a swirl of blades all around me, swords forming as they ready to strike. The slight lag for the Skill to take full effect is why I didn't start with it. Also, there's a certain lack of subtlety when you have a dozen swords around you.

When the Beacon of the Angels finishes, the Demon is snarling at me, crouched low as its body steams. Arcs of compressed power slash outward, edged with the light blue of my Mana Blade. One after the other, they impact the creature's body. Unfortunately, its health bar doesn't move, no matter how many blows land. I stare into the Greater Demon's glowing eyes, watching as its ability negates all the damage. Even as my Skill dies down, the earth around the monster is glowing and melted. The creature's health continues to tick up. Thankfully, Ali warned me about this, so I don't hesitate and toss a pair of grenades.

Rather than focus on my attacks, the monster throws its head back and howls. Ali takes position up high, watching for the minions that must be coming. He—and thus me—have the perfect Spirit-eye-view to see Mikito launch herself through the air, naginata pointed at the monster's back. Even as we watch, the blade of the naginata grows, dwarfing its original size and blazing red. The extended blade plunges into the Demon's back, parting skin and bone before the true blade enters, all powered by Mikito's weight and momentum. A little status update appears above the creature's head, a sign that it has been poisoned. It's only a minor debuff to slow the damn thing's ridiculous regeneration rate, but it's better than nothing.

The Demon roars, twirling and dislodging Mikito. She flips backward, just dodging the creature's arm as she does so. Already, the oversized blade is shrinking to a more useful size. I'm not letting up either, running forward as the grenades finally explode and pepper the monster with frozen metal and shards of elemental ice. I trigger the QSM as I run, letting the explosion pass through me.

Split off from its dimension by the QSM, I only have the barest presence and am entirely invisible to the Demon. I time my reappearance for when it's committed to an attack on Mikito, and I use a double-handed grip on my sword to chop into its hamstring. At the same time, I conjure up the remainder of my blades so that they can follow along.

Chopping into the Demon's flesh is like chopping into a particularly thick tree that burns back. Even leveraging my body and twisting with my hips, my blade catches halfway through the monster's body even as layers of skin, fat, and muscle part. The Freezing Blade spell I layered on takes effect, spreading a chill through the Demon and slowing it slightly. Flames erupt from the creature's flesh, wrapping around my blade as I struggle to free it. I throw myself into a twisting jump, getting my feet on the creature's lower back and kicking sideways and backward to dislodge the blade. I could abandon the weapon, but I'd have to layer my Freezing Blade spell on the newly formed weapon, wasting time and Mana.

"Oy! Shut up," Ali says, gesturing downward and sending a dozen Mana Darts into the Demon's still-screaming face. It's more distraction and annoyance than actual damage, but every little bit helps. *"As for you guys… incoming. I've got the east."*

I roll, coming up onto my knees facing the west of the clearing just in time to spot the first of the bobbing thralls. Their loping gait makes them appear and disappear. Each of the monsters are mini-versions of the Greater Demon, with smaller curling horns and longer, apelike arms.

Lesser Forest Demon (Level 47)

HP: 987/987

MP: 302//321

Conditions: Enthralled, Lesser Burning Aura, Flame Skin

Even as I stare at the monster, I can see out of the corner of my eye the heatwaves rolling around and attempting to burn down my Soul Shield. I ignore them, getting a quick count of the incoming demons as I move forward, charging up my spell in one free hand.

"Go die, you inconvenient monkeys." I raise my left hand, releasing the Enhanced Lightning Strike as the first monster reaches the ten-meter range. Lightning arcs outward, jumping from Lesser Demon to Lesser Demon as I extend a portion of my concentration and affinity to super-charge the Demons and the space between. I marvel at my ability to do so even as the spell flash-fries the creatures and my Mana drops like a rock.

"*Duck!*" Mikito shouts.

I duck low and flicker the vision options in my helmet. Nice little option, though I normally leave it shrunk. It's incredibly distracting in a fight. In either case, I get to see the Greater Forest Demon being shoulder-tossed by a tiny

Samurai into Ali, who gets bowled over. The Spirit, unused to being fully materialized, reacts too slowly, so he gets pancaked along with the thralls he had spell-shackled.

"Tell me you got that," I say.

"Recorded," Harry says as he tries to hold back his laughter.

I grin, turning my attention back to the twitching monsters. I disperse the last of the Enhanced Lightning Strike, and the creatures begin to recover until I throw my next spell—Ice Storm. As I guessed, the creatures are vulnerable to the cold spell, damage piling upon their smoking bodies. The lead trio collapse under the onslaught even as I pick off the rest of the horde with Blade Strikes and the occasional spell.

All the while, I hear the crunch and snick, the meaty thud of blade meeting flesh, and the roaring, panting growls of the Greater Forest Demon behind me. I focus on finishing my side as quickly as I can, knowing that if I leave these creatures alone, they'll regenerate before I can finish dealing with them.

Long seconds pass, each second punctuated by the battle behind me. In my antiseptic, filtered helmet, I can only rely on the noise, the vibrations of the earth, and the occasional gust of wind to inform me of what is happening. A final Blade Strike cuts apart the last monster, and I spin around to aid my friend, layering another Soul Shield on myself to deal with the flaming aura.

Mikito is doing well, engaged in exactly the kind of battle she excels in. A single humanoid opponent, bigger and stronger than her but certainly not faster. Her polearm gives her the reach to deal with the creature's attacks, and when it closes, her knowledge of close-combat martial arts lets her deal a series of blows before she disengages again.

All across the monster's body, red pus slowly dribbles from open wounds, the creature's yellow blood dotting the ground along with the pus. Even its massive regeneration seems to be taking a hit as Mikito's multiple stacks of poison take effect. Still, with nearly two-thirds of the monster's health left, taking it down would be a grind if she were left to deal with this alone.

Since Ali's finishing off his side of the thrall problem, I step in. Rushing forward, I dodge an outstretched leg and cut upward, scoring its buttocks and leaving a trail of ice. I skid to a stop and cut sideways again before I throw myself into a backflip to dodge a pounding arm. I stumble as the blow that was targeted at the earth forces cracks to appear in the ground—from which flames erupt. My Soul Shield fails under the sudden attack, and the heat scorches my skin.

"Goblin shit," I swear, getting my feet back under me.

I engage my Aura and the Vanguard ability, boosting everyone's abilities. My actions draw the monster's focus to me, and I trigger Society's Web for a second. Numerous threads reach out from the monster, leading to its various thralls. I watch as the threads jump and twitch as they close in on us.

"Tanking now!" I inform the group even as I rush forward to meet the monster.

This will be a grind. Its resistances and Skills force us to take this entire battle slowly, grinding it down rather than finishing it in one attack. And the longer we fight, the more Lesser Demons make their way over.

Time to pile on the damage.

***

Those who have never been in a duel or a fight think that they're long, drawn-out affairs. Part of that is the way fighters talk of their fights, outlining each punch, each kick. In the heat of the battle, each fight seems to take forever. Each punch, each cut, each blow is thought over, planned, and committed to with care if you're experienced. If you're not, the entire thing lasts an eternity—for very different, painful reasons. Each moment in a fight seems to last longer when you're fighting for your life. And yet when you're out of the fight, when it's over, that eternity could have been only a minute. Or five. Almost never more than that. Almost.

The Greater Forest Demon finally falls, Mikito's naginata stuck in its heart and three of my blades left in its body. Over half of its body is frozen from Freezing Blade while the red pus boils out from its nostrils and ears. The Lesser Demon thralls stumble to a stop as the boss falls, long hands hanging low as they gibber and jabber at one another. I stare at the dying light in the Greater Demon's eyes, the way its body slowly loses the green illumination that shrouded it.

The monster slowly topples overs, and the light of sentience in it flickers off like a flashlight. For a moment, a long-forgotten, long-lost emotion tugs at my heart. Pity. For the monster. Exactly where do we draw the line between needless cruelty and necessity? The Greater Forest Demon lived in this dungeon peacefully, a master of its environment. Then we invaders wandered in, killing and murdering its friends, its family, and the ecosystem until we found it. After which we froze, electrocuted, and poisoned it to death. For what?

A large chunk of experience, its loot, and its corpse? Standing over its corpse, I wonder what difference there is between me and the monsters I fought. What right did I have to think of myself better, to rage against their actions?

I loot the corpse, laying my hand on the creature's surprisingly smooth skin. I hesitate, then I make the corpse disappear into my Altered Space with a sigh. Perhaps I am no better. Perhaps I am but another damn hypocrite.

That's what the System makes us all. Murderers and killers, partakers of slaughter, and revelers of blood. Just another damn System-citizen. A partaker of cruelty and carnage. I draw a deep breath and stand, regret feeding my personal pit of rage.

"John?" Mikito's voice cuts through my thoughts.

I look at her, offering her a sad half-smile. "I'm fine. Let's keep going."

She nods and we lope off, heading in deeper. Looking for another fight. Another death. Like the hypocrites that we are. That I am.

Redeemer of the Dead indeed.

Chapter 8

"The Redeemer of the Dead. I expected you to be taller."

"Sorry to disappoint," I say, inclining my head slightly as I stand at wary rest. Wary because this appointment with the damn Representative for Duchess Kangana is not something I'm thrilled about. Even more so when it's not Priya I'm meeting but somehow, Hondo, the Weaponmaster, is still here. Here, present, and glowering at me with undisguised fury.

"Not your fault. I'm just surprised that someone so… small… was able to send the famed Master of Blades and Guns flying." There's nary a twitch as the Truinnar Envoy speaks. The dark skin, pointed ears, and pale white hair give the woman a stately, elegant air. It's a bit of a contrast to what she wears—a ball gown that'd be more appropriate in a Civil War movie with all its ruffles, hooped skirt, and corset work.

My eyes narrow, flicking to Hondo. But the Weaponmaster is too damn professional to show anything on his face. On the other hand, with my Social Web activated, it's easy enough to see his increased anger and deepening resentment. A lot of that anger radiates toward me, the Envoy, and so many other strings. It's kind of humbling. I often think of myself as this ocean of rage, but next to him, I'm just a little sea.

"If you're here to taunt the Weaponmaster, I really don't need to be here. If you're here to taunt me, I don't want to be here. So state your intentions or I walk."

"Johnathan!" Katherine says in a scandalized tone.

I shrug at the woman, unwilling to compromise.

"As blunt as your reputation," the Envoy says.

I sigh, taking the time to review her Status while she continues to patronize me.

Viscountess Oria Weekamu, Representative of Duchess Kangana, Envoy for Duchess Kangana, The Belle of L'mu, Thrice Chosen Dancer of the Leaves, … (Level 38 ???)

HP: ??/??

MP: ??/??

Conditions: ???

Typical. I wonder if it's a Skill or an enchanted piece.

"As for my reason to speak with you both, I wanted to verify why my cousin felt the need to invest so much of our influence and his personal attention on such a piddly little planet. Dungeon World or not, the returns on our investment of influence seem disproportionate. Still."

"Still?" Katherine says softly.

"Still, I will make full use of you." Oria leans forward, meeting our gazes. "There will be a need for your services. If you accept the request, you will be properly compensated. And, of course, your people will have access to the locations they have shown interest in."

Katherine smiles at that, obviously perking up a little. Me, I'm still wary since the woman is taking so long to get to the point.

"We want you to speak with the populace of the exterior rings of Irvina. We will make arrangements for such group meetings. You will sell the development of your world, the opportunities available to those who are willing," Oria says.

"Pardon?" I say, my jaw dropping. When she said request, my mind went to a variety of monster kill quests, maybe a collection quest, or hell, even a fight in the Arena. Public speaking was the last thing on my mind.

Oria snorts gently and waves a gloved hand, answering me with a notification screen.

Quest Offered: Increase the number of immigrants from Irvina

Visit the fifth and farther rings of Irvina. Meet with and speak to the citizens of these rings. Sell the opportunities and benefits of moving to the newly opened Dungeon World Earth.

Objective: 50,000 new immigrants above general trendline

"This is an interesting quest," Katherine says, her eyes going over the information. "But I'm uncertain why you are offering it to us."

"Politics."

We stare at Oria, who meets our gazes languidly. Katherine smiles slightly, sipping on her tea casually, patient as can be. I'm less patient by nature, but I've learned to manage that part of me. Also, my new Skill offers a myriad of interesting threads to look at. While I've gotten to the point where I can take in all the threads and get a general idea with just a glance at an individual, the details still take time to process. And it's in the details where you can see the intricacies.

The obvious big thread is between Oria and the Duchess. There's almost fanatical loyalty, love, and trust in there. A little envy too, but it's overshadowed by the deep, long-lying contract and obligation between the two. Obligations. My brows furrow as I stare, trying to assess the thread further. Surprisingly, unlike many employer-employee relationships, the obligations and contract seems to weigh down on both ends.

Interesting as that thread is, there are others of interest. The one between her and the Weaponmaster is laced with complex emotions. Obligations and duty, contempt and envy. It's multi-layered, but it's obvious Hondo is the servant in this relationship. If not for his control, he'd probably be snarling in her face.

Yet those aren't the only answers I get. The only clues. I see lines of obligation leading to individuals, groups, and organizations I've never heard of. And many that I have. I assess the way they tug at Oria, pull upon her, and the obligations that tie her up.

"It is rude to view another's secrets in that way, Redeemer," Oria says.

"If you're not talking, I'm going to find my own answers."

"Answers." Oria's voice is flat, but Hondo perks up a little, staring straight at me. "And what kind of answers have you found?"

"Well—"

"This is to help smooth out the issues we caused with the Fist, isn't it?" Katherine says softly, cutting in. "You're looking to shore up the position of the Galactic Edge at the same time. Your wish to reinforce the perception that Dungeon Worlds are good, that combat and the goals of the Fist are beneficial. Both of which are positions that both the Galactic Edge and the Fist hold."

"My, you are a smart one," Oria says. "But such a simplistic evaluation will do you little good in the arena you are in."

Katherine inclines her head, offering a courteous smile. "Of course. I'm still learning the details of the political situation. But if my understanding is correct, you also owe City Councilman Uss a favor. Whose main opponent's backing for the upcoming city election comes from the disaffected in the lower rings. Though fifty thousand seems like a small drop in the bucket."

Oria smiles at Katherine, not giving away a single hint. But with names and details provided, I can make a little more sense. I need a lot more context, but I get the feeling that Oria is playing both sides of the coin, or maybe all the sides of the hexagon. Repaying a little obligation here, getting a little favor from us there, removing some credibility from Uss's opponent, and more.

"You got anything to add?"

"Not really. Galactic Politics are a pain. The last time I was a companion to something in the game was over four hundred years ago. And by the time it died, it wasn't relevant anymore. Hadn't been for the last eighty years. Alliances and friendships change every damn week. But I'd say Katherine's only scratching the surface here."

"Sounds like this is a deal we can take," I say, mentally acknowledging the quest. Hell, if I don't need to kill anyone, this is certainly doable. In fact, it'll make a nice change.

"Good. Details will be sent to you," Oria says, dismissing us after Katherine acknowledges her agreement too.

We back out soon after, me having never taken a seat. Even that fraction of a second difference might have meant my death, with Hondo glowering as hard as he was.

Outside, in our private bubble car, I find myself questioning Katherine.

"I don't know, John," Katherine says exasperatedly. "I've only been here for a week. Working out the intricacies of the alliances and politics in this city in that time frame is impossible. Frankly, if we can manage not to get taken for too much of a ride in the next year, we'll all be happy."

"A year?"

"Yes, a year," Katherine says frostily. "What? You think getting a vote meant much? Sure, we now have control over Earth and some controls and regulations, but the politics are complex. There are thousands of seats on the Galactic Council and hundreds of votes every month. Earth has abstained from all votes thus far, but even keeping up with the reading for those is taxing my people. As for alliances and the deals they're all making?" Katherine waves to indicate the sprawling skyscraper city with its myriad jutting spires, floating squares, and flying ships. "We've just got to make do as best we can."

"Sorry." I incline my head, leaning back. It's not as if I didn't know how difficult it would be. But knowing and doing were two different things. "I just hate going in dark."

"Well, it should be mostly non-violent," Katherine offers.

I snort, my cynical side doubting that. But really, I'm just giving a few talks. How hard could it be?

***

"No. Not happening," Mikito states.

"Come on, just for a few of the first meetings?" I try to keep from sounding like I'm begging, even if I am. A bit.

"Do you expect to get into a fight?"

"I always expect to get into fights."

"Firstly, not true. Secondly, that's a pathetic attempt at a lie. Thirdly, with people you can't handle?"

I cough, looking slightly embarrassed. Fine. I'll be speaking to a bunch of Basic Classers. Even if they all ganged up on me, I was pretty certain I could survive. "Come on. They're asking me to talk about Earth. In public."

"And how's that my problem?" Mikito says.

"Because you're my friend?"

"No," Mikito says. "Now, if that's it, I need to make it to the Guild before all the groups looking for others are filled. You don't need me there. And I don't want to be."

"I do need you!" I protest. "For… moral support."

Mikito doesn't even deign to answer that, walking out of our apartment. I groan, leaning back in the chair, only to realize I'm not alone.

"How long have you been there?" I say, frowning. I'm still trying to figure out how Harry managed to get a room in the apartment, though I'm not exactly asking the question. Just idly wondering. The reporter's kind of like a bad foot fungus. Every time you think you've gotten rid of it, it reappears.

"Since the start of the conversation," Harry says. "Why did you want Mikito with you?'

"Why not?" I look over the list of speaking locations and times that prompted this conversation. Oria acted fast, sending this entire list a day after our initial meeting. The first of my scheduled appearances just happens to be later today. "If I have to suffer, it's good to spread the pain around."

There's a long silence after that pronouncement before Harry smiles. "No need to try to convince me. I want to see the sixth ring anyway."

"Okay."

"What's with the different welcome?" Harry says, crossing his arms.

"Eh, you're recording everything, right? Boy-o here's not a big fan of that," Ali says, cutting in as he stretches. "Also, you just ain't his type."

"I admit, I'm not as muscular or handsome as Lord Roxley, but… wait. Why am I arguing with you about this? I'm not even attracted to men," Harry says huffily.

"Not even a little bit?" Ali teases.

"Not even a little bit. Journalistic Integrity allows me to ignore mental and Charisma-based influences. I stacked that with Calm Mind," Harry says. "But out of curiosity, what is John's type?"

"I'm right here, you know?" I glare at the two of them. Not that me speaking will make them stop, but a man can hope.

"Taller. Also, you need to give him a little rush, you know? John's a bit of an adrenaline junkie. Likes the bad boys—"

"And I'm out," I snarl and walk out of the room.

Yes, I could dismiss Ali. But knowing the damn Spirit, he'd spill something even more private when I eventually dragged him back. And really, I sort of trust Harry to keep his correspondence to the relevant parts. The man has made a name for himself by reporting on actual wars and combat, real investigative journalism. Not the gossip pages.

***

The idiot pair catch up to me by the time I exit the private bubble car that took me to the outskirts. Thankfully, the System mixes nicely with the tech advances in Irvina, allowing something as convenient as sending the address to the car over the System. Once inside, the trip itself was uneventful.

Outside the bubble car, once I move away from the main drop-off location for this particular high rise, the environment changes entirely, a stark contrast to the second and third rings. The first thing that strikes me are the Levels. In another world, another time, going to the bad part of town meant the first thing I'd notice would be the strewn garbage and omnipresent graffiti, the smell of urine and feces, of rotting food and unwashed bodies. Here, all but the most depressed have access to the Clean spell. The System absorbs and clears out any building that is willing to tithe a small portion of its regular Mana upkeep. Since there's little that most buildings can do with that Mana, that means all buildings are clean and tidy. Even discarded refuse gets absorbed by the System.

In this System world, it's the people who tell the story. Levels are the first indicator—everyone I see is a Basic Class. A large number of those are non-combatants. And since combat, risking your life in dungeons and in the wilds, is the fastest and easiest way to Level, a society weighed heavily toward non-Combatants is going to be low-Leveled. Never mind the fact that you need a healthy proportion of combatants in any society, since they're the main resource generators of a System world.

Need food? Send a Combat Classer to kill a monster. Monster meat is both tastier and more nutritious than domesticated meat. Need materials for your craft? Send a Combat Classer to kill a monster. You could work with metal, but the returns from that end pretty soon. Need money? Send a Combat Classer to kill a monster.

Levels and Classes are a good indicator of the state of a group of individuals, but there are other signs too. In the third ring, every damn Adventurer is wearing high-class combat equipment. With the right Skills, you could even pull up their individual equipment stats and see that each piece is System-registered. Heck, many of the more successful Adventurers run around with handmade equipment, fully enchanted. Their clothing, their equipment is as much a public statement of their success as they are utility items.

Out here though, most of the clothing is mass-produced work made by machines that are barely registered with the System, if at all. None of the equipment has any stats or offers anything but a fig leaf of protection. In fact, considering how some fig trees have evolved, the equipment here offers less in some cases. No, the people in the seventh ring have no time or desire to buy "good" equipment.

"What a shithole," Ali says as he floats up to me. His loud and rude proclamation gets a few looks, but no one makes a move to deal with the floating Spirit.

In fact, a very excited gnome—which is the hallmark of tiny cuteness, by the way—is bouncing up and down and pointing at the floating Spirit. "Mama. Mama. Look! A Spirit. Just like the screens!"

"Oh, great gears above. Don't point. He's probably a bounty hunter. We don't want them to come after us."

I frown slightly, overhearing the conversation but dismissing it. Nothing I can do but move on, leaving the poor family to themselves.

As I walk, Harry rushes up, muttering softly, "They're afraid of you."

"Of us," I say and incline my head.

As expected, a bunch of toughs stand at the side, watching us carefully. They're not moving to obstruct us though—probably because the highest-Level tough is only in his high 30s.

"How the hell are their Levels so low?" I say softly to Ali and Harry. Jesus. I knew layabouts on Earth who had Levels like theirs. And we'd only been in the System for five years.

"Lack of motivation and opportunity," Ali says. "The first is self-explanatory. The second has to do with why we're here. As you know, if you're a Combat Classer, you can't get into dungeons without joining a guild, and most guilds receive more base-Level applicants than they need. So unless you've got a good Class or great base attributes, you're stuck running down vermin."

"Vermin?" Harry says.

"Mutated cockroaches, rats, and the like—alien version, that is," Ali says. "To keep the city expanding and the area controlled by the city orb in line, Irvina has increased the minimum threshold for Mana fluctuations. It allows the city to expand their borders faster but means that low-Level spawning still occurs in public areas. Every century or so, the city decides to create some robots to deal with the problem, but those robots get badly mangled."

"By the residents, right?" Harry nods as if that makes perfect sense to him.

"So everyone fights for the right to get into the guilds. And, what? The middle class buys their children better Skills?" I say, trying to piece together the logic.

"Definitely. You saw that with the Hakarta and Yerrick a little. Though they're a little more community-driven," Ali says. "There are exceptions to the dungeon rules to give the lower strata access though. Some of the lowest-tier dungeons host school days and dungeon runs for the kids to level. Then there are private dungeon runners. They're not as extensive or as good, but…"

"But they're available and will get people combat experience," I say, realizing the difference a little Credit can make. "What are these private dungeons like?"

"Depends. Everything from a single padded room with a monster they let you fight and kill for a fee to ones like the guild's training rooms, which actually run you through scenarios. No experience, but you get trainers and coaches' tips. The largest are multi-floor edifices that host a bunch of captured monsters. There are even monster breeders who work for them," Ali says.

"Weird. So, what? Don't people just kill the monsters and get better experience? Isn't that a way to buy Levels?" Harry says.

I get a moment of déjà vu, wondering if I've ever had this conversation, before Ali answers. "Sort of? Real monsters collect more unfiltered Mana, which gives more experience when you kill them. Also, don't forget that the System disincentivizes safe fighting. Private dungeons are literally the pinnacle of safe for a dungeon. There's a point where the experience penalties and experience requirements make it ridiculous to keep growing.

"And as boy-o will tell you, there's nothing like actually risking your life to hone your skills. Fighting and Leveling in a safe, happy environment won't do much for your skills. There's an edge you lack, and that edge matters at the highest Levels."

Harry nods and mutters to himself, making notes.

Meanwhile, we take the next left, heading down the long corridors as we tread through the building. Lining the corridor on both sides are retail shops, their windows doing their best to attract attention. It reminds me so much of walking in an eclectic shopping mall on Earth. The shops are varied and familiar—clothing, weapons, toys, more clothing, a blacksmith, a potionologist, a massage parlor, battle jackets, and a martial arts training center. Of course, there are stores that are a little more exotic—the full-body hair solution with award-winning scale buffing, the pet store with exotic pets including slimes, bred mini-manticores, and mini two-tailed cat-monsters. So many shops with people flowing in and out, getting on with their lives.

"So where are the Combat Classers?" Harry says, eyeing the area.

"Out. Grinding mostly. Or training," Ali says softly. "Even if the competition is high, you've got to be out there to find anything."

"And if you don't?" I say, cocking my head. Back on Earth, starvation took a while to set in thanks to our Constitution buffs. I assume it's the same here. Credits do make the world go around, and if you're a Combat Classer, killing things is how you make money. If you don't hunt, you don't eat. Add in the high cost of rent and I'm wondering how they're making ends meet.

"The Council has no place for the useless. Those who can't pay for themselves are made into Serfs and geaes placed on them to ensure they don't commit suicide. Then they're re-educated to become productive servants," Ali says, his voice growing entirely too serious.

"That's a messed-up System," Harry says.

"Oh? Is leaving them to fend for themselves on the streets better? At least we wipe out their Status ailments first, give them a mental or chemical rebalancing to ensure they're more stable," Ali says. "It's not permanent, but so long as it happens regularly enough, they can be productive."

"You keep using that word," Harry says. "Brainwashing people isn't right."

"Maybe not, but the boy-o can tell you it's for the best," Ali says.

"What? Don't drag me into this," I say, breaking off my window shopping. I really don't need a hoverboard. No matter how cool it looks. Or hoverboots. Well, okay, maybe those hover-cum-air-skating boots could come in handy. One danger of using Blink Step into the air is not being able to change direction. I've got my Flight spell, but it comes with the negative of using Mana and needing to be channeled. In the middle of a fight, it's more difficult to complete.

"John!"

"I'm curious why enforced slavery is for the best," Harry says, foot tapping as I continue to stare at the boots.

"Eh? Oh, it's a System thing. The more people there are, the more Mana gets processed out through the environment. The better the processing, the less strain on the ecosystem and the System itself. Sentients are filters, Mana banks, and engines. The Mana gets taken in by us, processed, and filtered back to the System constantly. It's why you've got a passive regeneration, because anything that overflows goes right into the System itself."

Harry stands there, mouth gaping.

"What?" I ask.

"How do you know this? And why am I getting so many experience points?"

"System quest," Ali and I say at the same time, then I chuckle at Harry's expression. "And it's because I read. A lot. It's also not particularly hard to realize if you keep track of things. Atmospheric Mana needs to be processed. Sentients are the best processors by far. The more sentients there are equals better processing. Less atmospheric Mana, less random mutations and weird temporal and dimensional hijinks."

"Temporal and dimensional hijinks?"

"Random monster teleportation, spawning, and lair creation," Ali replies for me.

I make up my mind, glancing at the clock in my status screen to verify there's enough time, and walk into the shop.

Harry hurries to follow, all the while talking to Ali. "Why does that sound like a Dungeon World?"

"What do you think Dungeon Worlds are? The Council picks a planet and floods it with Mana that should have gone to other locations, forcing those changes. That stabilizes Mana flow in other locations, creating an exit valve when the Mana flow surges. Unfortunately, if the Galactic Council doesn't expand the borders or the population fast enough, well, all the worlds become Dungeon Worlds," Ali says. "That's pretty much what the Forbidden Zone is.

Worlds where the ambient Mana levels have reached a point that they're basically considered a Dungeon World. Except worse."

"Worse?" Harry says, frowning. "And why not just expand the borders of the System?"

"Because we don't necessarily control the flow of Mana. We control the System boundaries, but not Mana boundaries. There needs to be a sufficient amount of Mana density before we can expand the System there. At times, there just aren't enough worlds. On top of that, while sentients are better, a Dungeon World is technically the best option. But if you leave a Dungeon World unchecked, it becomes a rupture in the System. So it's necessary to have both sentients and a Dungeon World. Well, not necessary, but well advised."

Harry nods, eyes focused on Ali in the way I'm fast coming to realize indicates he's recording.

I ignore the conversation, instead making my desires known to the proprietor of the shop. In a short time, I'm testing out a variety of hoverboots for style and fit. In the end, I end up with something black and boring and looking a bit like a motorbike racer's leathers crossed with cowboy boots. On the other hand, they're slim, can alter color on command, and most importantly, are the best boots the store offers.

Simalax Hover Boots (Tier II)

A combination of hand-crafted materials and mass-produced components, the Simalax Hover Boots are the journeyman work of Magi-Technician Lok of Irvina. Enchantments and technology mesh together in the Simalax Hover Boots, offering its wearer the ability to tread on air briefly and defy gravity and sense.

Effects: User reduces gravitational effects by 0.218 SIG. User may, on activation, hover and skate during normal and mildly turbulent atmospheric conditions. User may also use the Simalax Hover Boots to triple jump in the air, engaging the anti-gravity and hover aspects at the same time.

Duration: 1.98 SI Hours.

"Thank you," I say, slipping on the boots and dumping my old boots in my Inventory. I wave away their thanks, only showing my displeasure when I'm out of the store. "Ali, why were they so effusive in their thanks? They didn't look to be doing that badly."

"That's because you bought his best work," Ali says. When Harry and I continue to give Ali blank looks, the Spirit sighs dramatically. "He's a crafter in the seventh ring. You bought his best work. He's probably been sitting on that stock for months now and had to scrape and save to get the money to buy the materials in the first place. Now, with the boots sold, he can buy the material for another set, or for something new, and gain experience again for making it. Also, you bought them without bargaining."

"I was supposed to bargain?" I say with a frown, looking backward. "But it was so cheap."

"Nope. You overpaid by, like, twelve percent," Ali says. "We're in the seventh ring, not Earth. No long-range transportation cost, no teleportation fees. No extra hazard insurance. It's all cheaper here."

"Huh," I say then shrug. Ten thousand plus Credits was expensive, but just about what I got from running quests in the dungeon with Mikito. That doesn't include the thousands of Credits I received for the various loot pieces and corpses. In that sense, getting cheated wasn't a major problem. And if it makes their lives better, so be it. "Come on. We're going to be late."

"And whose fault is that?" Ali says.

I ignore the grumbling Spirit, picking up speed. Best make sure to arrive on time. Or early.

***

The first surprise is that the location is within a small corridor off the main thoroughfare. The second, that the address is for a meeting room rented out of someone's co-working space. I'm a bit amused to see that this co-working space mostly caters to crafters, with multiple desks and work areas cordoned off from one another via enchantments rather than a slew of random computers. Still…

"Redeemer of the Dead, John Lee? Yes. Meeting room three. Take the first right, second door on the left," the floating fish-creature that fishes the desk says through the electronic translator.

I'm a little surprised but follow its instructions. Ali's chuckling while Harry's peering around at the co-space, curiosity warring with his dedication to my story. Or Earth's story. Hell, I don't even know what he's working on now.

Opening the door to the meeting room, I'm a little surprised by how small it is. It's no bigger than a grade school classroom, maybe twenty feet across and fifteen wide. Numerous chairs are laid out, and a simple podium has been set up for my speech, but most importantly, the room is lacking a little in its most important characteristic.

"Where is everyone?" I say, eyeing the clock. We've got a good five minutes before the speech is meant to start, but seven people present isn't a particularly impressive attendance record. "Are Galactics prone to being late?"

Certainly in Whitehorse, I'd have to give everyone another fifteen minutes. They might joke about Yukon time, but not a single damn meeting or event ever started on time.

"Not really. Maybe by five or so? Galactics are pretty punctual. Comes from the HUD clock," Ali says.

I sigh and slump into a chair, letting my eyes drift downward. Fine. I can wait. Five minutes isn't that long, especially since the Galactic-standard five minutes is just a touch shorter than ours—3.8 seconds to be exact. For the most part, it makes no real difference, since Ali helpfully translates everything for me and rounds it up. Not as if I'm an engineer or anything.

I might have my eyes half closed, but in truth, I'm evaluating the few attendees. Quickly, I come to a conclusion that there are three groups. Those who are, quite obviously, here for fun and food. Initially there was only one of them, but soon enough, he's joined by a couple of others who hang around the free snacks at the side. The second group are those who look uncertain, individuals who have quite a few strong threads leading from them. Family, friends, obligations, contracts. I'm guessing they're here to look and learn but are hesitant because their lives are entwined with others.

Unlike the third group. These are the ones who are openly checking out Harry and me, eyeballing us and our Statuses. This group makes up the largest number, roughly two-thirds of those present. Of course, by the time everyone else streams in—most coming in on the dot or close to it—we've got a total of fifteen attendees.

"Well. I guess that's it," I say, still slouched in my seat.

I stand and walk up to the podium. Instead of getting behind it, I put my elbow on the side and lean, letting my gaze rake over the audience. They're a diverse bunch—male and female and things in between or just weird enough I don't even want to guess. Mostly non-Combat Classers, though a small group of four in a corner are fighters. Strong ties between each other, not much else otherwise. I see no Hakarta or Yerrick here, just a bunch of gnomes, Truinnar, Movanna, lizardmen, a Dullahan, and some other weirder species. The only person who seems out of place is the Kobold in a vest-and-suit ensemble, standing by the door. Still, I sense no hostility.

"You're all here because you want to know about Earth, the latest Dungeon World. My name is John Lee. I'm a human, a native of the Dungeon World. I'm also an Erethran Paladin. For those who don't know, or can't tell, that's a Master Class. I achieved that in five years of fighting on Earth." That last bit is a stretch, though most of my experience gains came from being on Earth. In fact, while in the Forbidden Zone, I never went up a single level.

"If you're looking for a change, for a chance to grow and Level, Earth offers a lot of opportunities. Even for those of you who aren't Combat Classers." I let my gaze sweep over the group, noting that I've gotten the interest of some of them. I relax my hold on my Aura, letting it turn on, and flash them all a smile. Then I mentally kick myself when I see one of the Galactics recoil at my brazen aggressive act. Oops. "Now, let's talk specifics…"

I talk about the changes on Earth, the numerous monsters and dungeons and wide-open lands. I talk about languages and cultures, of food and the various groups in the world. I try to keep the last bit broader since there's so much variation, but even then, the talk takes longer than I expected. After that, the questions come, many of them targeting areas I'd forgotten. For the most part, the answers are easy to provide. Then there are other questions which at first seem easy but get complicated.

"Which city do you think we should base ourselves from?" This question comes from the non-Combatant couple, an Alchemist and a Waste Processor.

"Where to ship in?" I frown, drumming my fingers on my leg. "That depends—"

"Actually, Redeemer, I think I should answer that. Wiza of the Third Pors Immigration Company. We're the one who booked this room," Wiza, the Kobold, says as he flashes a toothy smile at everyone. "If you sign up with the Third Pors, we'll handle all transportation, language, and cultural purchases required for a safe and ultimately fruitful immigration. Of course, we'll also help assign you to the most appropriate locations on Earth. We, in fact, have deals with numerous local governmental authorities…"

"I thought Oria booked this. And what's this about signing up?" I send to Ali as I half-listen to Wiza give his spiel.

"Normal immigration policy for those who can't afford it. They set up a Serf program for repayment, handle the employment and other skill purchases. Most of the people you're going to talk to can't afford the cost of flying themselves all the way to Earth," Ali says.

"No loans?"

"For going to a Dungeon World? Har. No self-respecting loan company will give out Credits to someone who might be dead within an hour of walking onto the surface. The few who do use a very high interest rate," Ali says. *"At least with a Serf contract, they can dictate where and how their Serfs live. Keep their risks down."*

I frown but don't interrupt Wiza's speech. I don't like it, not at all, but it's not as if he's forcing anyone to sign on. Then again, when your choice is a slow, grinding existence with little hope of ever getting better, is the only choice offered a choice anymore?

"For a group of Level 10s, how many Credits can we get per week? Safely, that is," asks the leader of the Combat Classers. I feel weird for moment when the speaker doesn't speak in broken English, considering he's got big long ears, stands about three feet tall, and is green.

"Uhh…" I try to figure out how to answer that. Considering I haven't been at that Level since, well, ever, it's not something I even considered.

"Depends. How hard are you going to work? Which city are you in? You know, the usual things," Harry says, stepping in. "But with a well-trained party of five, you could see two to three hundred Credits each." As murmurs break out at that low amount, Harry continues, unperturbed. "But you have to remember, if you're on Earth, your food cost is pretty close to nil. As for rent, it'd be maybe a hundred Credits each for a single detached house in a suburb."

That, of course, ends up starting a long discussion about what a single detached residence is. We even have to get Ali to show off pictures of Earth. I swear, those pictures of sprawling lands and houses that aren't connected to one another are what interest two-thirds of the group. And almost lose us the other third.

Conversations go on and on, and at the end, I spot Wiza passing on his contact information. Curiosity keeps me in the room until he's done, as I answer a few more personal queries. Some of which I have to confess ignorance to. Like, how would I know if there are underscale cleaners yet?

When Wiza is finally done with his conversations, I break off from mine by the simple expedient of shoving Harry and Ali into the spotlight.

"You wished to speak with me, Redeemer?" Wiza says respectfully, inclining his doggy head to the side.

"A bit. I'd love to see that Serf contract you're passing around."

"I'm sorry, but that's against company policy. Contracts are individualized for each contractee due to differences in Classes, Levels, and skills," Wiza says with a lolling smile. "There's no single contract to show, even if we were allowed to do so."

"Yeah, I've heard that one before." The gods know, employees the universe over love spitting out how there's no regular contract, how every applicant is different. And then when you push them, of course, there's a standard form everyone signs—with some minor concessions and a tiny band of what they're willing to pay and negotiate within. "Try again."

"It's not possible, Redeemer," Wiza says, straightening a little and meeting my gaze directly.

"Okay." Wiza relaxes a little, so I hit him with my next question. "Can you highlight on this schedule which talks you've sponsored?"

"I have not sponsored anything directly, Redeemer. The Third Pors are the sponsors, but I can highlight our sponsorships," Wiza says. A twitch of his fingers and the information is highlighted.

"Thanks." While the schedule is still shared, I send a mental command that wipes them all from my schedule.

"Redeemer? What?"

"I don't work with people who don't trust me," I say flatly, turning to walk away.

"Redeemer! Please. Wait. Let me talk to my supervisor…"

"Send me the contract. Then we'll talk," I say over my shoulder, walking out with a little saunter.

Yeah, it's a bit nasty to do that to an employee. But they're contracting Serfs. Even if it is the way things are done here, I still can't bring myself to like or accept the entire voluntary slavery thing.

Chapter 9

By the end of that evening, the multi-page contract arrives. Truth be told, any contract that needs a damn legal degree to understand always makes me wary, but this one is just plain painful to read. I have to stop numerous times to do the System equivalent of hitting the search engines to understand out what everything means. Well, understanding based off a layman's skill. It doesn't help that I'm doing most of it while wandering the sixth and seventh ring. A quick stop at the Shop helped solve the pressing issue of drawing too much attention.

Isekai's Mask of the Unknown (Tier V)

A basic piece of equipment that provides a modicum of privacy for those looking to hide their actions. This is the most basic mask on offer and is not effective under intense scrutiny.

Effect: Conceals status information from low-level Basic Class Skills.

Cost: 500 Credits

Of course I could have spent more money, but there's really no point. I'm not going to spend a ton of Credits trying to play rogue or assassin. My enemies will all send people with the appropriate Skills to break a casual purchase, and my Shrunken Footsteps Skill is already making it hard for others to track me. Layering another Skill on top of that, even an active Skill, would be a waste of Credits and Mana.

No, the mask is more a social convention. It's a way of saying "I'm here to do private business" rather than to actually stop people who are truly interested. It also has the benefit of hiding my race—or at least my facial features. While I do attract a little attention with my mask, with Ali in invisible mode, most people just leave us alone. Which is all I want.

"Harry, have you seen other contracts?" I ask. I mean, I know I sent others out to serve sentences while I ran my settlements, but most of our contracts are pretty straightforward. It's not as if we're actually trying to keep them as slaves forever. In fact, in some ways, giving them a job, a direction, and a goal in life might be better.

Or maybe that's my guilty conscience talking.

Harry's lips press together. "Yeah. This one's not that different. A few corporations were trying this on Earth about three years ago. Came through a bunch of major cities. Most of them were shut down pretty hard."

"Shut down?" I say with a frown.

"Taxes. A lot of the settlement owners didn't like their population being taken, so they taxed or otherwise restricted their operations. These days, they're still around but, well, you know. Dungeon World."

I nod, hating that Harry has a point. Earth being a Dungeon World means a lot of bad things happen. But one thing it provides that a world like Irvina doesn't is a raft of opportunities. Combat Classers are actively encouraged to go out and fight, to raise their Levels as fast as they can. Non-Combat Classers—especially in the Basic Level—swim in the loot and other materials produced from non-stop combat. It only takes a little motivation to do well in a Dungeon World. But then, a little motivation is all that most people have. The final resting point might be higher, but most people end up stagnating in their Level gains after a while.

Doesn't help that constant combat is a burden on the mind.

It's why so many of the surviving humans are switching over to non-Combat Classes. Most people can only handle so much bloodshed and danger. It takes a toll emotionally, mentally, and yes, on one's soul. With the slowly increasing number of Galactics, humanity has started offering quests and advice, guiding newcomers, and setting up stores. In many ways, I understand why they call us "NPCs"—Non-Participating Classers.

Non-participating in the greater game. Non-participating in the sludge and drudge of Leveling up. There's a point when growth becomes more hassle than it's worth for most people, so while they might continue to climb, they do it slowly, gently. A slow grind rather than the mad dash of the motivated and desperate. When the choice is not to level.

"So. This isn't that uncommon, but it still seems pretty horrible. Best I can see, even if it's not a non-stop circle of debt and penalties, it's a damn spiral," I say. "Am I wrong?"

"Not really," Ali answers. "These guys aren't the worst, but they're not great either. More reputable companies have better contracts, but because the contracts are better…"

"They can pick and choose who they take," I say. Of course, that meant that those who didn't get in then went to the worse groups, so companies like Wiza's had to acquire even higher costs to set up their new Serfs properly. That meant they had to get a higher return from any single Serf, resulting in stricter contracts and longer periods. It was a vicious cycle in a way, one that those at the bottom were forced to contend with.

"They're shady moneylenders. All we need is a pawn shop…" Harry shuts up when Ali flashes a new map, highlighting a half-dozen locations nearby. "The more things change…"

"It's not as if there are that many ways of working an economy," Ali says. "Especially when the System imposes its rules."

I nod and finally discard the contract. At the end of the day, it's not really something I can change. More importantly, the lack of audience today was a bit concerning. If we're looking at fifteen people each meeting, that fifty thousand number will be a very, very long time in coming. "Hey, Ali, anything we can do to increase the number of people attending?"

"Why ask me?" Ali says with a snort. "Do I look like an event organizer?"

I look over my stalwart and sturdy companion, the linebacker with a beard in an orange suit. "Yeah, okay. Sorry. Harry?"

The reporter smiles ruefully, making me sigh.

Fine. In the end, we spend the rest of the day wandering, getting a feel for the sixth ring. I leave my Social Web on, drinking in the sights and sounds while letting a portion of my mind go over the question.

***

"Dungeon?" Mikito asks the next morning, leg propped up on a chair as she stretches.

"Definitely. Let's try for deeper," I say, rubbing my neck.

Last night was… interesting. A night out with the boys ended up with us checking out the Galactic equivalent of a dive bar—not recommended—a pod-racing show—fun but expensive—and finally a Galactic strip joint at Ali's insistence. And we only ended up in the strip joint because Harry and I firmly turned down the suggestion of the brothel right next door.

"Okay," Mikito says. "How was your day yesterday?"

"Ummm…" I pause halfway standing and shake off the sudden bout of paranoia. And the rather vivid image of a cat-girl grinding on me while a pair of male Truinnar made out on stage. "Boring. I'll tell you about the speech on the way."

"Okay." Mikito sounds less than enthused but follows me out of the suite. "We leaving Harry?"

I cough, glad I'm not prone to blushing. "Yeah. He said he had more… research to do last night."

"So. We repeating the same quests?"

"Might as well."

***

Later that evening, we're back at the guild with our haul of the day. The attendant is categorizing and working out our earnings, which really is only slowed down by the speed of me hauling everything out of my Altered Space. Strangely enough, Draco is here too.

"A decent haul for a two-party team," Draco says, eyeing the screen in front of him. "That extra-dimensional storage space of yours is quite convenient. A lot of newer teams forget to account for the amount of space they'll need."

"Thank you. But I'm surprised to see the Vice-Guild Master on the floor personally," I say, eyeing the lizardman carefully. Intuition tells me this isn't a random visit.

"You shouldn't be. I'm here to offer you a quest."

Draco's left eye blinks, and suddenly, I'm staring at a new notification window.

Quest Offered: Train with the Devil's Flute and the Immortal Joes

The Devil's Flute and the Immortal Joes have recently been formed from the remnants of four previous Adventuring teams. The Vice-Guild Master feels they require additional training to achieve a B-ranking. Your job is to beat the snot out of them till they learn how to work better together.

Reward: +5,000 Credits per training session, battle experience

Penalties: Loss in Reputation. Loss in Fame for declining Quest.

"Interesting." I stare at Draco as I look over the information. "But don't you have other people who could do this?"

"I do. But I also promised you training opportunities," Draco says. "This is it. Both teams have very different makeups. It's about time you trained against other sentients."

I grunt, still not convinced.

"I'll also authorize your use of guild housing," he says.

Mikito's eyes widen, and she unsubtly elbows me in the side. "You've hit your limit training with me, John. A martial artist needs variety in their training partners to get the most from their training."

"I'm not a fighter," I grumble.

"Yes, you are, Paladin. Or shall I say, Duellist?" Draco says. "I'd also point out that while you might have won against many on Earth, they are, like you, specialized monster killers. On Irvina are many who specialize in killing sentients."

"You guys aren't going to let up, are you?" I sigh, letting my shoulders slump in defeat. "Fine."

Draco smiles while a new schedule appears in front of me. "Those are our current open slots in the training room. And those other schedules are the teams'. That is their contact information. I recommend you begin training as soon as possible."

"As soon as possible, eh?" I say, eyeing the schedule. *"Can you help?"*

"Ugh. You are so damn lazy. I really wish KIM was still here. This was his kind of thing," Ali sends back.

I can't help but smirk. Within seconds, all three schedules and my own are lined up.

"How often do you want to do this?" Ali asks.

"How often do you want to hit the dungeon?" I ask Mikito instead.

Draco leaves when he sees me taking the entire thing seriously, and the pair of us step away from the attendant's table to allow others access.

"I'm going in every day," Mikito says. "Well, except when I'm scheduled for the Arena. But that's very busy and I need to work my way up the rankings."

"Rankings?" I say, my eyes growing wide. "It's not dangerous, is it?"

"No, *oyaji*!" Mikito rolls her eyes. "It's nowhere near as dangerous as challenging a Weaponmaster. Or a dragon. Or taking on monsters thirty levels higher. Or—"

"I get it, I get it!" I hold my hands up in surrender. "Sorry. You show them what we humans can do, eh?"

"Of course." Mikito grows grim. "It's really good training. But the variety is a bit much sometimes…"

"Just… yeah." I shake my head, deciding not to add any more words of caution. The woman can kick my ass in a one-on-one fight if I don't go all out, and she's just getting better. Once she gets her Master Class, I have a feeling I'll be entirely outclassed in close combat. "Let's say every third day? For the dungeon?"

"Good enough for me," Mikito says.

In a moment, I've got the new schedule set up. There are obviously times when I can't do a full day with Mikito, and other times when I'm busy with my speeches. And of course I still want to spend time in the Questors' building. I wince slightly, staring at my suddenly-filled schedule, but push aside the hesitation. Really, leveling is important.

It takes only a single message before the rooms are booked and the Adventuring groups informed.

"Dinner?" Mikito asks, cocking her head toward me.

"No. I have a fight to get to."

"Already?"

I shrug. Coincidence and weird timing made it all work. That, and a little chicanery by Ali. But in truth, the Spirit knows me well enough. After my last disgraceful showing against an Advanced team, I'm looking for payback.

***

"Let's keep this simple for the first fight," I call to the group when they finally make their way in. To reinforce my point, I finalize the command, and every single obstacle, impediment, and terrain feature fades back into the floor and walls, showing off the bare room.

The Devil's Flute arrays themselves before me, finishing up their pre-battle buffs.

"Works for us. Let's get this over with," their leader, a Hakarta, says.

I scan the group, Ali translating their Classes to the closest human equivalent. The lead Hakarta's their Warrior Tank, geared toward eating damage. Next to him is a male Hakarta who's a Soldier with an oversized sniper rifle. A tall, thin, grey, elongated creature with a bulbous nose is a Summoner, while the Pooskeen next to him is a Spellblade. And their last member's a damn Healer, though weirdly, strings run from his fingers to all his people. Even weirder, the Healer looks like a damn puppet.

"When you're ready."

"Ready."

Ali's sitting out this fight for the most part, staying invisible and high above us all. I send a mental command to the room's system, and a big notification appears for all of us. The countdown starts from three seconds out. I watch as all of them tense, their eyes flicking over the room as their leader gives commands. I can't hear them, and the Hakarta's smart enough to drop his helmet so I can't read his lips either.

But I can read their body language, the way they move. I can see what they're looking for and what they plan. And so, the moment the countdown hits zero, I have a plan. Rather than spend time on the defense, I take the fight straight to them via a Beacon of the Angels.

I'm surprised when the Skill fizzles, canceled out as the Spellblade jumps up and cuts at the forming circle of power. I notice his Mana drop like a rock, but even as he falls, he's sucking down a new Mana potion. My lips pull apart in a snarl.

And while I'm distracted, the group is spreading out to make my attacks less effective. The Soldier snipes at me as he runs, his first bullet taking nearly half of my Shield's defense. The Warrior Tank is moving forward to meet me directly. The Healer's doing nothing right now, while the Summoner is staying behind the Tank and calling forth monsters.

"Ugh!" I say, when the Summoner's giant centipedes boil up out of the floor. At a glance, it's clear the Summoner has gone for the "quantity over quality" side of the pet equation. Which means…

"Ice Storm," I say softly, mostly because I can, as I release the spell.

The spell flies from my hand, but before it can reach the Summoner, it curves and falls into the Warrior's cupped hands. There, it swirls around and pulses as it tries to expand, contained by the Warrior. Even so, I can see the Warrior's health and Mana drain.

"Fine. Have two. No. Three," I snarl, flipping my hand forward as I chain-cast the spell.

Another hiss and crack as the sound barrier is broken, and my Soul Shield shatters under the Sniper's second shot. Slow. Powerful attacks but slow. Too slow. I throw another spell then have to retract my hand from getting cut off as the Spellblade literally appears in front of me, cutting ineffectually at my spell.

"Forgot about you." I grin. Fine. He wants to dance with the sword? We'll dance with the sword.

I conjure my own and we clash blades, all while I keep forming a spell in my free hand. That limits my fighting ability significantly, especially since I'm used to switching hands. Fighting single-handed is annoying, but lucky for me, the Spellblade isn't used to a bunch of extra swords joining the fight. That I occasionally throw and discard my weapon is messing with his rhythm, forcing him to constantly guess about what to do next.

"Stop that spell!" Tank screams when I lob it underhanded toward him.

It flies, only to be blocked by a giant swarm of centipedes that cover the area in front of the Warrior. The resulting explosion catches both the Spellblade and me, though the freeze effects seem to be negated by resistances from both of us. The centipedes, on the other hand, are turned into frozen statues, thin little frozen legs shattering and sending the creepy-crawlies crashing down.

Lobbing the spell makes me stop for a fraction of a second—long enough for the damn Sniper to take his next shot. The bullet burrows into my body, pain erupting as the bullet digs into my side. I ignore it and the way my body works to push out the bullet. Instead, I conjure another sword and lash out at the Spellblade.

Two swords in hand and a few more spinning around us, our blades clatter and howl, sparks flying as the Spellblade does his best to protect himself. As I'm getting the upper hand in the fight, the damn Warrior shows up, throwing a fist of ice at my head. Within seconds, I'm pushed back by the combined might of the two. I backpedal and swing, trying to keep the fast-approaching centipede swarm away from us. And each time I seem to be getting the upper hand, the Sniper fires again.

"He's not that tough. I thought he was a Master Class?" the Healer says, wiggling his hand and replacing the damage I've done to the Tank. I'm cutting the Tank's hands each time he punches or blocks, but the Healer fixes the damage within seconds, those strings glowing with concealed power.

"Hey, boy-o, if you're going for an attrition battle, you should know that the Healer's Mana has barely dipped."

I grunt, spinning away from the Spellblade's cut in an attempt to get around the Tank. The Tank falls back while the Spellblade ducks low and shuffles over to me. It's not the first time they've done something unnecessary, and I'm sure I know why. Those strings are how the Healer sends his Mana to them, keeping his Mana cost down. But it limits their movements somewhat. Since they've given me a bit of a break, I hop backward a couple of times and cut the next incoming bullet apart, watching my sword chip as the bullet shatters. I layer another Soul Shield over my body before grinning at the group.

"Okay. Let's start playing for real," I say. *"Time to come and play."*

As I cast a spell with one hand, the Warrior sets his feet to get ready to deal with the new problem. The Spellblade is moving forward with the centipede horde, wary of engaging me by himself. In the meantime, more centipedes crawl out of the hole in the floor and spread across the room in a wave as they attempt to cut off my line of retreat. The ones that weren't caught in the initial ice storm are converging around the back of the room, forming an encirclement.

One hand works the new spell, the second goes for something simpler. I toss out grenades. One goes directly toward the Spellblade, who bats the explosive aside. Annoying, but it doesn't matter. The smoke grenades spill colored smoke. With a snap of my hand, I throw my spell into the sky, watching as the spell container gets dragged over to the Warrior.

Too late though. I targeted it to go off about three feet above my head, so all the Warrior does is drag the entire thing over to him to center over the room.

Exactly as I planned. Polar Zone kicks in, lowering the temperature drastically and slowing everyone down.

More grenades come out, lobbed to skip across chitin toward the Summoner. They don't get far before they're swallowed by the centipedes. Sometimes literally. Too bad it won't matter.

F'Merc Nanoswarm Mana Grenades (Tier II)

The F'Merc Nanoswarm Grenades are guaranteed to disrupt the collection of Mana in a battlefield, reducing Mana Regeneration rates for those caught in the swarm. Recommended by the I'um military and the Torra Special Forces, these are the No.1 Most Popular Mana Grenade as voted by the public on Boom, Boom, Boom! *Magazine.*

Effect: Reduces Mana Regeneration rates and spell formation in affected area by 37% (higher effects in enclosed areas)

Radius: 10m x 10m

What happens next is not what I expected. The centipedes who slammed their bodies on the grenades twitch and scream, their bodies dissolving as the nanoswarm take effect. Literal holes open in their bodies, blood, guts, and chitin dissolving at a rate that's visible to the naked eye.

"What the hell?" I backpedal and throw a series of Blade Strikes to keep the Spellblade on his toes.

"Summoned creatures are made of Mana. Kind of like me. The nanoswarm are literally eating them to power their replication."

"Stop him!" the Summoner barks, twisting his hands and forming another pair of summoning circles to flank me. These look a hell of a lot bigger.

Another shot, this one punching into my Soul Shield. I drop a nanoswarm grenade by my feet, along with a smoke grenade, then engage the Spellblade in close combat once more. As the centipedes back off, giving me space, I grin. Isolate and win. The Summoner's out of play for a few precious seconds while the Sniper will have trouble seeing me. As for the Tank…

He slams into me, punching through my Soul Shield with a Charge and snapping back my head. I impact the wall hard, bending steel and cracking my helmet as I slump down the now-dented partition. Spitting blood from a cut lip, I draw and toss my knives at the Tank, letting the blades sink into his body. Of course, he gets healed within moments, but that's not the point.

As smoke engulfs the area, I let the pair close in on me before I trigger Blink Step. By that point, the first multi-headed chimera pokes its head out of the damn summoning circle. Luckily, dealing with Summoner is easy. I appear behind the Summoner, Ali having flown down and positioned himself close by to allow me to Blink Step in directly.

The first attack slices apart the Healer's thread. The second takes off a leg, and the third cuts across his upper body. The Summoner staggers backward then disappears in a flash, the room's System safeguards porting him out once he hits thirty percent of his total health. A sudden weight increase in my side tells me that my knives are back.

"*Go.*" Ali speeds off, headed for the second pre-designated target.

A baseball bat of force catches me on my right knee, forcing me to fall sideways as the Sniper continues firing through the damn smoke. I snarl, throwing on another Soul Shield and eyeing my health meter. Still good at just over two-thirds. As the Tank and Spellblade charge me, I raise my hands and trigger a Beacon from Angels. Already the summons are disappearing, forced out of our reality by their Summoner as per the rules of our engagement.

White fire blooms, and this time the Spellblade doesn't notice till it's too late. The Warrior sees it though, raising his hand to soak up the damage, forcing the beam to concentrate over him. His health yo-yos as the Healer desperately attempts to keep up his health. That's made all the harder as the Warrior is taking the combined force of my Beacon. Sure, it does 750 damage normally, but that's over a wide area. Concentrated…

I ignore the Warrior for now and turn to the Spellblade, who has managed to close to under five feet from me. He's fast, but my knives flash out behind my Blade Strikes, crossing the distance in a blink. The flashier, more powerful Skill hides the dark blades until they injure the Spellblade in the torso and arm. The third knife misses entirely, but that's fine. Already the Spellblade is reaching for a health potion, knowing he won't get help.

"Your turn." I grin as the Spellblade throws himself backward.

My body winks and disappears as I trigger Blink Step. High above him, I reappear to stare down at my target. Once more, I summon my swords, cutting at the form below me as I land.

The Sniper spins, blocking one of my blows with his rifle. The second catches him on the arm, tearing through armor and into muscle and skin. The Sniper snarls and disappears, reappearing at one of his set waypoints. I spot him on my minimap, but he's out of my actual line-of-sight.

"*Next one,*" I command Ali, who sends a raspberry sound over our mental link.

The Spirit is already on his way, flitting forward in his invisible form.

My hand rises and power forms as I recast Polar Zone, layering the freeze spell further. The Warrior is gone, overwhelmed by the damage he tried to stop. The Healer is busy trying to patch up his friends, but his Mana is nearly tapped out. Without passive regeneration, we're all getting low. But I still have more than enough in the tank to finish this.

***

"You're brutal," the Summoner complains, rubbing his reattached leg. A semi-clear bandage filled with a blue liquid surrounds the cut, bubbling and hissing as it works to reattach the limb. It's an interesting piece of technology, and I make mental note to pick up one. Probably faster and less painful than regenerating the damn limb by myself.

"It's the way I learned to fight," I say.

"Why bother with the Polar Zone?" the Healer says as he sips on elderberry mana wine. Unlike the normal Mana potions, this one is slow-acting, but it has the advantage of being useable even when you've hit your potion limit.

"Distraction. I also wasn't sure if it would break your strings," I say.

"Har. Not that easy to cut my Strings of Fate," the Healer says proudly, waggling threaded fingers at me. "They even reform if I put in enough Mana."

"Good to know," I say. *"Got the recording?"*

"Yup."

"All right, gents. I'll see you next time," I say, nodding to the group.

There are a few entreaties for me to stay and chat more, but I've done enough of the post-fight briefing. Now it's time for them to figure out how to beat me. And me, them.

I have to admit, Draco might be right. The fact that they've got Skills that counter mine, that they work together so smoothly, it throws me off. I do need to spend some time getting used to other ways of fighting, of winning with methods that don't involve hitting really hard. And I also need to remember that I actually have more toys. Like my hoverboots.

Time. I just need time.

Chapter 10

Soon enough, my life ends up being one scheduled event after another. Sparsely attended speeches to potential recruits are followed by turns in the guild for training interspersed with time off in the Questors' library and time in the dungeon. I start ignoring my friends, taking the time in transit to read and catch up on my real goal. Luckily, Harry gets bored with following me around to speeches and disappears to do his own thing. As for Mikito, neither of us were ever the most talkative, so a pleasant silence earmarks our interactions.

Days turn to weeks as we grind on. Sparring. Dungeon. Speeches. Reading. Again and again, round and round. It's a strangely peaceful life, a break in an otherwise hectic life that I sometimes find strange to believe is mine. Occasionally I walk around a corner and find myself conjuring my sword as I spot a particularly monstrous pedestrian, or I jump and roll, reflexively calling a Soul Shield, when someone screeches too loud. The peace that everyone seems to expect grates on me at times, forcing me to find refuge in my books and the violence of the dungeon.

As I stare at the passage before me one fine evening as we trudge back from the dungeon, I can't help but frown. It's an ongoing discussion about Skills, one that I decided to follow in my research.

"Skill evolutions continue to be a complex area of research. Numerous trials have been attempted, but thus far, no statistically solid research trial has been completed. While Grunter & Ross (document 1.82.5719.11) are the hallmark case in such trials, the data set is filled with significant sample bias. In addition, as many know, this data can only be held true for Basic Classes. Thus far, no trial has been successfully completed for Advanced or higher Classes. Researchers have cited the difficulties in gaining agreement from samples to use their Class Skill points in what can be considered a frivolous manner.

It is only via such institutions like the Erethran Army and others that we, the researchers, have been able to achieve a relatively consistent statistically relevant dataset. However, there are obvious concerns in drawing conclusions from such specific data sets, including sample bias and cultural and institutional influences on the System.

Still, it can be concluded that Skill evolutions occur when a significant number of Level-provided Skill Points have been dedicated to a single Class Skill. The number of Skill Points required seems to vary slightly from eight to ten points, depending on the rate and expenditure of such points.

It is believed, in this researcher's view, that the number of points and the requirement that they be Level-provided not be an artifact of the System but instead a requirement of the individual. It is believed that the individual's dedication to the Skill, the development of it and the acceptance of the Skill as an intrinsic part of their identity, triggers the Skill evolution. It is why Skill purchases from the Shop do not trigger the same evolution—as the purchases are, by virtue of their providence, an external bounty.

Now, it is clear that certain unique Classes, like the Shopper and Greed Pig, may set aside these personal requirements, as the foundation of these Classes lies in the acquisition of Skills and groups. But in this researcher's opinion, these very same Classes reinforce his hypotheses.

This research strongly disputes the prevailing belief that the current block on Skill evolution comes from a System edict to 'level the playing field.' It is clear, in this researcher's mind, that such an edict would be lifted on a case-by-case basis for interested and powerful parties. That we do not see such edicts is not proof that our Council members are above such petty power plays but that there is no such edict.

In terms of the increased power from a Skill evolution, further research should be conducted. But it is clear from the provided data sets that a minimum increase of two, to a maximum increase of ten, times the strength of the Skill can be seen. The volume and variety of these Skill evolutions can be seen as…"

I grunt, letting the book disappear. Sometimes I get really annoyed by how some of these researchers write, but information like this is important. And it's clear, as I eye my increase in experience, that this researcher has some truth to his assertions. Of course, my experience also increased the last time I read a document asserting the opposite. So what, if any, of the entire article is true, I'm not sure.

Pushing the thought aside, I check out the other notification that just showed up. Yay. Another addition to the immigrant list. I'm a little concerned that my quest numbers are creeping up so slowly. Even if Oria has opened the buildings to Katherine—allowing her to lease but not buy the space—I cannot dismiss the fear that she'll pull back on the invitation if we can't get more immigrants. Our problem isn't so much convincing those who show up to commit but convincing newer people. No matter how many speeches I give, it doesn't seem to make a difference. There just aren't enough people showing up to those meetings.

On the other hand, I can't help but appreciate Draco's quest. Training with the two Adventurer teams has been extremely useful. While I curb-stomped the second team when we first met, they've been the fastest to adapt to my techniques.

The Immortal Joes are a pure range combat team, with members all rifle, bow, or mage wielders. Together, they put out such a high output of firepower that they manage to take down most threats long before they close in. It helps, of course, that they've secured a variety of Skills like Dimension Lock, Sticky Floor, Surface Tension Decrease, and Web. In our first battle, their tactics were stupidly simple. They attempted to keep me from closing while hunkering down behind impromptu field defenses. What they didn't expect was for me to get grumpy after falling on my ass for the second time and spam Beacon of the Angels till all their defensive measures failed. Since then, we've switched things up and have included terrain. Once that happened, closing in on the Joes has become significantly more difficult.

Both teams have upped their Dimension Lock capabilities to the extent that it costs significantly more Mana and health for me to Blink Step or Portal to them. At best, I can only use either movement spell twice before things end. They've also started dealing with my grenades, throwing up targeted force fields or using portable slime eaters to remove my toys.

Overall, our fights have taken on a seesaw property where we figure out new ways of dealing with one another and enact that plan, gaining an advantage until the other party figures out a counter or comes up with a new strategy. Of course, such changes could happen multiple times through a single fight, but staying on the winning side is fast becoming an issue for me.

That thought troubles me, even if the gains from all that training has shown up in our dungeon runs. Learning to alter my tactics and use spells like flight or my new hoverboots has given me a new appreciation for terrain and three-dimensional fighting. During the last dungeon run, I barely touched the earth as I challenged myself to stay in the air. In turn, Mikito spent her time using a rifle to snipe attackers. Overall, it was a fun use of our time in the dungeon, even if it meant it took us longer than normal to clear the quests we received.

Rather than deal with it now, I decide to check into the guild the next day. And also to look into my on-going issue with the adventuring teams.

***

"The Vice-Guild Master will see you now," the secretary says, sending me in.

The big-chested lady is surprisingly beautiful in a very human way. If you ignore the extra pair of arms, she's utterly gorgeous. Even with the extra pair of arms—and the slightly longer-than-human torso—I can't help but plaster on a flirtatious smile. Not that she notices. Admittedly, that might be because I suck at flirting.

"Draco," I greet him. "Thank you for seeing me."

"My pleasure, Redeemer. You and the Spear were as good as your word. Your latest kill count came through, and we have reached a new Mana threshold with the city. Now, what is this meeting about?"

"Training. Or more specifically, my training with the teams." I run a hand through my hair before I drop it and squash the sudden bout of nervousness. "I'm running into a problem staying ahead of their tactics."

"What have you tried?" Draco says.

"Mmm… obscuring their vision, splitting them up using Mud and Metal Walls, creating extra chaos via chaos grenades or spell storms, hitting them with large-scale area-of-effect attacks, taking out the healer, hit-and-run tactics, grinding down their Mana, using throwaway gear to suppress attacks, direct charges…"

"And they've come up with ways to counter all of those tactics?"

I nod. "Yup. Last match with the Joes, I charged the group while fast-casting a bunch of fireballs. Those gave me the cover to drop a bunch of mines. After the Joes scattered, I pulled back over the mines and let them eat the damage and the webs, but that didn't last long. Even hunkering down and blasting them with Blade Strikes and my knives didn't go that well. Barely pulled a win that time, and mostly because they forgot I can fly."

"If you've gotten that far, then you are probably hitting your limits," Draco says. "I'll spend some time this evening looking over your fights, but I would not hold out hope for significant improvements."

"What? Come on. I'm a Master Class and they're, what? Level 40s at best," I say, crossing my arms. "I should still be able to win more often than not."

"It's true that most Master Classers require a pair or three teams of Advanced Class parties to beat," Draco says. "But you're not a regular Master Class, are you?"

"Exactly!" When Draco meets my own indignant gaze with his slit-pupiled, placid one, I rein in my pride and consider his words. "Fine. I'm missing a whole Base Class."

"Exactly," Draco says. "Never mind the significant loss in Skills, most of which focus on the improvement of an individual's base fighting ability, you are missing the attributes."

"But mine's a prestige Class."

"Which has given you the advantage you have needed to win against the groups. But they're learning your tricks, your abilities, and are developing counters just for you. A focused study like this will always create problems for a Master Class. You do not have the versatility of a Master Class Summoner or Technomaner, allowing you to adapt your drones and summons to their adaptations. On top of that, you face two additional disadvantages," Draco says.

"Pray tell."

"Numbers. You're two against five or six. While each single individual might not be your match, the advantage in being able to selectively counter your attacks is important," Draco says. "Some of the tactics you've mentioned are geared toward reducing or eliminating the options among your enemies, but that is insufficient."

I can't help but nod. It's true that the advantage in numbers is tough to deal with. Even if a single one of my attacks is more powerful, even if it takes two of them to neutralize my attacks, I'm still facing the rest of the team unarmed. There are ways of getting around that, but the teams are realizing their advantage in numbers and really focusing on zone defense plays. That's part of the reason why I'm finding the battles ever more difficult.

"Secondly, and more importantly, your Class is not geared for such battles," Draco says.

"Pardon?"

"The Honor Guard Class was never meant to be used sans support. Look at the Erethrans. They work in teams, often dedicating individuals within each team to specific roles. Damage dealing. Support and logistics. Bodyguarding and defense. It is partly why they are so feared. A dedicated logistics personnel with the Portal Skill evolution can put a strike team anywhere in the Galaxy. A bodyguard for the Portal specialist can take any and all damage thrown at the other and erect an unbreachable Sanctum in times of need. A mobile artillery personnel with the Army of One Skill. And that is just in a small team of five. Instead, you spread yourself thin with your Class Skills." When I move to protest, Draco snorts, body language that my new skill informs me is his race's way of holding up a hand. "I know you've alleviated some of that with Credits, but your opponents can do the same. Specialization works because there is only so much Credits can do.

"Even your Paladin Class is stretched thin. You've focused and taken points in everything, making yourself a generalist rather than specializing in any one aspect. That gives you flexibility which you've managed to use, but it also leaves you vulnerable to dedicated kill squads."

My lips press together, but I can't object. Even I know that spreading yourself thin is sometimes a bad move as a gamer. Min-maxing can provide significant benefits. Among them, Skill Upgrades and evolution. It's why an evolved Portal Skill could throw me across the galaxy, while my own can, at best, get me across the planet.

"Fair enough. But…" I try to figure out a way to explain my thinking.

"You have your circumstances. And being a generalist is not all bad. Being able to be flexible in a variety of situations is important, especially on Dungeon Worlds or in Forbidden Zones. The Guard is dangerous because they have each other to back them up. But you should understand your Skills, your

Classes—they're not meant to be used alone," Draco says, pointing at me. "Until you accept that and work with that limitation, you'll always be at a disadvantage. Now go. I've got more work to do. I'll send you my suggestions for your training later."

I draw a deep breath to quell my irritation and stand, bowing to him slightly. "Thank you. For everything."

It's only when I'm nearly at the door that Draco speaks again. "We've all lost friends. To time and blade. But refusing to take on more party members just puts the remainder at more risk."

I stand there, one hand outstretched toward the exit, for a time before I offer a nod without turning around. The door hisses open and I step outside, my thoughts plagued by the discussion.

***

The yellow Shop is the same as always. Foxy, my personal sales attendant, seems happy to see me and grateful that I've taken the time to actually port in to his interdimensional location rather than using the physical shop in Irvina. There are a few reasons I've done that, but one of them is the tall drink of water lounging in the waiting room chair.

"John," Roxley says, standing. His long hair is purple now, with light blue highlights. It sets off the mahogany skin beautifully.

I let my gaze drop to take in the strong, athletic form of the Truinnar and unconsciously find myself licking my lips. A shake of my head pushes the thought aside. Not the time. Or place.

"Roxley," I say, walking forward. The damn shameless hunk wraps me up in an embrace followed by a kiss, one that I enjoy before pushing him away. "Hey! Don't be so handsy. We're not doing that anymore. Remember?"

"It's traditional in Truinnar culture to greet one's ex-lover in that way."

My eyes narrow while Roxley gives me a perfect poker face. I snort, not believing him one bit. If I hadn't needed some background information on Oria, I wouldn't have called the man. Better to cut off what we had cleanly considering… well, we're galaxies apart.

"Right. Well, I need some information. Background on Oria," I say.

"The Representative to Irvina. I heard that she contacted you," Roxley says, leaning forward. "You do know that you are placing me in a very untenable position? I could get into trouble for speaking with you."

"I would never want you to get into too much trouble," I say sweetly.

Roxley rolls his eyes, but I know he knows I mean it. And that I trust him to watch how much he says to me.

"Very well. The first thing you should know of the Representative is that she speaks with the Duchess's voice. She holds an unparalleled position of trust within the organization."

"Why?"

Roxley visibly considers his words. "There are many reasons. But the most famous is what Duchess Kangana did for Lady Oria. It was eighty or so years ago, soon after Lady Oria entered service in Irvina. Her husband and firstborn had not returned from a Forbidden Zone expedition. The Lady went to the Duchess and begged her for help. In turn, the Duchess launched a full-scale expedition, including her own personal guard, and retrieved her husband and daughter."

"Huh. That's… kinda cool," I say.

"Many called it foolish." Roxley's lips pull into a tight smile. "The losses faced in the retrieval party significantly out-weighed the number that were retrieved."

"Ah…" I wince. I can see why Roxley mentioned this story. It sheds a nicer light on the distant overlord who messed with us, then helped Earth. I'm still not sure how I feel about the Duchess. Still, that matters little. I'm unlikely to ever meet her. Powerful as she is, she's just one of many powerful figures in the Galaxy.

"The Lady Oria swore unceasing loyalty to the Duchess, and she has become the longest-standing representative in Irvina for the Duchess because of that," Roxley says. There's a flicker, so fast and subtle that if I didn't know him intimately, I'd have missed it.

"What?"

"Nothing pertinent."

"Let me judge that."

"Lady Oria's husband was incensed that she sent others to retrieve him. He was so angered that he separated from her, took a pair of lovers, and eventually broke off contact entirely," Roxley says. "He died two decades later on another expedition."

"Oh." I offer Roxley a half smile. "Sorry. You're right. Not really relevant. So she's the Duchess's voice. What does Oria want from us?"

Roxley snorts, shaking his head. "From Earth? You should know that. Greater control, greater access. Credits and training grounds. The material resources and a location to shift overburdened populations. Everything that the Duchess desires."

"And from me?"

"To tie a string to you," Roxley says, pointing at my chest. "You and those of your ilk, the specials who break the System. You hold great potential."

I grunt. Over time, I've begun to realize I'm not as special as I thought. Oh, I'm a cheater—but in a galaxy-wide population, I'm not the only one. On Earth, there are two others who survived the cleansing that I know of. They're both

Champions of Earth. There are probably more individuals who have hidden their strength or just aren't as flashy. A certain Hong Kong Master comes to mind.

Galactically, there are those who have tried to "cheat" the System. Giving birth in high-Level zones, living in them for their entire childhood to ensure that when they gain full access to their Screens, they gain access to normally untouchable Perks. All of them taking risks and putting themselves in positions of danger or wealth to gain Perks like mine. Or, in some cases, just paying off the Council. Though that last one is as much rumor as hard fact. Some answers are too expensive to be bought.

Those who are "special" in that way are both lauded and feared. Minor Perks are something that most of the rich can acquire. Even some of the poorer individuals have lucked into them—whether through coincidence, fate, or planning. But like on Earth, becoming successful is not just a matter of luck. Too many gifted athletes have injured themselves, lacked the discipline or desire to become professionals. In a world where the fastest route to power is via combat, the losses are astounding.

"Har. That's it?" I say.

"For now," Roxley says, opening his hand. "Not everyone is useful. Not everyone is manipulable. Not everyone is trustworthy. A simple task like the one given to you helps create a precedent."

I grunt, crossing my arms. Right. Like you give a programmer a small job to start with then check their code or the final result. If they take too long, code sloppily, or don't put in comments, well, now you know. And for only a little cost. Doesn't matter how gifted a programmer is, if they don't comment in the script, you might not ever want to use them. Especially for big, complex projects.

"Thank you. So. How are the others?"

"Well enough. The Constable has been pushing me to reform the mounted police of your world. She's very interested in your Lana's griffon. We have been looking into the feasibility and have begun a pilot program," Roxley says. "Aiden has formed a magic academy in Kamloops. The number of students has ballooned, and they are hiring more faculty members. The school pays for itself via dungeon runs and live magical experimentation on monsters.

"Your friends Rachel and Jason? They are looking at a fourth spawn," Roxley says, distaste on his face.

I chuckle, recalling a memory of him being given their squalling firstborn child on one of his impromptu visits to Carcross. That had been a sight to behold.

I lean forward, asking questions. Sometimes about people I know, like Colonel Weir and the Champions. Other times about the politics on Earth. And for a time, I forget about the pressures of my quest and just enjoy the Truinnar's company.

But all too soon, we have to call an end to our visit. The Shop isn't meant for long meetings, and the longer we stay, the more expensive it'll be. Still, by the time I port back into Irvina, I find myself smiling. For all that has happened, life manages to find a way to go on.

***

As good as his word, Draco sends me a document listing my shortcomings and an analysis of the battle videos. As much as he downplayed the gains I could make, Draco listed a significant number of mistakes. Of course, some of them are so small that I'm not sure how I'd ever fix them—stepping a little too soon here, dodging when I should roll there—while others are more helpful and less precise.

Over the next few days, I fall into a familiar routine, but the problem of insufficient immigrants continues to bother me. I finally end up arranging a meeting with Katherine in her new offices.

Set in the second ring of the capital, the new diplomatic offices are part of a complex of buildings that ring a rare oasis of greenery. Well, vegetation at least. The offices for Earth take up a portion of one of the high rises with residential quarters situated at the top of the building. It's expensive, ritzy, and—in my eyes—no better than the simple guild quarters we stay in. Really, after a certain point, the levels of difference in comfort become too small to really count.

"Katherine." I sweep my eyes over the diminutive lady's form behind the large oak desk. I'm slightly amused to see an Earthen affectation, but the desk seems to be part of a concerted effort to give the entire area a human vibe. Though… "*The Scream*?" I incline my head toward the infamous painting.

"A personal favorite," Katherine says with a sad smile. "The Shop formed in the middle of the museum in Oslo, leaving the works untouched. It took a little negotiation, but we managed to retrieve it from the Movanna."

"Riiight," I drawl, not entirely certain what to say. The loss we've experienced in culture, in people, still aches.

I have to admit, compared to Katherine, I'm a bit of an uncultured boor. My favorite pieces of culture were mostly preserved by the System. Movies, anime, the text of novels. But I can see how the loss of priceless paintings, statues, and even architecture could hurt. It's nice to see at least some things have managed to survive. And maybe, in time, we might be able to get some back. Or create new forms of art.

"But you didn't come here to talk about art," Katherine says.

I flash her a grateful smile as she gets the meeting back on track. "Yeah." I sit down without prompting. "Have you been keeping track of our numbers?"

"The Quest numbers? Yes. Disappointing."

"I'm doing my best," I say defensively.

"Of course. I didn't mean it as an insult. But even Earth wants more Adventurers now. Especially if we can direct them to the right cities."

I snort slightly. How the worm turns. We fought to keep them out, and now we're desperate to find more of them to deal with dungeons, to help provide normalcy to the population, and because more Galactics means more money.

"I'm assuming you've got ideas?" I say.

"I do. I needed to confirm our budget and some other matters, but here's what I'm thinking…" Katherine says, leaning forward.

Hours later, we come to the end of our little tete-a-tete. While most of it was Katherine talking at me, I tried to provide my own feedback on what could be done. Over time, we refined the initial ideas, our implementation, and eventually our reaction to what we knew was likely to come from it.

At the end, I find myself offering Katherine my hand as I stand. "You know we're going to piss people off with this, right?"

Katherine stares at my offered handshake, raising an elegant eyebrow until I drop it awkwardly. "Of course. But it's why you fought so hard to get us a seat on the Council, right? A chance to make a difference on our own planet."

"Yeah…" A warm flush of emotions runs through me. Gratitude, happiness, and even a little fear. Because what we're about to do…

"Our choice, John."

"I know." I acknowledge her words with a nod. "How long?"

"Give me a day."

"Perfect."

I wave goodbye to Katherine as I exit the room, pushing aside my concerns. As Draco pointed out, I can't do everything myself. And pushing aside those who want to join me... well, it's self-defeating. So I take the help and bite my tongue because we're all adults.

***

A day later, I'm standing before a suddenly larger crowd. It's not a massive difference, but there are nearly forty people in the room—so many that we've run out of chairs and a few are standing in the back. The mix of aliens is different too, with a larger proportion of low-level Combat Classers. Wiza, who's been my main point of contact, looks elated, though he shoots a suspicious gaze at Harry, who has made an appearance for the first time in ages. Still, the Kobold pulls his lips into a wide grin. He's happy. For now.

At first, everything flows, the well-honed speech and show-and-tell portion going over as well as it usually does. There are a few chuckles, a few gasps as I show off the monsters that can be found, a few snorts of derision and moments of wonder as we pan over cities. We've honed my speech to focus on the common questions, making our presentation better and more effective. But when we've completed the rote presentation, things start heating up.

"I received a System advertisement saying that if we sign up with the Earth Council, you'll be conducting assisted dungeon runs in Irvina prior to departure. Is that true?" This comes from one of the Combat Classers, the insectoid rubbing two of its four arms in an unconscious act of nervousness and hope.

"Yes. I'm already part of Tig's guild, so we'll use my time slots with them to do the runs. Worst-case scenario, if that doesn't work, we'll pay for a dungeon use. Also, once you get to Earth, you'll be slotted into one of our regular city patrols if you wish, which will allow you to gain experience and Credits at the same time," I say.

"What?" Wiza says, jaw dropping and his tongue rolling out. "What Earth Council? What advertisement?"

Wiza's words get a few looks of pity and disgust. I kind of feel bad for the Kobold, considering it's not his fault we didn't tell him.

"And no Serf contracts?" someone else asks.

"None. Ali?"

A moment later, everyone in the room has new notification screens to review. They list the details of the contract Katherine has slaved over, tidying up the language and the necessary safeguards. That the entire thing is relatively short means the audience gets through the entire thing quickly.

"You'll provide us with housing, food, and a small stipend, along with materials for our production?" This exclamation comes from a Leatherworker, one whose pointed fingers must make punching holes to sew up leather super easy. I wonder if he wears multiple thimbles when he needs to work with care?

"Yes. Though only once you arrive on Earth. And we're going to restrict you from taking part in dungeon runs, at least until you've paid back your plane ticket. Shuttle. Spaceship," I correct myself quickly. "Obviously, the deal's slightly different for the Combat Classers. But after you've paid off the initial cost, you're welcome to join the protected runs or the patrols."

"What are you doing?" Wiza snarls, rushing up in front of me and revealing his teeth. He arches his back, looming over me as if he can intimidate me.

That lasts until I release my Aura and meet his gaze, staring down the salesman.

He shrinks back a bit, letting out an involuntary whimper. "Why are you doing this?"

"Because we're humans. And a Dungeon World," I say. "Now. Next question?"

"I'm a Technomancer who focuses on gravity fields. You going to supply me the tech I need?"

"Uhh… Ali?" I look desperately at the Spirit.

Ali snorts, fading into sight in front of everyone and getting a few gasps before he goes on to answer questions. Wiza, now ignored, looks between the two of us before he slinks out to report to his superiors.

Yeah. The shitstorm is coming.

"*You look happy,*" Harry sends over the party chat.

To that, I can only shrug. But this? This feels right.

***

"Evening, VG," I say, nodding to Draco. A little surprising to find him waiting at the bottom of the entrance of our housing, but only a little.

"We need to speak, Redeemer," Draco says.

"My residence?"

"No. I've secured a meeting room."

Draco leads the way into a portion of the guild housing that I've been to, a place I can only describe as a truncated business center. In the meeting room, Draco triggers a number of security measures to cut off outside communication and viewing before he pulls out another little device and waves it around. There are a few cracks and buzzes—even one on me—before the surveillance bugs surrounding us die.

"Ugh. On me?" I say with a snarl.

My Skill and the Brumwell Necklace of Shadow Intent might make my actions harder to track, but if a bug was on me… I sigh and make a mental note to go shopping for a toy like Draco's. There's no point in hiding from Skills if everything is getting recorded in a completely separate way. Thankfully, nothing I've been doing needs to be that secret. Still annoying.

"You still have a lot to learn." Draco leans forward, fixing me with those slitted eyes of his, a spark of anger flaring in them. "Along with the matter of asking permission first."

"Permission?"

"I have received numerous complaints about you offering to bring individuals of the seventh ring to the dungeon. Under the guild's name," Draco says.

"I said if I could get your permission," I protest slightly. Not too hard, because I'm not dumb enough to not realize that rumors and an individual's selective hearing could easily distort the message. Which, I'll admit, did come into our considerations.

"And you did not feel it wise to confirm with me before you announced the matter to the planet?" Draco growls.

"Well, I thought about it. But things were moving rather fast once we made up our mind. And we weren't sure how desirable the entire offer would be."

"I should kick you out of the guild for this," Draco says. "What makes you think you can do this?"

"Guild regulation umm…"

"137. Under Adventuring parties and guests. Part four," Ali helpfully supplies.

"Right. I may, at my discretion, party with other affiliated guilds so long as I'm willing to take full responsibility for partying outside of the guild. This includes entrance to dungeons. The only exception is if said individuals are not registered," I said. "And since we're going to have them register with NAGA provisionally, with myself as sponsor, it should be fine."

It's a workaround of course. The immigrants will be marked as the lowest Adventurer level possible—G—and even then, only provisionally. I'm required to provide them a significant amount of collateral too, but so long as I get their Levels and combat ability to F, I'll get the Credit deposit back. In many cases, a single dungeon run would be sufficient to prove that they had an F-level of ability.

That Combat Classers from the seventh ring have never done this before in large numbers is more due to the cost of joining NAGA—or the restrictions in any other guild—than any lack of imagination on their parts. It doesn't help that NAGA doesn't have open slots in the dungeons, which means that NAGA entrants either have to slot themselves in when time comes up or find another guild party to join. Not as much of an issue for me, as a Master Classer with friends, but more of an issue for an outsider from the sixth or seventh ring.

"Oh. Of course," Draco says. "I never realized you were a rules lawyer. You do know the guild does not get involved in faction politics? Or annoy large sections of our potential customer base!"

"It's not that big a deal," I say with a frown.

By my side, Ali snorts slightly as he spins in circles. On my minimap, I can see how Harry paces the corridor outside, obviously dissatisfied with being kept out of this conversation. But it's a guild matter and he's not part of the guild.

"I doubt we'll get more than a hundred people taking up this offer," I say.

"You doubt," Draco says sarcastically. "Are you being naïve? You are directly challenging the established mode of operation. Not only are you offering to train up the lowest Levels, you've offered those in the fifteen and higher range direct tickets to Earth with few strings!"

"Not a few. We've got them working for our city patrols for a good year, or until they pay back their transportation ticket with appropriate interest," I say.

"Exactly!" Draco snaps. "Your offer isn't just fair; it's downright generous. There are no margins for error. Your Contract has no insurance or coverage if they die! You don't even have a secondary signee, so all your funds are lost the moment they perish."

"That's unlikely to happen. We've gotten rather good at keeping our people from the really hard stuff. It's not like the first few years. Now we've got rapid response teams and experienced group leaders situated throughout our cities. Hell, some of the teams even have 'porters like me."

"Death still happens."

"Then I'd say they've already paid enough, no?" I say, leaning forward. "If they die while protecting our cities, it seems that wiping out a little debt is the least we can offer them. Anyway, why do you care?"

"I don't. Except everyone seems intent on whining at me about it. Your actions disrupt every small- to mid-sized guild or Serf-company that has use for these higher-Level Combat Classers," Draco says. "Our guild might not care. After all, we're looking for Elites and we offer the services and benefits to attract them. But the small- and mid-sized guilds? They thrive off these low-Levelers. That's how they make their money and fill their ranks. And now, you're offering to pull them all to Earth."

"Not all. Hell, I'm pretty sure we won't even get ten percent of everyone available." I smile slightly, opening my hands wide. "But yes, that's kind of the point."

"I repeat. Why the hell shouldn't I kick you out and save myself one Kelpie-birthed headache?" Draco says.

Strange. I stare at Draco, look at the way he's sitting, at the thrum of threads, and realize he's not asking this as a matter of course. He's asking because he wants me to provide him a good excuse. Because… "You like what I'm doing."

"It doesn't matter. What matters is your effect on this guild," Draco says. "If we don't take action, we're going to lose at least a fifth of our active contracts on Irvina."

"A fifth?" I frown, trying to figure out the value of that. After a moment, I discard that line of thought. It doesn't matter. "True. But do you really want them to know that the guild is willing to cave over a little pressure?"

"Over someone that everyone knows we have little ties to?" Draco shrugs. "I'd say we'd be hurting ourselves even more if we stayed with you."

"Fair enough," I say. "*Any ideas?*"

"*In or out. Sitting on the fence…*"

"*Mixing metaphors.*" My gaze sharpens as I look at Draco, resolving the answer in my mind. "You're right. Keeping me in the guild is a bad choice." I see Draco straighten a little, growing serious, but I don't stop talking. "But that's only if you're not supporting us."

"Supporting you?" Draco lets out a hiss-snort.

"Yes. Right now, you're collateral damage. So you either need to get out of the line of fire entirely by letting me go—or get in the bunker with us," I say.

"In the bunker?"

"Sorry. Place to—"

"I know what a bunker is. I want an explanation of what this bunker is about."

"It's a metaphorical bunker…" Draco hisses at me, and I stop teasing the Vice-Guild Master. "Easy. You help us. Earth will issue quests. You help run the recruits through the dungeons on the slots that the guild already has. You've got the extra slots since we breached the new Mana threshold." I wave my hand around, growing excited. "Not only do you make up for the loss in quests, you also get firsthand knowledge of potential new recruits.

"On top of that, I'm sure Katherine will be happy to negotiate additional discounts for the guild on Earth itself. I bet we could get you a few new Guild Halls. Find some great recruits, maybe even a few quests to escort the new recruits to the right cities. You can slot your new recruits right onto Earth, making even more money long term, and build up a great reputation here on Irvina. You can even start recruiting from our immigrants and the humans while having some great publicity. Trust me, we humans love an underdog story."

"And you think that'll be enough to offset the anger our actions will create?" Draco says.

"Maybe not from the corporations. But how many Adventurers have come from the fifth circle onward? How many of them would look favorably upon you?"

Draco crosses his arms as he leans back. "You think we'll be able to poach some other higher-Level Adventurers."

"Maybe. Worst-case, some of those other guilds have to answer to their guilds why they aren't doing the same."

"That's if this entire exercise works."

"There is that."

Draco falls silent. The lizardman stands after a time and walks toward the door. He leaves with one final, somewhat ominous, sentence. "I'll let you know what we decide."

"What do you think, Ali?"

"I think we should be looking at what it takes to establish a guild."

"Isn't it expensive? And hard to get a damn dungeon slot?"

"Yup."

Arse. I pull out a piece of chocolate, unwrap the velvety goodness, and pop it into my mouth as I stare at the exit, considering my options. In the end, I let out a little snort as Harry pops his head in, scanning my face for an answer. One that I can't give him.

Chapter 11

"This is not scalable," Mikito says, arms crossed as she eyes the eleven Combat Classers arrayed before us.

Unsurprisingly, the majority of the Combat Classers have normal non-prestige Classes, mostly in the melee and direct combat forms. It's one of the inherent disadvantages for many of these guys—even if they're guided by their parents, their options of achieving the necessary requirements for a prestige Class are nearly non-existent. On top of that, outside of the most basic long-range weaponry, it's hard to scale-up damage at the low Levels with crap tech weaponry. Tech at the higher levels requires a large influx of funds, access to the right people to build the weapon and equipment, and even more Credits to pay for the replacements. It's why melee and magic continue to dominate, except for certain groups like the Erethrans. Still, at least we have a pair of healers. But, of course, none of that is why Mikito is complaining.

"No, it's not," I agree with the Samurai. Only two of us here, so there's only so many people we can run through, especially with the slots we have. "But thank you for coming anyway."

"Ummm…" A short and busty woman comes up, her ears curved and overly large. She's an "elf" as per Japanese mangas, not like the *Lord of the Rings* movies. Being that she's so much shorter than me and wearing something way too low-cut, I'm getting quite an eyeful. Weird that there are so many variations on the elf idea, from Truinnar to Movanna to whatever she is. "Are we really going into this dungeon?"

"Yup. You guys need Levels more than combat experience," I say, eying the group again. A little piece of downloaded knowledge lets me estimate their ages, and what I'm seeing is a bunch of late teens or early twenty-year-olds. Which makes their single-digit Levels pitiful. "So we're going to get you those Levels."

"But, ummm…" Again, the woman looks at the dungeon entrance. "That's a Level 20 dungeon."

"Twenty to thirty, yup." I flash her a grin, which does nothing to reassure the woman. But that's fine. "All right, everybody. I don't care how you all divide yourself, except you healers. One each on me and Mikito. We're going in in five."

"Five seconds!" yelps one of the healers.

"Minutes!" Ali corrects.

As the group shuffles and prods one another, trying to divide themselves into a roughly equal split, I'm surprised by the results. Everyone wants to go with Mikito, which is a big and slightly hurtful revelation. I'm frowning, trying not to remind myself of dodgeball practice in grade ten, when I hear footsteps approaching. A turn of my head shows an interesting group of a half-dozen Adventurers coming up to us, arms crossed.

"And who says you're going in?" The speaker is rotund, bulbous like a beetle on hind legs. The fact that he's flanked by a frost giant mage makes me raise an eyebrow.

"Pretty sure that'd be the Irvina Dungeon Control," I say. "This is our slot and time. Cleared it all already."

"With those scum? You going to run a train for those vermin?" The rather high pitch that the beetle speaks in makes my ear hurt. I ignore Beetlejuice's Status, knowing I won't recall it.

"Yup. Mikito, you guys go first," I say.

The Samurai doesn't even give me a second glance, waving her group onward. As the troublemakers try to block them, Ali finishes a silent cast of Metal Walls, putting the metallic obstruction in their way.

"What are you doing?" Beetlejuice clicks, his friends glancing at their leader. Tearing down the wall would be easy enough for them, but they're hesitant to escalate the situation with violence.

"Well, I'm standing here in front of you. She's going in," I say. "And in about five minutes, we're going in."

"Don't you dare!"

"Or what?" I find myself grinning widely when I realize their threats are a bluff. They aren't willing to anger the authorities. Physically escalating this is a losing proposition for them—with only a bunch of mid-stage Advanced Classers—and outside of that, their options are limited.

"You—"

"Oh, be quiet," a familiar voice cuts over Beetle's chirping. Wiza lopes forward from where he's been hiding, the stealth Skill sloughing off his body as he becomes visible to everyone else. "I'll deal with this."

"Sorry," Beetlejuice says and backs off.

"Well, about time you came out." Not as if I hadn't noticed him, but I am surprised to see him make his presence known.

Mikito has stopped by the gates, a hand resting on the polearm as she eyes the newcomer. Those behind her group together, looking wary.

"Any of you who enter the dungeon will face sanctions by my company and all others. If you have any debts, we'll buy them. If any of you have family with debts, we'll buy them. If you have friends, we'll buy their debts too. And call the debts close immediately," Wiza says with a vicious snarl. "If you own anything on lease, we'll buy it. Your jobs, your families' jobs, your friends' jobs. They'll all be lost."

"You can't do that!" the little elf lady says, bouncing worriedly. "That's illegal!"

"Not the way we'll do it. It'll all be legal and above board. You think your contracts can't be sold? Think again. We'll buy them up and then consolidate everything for you," Wiza says, his smirk growing. "Of course, there'll be additional fees for all that, and penalties if you miss a payment. We'll even give you all the warnings we have to to make sure that you can clear your debts. Properly."

"We can't afford to buy out our debts. If we could, we wouldn't be here!" a Kobold says, his eyes wide as he grips the warped piece of metal he calls a mace.

"Exactly. Leave and we'll forget all about this," Wiza says.

"Sir…" The elf lady looks at me, giving me these big, imploring eyes.

I meet her gaze for a moment then sweep mine over the group, judging their resolve. A couple look bored, as if they're not worried. Most have concern etched on their faces, fear too.

"And if you think we can't stop you from leaving for Earth, you're wrong," Wiza says, smiling. "Anyone whose debt exceeds the primary threshold will find that we're more than willing to enforce the 'safe harbor' clause."

"*Ali?*"

"*Primary threshold varies depending on the value and income amount of the individual. It's a calculated threshold. But, umm, figure roughly around fifty thousand Credits. That allows the debtors to dictate that the debtees have to stay in 'safe areas' to safeguard the amounts owed.*"

I grunt to indicate I got all that. I hadn't expected this kind of problem, which is a big problem. I'm not sure how many people have that much debt— and it certainly seems pretty high to me—but it surely would cause significant problems. Still…

"Any of you who want to leave, go ahead. Let me know if you want to cancel your contracts too," I say. Wiza grins, gloating over his win, but I ignore the Kobold. "But realize that these assholes? They aren't going to stop pushing. Not now, not ever. Right now, you're in the front of the queue to change your lives. You leave, and someone else, someone with less to lose, less debt, fewer ties will take your place. And you'll lose your chance. Perhaps forever."

It's no St. Crispin's Day speech, but I see some faces tighten in resolve. Others continue to waver, while a few actually step away, shaking their heads. I understand. It's one thing to risk yourself, but your friends, your family? That requires a different kind of resolve, of bravery. Maybe even a lack of wisdom.

"Contact some of the others who signed up, especially those on the next run. Let them know what's going to happen, have them start coming now if they intend to stay. Whoever gets here first gets to do two runs if they're from the next batch."

"On it, boy-o."

We lose a good half of our people, ending up with just six. I send Mikito through with the remnants of the group and find my lips curling upward as Wiza takes note of those entering. I'm sure he's busy making arrangements to make a mess of their lives. As a thought strikes me, I touch the band that makes my helmet appear so that I can hold my next conversation in privacy.

"Katherine." Once the call connects to the lady, I fill her in.

She makes a face. Neither of us expected this particular method of persuasion. I admit, our inexperience at Galactic politics and how bare-handed they are is showing.

"Give me what time you can. I'll think of something," Katherine says.

While this might not cause too much problems for the middle-stage Combat Classers, it's going to play havoc for our recruitment of Artisans. Those fellows generally have the greatest debts, as they need to make better and better items to Level up. No surprise that it drives them into debt. It's workable debt, if you're smart about it, but it's debt. And while Combat Classers are nice, Artisans are where the volume is.

"Can do. Just don't overdo it," I say.

We're still a new planet with a lot of programs that need financing. Just the spaceship tickets alone will be a huge drain on our resources. Even though the new residents of our Dungeon World will bring taxes, security, and new skills to the planet, that doesn't mean those benefits appear immediately. We have a million and one programs drawing on our scarce resources, so we can't afford to devote too many Credits to this. Immigration might be a net positive, but it could take years before we see the results of it.

"Tell me about it," Katherine mutters. "I'm already getting an earful over the tickets."

"Problem?" I mutter, moving away from Wiza.

"Just a lot of complaints. Some valid—our resources are tight—and some, well, xenophobic," Katherine says. "Lots of NIMBYism going on too."

"You sound exasperated," I say.

Katherine makes a face. "It's familiar territory, except this is just driven by fear and hate. At least when it came to oil pipelines and dams, there was a lot to be weighed on both sides. Here, it's mostly just hate for the Galactics. It's not as if we don't have hundreds, thousands of empty towns. Never mind the millions of buildings and suburbs we need to take back."

I don't really know what to say. There is still a lot of anger and resentment over what happened, and much of that anger has pointed itself squarely at anything not human. There isn't a lot of in-your-face speciesism, but the undercurrent of distrust and dislike is there. It's not hard to understand, but it's not particularly useful either. We need the bodies to help contain the Dungeon World. While it happens a lot less frequently, we still lose settlements to monster swarms and burgeoning, unchecked dungeons. And it's not as if the vast majority of those who have arrived had anything to do with the choice to turn us into a Dungeon World. They're just immigrants after the destruction. Opportunists at worst.

But still, the anger and resentment, the unwillingness to let go of the past infects us all. We've lost so much, and some it will never return. Cultural touchstones, languages, skills. All of it replaced by, well, the System and the

Galactics. Is it any wonder that even the most enlightened are angry with the Galactics? Especially when they strut through our streets with their unconscious arrogance, some of them being blatant in their views of us as primitives?

Even when we want to use them for our purposes, it's hard to forget that it was the Galactics who made the decision to kill ninety percent of us. That these alien species, watched and betted on the outcome, laughed and cheered at our tragedies and triumphs. Enlightened or not, it's hard to forget our pain. Even if we know that some doesn't mean all, even if the one you're talking to is probably okay. And few of us are all that enlightened.

"Well, tell Lana I'm willing to use my investments on this," I say.

Changing minds, changing hearts, that's a job for someone else. Truth be told, I'm not that enlightened myself. I just found something bigger to hate. For now, all I can do is what I can. For now, building our world back up as fast as I can is my way of stabbing a thumb in the eye of those responsible. For now, fixing what was broken as best I can is how I can safeguard our world.

"Thank you, John."

"Yeah, yeah."

I kill the call then, since the next group of recruited Combat Classers is arriving. Seeing the group of helpless newbies stagger, some looking eager, others worried, I'm reminded of a time not so long ago when I dragged out a group of humans. A spark of understanding flows through me as I stare at creatures of skin and chitin, of blue and brown coloration. Maybe we're all just the same in the end.

We're all ground down under the System equally.

***

"Well, go on then," I say, sword resting idly on my shoulder as I nod toward the whale-like monster with its numerous-tentacled body in the water. Aggressive waving of its tail drive the monster toward us, tentacles waving as it charges our position.

Nima Whale (Level 23)
HP: 472/493
MP: 231/256
Conditions: Aquatic Mammal, Peerless Charge

The dungeon is a semi-aquatic one, which is partly why we could get in on such short notice. Aquatic dungeons are less preferred, since most Adventurers aren't suited to handling them. The few aquatic races that are in the System generally hog the aquatic dungeons. In fact, because of their ability to run aquatic locations at a faster rate than the majority of species, the aquatic races have a higher proportion of high-Level Adventurers than land-based species. Thankfully, due to the lack of conflict as we take on different terrains, they generally get on well with us non-aquatics. It helps that the System deals with pesky things like land-based pollution, so many of the major clashes in living arrangements between our species is minimized.

There are two major ways of completing this particular dungeon, 6-8. Hard mode, which is currently being completed by Mikito and her group, means submerging oneself in the water and dealing with the more numerous monster threats in their environment. It's good training and experience in abnormal environments, which is why this city has a few aquatic dungeons. I even hear there's a sub-zero dungeon.

The other path to completion is the one we're taking—the normal mode. This involves trekking across the dungeon via the floating platforms that dot the water. The platforms are somewhat unsteady, bobbing along in the water, and are not always connected. Occasionally, Adventurers have to either wait for platforms to float back to their correct position or take the quick swim to the next platform. Or fly. All of which adds to the fun.

"Shoot it!" Ali commands, having changed his clothing to a soldier's camo uniform. "All of you. Yes, you. The one with the sling. What do you mean you don't have a ranged weapon? What did you think you were going to do? Piss on it?"

Under the guidance of the Spirit, the group attacks. I watch with an amused expression as everything from slug throwers to slings and arrows lash out. The group even has a pair of beam rifles, though from the looks of it, they're rather poor quality. Weapons burn and tear, making the whale dodge beneath the water.

"You. Take this." Ali materializes and shoves my beam rifle into one melee fighter's hands. "And you, this." Next comes my pistol.

I grimace, making a mental note to get them back.

"You. Tank. Get ready for the wigglies," Ali orders.

Under water, the whale makes its way to us and pops up at the last second, long tentacles waving and darting forward in an attempt to pluck people off the walkway. The Tank moves, blocking a pair of tentacles with his body and slicing apart another one with his double-sided polearm. Another tentacle slips past, wrapping around a body. Since this is the first battle of the dungeon, it's a little too early to let one of them get dragged under. I lash out with a simple Blade Strike, cutting the tentacle off but leaving the monster mostly undamaged.

"You, Healer. What are you doing? Heal them!" Ali commands.

I step back, having done my part, and get back to watching. The group is significantly under-Leveled here, but with Ali and I helping out and lending a little equipment-based aid, there shouldn't be any issues.

"Why are you crying? You only lost half your health. Get back on your feet!" Ali roars. "Now kill that thing!"

***

"Ding?" I say, leaning around the large sasquatch-like Tank's shoulder to stare into the empty space he's focused on. Of course, I don't see anything.

"Ding?"

"Human term," I say, waving away Sasquatch's confusion. "Did you Level?"

"Yes!" Sasquatch nods. "I was considering where to put my attributes and Skill point."

"Nice. That's always fun. Except for two things," I say.

"Two things?"

"One. We're in the middle of a dungeon, in the middle of a walkway where monsters appear. You're on lookout. And have gotten distracted."

Sasquatch does the furred equivalent of blush—blue eyes turning red and pink—before he blinks quickly and looks around desperately.

"And two. You should use the resources at your disposal fully."

"Resources?"

"Me and Ali," I say, pointing between us. "Well, mostly the Spirit. He's got hundreds of years of experience under his belt."

"But he's your Companion," Sasquatch protests.

I stare at the Sasquatch for a moment before raising my voice, deciding to make the damn announcement for everyone to hear. "Okay, people. If you go up in Levels, don't allocate your points yet. Wait until we're in a safe point. Or enough of you are ready that Ali and I will take over watch. Also, you should seriously consider talking to the Spirit and me. We might not be as good as dedicated guild advisors, but we've been around the block or two."

"Or made a few blocks," Ali says with a harrumph.

"What he said," I say, nodding toward Ali. "Make use of us."

"Why would we trust you with that information?" a thin dwarf says, stomping over and glaring at us. "You could be screwing with us to make it better for your guild. Or planet."

"We could. And you don't have to. Your call. But it's worth thinking about what we'll get out of messing with you. It's not as if what happens to a bunch of non-prestige Basic Classers will ever make a difference for me. Or him." Not surprisingly, my words garner quite a bit of anger, but I continue on blithely. "On the other hand, the faster I get you and the rest up to snuff, the faster my quest gets complete. So. Do what you want."

They look between each other as they take in my pronouncement. In the meantime, I nod to Ali, who straightens up. I already see some of the kids peremptorily wincing.

He bellows, "MOVE OUT!"

***

"So. Uhh… about my Level up. Ups," Sasquatch says, looking at me nervously.

"You play tank, right? And you're a warrior type?"

Now that we've found a rather solid island and cleared out the mini-boss, it's quite a safe area to wait. The mini-boss—who would have been classed as an alpha if it wasn't in a dungeon—was a weird shellfish creature with long, stabby arms and a body configuration that made me wonder how it worked. I'd just finished announcing a quick rest and Level up before walking over to store the mana crystal when the Sasquatch came along.

"I am the Defender, yes," the Sasquatch says. I can even hear the capital letter the alien adds to the role.

"Then you should know to build up your Constitution primarily, with Strength and Agility next. If you're primary Defender, you're going to be eating a lot of hits," I say. "Any pain resistances?"

"No. But my species is naturally resistant to high levels of pain. We also receive a small bonus to our health and Mana regeneration in colder climates."

"Nice. Remind me to tell you about Canada. But you'll want to consider buying some pain resistances when you can. Chemical aids are fine, but they don't last long with the System. The more you fight, the more it'll hurt. Chemical aids end up being more expensive in the long term. So. Do you have a passive or active build?"

"My Class—Snow after the Solstice—emphasizes endurance over the long term, as the winter is long," Sasquatch replies.

My lips twitch in amusement, gratitude flowing through me to my annoying Spirit for translating that as "Warrior Tank."

"The first branch of my Class provides increases in my attributes and resistances," he says. "The second in passive regeneration. The third is damage dealing, mostly via damage reflection and a passive damage collection aura for friendlies."

I blink, never having heard of that. That sounds useful—an aura that collects damage from friends instead of you having to go to them. Too bad most auras conflict with one another.

"That's fine. Here are my thoughts. Firstly, do you have a regular group yet?" At the shake of the Sasquatch's head, I continue. "Then you'll want to consider forming one. It sounds like you can't do much damage without equipment, so I'd ignore boosting any of your damage-related Skills entirely in favor of good friends and good equipment when you can afford it.

"Secondly, consider specialization. Your Class might be racial specific, but it's not a prestige Class, is it? So your total attributes will be mediocre at best. Which is fine, but that means you need friends. Best way to get reliable teammates is being one yourself." I hear a mental snicker as Ali overhears that bit, but luckily, he's too busy to laugh at me directly. "So. Specialize. Figure out which branch you want to focus on and get that up as high as possible. Personally, I'd go down the one that gives you the aura and boosts to your passive regenerations. Especially if they're percentage-based."

"But they're less powerful than an attribute increase."

"Right now, sure. But you weren't born on a Dungeon World. You can afford to play the long game. And any percentage-based Skill will pay off by the time you become an Advanced Classer. Even when you get to Earth, we'll be keeping you on routine patrols so you can afford to play it safe," I say.

Sasquatch looks a bit startled, and I have to remind myself that the idea that they'd be able to become an Advanced Classer is as foreign to them as the idea of surviving the first year was to us. It was just something that we couldn't hope to believe in. Not really.

"I… yes."

"You know of Skill evolutions, right?"

When Sasquatch shakes his head, I sigh. Sometimes, I wonder about the public education system among the Galactics. Other times, I know. Then again, why should I be that surprised? Even with all the world's knowledge at our fingertips before the System, so many people never bothered to look up details about voting, or finances, or something as simple as a rental agreement. Why should it be any different for another species? Another world?

"Fine. Let's talk about that…"

***

"Kermit crab?"

"Hermit," I correct Ali as I stare at the giant conical creature breaching the water. Most of its body is hidden in the water as it paddles back and forth in front of us. The cream-colored spiral of its body is covered by a flowing, emerald liquid armor.

Hus Crab (Level 38 Boss)
HP: 947/947
MP: 478/478
Conditions: Water Armor, Reflexive Hydrospouts

"Are we supposed to fight that?" the thin dwarf says, fear threading through his voice.

I don't blame him. Even if the entire group has gained a Level or two throughout this dungeon, they're still miles away from winning against a Level 38 boss. I'm a little proud of the group, really. They've managed to handle the growing monsters better and better, with only three of their members ever getting dragged underwater. After babying them for a little, I started sending Ali down to keep a close eye on the submerged fool as an object lesson. Unsurprisingly, they got a lot better at avoiding the tentacles then. Even with all their improvement, expecting them to beat the Boss was a bit much.

"Nah, I got this." I raise my hand and call down a Beacon from Angels directly onto the bastard.

One disadvantage for a creature that large—it eats a larger percentage of the energy output, meaning that it takes a higher amount of damage than normal. Normally, its armor would decrease the amount of damage it took, but my Pierce attacks solve that problem handily.

When the beam finally fades, the group takes their hands away from their eyes to the sight of the hermit crab bobbing along the water on its side, armor shattered and flesh smoking. It drifts in the boiling water, dead as dead can be.

"Damn it. I barely got any experience from that," the skinny dwarf grumbles.

I snort. "Be glad the System gave you anything."

Ali flies forward to loot the monster, grimacing as he eyes the big corpse. "What'd you want to do with it, boy-o? Can't really fit this in the Altered Storage."

"Leave it," I say. A Level 38 Boss isn't worth the hassle of hauling its corpse.

That's when the group protests, shouting their objections. I wince, finally managing to shush them by detailing the problem to them.

Which is how we end up walking out of the dungeon, dragging a giant hermit crab corpse behind us to the awe-struck gazes of the next group.

Ali flits over to the new group, arching his back. "All right, you Gremlin-loving recruits. Time to gear up and buff out. We're moving out in two minutes!"

"You sure you don't want Credits for this?" Sasquatch says, his eyes wide. "There's at least three or four thousand Credits of meat alone…"

"Nope. And Ali will disburse your share of the kills later," I say, waving away his protests. It's not much to me, but the difference it'll make in their gear will be significant.

"Thank you. Redeemer."

Sasquatch runs back to his part of the rope and heaves on the line, answering questions at the same time. I can see the dwarf snorting and a few others looking at me skeptically, but I ignore them. Not as if I care whether they think I'm an easy mark or not. I've got bigger fish to fry.

"Let's go."

***

Hours later, we've run our groups through the allotment. Thankfully, enough people have heard about our offers and are still willing to brave the ire of the corporations and Sects to fill the groups. After we send them off to get their corpses processed, Mikito and I regroup, with Harry making an appearance.

"Any trouble at the butchers'?" I ask Harry. Just in case, I had the reporter poke around the butchering yards. Since the Combat Classers we're working with are all provisional NAGA members, they don't exactly have preferred suppliers. That means they can work with anyone, but they also run the risk of being locked out.

"A bit," Harry says. "Luckily they were willing to listen."

"Good." I turn to Mikito. "Any problems on your end?"

"No. They're better trained than most of the humans we used to run. The only issue was their fear."

"I get that," I say, shrugging. The fact that they're used to dealing with danger only in dungeons means that they're also used to controlling the amount of danger they're in. It leaves them unused to pushing their boundaries too hard. To those of us who survived the apocalypse, these guys play it too safe. "Can't do much about it. Think we can move on to phase two?"

"The guards should be able to handle them," Mikito says.

"Great." I smile and message Katherine. One of the few things we can do to speed up the process is to add Katherine's bodyguards to the rotation. It isn't the best solution, but it works. The more people we have running the recruits through the dungeons, the faster they'll level. For now at least. "So…"

"Dungeon run?" Mikito says, eyes brimming with real excitement now. "I've got an invite for 3-2."

"Isn't that a Master Class-only dungeon?" Ali says with a frown.

Mikito gives the Spirit a big smile then shifts her gaze over to me.

"Fine, fine. Let's go." Might as well reward the battle maniac. And I admit, I'm a little curious.

Chapter 12

Amusingly enough, Wiza and most of the other corporations that had sponsored the various meetings canceled all our bookings, and that turned out to be a good thing. Once word got out that we not only were serious but were coming through on our promises, attendance at our events bloomed. Katherine's aide found herself busy booking ever-larger meeting rooms and extending the times. As for Katherine, she and Peter found themselves besieged with complaints from half a dozen corporations, all intent on working with us if we would change our mind about the dangerous and destructive behavior Earth was showcasing.

Standing before a crowd of a couple hundred sixth-ringers, I found a sudden burst of stage fright attempting to overtake my senses. I fought most of it down with seasoned ease, mental resistances, and a constant reminder that getting eaten was infinitely worse. Slow, steady deep breathing fixed the rest.

"You know, if someone screamed fire, this would cause a stampede," I remarked to Ali as we stood in the wings of the stage.

"Why?" Ali said, frowning as he eyed the crowd. The fact that two fire elementals were seated near the front, hissing at everyone who came close, showcased why my attempt at a joke died a pathetic death.

"It's a saying. You know, shouting fire in a public place to create a panic?" I just get more confused looks from Ali and give up, deciding against trying to explain the matter to the Spirit who didn't have extensive experience with non-System-generated buildings and squishy humans. "Never mind. So. What do you think their next move will be?"

"The corporations?" Ali says before smiling grimly. "Probably the usual mainstay."

"Of?"

"Violence."

"Against them or me?" I say, concern tingeing my voice. If memories of Earth conditions are anything to go by, I'm imagining a group of union busters showing up to stop people from entering our talks. Not that this information isn't being disseminated in other ways.

"Probably you and Katherine," Ali says, his tone growing grim. "And any place where you intend to take recruits in person."

"So, here?"

"Unlikely," Harry says, smiling slightly. "No point in trying to hinder the flow of information when the entire story can be bought for five Credits."

"Five Credits?" My jaw drops slightly.

"Yes. Seems a farsighted reporter saw the need to head off future conflicts by releasing a detailed analysis—with video and audio recordings of previous speeches and meetings—of this unprecedented offer to the masses. It's been picked up by quite a few news organizations," Harry says, looking quite pleased with himself.

"Why is it so unprecedented?" I say. "I mean, we can't be the only ones to have seen the advantages of doing this."

"I might have been exaggerating a little," Harry says, offering a slight shrug. "But not by much. There have been organizations—mostly charities and non-profits—who have made similar offers, but most of them ran into a few major problems."

I grunt for Harry to hurry it up, considering the crowd is getting restless as the start time gets closer.

"Credits. Or specifically, the return of it. Wiza wasn't exactly wrong about the fact that what we're doing guarantees us a loss. Once you factor in losses from death and slow Level-ups, your rate of return looks dismal, especially compared to other options. In most cases, the repayment period stretches out too far to be viable," Harry says. "Governments that have looked into these programs aren't interested in adding more to their own population. Even border planets often struggle to feed and train everyone on planets that are being terraformed. They have better things to do than bring in low-Level individuals."

"We're also a Dungeon World," Ali chimes in. "Most planets are flooded with more Combat Classers than their dungeons can handle. Everyone gets put on a rotation, so adding more people to the list is a bad idea. But Earth? We just go for a stroll outside a city's borders and bang! We've got monsters galore."

"Right. So, basically, because we're the only actual planetary government with monsters galore, we can make this offer and potentially make a profit on it." I recall that the total number of aliens we saw on Earth was relatively low at first. Costs, bureaucracy, and the ability to exploit other locations meant that many groups were slow to move in unless they had a vested interest in the planet, like the Truinnar and Movanna. But in the four years that I was gone, the number of aliens had increased. In time, as more and more trade routes connect and the cost of flying over decreases, we'll see even more aliens arrive.

The clock turns over in my mind's eye.

Time.

I walk out to the stage, letting my aura turn on and shutting up the crowd. "Thank you all for coming. Ladies, gentlemen, those in-between, and those who laugh at us with our weird gender issues…"

Laughs come from a small smattering of the audience, and I fall into my usual spiel. If our world is to be flooded, better for that flood to be controlled by us.

***

Harry and I are sitting in the bulbous little vehicle that makes up part of the transportation network here, zipping past high-rise towers at rectum-clenching speeds when things go to hell. The first thing I notice is the minor change in velocity of an oncoming bubble. But that minor change is all that's needed when vehicles pass by each other by centimeters.

I reflexively throw Two for One on Harry before casting Soul Shield on him. That's all I get to do before the two vehicles slam into one another. Metal screeches, plastic shatters, and the body of the bubble vehicle warps, jagged edges of ultra-tough metal twisting and spearing within. The inertial compensators give way, throwing us toward the metal even as my Soul Shield Skill snaps into place around Harry. My contingency ring activates too, covering my body as we both are pin-cushioned by the metal and crushed.

The vehicle directly behind us fails to stop. Again, the screeches of failing metal and plastic erupts as the abrupt cry of surprise still issuing from Harry's lips cuts off as he bounces around. The Shields give way, shattering beneath the massive forces. Surprisingly, not a single safety mechanism activates in our vehicles, forcing us to withstand the damage directly. Already I feel pain shooting through my chest, arms, and foot as Two for One shares Harry's damage with me. I'm not even sure where his injuries end and mine begin.

Next to fail are the magnetic grips holding the bubble cars in place. The compressed mess that is the remains of our vehicle gets clipped again by another vehicle from behind, sending the remnants of the car breaking apart as gravity takes us.

As we spin around and around, I manage to get up my Harden Skill, toughening my physical defenses further. Once that's up, I layer Soul Shield on Harry again, offering him additional protection while absently noting he's begun healing himself. Soul Shield goes on me too. All of this is accomplished in seconds with the exertion of will and Mana. Damage accumulates even through the Shield as Harry bleeds and tears from the metal embedded in his body forcing its way out. I share the pain and injury through my Skill, sucking it all in as I focus on more important matters.

"*Status?*"

"*This is definitely an attack. Goblin's arse! Brace!*"

I don't even know why Ali bothers saying that much, crushed as I am within the damn vehicle. But the reason for his sudden declaration makes itself known a moment later as a rocket punches through the mangled mess before exploding. I get to watch it work, my mind processing the danger of the empowered weapon before the explosion tears apart the mangled vehicle. Last I see of the reporter, he goes through a nearby wall into one of the high rises, skipping along inside the melted and burning remnants of the vehicle.

Seconds. Everything has happened in seconds.

Dimension Locked!

Reality has been stabilized in the immediate area. You may not enter another dimension or pass through space while this status is in effect.

Note: Dimension Lock may be breached using a Master Level (4) Skill

I get thrown into the air, where additional rockets home in on me. I throw up another Soul Shield, my hoverboots engaging as I literally find myself jumping through the air and cutting apart one rocket. I dodge one only to be struck by another. Explosions ripple from the one that hit and the one I dodged, throwing me around. More rockets fill the air, along with high-powered beam rifles. I'm still falling, but my entire body is buffeted by shrapnel and continuous explosions. I cut and twist, doing my best to dodge even as I fall.

"*Unlocked. Go!*"

My lips pull back as I engage Blink Step, reappearing out of the blast zone and higher in the air. I spin, engaging my hoverboots as I kick off again. Seconds later, the same dimension lock status appears as beams of fire point at me, but I'm right next to one of my attackers now.

A spider-human hybrid, an Uttu, is standing next to a field artillery beam weapon on the edge of a skyrise, the weapon pointed down towards where I was. As I drop, I can see the muzzle of the weapon swing up as the artillery piece tries to retarget me. The Uttu itself is covered in a silver-and-grey armored jacket, protecting its body and fractal eyes while a portable force shield covers portions of the weapon itself. None of that matters.

A Blade Strike shatters the barrel, and a portion impacts the force shield, which quivers. I throw myself aside as the hover boots whine, their engines badly damaged from the numerous explosions. But they hold for now, allowing me to dodge an incoming beam attack. Another Blade Strike shatters the shield. Then the remaining beam attacks find me.

My skin bubbles, armor melts, and cuts cauterize under the attack. Even as I struggle to get away, I'm caught in another explosion as an arrow I never saw slams into me, wrapping me in green flame and acid. As I fall, my hoverboots finally give way, dropping me faster toward the ground. My throwing knives flash outward, catching the Uttu even as the assassin leans out to continue its attacks.

Down, down I go, spinning and twisting as I streamline my body in an attempt to get away from the incoming rockets and the area lock. My mind splits, one portion tracking the attacks, the other fast-casting the Improved Flight spell, though I hate to waste Mana right now.

"Shit. They locked the area right below you too, boy-o."

My eyes widen. My health is already down to half of what it should be. Even layering on Soul Shield does little to slow the accumulation of damage as more attacks land on my falling form. My armor is shredded, my body wrapped in caustic acid. Harden does nothing because my defenses are crumbling nearly as fast as I get them up. They have me cornered, and I'm falling too fast to deploy things like smoke.

I finally catch a good glimpse of what's attacking me from above. A floating gunship, one that uses mundane rotors, anti-gravity skids, and magic to keep it aloft. Beneath its stubby wings are rocket tubes spitting out more firepower than should physically be possible. And in its front are individually tracking beam weapons. There's no convenient window to show me my attackers, but my minimap tells me there are three within.

I use the sudden increase of thrust as my spell kicks in to send my body toward a hole in a nearby high rise. Another explosion from behind shatters my Soul Shield again, sending me through the hole faster than expected. My hand grips and grabs at floor as I skip along, a sword conjured and plunged into the floor to slow me down. As I skip along, I flex my Elemental Affinity to loosen the bonds of the flooring, allowing me to crash through the floor on my next skip and the one after that. That puts some distance and visual impediments between my attackers and me.

I finally come to a halt next to a reinforced wall, my health down to a fifth, even with my regeneration. I push myself up, groaning slightly as the weapon shop's interior vault creaks alarmingly. With an exertion of will, my spells are released, allowing my Mana to begin its slow regeneration. Another exertion of Mana and I layer another Soul Shield before I cast my other buffs and scramble for a health potion.

"You guys might want to clear out," Ali says, making himself visible as he darts in. "You don't want to get caught in this."

The employees don't need another warning. They rush out as fast as they can.

A second later, the roar of engines grows louder. Explosions and beam weaponry chew their way through the building, forcing me to run again.

"Are they insane?" I snarl, wondering how many people have died by now. How much destruction have they caused just trying to get to me? I can't help but wonder where Irvina security is. Or who was paid off to stay away. "Ali, can you take out the ship?"

"No chance," Ali says as he floats beside me. "The Machine Meld piloting the gunship is soaking up any damage it's receiving. And the Master Class who's sitting shotgun will tear me a new one the moment I start attacking."

A beam punches through the air ahead of us, cutting across the corridor and burning to death a non-Combatant who hides behind a wall. I snarl, throwing a series of cuts into the floor, and drop through the newly created hole, putting more walls between the attackers and me. "Damn it. Security?"

"On their way. Six minutes for anything effective."

Effective is the right word. As I run, I scan the information dump Ali is feeding me of what's happening outside. Automated defenses, robots, and other sentinels have already started their attacks on the ship. But it's too well-armored, too well-defended for automatic defenses meant to suppress Basic Class troublemakers to hinder it. For that matter…

"Can you channel Beacon?" I say as I stop cutting and head deeper into the building.

I'm safe, for now at least, as I put more masonry between my attackers and me. I pant, eyeing the minimap, and grimace. Too many dots, most of which are color-coded grey for unknowns. Trouble could come from any direction now, and I'm not sure which way to run, even if the dimension lock is gone.

"Possible. But you'd be stuck with the collateral damage from fighting back," Ali says. "There's… a lot of people."

"Yeah," I exhale, slowing my run and slamming down a healing potion. I watch as flesh and skin knit together, wounds slowly closing as my body fixes some of the damage.

I hate running. But backing off now is the best idea. I form a Portal, picking a location far away, and figure I'll pay the fine later for Portaling in the city.

"And there they go," Ali says, interrupting me.

I blink, staring at the information as the red dots pull back. The Uttu disappears from the map entirely while the three in the gunship burn oxygen and run for it, fast disappearing from my minimap.

"That's it?" I mutter, staggering to a halt.

But it makes sense. They could cut through the building again, but I could easily run. Each angle change forces them to blow up even more areas. And with security on their way, they don't have the time. They must have banked on finishing me off quickly and didn't realize my defenses were sufficient to hold them off this long.

Or this could have been a warning. An elaborate and destructive warning.

***

"Think we should go somewhere else?" I say, cocking my head at Ali, who keeps floating in circles above me, looking uncommonly serious.

"Go where?" Ali says with a snort. "You're the victim, not the perpetrator. Nor did you try to hide your identity."

"Yeah…" I say, calling back up the notification when I viewed the Uttu.

*??? ????, ???? ???? (???? **Level** ???)*

HP: ????

MP: ????

Conditions: Masked, ????, ????

It did tell me a few things. For one, either it or someone in its party was at the Master Class Level to be able to hide their Status from me. Eye of Insight might not seem that powerful on first look, but its ability to cut through stealth-based Skills of a lower rank means that surprise attacks are much harder to pull off. So I'm facing at least two Master Classers—one who can lock down space and another who can hide their abilities. Potentially one, but I'd be surprised if that's the case.

"That Machine Meld guy, how'd you know?" I say, realizing something.

"They forgot to shield the vehicle itself," Ali says. "And I know the ability the Master Class was using. It's a Mastery Skill."

"Right," I say, rubbing my face. "The Uttu?"

"No idea. It was hitting you with empowered attacks, but I didn't get a chance to dig into the details."

"John?" Katherine's voice cuts in, resounding in my ear.

It's an emergency line that patches her directly into my helmet, making my eyes widen. Shit. Did they attack her? "Trouble?"

"Yes"—my hand rises, a Portal forming even as I ping the map for her location—"but it's over now."

I drop my hand, my chest relaxing.

"They left a warning at the front doors of the embassy," she says. "And killed Kylie and Meo."

"How?" I snarl, my hands clenching.

"They were attacked on their day off. I've recalled everyone and rescinded leave for now. Are you all right?'

"We're fine. Harry triggered his Skill and disappeared once we broke apart, so they never went after him," I say, recalling the party notification I had ignored while fighting for my life. "Mikito's out of contact, but she's in a dungeon with others from Tig. She should be fine." I doubt they'd drag in the guild with attacks like this. "I hope."

"Stay safe, John."

"I will."

We cut the call as I hear the tramp of boots making their way toward me. Ali even nicely highlights the security forces in blue on my map. As they close in, I dismiss my sword and layer on a Soul Shield, getting ready to greet them.

***

Hours later, I'm finally free to leave the scene of the attack and make my way back to my residence. It amuses me somewhat that the investigators felt the need to play good cop, bad cop, even with the use of Skills and all the technology that showcased exactly what happened. I wonder if that's just a way to extract more information. Or are there enough people lying and setting up fake attacks that it's something they need to do? That's a rather disturbing thought. In either case, I ended up spending a lot of time answering the same set of questions, all phrased a little differently. It's only when I threatened to get up and leave that they finally let me go.

Harry finds me soon afterward, a flask in hand and a slightly glassy look in his eyes. Not too inebriated, but "tipsy" as his status condition says. That amuses me, as does the large and obvious security force that brings us home eventually.

When we're secured in the flying car, I turn to the reporter. "You okay?"

"Just fine. Takes more than a few overenthusiastic buggers shooting me down to stop me. Not exactly the first time either," Harry says. "Did I ever tell you about the time Daesh took a shot at the army 'copter I was in? Took out the tail rotor. Bam! Lots of screaming then too. The pilot had to do an autorotative landing. Threw up so much that time."

"And the drink?"

"Steadies my nerves," Harry says, offering the flask to me.

"No thanks. I'll wait until we're back safe," I say.

"Don't trust the security?" His wave encompasses the multiple flanking vehicles and the security officer in the back with us.

"Don't trust our attackers," I say.

A downloaded memory presses into my mind, reminding me that a common advanced ambush tactic is to launch a second one after a failed first. Most untrained individuals would, like Harry, expect that the attack is over. The second ambush catches them by surprise, finishing the job. Of course, I wonder how untrained Harry is. Maybe he knows and doesn't care.

Of course, under the System, the second ambush would need to happen a lot sooner. Otherwise, outside of the psychological blow and some minor drop in consumables, the effect of a second attack is mitigated. After all, in ten minutes, all the wounds and Mana would have regenerated fully. Which means another attack is unlikely. But, perhaps they could be counting on that.

"Coward!" Harry chugs down the drink again. "Wait till I put out a clip on them."

"You have a lead?" I say, my eyebrow rising.

Unfortunately, I was too busy running to pay attention to any of their threads. Even the Uttu only left an impression of her connections, one that ensured I would never miss her again if I saw her. But it was insufficient for me to track her down.

"Lead, smlead," Harry says. "I'm a reporter. Finding sources and investigating is what I do."

The security guard with us snorts through its big, piggy nose but doesn't say anything else.

Harry still catches it and stretches himself upward fully, fixing the alien with a serious gaze marred only by the slight green around his eyes. "Just you wait."

"Of course. Of course. Not as if we don't have hundreds of investigators of our own. Master Class ones," the demihuman says.

I sigh, doing my best to ignore the byplay. "Fine. You go do that." I lean back, half-closing my eyes. "*Can you contact all the people who we've signed on? Tell them to be extra careful. And let's look at moving up the timeline for shipping them off-planet.*"

"*What if they get hit en route?*"

I'm unsure what to say. Insurance helps, but that's no guarantee that the pirates won't ignore the damn insurance and go ahead with physical attacks. Especially if they're being paid more to attack than the insurance would pay out. "*Find better armed transports.*"

"*Sure. I'll just click my little red heels and wish them up.*"

"*Ali…*" I send warningly.

The Spirit sniffs. "*You're always so uptight when you don't get a chance to hit back.*"

Ignoring the Spirit, I close my eyes, reaching out with my Skill to check on the threads that run from me. If someone wants to target me, let's see if I can find them. And maybe make their day a little bit worse.

Chapter 13

An hour and change later, I'm standing in front of Katherine, having opened a Portal directly into her office. Between the exception granted by the ambassador into her offices and the one offered by the security forces, I'm now allowed to pop between locations with less hassle. While Portaling isn't exactly banned, it is significantly discouraged via the requirements for a license. One that, until just recently, I had not been granted. Amazing what the destruction of a large swath of a neighborhood and just over a hundred civilian deaths can do to the wheels of bureaucracy.

Interestingly enough, Oria is here too, seated across from Katherine when I walk in. Hondo has his hands behind his back, glowering at me as I step through the shimmering black Portal. I don't miss the way his hands twitch, sliding a pair of knives back into their sheaths once it's clear I am who I am.

"Representative Oria. Perfect," I say, offering her a half-smile. "I was hoping to speak with you."

"And I, you," Oria says, fixing me with a disapproving look. "How is it that a simple request has become the talk of the town?"

"Talent."

"Do you think this is a laughing matter?" Oria says, eyes glowing. "Lives have been lost, property damaged, reputations sullied. All because you people could not do a simple task without complicating things."

My lips curl up slightly as her words dig into my guilty conscience. "You wanted a Dungeon World. You have one. What's the use of having a Dungeon World in the Edge's corner if you aren't going to use it to its full potential? We could easily take hundreds of thousands of people, grind them through all our monsters, and spit them back out to be productive members of society. But you're too scared to take the steps, too scared of the Traditionalists, the corporations with a stake in the unfair institutions. Well, tough. Time to ride the tiger."

"Ride the wha… ah. Right." Oria's eyes flash as information is injected or searched or something. Her cold eyes regard me as a finger slowly moves in a circle on the armrest. "It seems that Graxan's warning that you're a troublemaker and foolhardy actually understated the matter."

Katherine looks between us before leaning forward, coughing gently to attract our attention. "Whether the actions taken were wise or not, rescinding them would be an admission of defeat. It's not something my government is willing to do. Nor, I think, something that your Duchess or the other members of the Edge desire. We would be losing reputation with no gain."

Oria looks at Katherine before she finally inclines her head slightly. "No. We would not want you to rescind your offer now."

"*Yes!*" Ali crows.

"That does not mean we are happy with what you have done," Oria says. "Still, we shall set that aside and discuss appropriate compensation later."

I growl slightly, but Katherine shoots me a look that tells me to stay silent. I cross my arms and press my lips together. I'll tell Oria where to shove it later.

"In the meantime, we need to deal with these attacks," Oria says. "I understand you've seen a drop in your recruits since the incidents?"

"We have. There are scattered reports that Artisans are facing additional violence. Some have had their workshops and wares destroyed. Others have been fired. And of course, the companies have been purchasing debts, as they have promised," Katherine says. "Couple that with the reduction in recruits from the Combat Classers after the most recent incident and we are down by around thirty-eight percent."

"Not as bad as we feared then," Oria says. "We have arranged for a few of our troop transports to arrive soon. Those transports will take all your recruits directly to Earth. In turn, Earth will pay a premium on their transportation to cover the dangers we expect to see in space.

"In addition, the Duchess has made arrangements for any of your Artisan recruits to draw upon an interim loan program to cover any increases or repayments needed. If the Irvina have decided to give us such good clients, we will take them. As for the Combat Classers—"

The woman's shark-like grin reminds me that I do not want to get too far on her bad side. There's a killer instinct in her, one that has nothing to do with blades or spells but is just as deadly.

Still, I have to chime in. "Let the ones who want to go, go.."

"Pardon me?"

"We don't want any Combat Classers who are scared away by a little blood in the operating room. They're going to see a hell of a lot more of it on Earth. If they aren't cutting the mustard now, they won't do it on Earth. If you don't believe me, ask Hondo." I nod at the glowering Weaponmaster who reluctantly nods in approval of my words.

"Very well then. That shall save some Credits. The ambassador and I will discuss the details of the arrangements to provide additional protection for the Artisans, but there is one last matter," Oria says.

"The Master Class attackers."

"Yes. Preliminary investigations and analysis show you were targeted by at least three Master Class attackers," Oria says. "You are, I must say, fortunate that they decided not to unleash their full array of attacks."

I grunt but have to admit she's correct. If they had access to high-Level damage Skills like mine, they sure as hell didn't use them. Then again, not all Master Classes are geared toward battle. The fact that she knew enough to say what she did means… "You have more details about the attackers."

"Yes." Oria's lips thin for a second. She looks at Hondo, who waves, sending over a series of notifications.

"The attackers you faced are a known for-hire network team currently working for the opposition. While we know of their identities and Skills, their location continues to be hidden from us. The current Credit cost of locating the Wolves of the Air Team stands at just over fifty million Credits," Hondo says. "Two attempts have been made to take them down. Both have failed."

"Oh shit. I know that name. One sec… goblin's children. That explains a lot."

"Explain."

"You can stop asking your Spirit to research the matter," Hondo says stiffly. "I was on the second team to take action. What we did not know was that they had set up a counter ambush. Our team was destroyed, leaving only me alive."

"How…?"

"I was left alive as a warning," Hondo says, his fists clenching. "As the lowest Leveled member of the team, I was considered the most… insignificant."

"Thus your fall from grace," I say, slowly nodding. "And your bad temper."

"To scum like you…"

I wave away his words, ignoring the man as I look over the team details he has sent. That makes him growl more, only to be shushed by Oria.

Evanline Brae; Scourge, Lady of Many Rooms, Monster Hunter (Goblins, Hakarta, Truinnar,…), more… (Space Lord Level 14) (M)

HP: 1280/1280

MP: 5280/5280

Notable Skills: Space Lock, Aura of Reality, Spatial Prison, Off to the Side, Dimensional Shards, Squish Your Head. Illu's Blessing of Mana Regeneration

"Care to explain? Some repetition here."

"Space Lord—Master Class version of the Space Mage specialization. Concentrates on altering and shaping space itself and, to some extent, the dimensions that intrude on that space. Space Lock is your everyday Dimensional Lock, just slightly differently flavored. Off to the Side is a wide area spell that isolates a location from outside interference, putting the entire location just a bit off from every other location. That's how she isolated you during the attack. Threw the area around you a kilometer out of whack from reality, making sure that reinforcements couldn't just portal or teleport in," Ali explains, shedding a little light on something I hadn't even thought to question. Old assumptions about how long it takes police to respond conflict with my own learned experience of jumping from place to place.

"How come I never got a notice that was happening?" I say.

"Didn't affect you directly, just the area. It's so wide-area that there's no warning until you bump against the edges. It shifts the entire space, but the rules are still the same. Part of the reason why she needed to use Space Lock independently too," Ali says.

I grunt, making note of this problem. *"Is this why it's so expensive to find them?"*

"Partly. Pretty sure the entire team is also decked out and counter-intelligenced up the wazoo. But if where they're staying is out of sync with normal reality, a lot of normal tracking spells and Skills won't work."

I ask, as a thought strikes me, "Is that fifty million Credits also due to politics?"

"Yes. The factions that make use of them have invested a significant amount of funds into ensuring their continued existence," Oria says.

"Got it." I turn back to the information as Ali continues.

"Aura of Reality is the one that forces people back into normal dimensions and also makes Stealthed attackers appear. Space Prison is an extremely hard-to-escape trapping spell that slides you into your own warped space. She used that to great effect against Hondo's team. The other two are wide area and individual attacks."

"Evanline looks to be a pain," I say.

"She is," Hondo says. "Powerful and smart. She split my team, took out our frontline till it was too late."

"Damn," I say, rubbing my chin. "Recommendations?"

"Your resistances will help against her direct attacks. It won't stop her prison, which is what she'll likely use against you if she's looking to isolate you further," Hondo says. "Don't let her."

I stare at the rather unhelpful Weaponmaster before snorting. Fine. Time to go shopping then. Next up is the Machine Lord.

S'Baxu; Exploit 3-x-189, Monster Hunter (Goblins, X-23, Slimes,…), The Lumierre Prize of Artisanal Excellence, Grandmaster Brewer, more… (Machine Lord Level 21) (M)

HP: 1830/1830

MP: 3210/3210

Notable Skills: Machine Meld, Overdrive, Boosted Performance, Gift of Sentience, Networked, MagiTech Rules (3)

"That's the gunship pilot, right?"

"Yup. He's the most flexible since he can change his gear to suit the situation. Like a gunship to deal damage and run away. He's also the one who hacked the bubble cars and crashed you."

I recall the damage notifications and the volume of fire from those rockets. I assume that's where things like MagiTech rules come into play. *"Lots of firepower, not a huge amount of damage."*

"Har. That's because you had Harden, your damage resistances, and gear on. Without it, you'd be singing a different tune. But yes, his max damage is lower overall. He's more a high-volume-of-fire kind of guy. Less effective against you, but better for dealing with softer

targets or Summoners. Overall, he's probably the least worrisome since he's not technically a direct Combat Class."

"Like Sam."

"Like Sam was."

I dismiss the status information. If he's anything like Sam, I could expect a completely different loadout and vehicle the next time we clash. Frustrating that taking out his vehicle would be harder than normal, but nothing to get too worked up about.

Hurquji Sani, Son of Ze'us, Monster Slayer (Hydra, Goblins, Kobold, Bulls, Harpies, …), Blood Drenched, Duellist, Winner of the Four Ivies, more… (Titan Spawn Level 13) (M)

HP: 7830/7830

MP: 3810/3810

Unique Skills: Demigods Body, Resistance to Pain, Father's Blessing, Gifted Strength, Demigod Regeneration, Ares' Blessing

"Titan?" I say, my eyes widening slightly.

"Elder race. Not many of them left, since their planet got destroyed."

"The System?"

"Nah. Ze'us, Poseidon, and Hades got into a three-way tussle and ended up destroying the planet. Happens when you've got three Heroics who are relatively balanced," Ali says.

"Is Zeus going to be a problem?"

"Ze'us. And nah. He's a rather famous negligent dad. Has to be really, with the way he acts. When your spawn number in the tens of thousands—"

"I thought you said they're a dying race."

"Sure. From a few billion to less than a hundred thousand. That's one heck of a drop."

I give up on arguing with Ali and turn my attention back to the room. "Correct me if I'm wrong, but Hurquji's your basic brawler?" If so, that'd explain his lack of interaction in our latest fight. No place for a guy who punches when we're fighting mid-air.

"If you call a Titan 'basic,' certainly," Oria says.

"Do not underestimate the Titan," Hondo says. "His abilities give him unending Stamina and incredibly high resistance to damage. While he might not be able to alter the trend of a battle at the snap of his fingers, the Titan can finish the entire battle by himself if left unchecked."

"Hits hard, soaks up damage even better. Got it."

My words make Hondo glower at me even more, which I admit is part of the point. Objective complete, I return to my perusal of the Wolves.

Trols Vroldrons, Webweaver, Monster Slayer (Kobolds, Ussma Flies, Samak Vipers), One Shot, more… (Ryou-ri-rr Level 48) (A)
HP: 3870/3870
MP: 2840/2840
Notable Skills: Target Lock, Charged Shot, Lurker in the Web, Spider's Camouflage, Weapon of Choice, Stamina to Power, Mana to Power, Triple Tap

"The Uttu?" I say. *"I don't like that One Shot title."*

"Relax. She tried it already and failed. She probably got that earlier on. It's one of those conditional titles—kill a hundred people who are twenty Levels above you with one attack. Nothing that impressive." I kind of want to protest that yes, yes, it is impressive, but Ali continues. *"I'm more interested in that Weapon of Choice Skill. Makes her significantly more dangerous when she's using a specific weapon, and it's also a little more flexible than your Soulbound weapon. So long as she designates it beforehand with sufficient training time, it increases damage output by eighteen percent. But they aren't indestructible. That means if you destroy the weapon…"*

"Boom." I get more than a few exclamations of surprise from the crowd around me and I offer them a slight smile. "Sorry. Reading. All right, it seems I've got a rough idea of what we have here. No dedicated healer, but it seems that's not been an issue."

"They're an assassination team. They hit hard and fast. And then they use Evanline's and S'Baxu's abilities to leave. It's extremely hard to lock down a Space Lord." Hondo grimaces slightly. "It limits our tactical options because we have to take her down."

"Why?" I say. "They're mercenaries, right? Isn't making it too expensive to deal with us the better solution?"

"What are you suggesting?" Oria says while Hondo bristles.

"Focus fire on the weakest. Take them down the next time we have a chance. If they start losing people each time they attack, they're going to be a lot less likely to keep the contract," I say.

"Losing an Advanced Classer means nothing to them," Hondo says. "The loss of the Webweave is negligible. They have churned through many others since my disgrace."

"But my point still stands," I say. "Your way hasn't resulted in any wins. Also, what's with this we?"

"I have been tasked by the Representative to aid you in dealing with them," Hondo says. "From now on, I shall be accompanying you."

"Hells to the no."

"John!" Katherine's voice rises and she slaps the table, drawing my attention to her. "You will take the offered help."

"You think I can trust this guy not to stab me in the back?" I say, ignoring the way Hondo bristles.

"The Weaponmaster will not betray his honor. He has never betrayed his honor," Oria says, her voice as cold as the wind over a Yukon lake in the middle of winter. "Even the mildest scuff on it sends Hondo into a tizzy of anger and recrimination. His job is to guard your back and kill them. He will not touch you."

"Take the Weaponmaster, boy-o. That's three sentient-trained Master Class killers after you. You can't win without help," Ali says. *"If you don't recall, the best we could do was run like hell."*

I want to object, but the Spirit has a point. I did barely any damage to the Uttu, and I never even got a chance to leave a scratch on the others. The best option I had was to run, and as Oria has already pointed out, it's likely they weren't actually trying to kill me. Just pass on a message to back down. Kind of stupid really. If they had done any research, our opposition would know I don't back down.

I draw a deep breath, looking at Hondo. There's a burning anger in there, a sneer that he does not hide. But beneath all that, there's a solidity to the man too. A bone-deep stubbornness that's comforting in a way. He won't run, he won't bow. He has a personal grudge in this, one that transcends the one he has with me. He's also probably skilled enough to handle at least one of the Master Classers.

Which means…

"Fine. Now, how do we find them?" I say.

The silence that follows is quite telling.

***

Portaling back to our residence takes only a fraction of a second. Mikito is absently walking out of the bathroom, playing with the clasp of her nano-formed collar helmet. She offers me a smile that freezes before she explodes into action, Ghost Armor forming as she moves sideways, polearm appearing in her hand as she points it behind me. I twitch and shift, sword forming in my hand as I spin about before thought catches up with reactions.

"Hold!" I roar, making my sword disappear.

Hondo sniffs, one hand raised only slightly to ensure that a lunge doesn't catch him completely unprepared. But otherwise, the Weaponmaster looks entirely unimpressed by Mikito and her actions.

"What is he doing here?" Mikito says, lowering her naginata but neither dismissing her armor nor putting away Hitoshi.

"He's our newest buddy." I walk over to the kitchen and poke around the Galactic equivalent of a refrigerator, looking for something to eat. The first shelf carries a series of flat, metal-coated pre-packed meals that I recall being particularly tasty. One advantage of the pervasiveness of sci-fi technology and System Classes is that Cooks and Chefs are very, very talented. I pull out three of the pre-packed meals and walk over to the dining room, eyeing the pair in their silent standoff. "If someone wants to grab the alcohol from the fridge, we can eat and talk."

"With him?" Mikito almost snarls.

"Oh, come on. I've gotten over it, and I'm the immature one here," I say.

"He really is." The grumpy Spirit glares at me and floats over to the fridge before yanking out another pair of meals and a case of beer. "Mikito, Hondo's given his word that he won't harm John. And now Hondo's going to give his word not to harm you or anyone else in the party. Right?"

Hondo hesitates before he inclines his head. "I do. For as long as we share a common enemy, and until we have provided an in-person report to our respective masters, I shall undertake no adverse action against you or members of your party."

"See? All good." I push the meals across the table. "Now, sit down, eat, and let's talk."

I tap the seal on my meal and sit back, crossing my arms as I wait for the meal to be properly heated. While it does that, I fill Mikito in on what happened at the meeting. The Samurai looks less than happy even when she gets the information on the Wolves, but she relents enough to sit down and eat.

"Where's Harry?" I ask, looking around. Don't want the reporter randomly walking in on a conversation he shouldn't hear.

"Out."

"Is that safe?" I say, frowning. Then I realize who I'm talking about and shut up. If there's anyone in our group who would be safe, it's Harry. Not only do his Skills provide a measure of protection from being targeted, the guild he is in frowns heavily on attacking their people and have, at times, taken steps to make their displeasure known. Of course, if he's actively looking for the Wolves of the Air and feeds information back to us, it'll be a problem for his professed "neutrality."

"He said so. Wants an interview with them, he says," Mikito say, meeting my gaze. I see the worry in her eyes, the concern for our new friend. But his job is dangerous, no matter what choices we make.

"This is the reporter?" Hondo asks.

I nod. The Weaponmaster snorts loudly, tapping the ready meal and letting the metal roll backward to showcase slabs of meat and carbohydrates. There's even a good mixture of weirdly colored vegetables, neatly sliced. And of course, the *piece de resistance*—a triple-layered dessert.

"You have a problem with Harry?"

"I have given my word to cause no problems."

"Wasn't the question. What's your problem with Harry?" I ask.

"Nothing. I just dislike such creatures."

"Creatures?" I frown.

"Reporters, John," Ali says around a mouthful of the dessert. As always, the Spirit has started with the sweets. In fact, he's got both meals open, the desserts from both trays in front of him.

"What's your problem with reporters then?"

"They are the most useless Class. Less useful even than Slime Trainers," Hondo says. "They spread refuse as badly as any Sanitation Worker and constantly agitate the commoners. They provoke the Combat Classers, delude the Artisans, and embarrass our proper rulers. Well. Perhaps they are not all bad."

His last words are met with stony silence before it slowly dawns on us that the Weaponmaster made a joke. By that point, it's a little too late to laugh, so we end up staring at him in shared embarrassment. In unison, Mikito and I duck our heads and chew on the monster meat.

A few minutes later, after I come up for air, I look at the strange group that makes up my dining companions. The sight before me makes me blink, but I push the thought aside and sip on the Apocalypse Ale. "So what do we know about the Wolves?"

"We have our contacts looking for them, but…" Hondo shrugs.

I have to admit, I understand his reaction. After all, they've been looking for this group all this time. It's not as if looking a little harder will make a difference. Probably.

"Hondo, have they ever been this blatant before?" I say.

"In their attacks? No. But you underestimate the anger you have generated. Local law enforcement might desire them caught, but they have neither the Skills nor the Credits to do so, not while stymied by those with vested interest. As for the Master Class bounty hunters, few will take a commission on a team this powerful."

"How about Heroics?" Mikito asks.

Hondo shrugs.

When he provides no further answer, Ali butts in. "Heroics kind of do their own thing. Or whatever the organization they chained themselves to tells them to do. While Irvina has three Heroics, they're mostly dealing with other problems. Unless the Council decides to set them loose, you won't see them move."

"And the Wolves are under the thumbs of the Irvina already. I'm guessing the Edge has their own Heroics. So… what? A cold war situation where the Heroics are never put in play?" I say.

Hondo inclines his head slightly, and I sigh. Joy.

"Bait?" Mikito says, deciding to shift the direction of our pointless conversation.

"Probably." I lean backward, sipping on the beer, and pull some whisky-infused chocolates from storage. I offer the pieces to the others before popping one in my mouth. "Obvious but…"

"But if they don't take it, they'll fail to finish their mission," Hondo says.

"Do we know if they're contracted to keep coming at John?" Ali says, raising an eyebrow. "I mean, their attacks and other actions are already having an effect on recruitment."

"We do not," Hondo says, "but we must assume a contract is in effect. Slowing down the recruitment is insufficient for their ends. They must destroy the program and make an example."

"Katherine? If they go after her—"

"Unlikely, but we have added to the defenses your people have set up," Hondo says. "Attacking an ambassador on Irvina carries significant penalties. It would—at the very least—increase the bounty on the Wolves to the point that other groups would target them. In such a case, I would not be surprised if some of the more proactive Heroic Combat Classers bumped them up on their list. Or the Council even authorized some of the local Heroics to take action."

"Wait. Heroic Combat Classers have a list?" Mikito says, eyebrow rising.

"There are… individuals who feel that their position allows them to right wrongs," Hondo says, his nose wrinkling in disgust.

"Wannabe superheroes," Ali adds in his two cents.

"That's amazing," I say.

"Oh please. Paladin." Ali points his wrapped-up meat-meal at me. "As if you aren't going to become one of those."

"Hey! All I was doing before these guys bothered me was reading," I say.

"It's true. He was very boring." Mikito nods sagely.

"Exactly. Wait." I glare at the little Japanese woman, who flashes me a smile, before I change the subject back. "So Katherine's relatively safe. The rest of the diplomatic corp are in lockdown. How about the combat teams?"

"Portal."

I nod at Mikito's short and entirely reasonable suggestion. "Good call. All right, then we have a game plan? Or at least, the outline of our strategy?"

"This is no game. But yes, I believe so," Hondo says. "I shall be accompanying you in any dungeon run."

"To the dungeon entrance. But you're going to run a dungeon and a team yourself." When he moves to say something else, I shake my head. "We'll use ones with clear boundaries so we can't be attacked while running them. In the meantime, you'll help run as many people through as possible."

"That is not my job," Hondo says with a snap.

"Maybe. But it'll help us finish this faster. The higher Level we get these recruits, the better the campaign looks. And that means the more pressure the Wolves will be under to finish this."

Hondo stays silent for a time before he speaks slowly. "Very well."

After that, we talk details. Both where and when we can expect to be attacked as well as how we should handle matters. We talk about our strengths and the Wolves' strengths, as well as potential weaknesses. It's almost nice, working with Hondo. He's vastly more experienced and offers some great suggestions. But a portion of my mind can't help but think that we're asking for trouble in the future.

Ah hells. What is, is. And what it is, is that we need him. And him, us.

For now.

Chapter 14

Walking out of my Shop the day after, I find Hondo standing impatiently in front. I was amused when I got to the Shop and found out that the Weaponmaster did not have the right to enter. Rather than give him a guest pass, I left him outside to stew.

"Did you get what you needed?" Hondo says, and I nod. "Then let us go."

"On it," I say, raising my hand and opening up the Portal to the dungeon.

Seconds after we step through, I've got another Portal open for the other members of the security team. Hondo organizes the crowd of Combat Class recruits who have been waiting for us under the watchful eye of the local security forces. Due to the potential for conflicts among the guilds and loot stealing, security around dungeon entrances is always significantly higher. Since the attacks, the security teams have been doubled.

"About time," Mikito says grumpily as my last Portal pulls her from our guild entrance.

Surprisingly, Draco comes out of the Portal too, eying the crowd. "Redeemer. I would like a word."

"Right. Can I send the others out first?" I say, nodding at the groups who have mostly organized themselves.

Draco accedes to my request and soon enough, everyone's lined up and pushing into the dungeon.

"Thanks. Now, what's up?" I ask.

"I have received word from Tig himself," Draco says, his eyes gleaming slightly. I fail to read them, uncertain if he's amused or interested. "In short order, a citywide announcement will be made. Any attacks on dungeoning parties that contain members of our guild will be dealt with directly by Tig and his party."

"Dungeoning parties?" I frown.

"Aye. On that note…" Draco tilts his head, and I follow his gaze to a group of other aliens arriving. Surprisingly, their Status information publicly displays our guild affiliation. "Say hello to your new volunteer dungeon party leaders."

"Why?" I frown at Draco, a bit concerned by this sudden change.

"Three reasons. Firstly, we're going to be recruiting directly from your people. I understand that Tig has already discussed a number of additions to our Guild Houses on Earth. Secondly, allowing attacks on dungeon parties—for any reason—is a bad idea. That's why our guild will not be the only one making their stance clear. The second and seventh guild wars are not something we want to see repeated. Lastly, and Tig wanted me to emphasize this." Draco falls silent, letting the silence stretch out between us. "You owe us."

I let out a surprised bark of laughter at those words and the all-too-serious look on Draco's face. When the lizardman doesn't change his features, I sober up. "Of course."

"Good. Try not to die. We've invested a lot into this experiment of yours."

"You know, I could use another Master Classer…"

"Not happening," Draco says, shaking his head. "Supporting you in the manner we're doing is already stretching matters. Directly providing you with individual help would be… well… a Skill too far."

"Fine, fine," I say, waving off Draco and gesturing for the waiting group of recruits to come over.

In the meantime, Ali's been sorting out our help and sending out notices to the bodyguards and our recruits.

I'm about to enter the dungeon when Draco calls, "But that wasn't a bad idea."

"What?" I say, confused as my mind is wrenched from working out the most optimal formation for these new recruits.

Draco doesn't answer me as he wanders away, chatting to his own people.

I stare briefly at the lizardman's tail before throwing up my hands and pointing at a laggard recruit. "Come on, we don't have all day. Trust me, the monsters don't care what color your skinsuit is. You're all red on the inside."

"Actually, Oeonae muscle is yellow in color and our blood is green," the fussy humanoid with a hard-shell frill across his head and extra-large jaw says.

"In!" I roar.

***

"Oy! Pretty boy," I say, pointing at the Oeonae. "Get your ass back in the line."

"But I've got to heal her—"

"In. Line!" I shout, grabbing his shoulder and tossing him back in line. I wince as I overuse my strength, sending the poor bastard bowling into the group of robotic monsters charging the group.

There's stunned silence among the adventuring team while the robots swivel, taking the change in circumstances and rolling with it, like the robotic monstrosities they are.

"Did you fall asleep and get switched out for a Changeling? Get moving, you bunch of Goblin asses. Back up your friend!" Ali says, his gestures even more agitated.

The group of beginner Adventurers jerks into motion, launching themselves at the robots in a frenzy. The lead Warrior uses his halberd to bash away a pair of robots while a red-skinned devil poofs and reappears next to the downed Oeonae to jab electrified gauntlets into an attacking robot.

"And you!" Ali spins to me and points a finger. "Stop helping."

"Fine," I growl and cross my arms. Beelzebub flips over the shorting monster and sweeps another robot off its feet with his tail. "Some good talent here."

"If you don't kill them," Ali retorts.

I grunt and step back, leaving the Spirit to harangue and generally train the kids while I walk the line, watching as they battle the Level 20+ monsters. This is one of the strangest dungeons I've ever been in. Here, you walk into a room that rotates, moving on its own accord. Monsters stream out while obstacles and other objects pop up, giving new terrain features. The entire room assembly moves up, down, and sideways through warped space, connecting to different corridors depending on some esoteric puzzle mechanism that involves killing monsters in the right sequence to get to the end of the maze. Or, as we're going to do, just killing everything along the way since there's a max number of changes allowed per session.

"John. They're tapping out," Ali calls.

I take my time conjuring my sword as I eye the group. The support members of the party are nearly out of Mana. The front-line fighters are panting and groaning from numerous injuries, Stamina nearly tapped out and, in some cases, Mana too. I watch as the purple-clad Oeonae gets swarmed again by robots that punch and stab with their drills while Beelzebub gets tripped up and smashed into the ground.

"John?"

"Redeemer!"

I swing my blade three times, Blade Strikes flashing out to tear and rip, cut and dismember. And then it's over. I could have done it in one, but then I'd cut apart the team.

"What in the System's name was that!" The Oeonae pushes himself upward, flecks of acidic spittle flying from his mouth.

"Pretty sure that was me saving you. All of you," I say.

"You could have acted sooner. The Spirit told you to act faster," a female Yerrick says while bent over, sucking in deep breaths. Her compression clothing is torn, showcasing fur on her stomach. It seems the Yerrick has invested in self-repairing armor, so everything is slowly getting put back together.

"This is the third fight. None of you have been conserving your Stamina or Mana." As I speak, the robot remains slowly fade into the ground, their bodies broken up by the nanites that live in the room itself. A slight shudder runs through the room, then we're moving again, shifting to a new location. "And we're about to enter the fourth fight. Exactly how are you expecting to survive this?"

"With you," Beelzebub says as he bandages his leg. "Isn't that what you promised?"

"We did. But what's the point of me doing all the work? If I do that, how much experience are you all going to get?"

There's a long silence as they consider the question. As the room clunks to a stop and metallic pillars rise, I raise my hand and cast Metal Walls. The newly formed barricade blocks off what's coming and gives our people time to rest.

The Oeonae looks at me, firming his stance. "But what can we do? We're out-Leveled by a significant margin."

His words get the group nodding, and I find myself sweeping my gaze over everyone. When I see them actually listening, I point at each person in turn. "Stick to your roles. No running back and healing people, even if you can. Use your healing on yourself if you need it." This to the Oeonae.

"Use your spells to hinder and bind instead of damaging." This to the gnome, who blushes, setting off his cute freckled nose as he does so.

"And, for god's sake, don't step out of line if you intend to hold a melee line." The Yerrick snorts in acknowledgement.

"Next"—I cast a second Metal Wall to keep the monsters back—"you guys aren't helping each other. You're meant to be a team. Start acting like one. And yes, I know you're a random group we picked up. But that doesn't mean you should act like a bunch of independents.

"Also. Slow it down. We change rooms each time we clear it. So why are you rushing the battle, especially the last kill?"

"Mother's udders," the Yerrick swears, breaking the stunned silence.

I glare at the group before I sigh, raising my finger. "Last thing, people. Stop panicking. You're going to Earth. It's going to get hairy. It's going to get tough. You need to keep thinking, keep on the balls of your feet. Or hooves. Whatever you've got. Sure, this is your first time in this dungeon. But if you stop trying to figure things out, you're going to die."

When I see my words sink in, I flash Ali a wry grin. Weird to play the good cop in this relationship, but drill sergeant Ali is not the right person to tell them this. Not and keep them moving and fighting when the walls come down. So here I am, teaching a bunch of kids how to fight. Again.

***

Six rooms later, the kids are getting the hang of it. They've got the latest final robotic creation down on the floor, attempting to pick up its pieces. The robot keeps attempting to regenerate its accordion arms to prop up its saucer-shaped body, but every time it manages to get a second army fully created, either the Yerrick or Beelzebub takes out the other arm, dropping the robot to the floor. The rest of the group is drinking water, chewing on regeneration food aids, or just resting.

"How about you, Eezoo? Why are you going to Earth?" the Oeonae asks the little gnome.

"Credits, what else? My pod family were caught in the Iuwil outbreak four years ago. Nearly all of them had their Mana channels damaged. We've scraped enough together to get my second ma the healing she needs, but my first ma and third pa have it worse," the gnome says. "Getting to Earth will give me more Credits to get them a proper healing. Otherwise, we'll be stuck constantly buying the Looma freshers."

"Double-orificed worms, those freshers." Oeonae spits to the side. "Fix you up for a few months but then you have to buy them again."

"Yeah. But at least they're cheap. What about you?"

"Nothing so noble," Oeonae says. "Just got married and a litter. We need to make enough to eat, you know? Can't own a place on the scraps you pick up here."

"She a Combat Classer too?"

"Ja. We decided it's best not to be on the same team. That way there'd be one of us for the litter. The slimeballs are with the parents right now. Hopefully we'll be able to Level up enough to bring them to live with us before they get out of the larvae stage."

That image makes me shudder internally, so I stop eavesdropping. They're already turning to talk to the next person in line, but I decide even my curiosity has limits. I'm an open guy with a decent level of respect for our new alien brethren, but there are limits. And so I resolve not to pay further attention to this discussion while I concentrate on the next step of our dungeon run.

***

The room lurches again, coming to a shuddering halt. The entrance doorway twitches and flows, expanding as the nanites that make up the room eat away at the metal walls and replace them with larger blast doors. It was strange to watch the first few times, but by this point, we're used to it. Even if this particular door is significantly larger than anything else we've dealt with thus far.

"All right, kids, get your long-range attacks ready. Power them up if you can because you're going to get one shot. Then boy-o here is going to finish this," Ali says.

"Really? We can last longer than that," the Yerrick growls, hefting her axe.

"You've done well. But there's no point in chancing a death now," I say, stepping forward. "Boss monsters often have nasty one-shot kills, so better to just take the experience. Anyway, you'll all be getting his loot."

"Really?" Beelzebub says. "I mean, the others mentioned…"

"Yes," I say. No point in trying to insist on the truth. Better to let them experience it.

The group gets ready while I turn to the blast doors. They slide up to reveal a robotic monster that could only be described as the bastard love child of a dump truck and a mecha. The moment the monster makes itself known, a wide array of attacks hit it, from beam rifle shots to spells. Beelzebub disappears, reappearing in a puff of smoke right above the monster, daggers stabbing deep into the Boss. The Boss glows, electrifying its body and sending Beelzebub into spasms, his health falling precipitously.

"Nooo!" the friendly gnome screams as he sees Beelzebub fall.

Blink Step takes me to the Boss, where I snatch and throw the falling body. Unfortunately, that puts me way too close to the Boss. Electricity arcs, jumping through my body and making my muscles twitch.

Too bad for the Boss that lightning is one of my highest resistances. It's annoying but not painful. Not yet at least. Lips pull into a grin as I conjure my sword and thrust it into the monster's head, cutting through armored skin with ease. The Boss throws itself from side to side as it attempts to dislodge me, but it's too late. I trigger Blade Strike after Blade Strike with my sword embedded, my other hand gripping a convenient handhold to keep my balance.

The entire fight takes half a minute at most. Blade Strikes eat away at its internals, shutting off the electricity before the Boss mecha falls, lights dimming. A moment later, I have the monster looted while everyone gathers around to berate the experience-stealing idiot of a devil. The fact that Beelzebub managed to do more damage than the rest of the melee fighters means he received a large chunk of the experience. Especially since he risked his life.

"Well, that could have gone better," I say.

"You okay?" Ali says, floating over to me.

"Just tired," I say, waving away Ali's concern.

There's not much to be said. Beelzebub was stupid to take the risks, but the System rewards such behavior. So chances are he'll probably do it again. And sooner or later, he's going to die. Sometimes, I really wonder who built the damn System. Idiotic, stupid-ass counterintuitive rewards and benefits.

"All right, children, time to go. You can kick Red's ass later," Ali calls, waving the group to the newly created entrance.

I follow, the boss monster already fading into the ground. No convenient Boss monster corpse to loot this time.

As I walk out, I stretch and get ready to do it all over again.

Chapter 15

Hours later, our timeslots have been used up and everyone who could be run through has been. Thankfully, with the guild's help, we managed to process a much larger than normal number, with many runs giving at least one if not two increases in Levels. Of course, with so many people going through, and some of the helpers being lower Leveled, there have been a few unfortunate accidents and one death. Unsurprisingly, the news of the loss was a blow but one that most took well. Our job, our lives as Combat Classers can only be described as dangerous.

"Are we done yet?" Hondo says, arms crossed grumpily.

For all his complaining, the group the Weaponmaster dragged out all went up by two to three Levels each. It seems some of the Weaponmaster's passive abilities not only increase the stats of those in his party but also increase their Leveling speed by distributing some of the experience he would gain to them.

"Almost. Just waiting for them to get home." I shut down the Portal after the last of the recruits step through. "And done."

"Pretty sure when they gave you the clearance to use a Portal, they weren't thinking about you using it for others," Ali says.

"Then they should have specified their intentions," I say, sniffing slightly. As if I would make people walk around in danger of being ambushed if I didn't need to.

"Very well. Open one of your Portals to the prime dungeon," Hondo commands.

"Sure… wait. No can do. Not been there," I say.

"Closest point then."

"Okay…" I pull up the map and look around. There are a few areas, though some of them are in high-traffic locations. Then it hits me that I have another option. "Or I could Scry it. One second…"

Hondo snorts and crosses his arms, waiting for me to cast the spell. It takes a little bit of adjusting, but eventually I not only locate the entrance to the giant hole in the ground that leads to the prime dungeon but also the location meant for those teleporting in. I mentally snort at seeing the location, realizing that once again, Galactic Society really has two sets of rules.

"Why are we going here?" I say as we walk through the blank oval and take in the relatively quiet dungeon.

In the distance, a score of Advanced Classers stand around, packs, floating gravity trains, and a pair of mechanoid animal drones beside them. A short distance away is a platoon of armed and armored soldiers, all of them clad in the same uniform and weaponry, listening to their officer detail their attack plan. As for dungeon parties, that's it. Unlike so many other dungeons, the prime dungeon is sparsely populated at the top.

"Training," Hondo says. "We need more Levels."

Hondo's words make me really look at the man, taking in his Status. Nearly five years since we've seen each other, give or take a few months, and in that time, Hondo must have trained like crazy to reach the Level he has.

Hondo Ehrish (Weaponmaster Level 48, Master of Blades and Guns, Slayer of Orcs, Goblins and Unika, Destroyer of Monsters, The Unbroken Warrior)

HP: 4,510/4,510

MP: 2,070/2,070

Conditions: Weapon of Choice, The Master's Body, Battle Flow, Greater Regeneration, Greater Mana Regeneration

"Looking to Class up?" I say.

Ali giggles while Hondo and Mikito look at the Spirit flatly. Obviously he's the only one who got the pun. I'll take it, considering I'm punning in English but speaking in Galactic.

"As is your friend," Hondo says, inclining his head toward Mikito.

I look at her Status Screen and find my mouth dropping in surprise.

Mikito Sato, Spear of Humanity, Blood Warden, Junior Arena Champion of Irvina (Middle Samurai Level 48)

HP: 2030/2030

MP: 1440/1440

Conditions: Isoide, Jin, Rei, Meiyo, Ishiki, Ryoyo

Galactic Reputation: 15

Galactic Fame: 6,323

"Wait. You went up two Levels?" I say as I find my voice. "And what's this Champion title?"

Mikito rolls her eyes while Ali cuts in. "Took you long enough. She's had that title for two weeks now. If you'd just been oblivious for another two, I'd have won the bet."

"I earned it a while ago. While you were busy in your Questor library," Mikito says. "The championship came with a very nice experience bonus."

"Oh. Wow," I say, scratching my head. Damn. Now I feel like a right slacker. "Congrats."

"No need," Mikito says, waving away my words. "It was only the Advanced Class portion of the junior level."

"Still, that was well done."

Hondo coughs, drawing my attention back to him. "We do have a deadline. We are on a limited access pass. In five hours, we'll be teleported back here. I would prefer to actually make use of this pass."

"Fine, lead the way, honcho."

"It's Hondo."

"Right, right. Sorry," I say, flashing a slight smile to Mikito.

She sniffs at me, and I flush guiltily. Okay, maybe I'm teasing the Weaponmaster a little too much. I kick myself mentally for being so juvenile and resolve to be better.

Hondo leads us to a group of freight elevators, where he flashes a pass at the console. A second later, we're all speared by beams of light and a new Status Condition appears for us. It's a limited access pass to the prime dungeon, along with a tracking and teleportation spell. Once the doors slide open, we enter the freight elevators and are lowered at ear-popping speed.

"So… details on the dungeon?" I say. It's not as if I ever did any research on it. Beyond the fact that the dungeon was Irvina's first, and thus most powerful, dungeon, I have little information on it.

"The prime dungeon is the first dungeon ever created in Irvina. It was initially located outside of the city, with the dungeon built as a classic dungeon format. As such, it extends deep underground," Hondo says. "The hole you see is to allow airflow to the lowest parts of the dungeon. If you were cognizant of space manipulation, you would feel the way the space itself is manipulated around the dungeon, allowing it to continue growing without impacting the city. Understand that the dungeon itself is many times the size of Irvina."

"It's bigger than Irvina?" I say, my jaw dropping slightly. That's kind of hard to imagine, considering Irvina is what we poor humans would consider a megacity.

"Yes," Hondo says. "During the delve, if you are ever lost, make your way toward the air intakes. That will lead you to the exit and the way up. This will hold true in all locations but the labyrinth floors. We will not be visiting those floors.

"Like any good dungeon, it is more dangerous the deeper you delve. As such, we are entering a floor midway down. Floor sixty-seven. If we do well, we'll enter floors sixty-eight and sixty-nine. Every ten levels or so, there is a major boss, but unlike static dungeons, these zone bosses wander. As such, care must be taken while engaging in battle."

"Right, big nasty monsters wandering around. What kind of Levels are we looking at?" I say, stretching and layering buffs on myself. I eye the slowly ticking floor counter, amazed that we're still going down. Each floor must be huge.

"Level 90 to 100. The Zone Boss is expected to be in the Level 110 region," Hondo says.

"Expected?"

"They evolve," Hondo answers. "It is why quests are regularly issued to clear the dungeon. Left alone too long, the prime dungeon becomes even more dangerous."

"Interesting. I wonder if that happened in Vancouver." Frustrating that I never had time to learn more about dungeons. I know about them in the most academic of senses, but details like their continued evolution have eluded my study. Most of the details about dungeons for the System quest were easy enough to locate, with many researchers already having drained the well dry. There are, basically, no easy research studies to be done for the System Quest. Dungeons might be an artifact of the System, but they are not, as far as we know, central to the mystery of the System itself.

"Monster types?" Mikito asks as the elevator jerks to a halt.

Hondo touches the side of his neck and a helmet forms around his face.

The doors slide open, revealing the most messed up thing I'd seen in a while. Take a horse, skin it, and meld a humanoid torso where a rider would normally be. Give said rider long arms with black-tipped claws that drip acid and can reach past the horse's eyeless eyes, then add a stench that makes me gag. Mikito reflexively has her Ghost Armor formed, protecting her even while my eyes water.

As I put on my helmet to protect my sinuses, I scan the creature for details.

Nuckelavee (Level 87)

HP: 2140/2140

MP: 390/390

Condition: Odor of Disease, Aura of Decay, Body of the Grave

Aura of Decay

In the presence of an individual with an Aura of Decay, all will crumble and fall. In death, there is decay. In decay, there is peace. Rest, mortal, knowing your demise is part of the inventible.

Effect: -20% to all resistances. Negative resistances invoke damage over time effects

Hondo doesn't even hesitate, obviously expecting the creature. He explodes into action, rushing the Nuckelavee as the polearm he uses appears in his hand. Mikito follows, the pair proceeding to cut and slice the monster apart. I hang back, looking at my sword then at the long weapons the pair wield, trying not to feel out of place. But…

"I'll get the next one then," I say, mostly to myself.

I catalogue Hondo's Skills, eyeing the things he can do. Like Mikito, he has a Skill that extends the blade of his weapon, making it bigger and sharper. There's definitely a penetration Skill or two in his repertoire, which explains the way he peeled apart my Shield and Sabre's armor the last time we clashed. I don't see the speed boost he used the last time, but it's frightening how fast the damn Truinnar is naturally. But I see nothing of his greater Skills, none of the third- or fourth-tier sure-kill attacks.

"Pick up the corpse," Hondo says, looking over his shoulder to me. "And stop hanging back. You need the Levels too."

I grunt, sauntering forward and dumping the corpse in my Altered Space. Right or not, I'm not entirely sure I like being ordered around by the

Weaponmaster. Still, I follow along until we hit the next bend in the earthen corridor, which expands into a full-sized cavern. There, a full half dozen of the monsters stand, waiting for us.

The next few seconds are filled with bright lights as we trigger our long-range attacks. Blade Strikes or the Class equivalents flash forward from our weapons, Mikito's and mine moving in arcs of power while Hondo holds his polearm under his armpit and fires a concentrated beam directly from the head of his weapon.

Two of the Nuckelavee drop before they reach us. Then we get to experience a whole new slew of unpleasantness as the monsters' overlapping auras actively work together. Along the way, the other carrion monsters make their presence known. Small, crawling insect-like figures nip at heels, bite the corpses, and glow with power.

"Thousand hells," I snarl, Blink Stepping away from the group then throwing Blade Strikes.

I reappear too close to a mushroom-like object that explodes, coating me with some pollen substance that burrows into my Shield, draining its integrity. I yelp, jumping into the sky and triggering my new hoverboots. High above the fight, I attack the monsters, spamming my cutting attacks into the group's backs and staying away from the overlapping decay domain.

Mikito and Hondo split apart slightly, giving each other enough space to wield their polearms effectively. Mikito's Ghost Armor cracks and fades before rippling and refreshing in a constant battle against the auras. The Japanese lady ignores the byplay, her naginata dipping and cutting, lopping off legs and tearing off arms as she fights. Not surprisingly, Hitoshi doesn't seem to be affected at all by the Aura of Decay.

Hondo ducks a blow, catches a second on the haft of his polearm, then twists, kicking one of the monsters in the chest. The Strength he wields is incredible. While leaving the ground Hondo stands on unmarred, he sends the monster flying all the way to the other side of the cavern to pancake against the wall. The man never stops moving, ducking and cutting, shrugging off glancing blows to land deadlier, critical wounds on the monsters. When his polearm breaks, he stabs the broken haft into a convenient leg and pulls another, the weapon glowing with the light sheen of power that covered his former weapon.

My eyes narrow slightly as I watch, Eyes of Insight hinting at something…

"He's got a targeting Skill," I send to Ali.

"Weakness Must Be Driven Out. It's a first-tier Advanced Class Skill for a Weaponmaster. More powerful than the basic Trainer Skill of the same type. Allows a Weaponmaster to see the flow of battle and where their opponent is more vulnerable to attacks."

A twitch of my hands and I send my knives flashing forward, lodging in a Nuckelavee horse skull. It thrashes, and long fingers dig into its own skull as it attempts to rip out the daggers. As the monster deals with my distraction, I continue my conversation.

"Old school training."

"Just like toots."

I wince at Ali's reminder. Mikito grew up under the kind of strict tutelage that valued beating a weakness till the recipient learned to deal with the flaw in their defense. And since I'd spent uncountable hours training with the woman, she'd beaten me down too. One last slice of my Blade Skill and I send the Nuckelavee attacking me to join its dead comrades. A gesture sends a slew of Mana Darts to join Ali's, ending the last of the spore trap. Once the floor is clear, I drop down and pick up the corpses.

"Why did you leave the line?" Hondo snarls at me.

"Stacked auras. Also, between the two of you, there's not much space for me to fight," I say. "And this way, I could contribute and not get attacked."

"Cowardly."

"Effective," I retort.

Hondo glares at me and I shrug, waiting. Eventually, Hondo leads us down the corridor while Ali finishes putting away the corpses. I chuckle but take the time to switch out my nice jumpsuit for one of my less-pricey versions. If it's going to get destroyed, I might as well make sure it doesn't cost me too much.

***

Over the next three hours, we tear through the dungeon at a good clip. Eventually, we fall into a routine of fighting and I even join the pair on the front line, dishing out damage. Since we're all melee combat fighters, this only happens in the biggest rooms, where it's possible for both polearm wielders and myself to stand in line. The stacked damage from the aura is bad enough, such that I find myself storing the hoverboots and anything not directly necessary for modesty. Even my soulbound sword slowly degrades over time, forcing me to resummon it occasionally.

As for the other two, they deal with it in their own ways. Mikito's Ghost Armor Skill seems to be absorbing the majority of the effects of the aura, leaving her clothing in one piece. Her naginata, Hitoshi, is special of course. Hondo, on the other hand, tosses the broken weapon away each time it gives up the ghost, drawing a similar weapon from his inventory. As for his clothing, it seems to have a passive resistance ability that defies the aura.

We head down the moment we find the descending tunnel, content to leave for more difficult environs. Outside of the vermin monsters who Ali seems to have a hate-on for and the spore mushrooms, the Nuckelavee are the main opponents here. Fighting higher Level Nuckelavees and variants of the damn spores and vermin still hasn't pushed us to our limits. I hate to admit it, but I'm getting bored.

That is, until we end up in a large, empty cavern that hosts a single pillar of crystal. There is a small ledge leading up to the pillar and a couple of stalactites on the floor, but for the most part, it's just a giant cave. We cautiously enter the cavern, finding nothing extraordinary until we're next to the column of crystal itself.

"What is this?" I say, tapping on the crystal with a bare hand. The hiss from Mikito and Hondo comes a little too late. The crystal resonates from my tap, a slowly growing noise that fills the room, increasing in volume and sending a thrum straight to our bones. It's not painful, just slightly uncomfortable. "Huh."

"What are you? A child?" Hondo snarls. "Never touch strange things in a dungeon."

"Oh, come on. Worst-case scenario, it just dumps some light or blasts us with acid. Nothing we can't handle," I say defensively.

Mikito growls at me, the tiny Japanese swivelling her head toward the numerous exits then the resonating pillar.

"You have thought of something, Spear?" Hondo says.

"Trap." Mikito points at the entrances.

I open my mouth to point out that there's no such indication on my map, only to be forced to shut it as dozens of dots appear.

"Goblin shit," Ali says.

"Yes." Mikito twists her hands, withdrawing items from her inventory. Underhand tosses send webbing grenades to the entrances of some of the smaller locations, blocking them off.

Hondo is doing the same on his side of the crystal. I move away, reaching into my inventory to check what I have.

"Ali, go high please," I say.

Right. Let's see. Webbing grenades and fast-forming foam walls are perfect for the smaller entrances. I have three portable shield generators too, but they're too low tier to do anything but annoy the Nuckelavee for more than a few moments. Better to save them.

Oooh. Mines.

Ali shoots upward, headed for the few entrances that are above ground level, and drops off foam-covers and webbing grenades. I do too but also add a series of portable mines to the area in front of me. I make sure to key the mines to go off on command only though.

Not that I've got a lot of time to get all this sorted. By the time I've got the barest defensive line up, the Nuckelavee are on us. That's when I channel my Mud Walls, focusing on the two largest entrances in sight. Those have been left alone thus far. As the Nuckelavee charge, I release my spell, earth rising from the front of the entrances to envelop the horse-demons.

Screams and choked cries flood the room, but I'm too busy paying attention to my side to deal with it. I shape the walls, flooding the entrances as best as I can with the conjured matter. Even so, the leading edge of the Nuckelavee wave have broken free from the webbing grenades and other blockades at the other entrances.

I tie off the spell, leaving the Mud Walls in place, and step forward, sword in one hand and throwing knives in the other. Within seconds, the monsters are on me and I dance, Thousand Blades and my original blade clashing with Nuckelavee claws. Sharp claws cut at bare skin, tearing through rotting clothing even as my body attempts to fight off the rot. The stacked auras of decay attack from within, corrupting organs, weakening bones, and rupturing blood vessels as I move. Blood drips from my nose, blocking my breathing and leaving a salty taste in the air. Back and back again, they push me.

"Enough!" Hondo roars.

The command washes over the room, freezing the Nuckelavee for a few seconds. I trigger the mines, only to realize that two-thirds of them no longer work, their mechanisms destroyed under the demonic aura. The pitiful explosions do little but wake the monsters from Hondo's Skill. Mikito uses the break better, forming a twenty-foot blade with her weapon and sweeping the extended cutting edge across multiple necks. Blood fountains and the stench of decay and disease expands.

"Frack it. Beacon from Angels," I say, thrusting my hand toward the sky.

I layer the attack again and again, its power reduced in these tight, underground confines. But the damage spreads across the group, those near expiring falling over. As the bright beams of light and golden glyphs disappear, a louder sound appears.

A creature, a distorted mass of flayed humans and beasts, crawls out of the largest tunnel. Multiple heads stick out, most missing eyes, just gaping wounds that pour pus and blood. From a few of those wounds, alien insects emerge, boiling around the monster before burrowing back into its red, distorted flesh.

"Goblin shit." Ali flies down, coming to a standstill next to me as he finishes throwing a lightning bolt. "Boss."

Mother Nuckelavee (Zone Boss Level 113)
HP: 11830/11830
MP: 3218/3218
Conditions: Pregnant, Aura of Greater Decay, Disease Vectors

"Armory of the People," Hondo intones as he raises his hand. Gold and silver ritual circles with weird glyphs appear, hundreds of them rotating above the Truinnar. From each circle, a weapon emerges. Sometimes it's swords, axes, polearms. But more modern weapons appear too, including rockets, grenade launchers, beam pistols, slug throwers, and more. With a sweep of his hand, the weapons unleash their fury at the Zone Boss in a furious roar.

The suddenly compressed air from hundreds of weapons firing staggers me backward, pressuring my already weakened eardrums. They pop with a tear, and blessed silence appears while the Nuckelavee caught at the edges of the attack are torn into pieces. Swords bounce, arrows burrow, and rockets explode as Hondo unleashes his attack. Those within the actual blast edges aren't just ripped apart but turned into bloody mist.

Out of the cloud of blood and dirt, the Mother Nuckelavee staggers forward. It's lost nearly two-thirds of its life but is still alive. The Mother gestures with a few hands, fingers shaping arcane motions. The air swirls toward her, sucking in floating pieces of her body and other Nuckelavee. As they reach the Mother, the creature's health ticks upward.

"Redeemer!" Hondo snaps.

I growl in acknowledgement, bringing my sword forward. But Mikito takes off first, her Hasted form blurring as she rushes through the crowd, polearm extended.

"Right. I guess I'm on support then. Fastball special, Ali," I say, charging up the Enhanced Lightning Strike spell.

I grin slightly as the Spirit floats a short distance away, his body glowing. As I form the connection of electrons between the Spirit and myself, I unleash the spell, converting raw Mana into electric potential. The blast strikes Ali, who takes the channeled energy and directs the bolts of lightning at the remaining Nuckelavee and particularly large, floating masses of flesh that the Mother is pulling back into her body.

While I deal with the riff-raff, Mikito is dancing through the lightning, her blade leaving trails of blood and light as it cuts the Mother. At times, it looks as if Mikito is literally dodging lightning, her movements so fluid and fast. It's a ballet of death that ends with the Samurai jamming her polearm deep into the Mother's chest, the weapon extending within the creature and exploding out its back.

It screeches, pounding the ground and sending another wave of exhaustion and dizziness through us all as it dies. I cough, spitting out blood, and eye Mikito's health bar. Of us all, she's nearest to bottoming out. With a wave, I cast a Greater Healing on her. Her health creeps up a little before it stabilizes, the lingering effects of the aura still warring with the woman's natural regeneration.

"Well, that was fun," I say.

Mikito shrinks her blade, kicking the corpse off her polearm, then spins it around, flinging droplets of blood and rotten flesh from it. Ali tosses a last Mana Dart to finish off a crawling, dislimbed monster, then eyes the swirling bat creatures above. None of them come down, instead fleeing the room.

Hondo glares at me and stalks away from the crystal pillar trap, making a circuit to check each entrance. I sigh and slump against the now quiet pillar, mentally requesting Ali to deal with the corpses. As he does so, I pull up the notification I've received.

Level Up!

You have reached Level 26 as an Erethran Paladin. Stat Points automatically distributed. You have 14 Free Attributes and 1 Class Skill to distribute.

I get that little rush of dopamine from achieving a new Level and find myself smiling slightly. Good reminder that I have a Class Skill still to assign. Along with the attribute points. Truth be told, I wanted to hold off on the Class Skill point until I managed to get to the third tier. Or at the least figured out a more thorough build. Part of the reading in the Questors' library was meant to help with that a little.

Now, here I am, expecting to fight three Master Classers, which means I need every edge I can get. In some ways, I'd love to up my Advanced Class Skill Portal. Or perhaps Army of One. That's a nasty sure-kill attack. But using my Paladin Class Skill on it would be a waste. Better to focus on my Paladin Skills.

On that note, I eye the columns in my Skill Tree. The third branch is all judgment-related Skills, and those make no sense to upgrade. Well, perhaps Eye of Insight. Upgrading the Eye might give me a chance to break through their Stealth Skills. But I think that's still a relatively low chance.

My aura and Eye of the Storm Skills are great, but more meant for large fights. Paladins are meant to be standing in the middle of a war and rallying their side to them. Vanguard could be useful though—the additional damage and boost in Physical Stats could make a huge difference in a very short timeframe. I don't use it as much, due to the cost, but if I'm going one-on-one with the Titan, it might make sense.

Penetration is so damn useful, but I've already dedicated quite a few points, relatively speaking, to it. Adding more seems like a marginal increase to an already useful spell. On the other hand, Beacon of the Angels has been my go-to wide-area Skill. Hell, it's my only wide-area Skill. Unlike spells, it takes almost no time to put in motion. Even if there's a minor delay, it's still better than standing around trying to cast a spell. Adding another Level to it might give the Skill the punch to do real damage.

Eye of Insight or Beacon of the Angels. They both have good points to them. Eye of Insight might be more useful long term and over multiple situations, but Beacon of the Angels seems to be a decent Skill to shore up my weak area effect damage. Resolved, I dump the point into the Skill and eye the new information.

Beacon of the Angels (Level 2)

User calls down an atmospheric strike from the heavens, dealing damage over a wide area to all enemies within the beacon. The attack takes time to form, but once activated need not be concentrated upon for completion.

Effect: 1000 Mana Damage done to all enemies, structures and vehicles within the maximum 25 meter column of attack

Mana Cost: 500 Mana

That's what I call a satisfactory increase in damage.

After that, assigning attributes is easy. I split them evenly among my go-to combat attributes. Once that's done, I eye the newly developed Status Screen, soaking in the details.

Status Screen			
Name	John Lee	Class	Erethran Paladin
Race	Human (Male)	Level	26
Titles			
Monster's Bane, Redeemer of the Dead, Duelist, Explorer, Apprentice Questor			
Health	3650	Stamina	3650
Mana	3440	Mana Regeneration	287 (+5) / minute
Attributes			
Strength	249	Agility	329
Constitution	365	Perception	186
Intelligence	344	Willpower	372
Charisma	124	Luck	74
Class Skills			
Mana Imbue	3*	Blade Strike*	3
Thousand Steps	1	Altered Space	2
Two are One	1	The Body's Resolve	3
Greater Detection	1	A Thousand Blades*	3
Soul Shield	2	Blink Step	2
Portal*	5	Army of One	2
Sanctum	2	Instantaneous Inventory*	1
Cleave*	2	Frenzy*	1
Elemental Strike*	1 (Ice)	Shrunken Footsteps*	1

Tech Link*	2		Penetration	3
Aura of Chivalry	1		Eyes of Insight	1
Analyze*	2		Harden*	2
Quantum Lock*	3		Elastic Skin*	3
Beacon of the Angels	2		Eye of the Storm	1
Vanguard of the Apocalypse	2		Society's Web	1

Combat Spells	
Improved Minor Healing (IV)	Greater Regeneration (II)
Greater Healing (II)	Mana Drip (II)
Improved Mana Missile (IV)	Enhanced Lightning Strike (III)
Firestorm	Polar Zone
Freezing Blade	Improved Inferno Strike (II)
Elemental Walls (Fire, Ice, Earth, etc.)	Ice Blast
Icestorm	Improved Invisibility
Improved Mana Cage	Improved Flight
Haste	

As I eye my Status Screen, my gaze falls back on the Aura and Eye of the Storm abilities. I don't use them much—mostly because thus far, my enemies have been either too strong or too weak to bother. But perhaps it's time I look at them as boosts for my friends. Not that these two need it necessarily. Yet thinking of Hondo's experience Skill, of the way he led the kids—and hell, us—perhaps it's time to look at how being in a team changes how I fight. Especially with my new Skills.

Mikito rests on her polearm next to the Zone Boss. I catch her eye and find her smiling slightly. I return the smile, basking in the shared sense of accomplishment of raised Levels. One Zone Boss down. Next time, we'll have to go deeper.

Chapter 16

For all our caution and concern, the next few weeks are quiet. Oh, the corporations and the sects keep pushing at our recruits, buying up debts and occasionally laying into them physically. But a few well-placed quests, along with the movement of many of our recruits into holding areas, mean that the number of incidents has decreased. Our recruitment numbers grow, such that we'll easily meet the initial quest numbers once these immigrants actually set foot on Earth.

There are a tense few days when the ships arrive and everyone is transported onto the ships. Needlessly stressful since there's little chance of an attack on the station or the beanstalk itself. Irvina's System Commander is infamous as one of the highly active Heroic Classes in Irvina. The Eye of Heaven. The Watcher of Watchers. His Heroic Class Skill All Seeing Eye means he knows everything that happens on his station and, if he pushes it, in the entire damn Solar System. Add that to his ability to teleport himself to any location in his domain at will—bypassing any Dimensional Locks in play—and no one tries anything on the stations under his watch. Much, much better to wait until everyone is on the ships.

Still, we worried. To that end, we shuttled people back and forth to the beanstalk with care, eyeing everyone and triple-checking the loading of the ships for bugs and smuggled bombs.

In the end, the ships leave the solar system without a hitch. After that, it's a multi-week journey where the ships will travel to Earth via a series of random jumps. Without a logged or planned shipping route, it's impossible to purchase their route information beforehand. That still leaves some viable options for attack—Forecasting and Divination Skills being among the most likely culprits—but it does make things a lot harder. And harder is all we can hope for.

After that, we start the entire process again. Training ourselves and new recruits. Putting them in sponsored and guarded locations. Offering loans when necessary. We're watching and waiting. The only thing we know is that there's still a contract out on me and Katherine. But when, how, they'll be put into play is unknown. Even getting that amount of information from the Shop was expensive. And so we wait.

Weeks pass by. One morning, I'm staring at the gruel I somehow inflicted on myself for breakfast. For the life of me, I can't recall why I thought gruel was a good idea. Porridge I can do. Rice porridge is good, tasty food. Perfect for breakfast, especially when combined with some fried breadsticks. But that hasn't arrived yet. Sooner or later, I'm sure. But gruel? Gruel the Galactics have a version of. And seeing it, I somehow thought it'd be a great idea to try it. Somehow.

The doors slide open, and I eye Harry as he saunters in. The reporter offers me a weary grin as he drops into the chair beside me and takes my bowl of gruel, spooning my food into his mouth without a word. I watch, bemused, as the reporter swallows the meal down before he leans back, letting out a little burp. One hand comes up, wiping dark skin clean.

"Nice to see you too," I say.

"Thanks."

"How are you doing? What have you been doing?" I say.

"My job. Just finished my interviews with the Wolves of the Air," Harry says. "Fascinating group."

"Did you now?" I say, forcing my voice to be light.

"Oh yes. Took weeks to set it up, weeks to get their trust. Got to cut and sculpt the episode, but it's fascinating really," Harry says. "Utterly fascinating. The world they live in as hired assassins is such a different world. Do you know, they have to walk a very fine line? Can't get too flashy or else the Heroic Classes get annoyed. Can't turn down too many jobs or else, well, what's the point of such a team? Really polite bunch too. Very apologetic about the attack on me."

I blinked, trying to figure out Harry's angle here. Their angle. I knew he had meant to go speak with them, but now he sounds a little like a fan.

"Oh, they also wanted to say they were quite impressed. Fast thinking on your part, running into the building," Harry says. "But they wanted you to know that if you don't make yourself available to be assassinated soon, they're going to have to take steps."

"A threat. How novel," I drawl.

"Just completing my part of the deal." Harry sits up properly, looking at me seriously. "They're not going to stop. They didn't mention it directly, but their last job went badly. Tried too hard and well…" Harry shrugs. "Let's just say they need a win."

"Isn't that a little too far?" I say, touching the table. I don't know how he edges around his non-Combat status or what his various rules are, but what he said seems a little too pointed.

"It's a little close," Harry acknowledges. "About as much help as I can give. I will say that you should watch part one when I'm done."

"Only part one?"

"Well, part two will depend on what happens. With you," Harry says, pushing back from the table.

I chuckle but take his point. I'm sure something in his exposé will be of use. Though I'm still amused that an assassination group was willing, even happy, to do an interview. Cloak-and-dagger kind of loses its meaning if you shine a light on it. Then again, if you're an assassin, once you're down that road, it might be hard to find a new job. Not without some major time repairing your reputation.

I watch the reporter go and sigh, half-closing my eyes as a sudden wave of weariness washes over me. Another threat. Another fight. More loss. More death. More blood. And all I wanted to do was read. Just find an answer…

"John?" Ali's voice cuts in, jarring me from my spiraling pity party. "Time to go. Or else you're going to be late."

"Yeah. Sure."

I shake off the darkness in my mind, push it aside, and compartmentalize the feeling. Easy. So easy after so many years. Even if doing so always leave a smudge of it behind, a trace. It's not necessarily healthy, but sometimes, all you can do is keep moving. Because the other option is stasis. And stasis is not death. Death is decay, destruction, dispersal. No, stasis is worse than death. It's the end of everything useful or good. Just a pause without hope of rebirth or renewal. Not without breaking it, not without momentum.

A hand rises.

A Portal opens.

And the day starts.

***

The Portal opens back into our apartment, and Mikito walks through first. I follow, nodding goodbye to Hondo, after Ali finishes a quick check of our apartment. No lurking Master Classers, so I shut the Portal, leaving the Weaponmaster to his evening.

Three steps later, as I'm headed to grab some grub from the fridge, I get a notification. I blink, surprised to see the name, and find myself hesitating. A com-call isn't unusual, but the caller… I push my doubts aside and take the call, smiling slightly at the redheaded beauty on the other end.

"Lana. Good timing. Just got out of the dungeon here," I say.

"I know. I tried earlier and got a no connection signal," Lana says. "You're pretty busy."

"I am. Got a bunch of newbies to Level up. There a reason for the call?"

"That hurts!" Lana says, touching her chest. "So much for staying friends…" The redhead pulls a face and long-buried emotions twinge. But only a little, because I can tell she's teasing me. "There're a few things I need to talk to you about for the investment business."

"Go for it." I know that the cost of such a long-distance call through the System's comm networks is high. Instantaneous communication should be impossible, but so should a million other things. Though… I note that as another area to look into in the Questors' library.

Lana quickly outlines the issues—mostly director-level stuff that I either need to grunt and assent to or rubber stamp decisions on. A good thirty minutes later, we're done.

"See. It wasn't so bad," Lana says, flicking her fingers to dismiss notifications. "How have you been otherwise?"

"Not bad. Better before all this quest rubbish but…" I sigh. "But not bad."

"Only you could say being targeted by three Master Classers is a 'not bad' situation," Lana says with a roll of her eyes. "How's Mikito?"

"Good. Do you want to talk to her?" I say, seeing an out.

"No. We'll chat later. So…" Lana seems suddenly uncomfortable. Ever since our breakup, things have been a little more strained. Hard to find a balance, especially now that work talk is over. "Roxley asked about you. Mentioned he talked to you a few weeks ago."

"Yeah. We caught up in the Shop. Had some loot to sell." Silence falls between us, and I consider breaking the connection. But she's a friend, someone I cared about. Care about. And if I don't try, I'm not sure if we'll ever have a relationship outside of what we were. "How's your boy?"

"My boy?" Lana's eyes sparkle, but she doesn't offer a name. She knows me well enough to know that I'd promptly forget it. "He's good. He actually moved up here. I have him running our land reclamation efforts."

As mundane as that sounds, I know the truth behind the prosaic-sounding name. The lands we're trying to reclaim, like infrastructure and the surroundings that connect our settlements, are areas often overrun by monsters. Dungeons have taken over important areas, like the dams in northern BC. The job is as much about fighting as it is infrastructure reconstruction.

"Good for him. And you." Obviously things are going well. Once again, things get awkward. "So. Everyone doing well? Jason and Rachel? Their kid?"

"Kids," Lana reminds me. Right. There's an unborn one in there too. "They're good. Amelia and her wife ended up adopting their third. This one's a baby actually. Found abandoned."

I smile, listening to the gossip. I'm grateful to hear about the mundane and dangerous lives of our friends. It's strange to think that five years after the apocalypse, the world has begun to stabilize. A strange, violent, and different world. But more stable.

***

Time moves on. Two days later, I wake up to a new notification from Ali. He's floating next to me, a bowl of popcorn in hand, watching something. Rather than answer my question, he maximizes the entire notification until it takes over my vision.

Harry's report. It finally dropped.

The first portion of the report is background information. Harry builds the tension, discussing unsolved cases, assassinations. Occasionally there are voice-overs, the Wolves mentioning a detail or two about the case. It builds the story, informing without revealing. It's a masterful work of directing, and I find myself drawn in.

The next portion is about the attacks, successful and not. Again and again, voices overlay footage of the battles. Sometimes its footage from after the assassination. Other times, it's clear footage of the attack itself taken from security cameras and other nearby recording devices. In a few surprising instances, the footage comes directly from the Wolves, often from the mecha's point of view. Or the view of the sniper scope. The Wolves speak of the attacks in a detached manner, talking of business, of their successes and their occasional failures. I soak in the details, chocolate sliding down my throat as I watch.

An Advanced Adventuring Team that broke away from their guild over a dispute over spoils. Tracked down when they left for a Dungeon World, attacked after exiting a particularly hard lair, and bodies disposed of without trace—till now. Their disappearance had been taken as a matter of course.

In Irvina, an apartment building at night in the second ring. Home to the vice president of Jimee Artifacts. Security bypassed by the Machine Lord. Space Locked by the Space Lord. The Titan Spawn enters with another, and they kill everyone in the building, splashing the walls with blood and covering the floor with viscera. Long before the Skills fail, before security can react, the Wolves are gone in their gunship. Only a single son lives, the eldest, who was on a school trip with friends to a pleasure planet. Cut off-screen to an interview with a security consultant who discusses some of the ensuing security upgrades in both the second and third rings.

The Weez Guild, an up-and-coming Artisan guild. Built like a cooperative, with an extremely low overhead. Set up in the seventh ring. This time, no Space Lock is required to seal the guild headquarters. Instead, the low-slung building is engulfed in a firestorm, a Space Prison, and Dimensional Shards. The destruction is complete, and the guild disperses the next day.

Successes. More successes than failures. And then, their last mission before mine.

An attack on Kalidia, the Heroic Wendigo of the Beast Plans. The initial attack goes well. Space Locks keep out trouble. A Dimensional Lock stops Kalidia from fleeing. A plasma cannon fires upon the Hero, peeling away a quarter of her life. Immediately, her health regenerates at a visible level, but the Titan Scion and two other Wolves appear, moving to suppress her regeneration as the mage pelts her. Magical restraints, web grenades, and abyssal chains are all used to slow down Kalidia. It works. Until it doesn't.

The video shorts out then, the view growing blurry. The entire view pulls back, clearing up some of the graininess. In the video, things boil out from the ground, from the sky, cracking open space itself. Inky, two-dimensional figures crawl and squirm into the air, pulling down the Wolves. The fire mage goes down first, its slug-like body torn to shreds as one of the creatures crawls into its body from its mouth. The Wendigo pulls another fighter close, using their mouth to tear open their chest as it feasts. The Wolves fall back, forming up around the Space Mage. She dismisses her Space Lock and recreates it, forming a protective barrier. Long enough for them to disappear, but not before leaving another of theirs behind.

Leaving only the three Master Classers. And an abject failure on their record.

The documentary moves on to a wider perspective. Of the effects and uses of such teams in the Galaxy, interviews with past victims and the individuals who have left, escaping the dangers of Galactic Society and the threat of such groups. I soak in the information and let my mind turn over the documentary.

***

Days later, the Portal opens back into our apartment and Mikito walks through first. I follow and, surprisingly, so does Hondo. It's unusual for the man to follow us after a dungeon run. I tilt my head, letting the Portal disappear even as a ping arrives from Katherine. At her request, I open a new Portal, one that allows in her stream of bodyguards before the Ambassador walks in herself.

Immediately, it's clear that something is wrong. Katherine looks haggard, her normally perfectly coiffed hair disturbed, stray locks escaping a tightly wound bun. There's a frown on her face, and her eyes are red-rimmed and grief-laden.

"*Beer. Now.*"

Ali flies off to the fridge and grabs cases of Apocalypse Ale while Katherine sits down.

"What is it?" I ask softly.

"They hit Earth."

My chest clenches, squeezing air out of my lungs, and Mikito lets out a little gasp. Too shocked to speak, I wait for Katherine to continue.

"A half dozen cities. Ten towns. And we're still trying to get the numbers on the villages. All attacked. Civilians. Adventurers. Combat Classers. Everyone was a target. They went after our people too, with numerous assassination attempts."

"Lana? Roxley?" I ask. "The others?"

"Roxley is fine. They didn't touch him or the Duchess's holdings," Katherine says. "Lana was injured, but she's fine now. Shadow saved her while Roland and Howard finished her attackers. Rachel…" She coughed, her face freezing. "They hurt her. And the child. She miscarried."

I freeze, pain for my friend, for their loss, engulfing me. It cuts deep, opening old wounds. So many losses. And I realize this time, it's my fault. If I hadn't pushed for this, if I had just done the job without adding my stupid little flare to it. Without deciding to poke Galactic Society and its stupid notions in the nose. If I had just stopped when they told me to.

"Who else?" I ask softly.

"Aiden's fighting for his life. He was hit with a parasite that's fighting to take over his body. Last we heard, he's comatose. They can't extract it, not easily. They intend to move him into the Shop, but there are complications," Katherine says softly. "They killed Rae. Rob nearly died. They took out half of his security group. If the Champions hadn't teleported in…" Katherine shuddered, shaking her head.

"I'm sorry," I say, my eyes closing. Damn it. I knew our security was less than adequate. Especially compared to many of these older, more secure states. I knew we needed time to get built up. But I never thought they'd attack us on Earth. Here, sure. But Earth… "Has Rob changed his mind?"

"I don't know," Katherine answers, her arms crossing. "He's dealing with Earth and the representatives. Dealing with the attacks."

Mikito grabs a bottle of beer and pops off the cap. She shoves the alcohol toward Katherine then opens another for herself. Ali stares at the bottles before he opens one for himself and me. I watch as he floats the bottle over before I snatch it from the air and down the bottle. Eyeing the two cases on the table, I twist my lips slightly. I glance toward Ali and the Spirit bobs his head, eyes unfocusing as he puts in an order for delivery. We're going to need a heck of a lot more alcohol.

This. This could change everything. But I'm too tired, too hurt to think about it. So I sit, and for tonight at least, I drink with my friends for the memory of what we lost. Around us, Hondo and the guards watch.

***

Night turns to day. Katherine doesn't leave our apartment as the day drags on. She stays for safety, for comfort, for convenience. We get information in dribs and drabs, news arriving via Galactic news services and, later on, Harry.

The attack was shocking, it was painful, but it was, thankfully, a single-day affair. There are no follow-up attacks, no expenditure of even more lives. Katherine believes it is because they want us to reconsider, for those who lost something in the attack to pressure Rob and Katherine to stop. Representative Oria calls, speaks a little with Katherine, then leaves, promising help and security. For a price.

When the news explodes across the city, things truly heat up on the political front. I end up porting Katherine back to her office, where her staff are already hard at work. Harried staffers shift video calls around, doing their best to appease those on the line. The calls are varied in tone and message. Peter watches over the entire dance, making note of each missive.

Some are the usual messages of condolences. Those are noted and marked into the friendly column.

Others are condolences with threats. Those Peter sends to a few well-fortified and cold staffers who handle them with simple efficiency.

Offers of help for a price are sorted to another group, the harried staffers making quick notes and adding to the growing column of potential resources we can draw upon.

The buzz builds and builds, and I watch silently from my corner as the ambassador is swamped, doing her best to stay ahead of the questions. She handles those few groups willing to offer help without price first, and after that, the ones offering help at a price. Because we need them.

I watch in silence, pain and loss turning slowly to rage.

At myself for putting my friends, and others, in a position where they could be attacked. It's unfair to them and to myself. But feelings are not fair.

And my anger is not just internal. It soon turns toward the corporations and sects who felt the need to push things to this extent. At our allies who are willing to stand aside, allowing us to get hammered while they pick up the benefits. And at the vultures, the many, many vultures, who just want a piece of the fallout.

Anger wraps me in a comforting blanket, allowing me to stew in its comforting burn rather than feel the grief that threatens to eat me alive. But anger without action is the senseless bragging of a fallen monkey god. In time, I push from the wall, turning to leave.

Katherine doesn't see, but Hondo, who has been standing by, does. He follows me out of the room and through the Portal home. Mikito's sitting on a couch in our living room, legs crossed, clad in full battle armor. She looks up when I come through, her eyes flat, cold, and deadly as the arctic winds.

"Are we going?" Mikito asks.

"You knew?" Knew what I was going to do. Knew my reaction.

"Of course."

"What exactly are you planning?" Hondo says.

"I'm taking the Wolves up on their challenge. And then after that, I'm going to take the bounties on their heads and use it to find who, exactly, assigned the hits. Then I'm going to see how they like having assassins sent after them," I say heatedly.

"This is a bad idea."

"You don't have to come," I say to Hondo while turning to look at Mikito. "Suggestions?"

Rather than answer me directly, Mikito sends over a map. It's a location well outside the rings of Irvina, in the middle of nowhere. A location outside of the jurisdiction of anyone who could stop this fight. Or who would want to. Rolling hills. Forests.

In other words, perfect.

"It'll do."

Mikito hops up, swinging her naginata onto her shoulder. Harry comes running out of his room, a trio of floating camera droids joining him. I raise an eyebrow and he puts his hands together as if begging. But there is no humor in his eyes, no matter his actions.

"Make the call."

Harry's face twitches, but he nods, his eyes glazing over. Ali does the same, lips compressed as he gets things ready. Hondo lets out a loud huff, but he doesn't gainsay our actions. Perhaps he's tired of waiting too.

No more second-guessing. No more questions. Time.

I open the Portal and we step through. Time to end this.

***

Rolling hills. A forest to the right of us. A lake and the river that feeds and leads from it to the left. Behind and ahead of us, more gentle, charming land. The city ahead of us in the distance—the far distance.

This is technically public land. Land yet to be fully claimed but thinned out of monsters regularly. There's nothing here above Level 20. And nothing comes near us, not with my Aura unfurled, its pressure beating upon unseen wings.

"Think they'll come?" Ali says, spinning slowly.

"Yes," Harry says. "Especially since you haven't set up any traps."

I shrug. A neutral fighting ground is the best we can hope for. If we keep waiting for them to attack us, they'll find a time and place that works for them.

"We could have called the authorities," Harry says suggestively.

"Then they wouldn't show up," I say, shaking my head. "No. Leave it be."

"Relax," Mikito says, nodding toward the city. "Eat a little. What will be, will be."

"Que sera sera?" Harry snorts.

Hondo looks at us flatly, disdaining to show confusion. But if the Weaponmaster is worried, he does not deign to show it to us lesser mortals.

"Wish they'd let us Level up though," Ali says, looking at Mikito and Hondo.

Both are so close, sitting at Level 49. There's a lot of ground to cover in a single Level at this stage, but we're so damn close. But that's the other reason we need to act now. Otherwise they will. There's no way they're going to let us Level in peace.

"No more innocent lives," I say softly. "This ends. Today."

And after that, there's nothing more to say.

Chapter 17

Time creeps by slowly. I'm on my fourth chocolate bar and even Hondo has unwound enough to test out a bar when Ali stops his spinning abruptly. The orange-clad Spirit stares at a new notification screen and holds his awkward, legs akimbo, partially inverted position before he grins savagely.

"Got you!" Ali says.

I swallow my last mouthful as I tense. "They're here?"

"Space Lock is in place. I just lost all connection to the outside world," Ali confirms. "The Uttu is probably on her way to a good position to snipe, if not there already."

"Titan," Mikito says, drawing our attention to what is in front of us.

A single figure saunters forward, metallic bands that act as knuckle dusters gleaming in the sunlight. I twist and turn my head, searching visually for the Machine Lord but finding nothing. Rather disturbing how I can see the Titan but I get nothing on my minimap. From his mini-bunker on a nearby hill, Harry waves and gives us a thumbs-up before he shuts the door, hiding from the ensuing battle.

"A bit brave, no?" I say.

"He is a brawler," Hondo says, cracking his neck. "Mine or yours."

"Hey!" Mikito protests.

"You're on sniper duty," I say.

"Not me?" Ali says, playing hurt.

"Fill in when you can, but I want you near me. We might need to do a fastball special if the Machine Lord goes swarm."

"Not his style," Hondo contradicts me.

"Exactly." I shrug, loosening up my shoulders before I jerk my head toward the Titan. "Yours."

"Guess I've got the Space Lord," Ali says, frowning slightly.

I understand his hesitation. This is insane. We're out-numbered, out-Classed, and I'm sure they've only come because they think they can win. The only uncertainty is the same one any fighter faces during a battle—a bad roll of the dice, a lousy call. There are few guaranteed wins in fights, even in a System-adjusted world. Just chaos and blood. For now, all we can do is roll with the punches.

Something pings on my minimap as my Greater Detection picks up new figures. I frown, curious how they only now made an appearance. The inquiry sent to Ali gets a quick answer.

"Whoever was hiding them has dropped the upkeep. Looks like they were a little slow. Or might be on a cycled timer."

I grunt, using a small exertion of will to send the notifications to the team. Four more figures, all Advanced Classers. Two with large Mana pools, with Classes that blend out and get replaced with Healer, Healer-Support, Ranger, and Whipmaster. That last one involves a buxom flame-haired lady clad in the usual Adventurer one-piece armored skinsuit. Of concern is the fact that all these newcomers are Advanced Classers in their high 30s. By themselves, they would be of little concern. But with the rest of the Wolves in play, this team could lock down one of us.

"Uttu or newcomers?" Mikito says, her tone chilly.

I grimace, considering our options. Blink Step should, theoretically, allow me to get to the Uttu first. But that's only if they don't throw up a Dimension Lock. And past experience tells me that they will. All that means is we have to make our way to her position manually when she takes her first shot.

"Focus on those here first. Healers, then ranged. We'll stall," Hondo pipes up, flexing his hand.

I consider his suggestion then nod. We'll have to play the Uttu by ear.

We finish layering our buffs, adding whatever bonuses we can to each other and ourselves. Eye of the Storm is already active, giving everyone a little higher regeneration while I layer on Soul Shield. I'm tempted to add Harden, but the cost is too high. Until the fight actually begins, I don't dare use that Skill.

By this point, the Titan and his backups are a few hundred meters away. Distant, but with all our attributes, more than close enough.

"You finally came." Surprisingly, the Titan has a high, squeaky voice. His accent reminds me of a blond, cheerleading Valley girl. Entirely at odds with his big, rippling muscles. Though he does have the long blond hair framing his three eyes. Each of those eyes is a different color. Purple, red, and green with the barest hint of yellow on the edges. Handsome, if you're into that. "Tired of hiding?"

"Figured you'd hit us at home sooner or later. Once you figured out how to breach the new defenses at our home." I don't raise my voice like him, but increased Perception means we all can hear each other perfectly fine.

Hurquji grins. "We would never think about attacking Tig's guild residences."

"Uh huh." I don't believe him, but I can see why he'd say that. "You know, you could just walk away. Earth might decide to kill the program, whatever I decide."

"Contract hasn't been canceled."

"Good." My heart speeds up at those words, pumping more blood into my body. I unconsciously lean forward on the balls of my feet, bending at the waist as I ready myself. Anger, leashed till now, bubbles forward, filling my veins. The losses from before, the hurt over the injustice of this world wraps around me, armoring me in its hate as much as my Soul Shield does.

Dimension Locked!

Note that reality has been stabilized in the immediate area. You may not enter another dimension or pass through space while this status is in effect.

Note: Dimension Lock may be breached using a Master Level (4) Skill

As if that were the signal, the battle begins. An overpowered beam attack strikes against the layered defensive shields we've placed around us. It shatters the first, second, and third shields before splashing against Mikito's body. My Soul Shield absorbs the remainder damage, leaving the Ghost Armor-clad Samurai untouched.

Mikito and Hondo take off, blurring as they run and leave me behind. I haven't triggered Haste, preferring to keep my Mana for now. Hondo pulls ahead of her as his damn passive speedster ability is kicked in full bore, covering the hundreds of meters in seconds. Spikes of obsidian stone erupt from the earth, forcing them to duck and weave through the new impediments while I jog behind, calling upon my own Skills.

A formation appears above the group, gold and silver glyphs forming as a column of power slams down. One of the Healer-cum-support players throws up their tentacles, forming a dome of power that stops my Beacon. It's a powerful defense, but I see her Mana bar shrink as she defends the team, even while the dome cracks under the onslaught. As I raise my hand to throw another Beacon, the world lurches and all noise cuts off.

I blink, thinking that my eyes are playing tricks on me, but they're not. There's suddenly a pane of glass between the world and me, and as I watch, that pane grows denser and denser, the other side fading in clarity. A hand pressed against the glass finds it unyielding.

"What the hell?"

Nothing.

I slam my fist into the wall, achieving only aching knuckles. My sword does little better, bouncing off my prison. There's not even a scratch on the glass-like substance before me. I stretch out my Mana Sensing ability and see the way Mana interacts with the wall, converting itself into whatever the "wall" is. Without me noticing it happening, I realize I'm in darkness now, no longer even vaguely connected to the world. Only the automatically turned on lights of my helmet provide illumination.

"So. This is what the Spatial Prison is like," I say to myself.

That explains why hitting the wall made no difference. Why would hitting "space" injure it? Admittedly, with my Mana Sense, I could tell that the Mana Blade portion of my attacks were doing a little damage, but it was so low that it doesn't show up under anything but my extended senses. If I had to rely on my blade or Mana Darts to escape, this could take a very long time.

Good thing I planned for this with my shopping trip weeks ago. A slight focus and I pull my Quantum State Manipulator from my bag. I grin, slapping the QSM on my wrist then activating it.

Getting the exact details of her Spatial Prison Skill cost me a pretty penny. The Space Lord doesn't actually trap someone in a different dimension, but instead displaces a specific portion of space into that dimension. Attacking a Spatial Prison like the Space Lord's is actually dangerous, as the walls are the only barrier between you and the other dimension. Breach the Prison and you suffer the consequences of an explosive and violent introduction to the dimension you're trapped within. If you're lucky, you then receive an abrupt and painful return to your own dimension as you are ejected backward. If you're unlucky, you're stuck. It's a nasty, nasty Skill. It's biggest weakness? It's a channeled spell that costs a significant amount of Mana.

Knowing what she could do, I had the QSM adjusted to locate the very thin line that connects the space I'm in to my original dimension. Once the QSM locks on to our home dimension, it's a simple matter for it to shift my body. In theory.

The QSM chimes, pinging me that everything is clear and ready. I draw a deep breath, hoping that the work done on the equipment was done right. I had no way to test it beforehand. Even if I've paid for the best I could afford, if the Space Lord knew about my intentions and took steps…

I step forward, passing through the previously immovable barrier, and find myself back on Prax, in nearly the same spot I left. In my brief absence, the terrain has changed significantly, as has the status of the battle. All around me, once-pristine grassland and rolling hills are blasted and torn, the smell of freshly churned earth and charcoal grass breaching my helmet's filters. The clash of battle resounds through the dimension, and I quickly take in the changes.

Off in the distance, Ali is tangling with the Space Lord. Her abilities have pulled him into this dimension, but the Spirit doesn't seem to care, weaving between shards of spatial distortions. His fists are charged up with power, lightning and Mana arcing around them as he occasionally thrusts a hand forward, unleashing his attacks. Only a thin layer of a spatial disturbance seems to stop the attacks from impacting the woman, but each second, her Mana drops. Truth be told, Ali is out-classed, and if she wasn't keeping up the Spatial Prison, she'd probably have wiped the floor with the Spirit already.

Hondo has his hands full dealing with the Titan and the Machine Lord. The Machine Lord is clad in what I can only call a full-on mechanized and armored suit. It's not a mecha, because the thing is only nine feet tall all in, but it's not just armor slapped on the body either. I can see servos hidden behind segmented armor plates, corded steel muscles propelling the Machine Lord forward as a plasma glaive comes crashing down on Hondo. The Weaponmaster blocks it with a sword, discarding the already melting weapon into the face of the charging Titan even as he makes a chain appear, catching the Titan's punch and wrapping around the extended arm. Hondo slides beneath the Machine Lord's legs, dragging the Titan toward his friend and wrapping the chain around the Lord's legs. He then releases the chain, letting it constrict the Lord and Titan together. While the pair struggle to free themselves, Hondo conjures a large knife and stabs it into the Titan's free arm.

Before Hondo can follow up, the Machine Lord's gunship—which has been hovering ahead—manages to shift position sufficiently to bring its beam cannons to bear and blasts Hondo away. Even as Hondo flies through the air, the Weaponmaster is activating his ultimate kill Skill, gold and silver circles forming as the arsenal appears.

I turn away, checking on Mikito. The Samurai is glowing, a golden sheen covering her ghostly blue armor. The Samurai's form blurs as she fights the entire Advanced Class team. As I watch, an overcharged beam cannon shot impacts Mikito's golden form but breaks apart with no effect.

Damn. Mikito has triggered her penultimate defensive and offensive Skill—Chugi. It's similar to my Sanctum, blocking all incoming damage, but it has an extremely high on-going cost. Unlike my purely defensive Skill, Chugi covers only Mikito and allows her to move and fight while boosting her basic attributes at the same time. There's a cost to this Skill, over and above the Mana cost. Mikito must have been pressed to the extreme to use her Skill so soon.

But…

Grinning, I trigger Beacon of the Angels over Mikito's location. Even before it finishes, I begin a second activation of the Skill.

"*Mikito. Incoming,*" I send over the party chat. Wouldn't want her to drop her Skill at the wrong time.

Light then fire. The Beacon of the Angels smites the group crowded around the Samurai like the hammer of the System that it is. Of course, as the group splits and moves, I don't catch everyone with the first Beacon. It doesn't matter, as I layer the attacks over the area.

Armor melts, force shields shatter, skin and muscle burn. Screams resound through the hills, informing everyone that I'm back. My grin widens as I take off running. Through Ali's eyes, I sense the way the Space Lord snaps her head toward me, surprise etched on her face. She pays for her distraction, Ali blasting her full-on with one of his lightning bolts. As the attack lands, her body arcs in pain as muscles clench tight. Leaving the Spirit to slow down the Space Lord, I use Haste and Thousand Steps to carry me closer to the fight. The sudden burst in speed makes the Uttu's next shot miss me.

By the time I reach Mikito, she's put down one Healer while the Healer-Support falls back, hands up as she tries to clear the fight. A glance shows she's at zero Mana, and that's probably the only reason any one of us is letting her leave. Even if she manages to get a Mana potion down her chest, zeroing out your Mana is a good way to get a Mana Withdrawal condition, wiping out any possibility of spells. On the other hand, she's done well considering she's sucked up two of my Beacons of the Angels.

That, of course, leaves Uttu, the Whipmaster, and Ranger. The peak-capped Ranger looks the least scorched, having been on the edge of my attacks. As I watch, the repeating-crossbow-wielding, jackal-headed Ranger's health pool is recovering at a visible rate.

As for the Whipmaster, her whip spins toward me. My attempt at a dodge fails because the semi-sentient weapon shifts trajectory in mid-air to wrap around my leg. I find my feet pulled out from under me, slamming me into the ground and eliciting a grunt. Vines, dripping with poison and acid, crawl up from the whip, layering over my Soul Shield and chewing through the defense.

Fingers dance across my torso as I pull and throw my knives. The weapons dart through the air, only for the first two to be blocked by a hexagonal shield

of force. But the first two were a distraction for the third, which cuts the whip apart, sending the vine around my leg thrashing. I rip the freed whip-vine from my body before doing a rolling recovery. As I stand, I watch with horror as the vine end and whip remnants twitch and crawl, reforming themselves.

"Ewwww," I exclaim.

"*Above!*" Ali sends.

The warning is a touch too late. Rockets throw me sideways, tearing the vines and my shield apart in flame and concussive blasts. Beam weapons slam into me, heating up armor and burning flesh. I snarl, rolling aside and throwing up a hand to call forth a Mud Wall. It blocks the attack as I move, but the wall won't last long. Nor will the gunship hold its position. Mikito, now free of the slain Ranger, throws herself at the Whipmaster, leaving me time to deal with the gunship.

Sideways, blade coming into my hand, I turn, throwing a Blade Strike at the floating gunship and bouncing across the ground and into the air with my hoverboots, screwing with the AIs targeting algorithm. Blades of force shatter against the ship's force shield, ripping through the fast-regenerating defense. I can tell it's weakening, that the shield will go down. If I'm given enough time.

"*GOBLIN'S AAARRRRSSSSEEEE!*"

A scream. A searing flash of pain through our mental connection. Then Ali is gone. Banished. One of the real dangers of fighting a Space Lord. Their abilities deal with dimensions, and those not inherent to this reality are particularly susceptible to banishment.

"Damn it," I snarl. But no time to waste.

I eye my Mana bar, noting that over this period, I've burnt through nearly half of my entire bar. I grit my teeth, plunging a Mana Regeneration potion into my body to kick up the speed. It's a short-lived increase, but I get the feeling this fight will be pretty short. A mental command turns off my hoverboots,

letting gravity drop me faster than ducking down myself would. Beams blaze over my head, and I toss my knives at the ship underhand, hoping to cut through the gunship's walls.

Space warps, twisting like a heat mirage. My knives slide into the mirage and never come out. I can only hope the recall spells brings them back. A follow-up Blade Strike disappears just as cleanly, leaving our reality without a ripple. My feet hit the ground, flexing and taking in the fall before I kick off, dodging rockets. I channel Mana once more, triggering my Blink Step Skill, and watch as my Mana and will battle against Evanline's Dimensional Lock. The Skill falters, but not without result—the Space Lord's Dimensional Lock disappears too. Specialized Master Mage or not, her Mana reserves have a limit. I reach out again through the dimensions and find the edge of her Skill, find where it interacts with my Mana and soul, where it works with and against the System, and I push, feeling Mana flee my body.

An ear-shaking boom erupts, reminding me of the other fight. Hondo has taken a full-on blow, shattering armor and his chest as he flies backward and through the curve of a hill. Hondo keeps going until he pancakes upon hitting the next hill, coughing out blood. Even as Hondo squirms out of the hole, railgun pellets slam into his body, tearing off a leg. The Weaponmaster throws up a hand and casts Mana Shield, forming a temporary wall of protection. The Skill is a life-saver but trades Mana for shield integrity on a direct basis, and Hondo's already low on the precious resource.

"Thousand Hells."

I take the momentary gap when the Dimensional Lock isn't active to Blink Step. I can't reach Hondo himself, but there's nothing stopping me from putting myself in the way of the pellets. I appear between Hondo and the Wolves and throw out a hand and a portable shield generator, watching the entire thing appear in mid-air and form its force shield. The pellets are stopped

for the second, the Machine Lord's shoulder-mounted railgun continuing its attacks and wearing down the defense. As I ready myself, the Space Lord recasts the Dimension Lock, forcing me to stay where I am. As the Titan jumps, landing a short distance from me, I realize I'm now facing all three Master Classers.

It's not all going their way though. As I throw up another Soul Shield, the howling fire from the gunship dies. Ignored for a short time, Mikito managed to climb on top of the gunship. The Samurai is no longer glowing and has only a small thread of Mana left, but she's still in play. With Hitoshi in hand, Mikito doesn't need much Mana to do damage. Her polearm cuts right through the armor, hits a stabilizer, and sends the gunship spinning through the air. Defying all logic, Mikito manages to straddle the spiraling, falling gunship as she continues her attack.

I turn back to my opponents, my lips curling upward as blades form around me, a precursor to my final attack. The sword in my hand swings down, followed by dozens of conjured blades. Army of One cuts through the air, light hurting my eyes as the Skill homes in on the Machine Lord. Powerful as his machines might be, they aren't up to taking my Skill head-on. My lips pull apart in a savage grin—then fall as the Titan interposes himself between the Skill and the Machine Lord.

Blood flies, dirt kicks into the air, and the world shakes. I don't stop moving after using my Skill, narrowly dodging the first of the spatial shards Evanline throws at me. I don't manage to dodge them all though. A particularly hard-to-see shard catches me high on the body and tears away my Soul Shield. I scream as my muscles, tendons, and molecules are rearranged by the Skill. Just a little, but enough that the pain from the wounds makes me stumble and fall.

As I stagger upward and the dust settles from my attack, a cold dread grips my stomach. The Titan strolls out of the damaged earth, wounded flesh closing before my eyes. There's a wide grin on Hurquji's face, his eyes darting between Hondo and me. Behind the Titan, the Machine Lord walks out, the myriad weapons on his armor pointing at me.

I'm down to less than a quarter of my Mana, my Soul Shield gone. I have the contingency shield from my ring and some Mana left, but that's it. Even as I desperately refill from the Mana Battery, I know it's not enough. Not by far. Not against three Master Classes.

"Pitiful," Hurquji says. "Did you think you, a single Master Classer, could beat us? You should have kept hiding. Run. Get your last Levels."

"You weren't going to let us," I say, forcing myself to my feet. Two-thirds of my life left. Less than a quarter of my Mana. I could go for a Mana potion, but I doubt they'd let me. Three Master Classers, most at nearly full health with Mana ranging from close-to-empty to two-thirds. And the Uttu, somewhere close, ready to fire again.

"Will you stand down or continue this senseless struggle?" S'Baxu's voice is loud, though his words are punctuated by the secondary explosion of his gunship in the distance.

I wince, seeing Mikito's health take another dive. S'Baxu looks in her direction and a portion of his armor detaches, the rocket launcher and beam pistol drone flying off in her direction.

"Senseless," I say, closing my eyes. Exhaustion slides over me as I taste the word. "Maybe it is senseless. Hondo?"

"I will not give up," Hondo grates out.

I sense his presence and turn. The Weaponmaster slowly makes his way over to me, using a new halberd as a support for his missing leg. A quick perusal reveals the hastily applied plastiskin bandage that has molded itself to the remnant limb, stemming his bleeding.

"Better to die than fail again," he says.

"Well, that's his answer." I push against the weariness that grips my soul and body. It refuses to yield, so I let my anger burn it away. My lips twist into a half smile, one that they can't see behind my helmet. "You guys don't want to pull back, do you?"

Laughter from S'Baxu. Evanline and Hurquji do not laugh, their eyes narrowing as they realize I'm less afraid than I should be. Tired perhaps, but not afraid.

"You have a trick." Evanline's voice cuts through the air, reaching all of us as if she's standing right next to us. Neat trick.

"Always," I say. "Last chance."

"He's bluffing," S'Baxu says.

"Do your worse," Hurquji replies, smirking.

The Titan kicks off, speeding toward us even as S'Baxu opens fire, beam weapons and rail pellets tearing up the earth and lighting the sky in flashes of white and purple. I twist and jump, my Elemental Affinity tingling as space twists and warps. The Space Lord's hidden attack misses by millimeters.

We can't win this. Not with Hondo out of Mana. Not with Mikito injured.

No way to win.

Not alone.

Chapter 18

Chaos. All fights are chaos. Even more so when one side is attempting to make it even more chaotic. I gesture with one hand, opening up my Altered Storage. From it, hundreds of tiny drones emerge. They spin through the air, zooming directly toward the Space Lord. As they fly, they explode with a million watts of lights in all the colors of the rainbow, miniature suns in daylight.

Hondo shifts sideways, darting farther away from me as best he can on one foot, a beam pistol firing from his hip at the Machine Lord. Huquji kicks off, charging us as S'Baxu keeps ups his attacks, the beam pistol doing little to his armor while his own beam weapons and rail cannons churn the earth and burn the air. S'Baxu targets both of us at the same time, throwing firepower with indiscriminate care, like a Mardi Gras floater discarding beads in New Orleans. I twist and jump, my Elemental Affinity tingling as space twists and warps, a new Spatial Prison almost catching me. Perhaps the blinding lights slowed her down, or perhaps just luck. I trigger my Haste and Thousand Steps spell, speeding up to avoid being targeted again.

Hondo has discarded the beam pistol as he comes to a stop. In his hand is a belt-fed grenade launcher. The deep thump of the rocket-propelled grenades beats through the air, punctuated by the crack of rail pellets breaking the sound barrier. Many of the grenades are intercepted, their payload exploding too soon.

Chaotic energies swirl, some of it creating tantalizing, narcotic-laden smells. Other energies twist time and space in ways that hurt the brain to look at. A rent in reality opens, sucking up air and smoke grenades, then snaps shut a second later. From open air, a squirming whale-like creature is deposited on the ground, its form still crackling with the chaotic energy that brought it to our dimension. Sixty feet long, the blue creature flops, mouth opening and closing in a silent scream. Bullets and beams smash into it, its sudden appearance blocking the Machine Lord's view for a second. The next moment, the blue-whale creature warps, twisting and shrinking as it is caught in the vortex of probability.

In the meantime, I'm throwing Blade Strikes as fast as I can at the Space Lord and flipping my returned throwing knives at the Titan. The enhanced Penetration effects, along with my Skill, are causing the Titan problems, as is the quick-cast Freezing Blade enchantment. The effect hurts the Titan, slowing its mad rush toward me. Strong and resistant to damage the Titan might be, but fast he is not. But I can't afford to stay ahead of him much longer as my Mana bottoms out.

I don't even see the next trap coming. The wall erupts in front of me, forcing me to smash into it. Reinforced via Mana, the spellborn Earthen Wall bounces me backward. Before I can focus and break it, Hurquji shatters my freezing spell and triggers a Charge ability, appearing by my side in a blink of an eye. I barely get my sword in the way before a fey-metal-banded fist slams into me, sending me through the Earthen wall. Only to be pancaked against an even harder Spatial Wall.

My sword is pressed into my body, cutting into my own flesh from the block. My helmet is shattered, my armor broken. Blood runs down my chest even as my vision fades at the edges. An alert flashes across my eye, a simple notification.

Critical Damage Dealt! Status Condition Overridden
You are Stunned! You will not be able to move, use Mana, or react in any way while Stunned.

I try to move, try to shift my body, and fail. I pull at my Mana and I can feel it, sense it, but a wall blocks my way. It's a wall that I know instinctively is created by the System as it overrides my body control, overrides my ability to reach for my Mana. I grunt, straining as the Titan jumps, lands beside me, and shatters the earth beneath his feet. I'm pushed out of my hole and fall to the ground facedown. The first punch takes me from behind, pancaking my nose and breaking my teeth. The next blow cracks my skull, adding another debuff, and shatters cheekbones. Pain encompasses my existence as the debuff renews and Hurquji's attacks override my resistances.

A meaty hand picks me up and turns me around. Blood dribbles down my face, coating my jumpsuit, the cracked helmet doing nothing to stop the flow of blood. Hurquji stares at me, no pity, no mercy, no regret in his eyes as a hand pulls back.

I have no access to Mana. No ability to move my body. Just my mind. And something else. Something not given by the System. In the corner of my pain-filled and shocked mind, I feel it. The connection between Hurquji and me. Between every single being, every single atom in the world. The forces that bind. And loosen.

Just a little prod, a push using something that was given by the System but is not part of it. Not enforced by it. It's a power that is mine and Ali's. I feel the System try to stop me, try to block it, but the power is not part of the System itself. Only categorized, only noted.

I push, and the large, meaty paw that flies toward me misses, flying past my body by inches. I've taken away the friction between myself and the Titan's hand, making me so slippery that I shoot out of his grip like an oiled sardine. As I shoot downward, the Titan's fingers clap shut in surprise. Along the ground I skip, my Elemental Affinity adjusting the friction between the ground and me as I land, sending me moving like a hockey puck on fresh ice. Soon enough, I come to a stop, because even reduced, friction is still in play.

The surprised Titan stalks over to me, my body still paralyzed by the System. "Interesting trick. But not good enough. You're just delaying the inevitable."

I grunt, some of my control over my body returning. A hand, a knee. I push myself upward, forcing my body to act, pitting will against the System and winning. A pitiful victory as my health flashes in the low hundreds, as shattered bones, bloody vision, and crushed organs decry.

"Delay." I cough, watching as the Titan stops, staring at me. "About. Right."

"Do you think there's someone who is going to save you?"

"Behind. You."

Hurquji pauses, eyes darting upward and sideways to look at his own minimap. They widen and he spins around, seeing what I see. Evanline is gone, a bubble of pink and orange where she was. No sound, no light escapes from the bubble. She's gone, and with her, the Dimension Lock. On the other hand, what is happening to the Machine Lord is quite, quite visible, if not audible. S'Baqu is no longer fighting just Hondo but another five individuals, one of whom has a yellow stream of energy connecting him and S'Baqu's armored suit. Even from here, I feel the way power shifts and drains from the suit.

"Hera's scorn!" Hurquji says, eyes widening. The Titan hesitates then raises his hand, attempting to active his Skill. Only to pause and look back at me with wonderous surprise. "You're blocking me?"

"Yes." I'd smile, but it hurts too much to try. The damn Space Lord is not the only one who can lock down a location.

Once I answer, the Titan doesn't hesitate, his fist flashing forward. I finally activate the contingency Shielding ring, and it blocks the attack but sends me flying backward. The Titan isn't expecting me to survive and delays moving for a fraction of a second. A fraction too long. Too late.

By the time Hurquji reaches my prone form, he finds another figure before him. The last arrival to the party. The star of the show.

The Wendigo catches the Titan's fist in his. Even his block is sufficient to bend and warp the fey-steel knuckle dusters.

"I've been looking for you," the Wendigo rumbles, his voice low and bestial. There's a hunger in the voice, a bloodlust I recognize all too well.

"About time," I mutter. Not that anyone's paying attention to me.

The Wendigo and Titan explode into action. The sheer concussive blasts of their fight strip my contingency shield from my body and then, even more of my precious health. I tumble across the ground as the backlash of their battle kicks my body around. I'm saved only by the fact that the pair move their fight away from me, probably unintentionally. As I lie in a pit of churned and broken earth, my body too broken and shattered to move, a figure appears.

"Here. Dri… never mind. I'll get the injector," Harry says.

The reporter drops to his knees and stabs me with a health potion It's a lesser health potion, offering only a few tens of health points, but it's the best we can do. Too much more and I'll suffer from the effects of overuse. Instead, Harry channels a healing spell into my body.

I stare at the man for a second, taking in the double, triplicate forms of him that fade in and out. I want to ask about the fights, about how many more we can expect. About the Uttu. And Mikito. But the part of me that knows this fight is over, that my part is done, pulls the darkness in the corners of my vision close. It wraps me up in comforting numbness and dismisses that harsh mistress consciousness.

***

The System is so messed up. In twenty minutes, I wake up again, my body healed, teeth regrown, bones replaced. There's lingering pain, but it's all in my mind. I know, soon enough, that even that will go. The resistances, the System-given abilities, will wipe them away. Making me… functional. A series of notifications from the fight wait in the corner of my vision. My share of the experience for the damage I caused, the deaths here. But I can find no motivation to read them. Not yet at least.

"The fight?" I say as I change out of my torn and blasted clothing.

"Done," Ali says, floating beside me.

I smile slightly, grateful to see the little bastard. Pulling him back earlier outside the edge of her Dimensional Lock meant he could help the others bypass the Space Mage's Skill. "Harry?"

"Getting last-minute interviews."

"Cutting it a little close, weren't you?" I say, sliding on the new skinsuit and hoping that my expensive set fixes itself as advertised. I'm not entirely sure it can, not with the sheer amount of damage it took. Then again, look at me. Fit as a fiddle.

"Wendigo took a bit to get here. Seems like he wasn't watching," Ali says. "Anyway, you guys took too long to take her Mana down."

"Yeah," I say, shaking my head. One of the keys to the fight had been breaking the Space Lord's Off to the Side Skill without her knowing. That, or making her drop it voluntarily. To do that, we needed to reduce her Mana to a point where she would no longer dedicate Mana to reinforcing it, allowing Ali to breach it when I pulled him back into this world. "Things didn't go exactly as planned."

"When have they ever?" Mikito says, walking over to me with her naginata over her shoulder. She looks calmly around the burnt and blasted wasteland that was our battleground before her gaze fixes on a particular spot. "You nearly died there."

"You too."

Mikito shrugs. "Did you know? That they'd all be watching for Harry's next segment?"

"Know? No. We tried to contact them, leave them hints. But there was no way to really know," I say. "If they'd watch. If they'd come."

"You gambled."

My lips twitch. "Revenge is a very universal desire."

Mikito stands in silence for a time before she meets my gaze with her brown eyes. She stares at me, searching for something for long seconds. Eventually, she turns away and walks off.

"Mikito?" I call hesitantly.

"You lead. I follow." When she turns around, her gaze lands on me with a weight that takes my breath away. "That's our deal. Win or lose."

I want to protest that we never discussed that, never agreed. I didn't ask her to come. I didn't ask her to join me. But that's a lie. I assumed she would be here. I took her help without question. I could have left her out of this or trusted her with more details. But I didn't. Not because I didn't trust her, but because in the System, anything said out loud, any information passed on to others is purchasable. I already risked a lot by checking that Harry would broadcast our fight live. Even more when I had Ali ping the previous targets of the Wolves via an intermediary, telling them to watch.

If the Wolves had learned about the trap beforehand, it would have all been for naught. If I had coordinated directly with the victims, I likely would have failed. In truth, if it were not for how passionate Hondo was about dealing with the Wolves, I would never have taken the risk. Yet I could think of no other way to win. And we needed to win.

Because this was just the start.

***

Hours later, we're back with Katherine. The ambassador looks relieved to see us, tension held in her shoulders disappearing. I offer her a half-smile, slumping into one of the proffered chairs while Hondo looks at Mikito and me.

"Thank you," Hondo says.

"Pardon?" I say, sitting up.

Rather than answer, Hondo walks out of the door—heading to see Oria, I'd guess. I stare at the Weaponmaster's back, scratching my head absently, amused to note that he's already got his leg back. Mikito has a wry smile while watching Hondo leave before she turns back toward Katherine and Peter.

"How are things?" I say, the wash of happiness from beating the Wolves now shifting back toward grief as I recall what happened on Earth.

"Stabilizing," Katherine says. "Rob has decided to continue with the program. We have numerous law enforcement personnel scattering planetwide to look for the attackers. A bounty tax has also been instituted planetwide, and that tax is being used to fund quests to deal with the attackers. These quests have also been passed on to any guild willing to take them.

"Rob is looking at what additional tariffs and other penalties we can levy on those we find connected to the attacks. In the meantime, the Galactic immigrants will be concentrated in a few locations that have volunteered to take them. The Duchess's location is one of the prime areas."

I nod, accepting Katherine's words. We might be stabilizing for now, but if the attacks continue, there's no guarantee that Rob will be able to hold the planet together. And while he might not be up for reelection for a few years, ignoring the wants and needs of the settlement owners would be an extremely bad idea.

"Security?" Mikito says, picking up on the unanswered question.

Peter grimaces, but he finally speaks up. "We're looking into a planetary-wide security net and dimensional blocker. And a temporary mercenary corp. The Erethrans have offered to send a fleet of theirs to aid us. For concessions."

"What concessions?" I ask.

"They want New Zealand," Peter says.

"Pardon?"

"The country. They want it all."

Silence descends as I struggle with that idea. I open my mouth, then shut it, then open my mouth again before giving up.

Ali snorts, filling the silence. "Eh, good deal for you guys. Not as if many of their population survived."

"No?" I say. Come to think of it, I never did visit New Zealand.

"Remote island. Lots of monsters. Including a dragon that you all decided to call Smaug for some reason. That lost you a whole city when he found out," Ali says with a sniff. "Really."

"So what? We just take the entire country and give it to the Erethrans?" I frown. That doesn't sound right.

For one thing, I'm not sure it's our land to give. Then again, there are monsters there, and without a high enough population keeping them in check, those monsters will keep getting stronger and stronger. Already the Caribbean is a no-go zone. Between the sheer number of monsters, their strength, and the elementals who have taken residence among the hurricanes, it's a treacherous land. If we leave New Zealand alone too long, it'll just be another lost island.

Still, it sits badly with me.

"In essence, yes. Rob is speaking with their representatives now. The Erethrans have promised to arrive the moment the agreement is made," Katherine says, her eyes tight. She meets my gaze and I can see that we share some of the same feelings. But on the other side of the equation is the simple need for security.

Compromise. Politics is all about compromise. Once again, I'm grateful that I'm not forced to take part in it. Perhaps it's cowardice on my part, but finding that compromise, choosing the least of all evils…

"John?" Peter says, and I blink, looking at the man. "There's something else we need from you."

"Oh?"

"Yes. As you know, this isn't over. Not by a long shot. A large number of those who attacked us on Earth have left the planet already," Peter continues. "And while the guilds might get some of them, the ones who attacked Rob, who attacked Lana, are at least Advanced Classes."

"I see…" I say slowly, leaning back. "You want me to go after them myself."

"Yes. You're out here in the Galaxy already. You're also…" Peter waves toward my Status Screen above my head.

I get it. As one of Earth's few Master Classers, I'm in an enviable position of being able to kick ass. Only leveling fanatics like Mikito are anywhere close to breaking the last Level barrier, and even she would have found it hard to do without the Arena. Out here, in Irvina, where the fights are broadcast over a large area, the potential experience increases from the watchers' tithe is significant.

Even so, for all the allusions that we have made, what Peter is asking me to do is to be Earth's hitman. Their Galactic bounty hunter. It might leave me free to set my own hours, but Katherine at the least knows I'm not one to do things halfway. If I agree, my time researching quietly is gone.

If I don't…

A memory of friends in a city by the water. Of a lonely mountain range where I woke up over five years ago. A lake and blue boxes that changed my world. Strewn corpses. Laughing faces. And I know, for certain, that more will be lost. If I refuse, I open Earth up to reprisals. Even if I agree, I leave them open. But at least they'll know that anyone, anything going after Earth will face me at some point.

"Mikito?" I say softly, looking at the Japanese woman.

"You lead. I follow," Mikito says simply.

I feel that burden sink further onto my shoulders, my chest tightening as she lays it on me. She sits there, weighing me, judging me by her very presence. Asking me to live up to that level of faith she has shown me.

I shut my eyes, the weight of the responsibility that I tried to set aside pressing down once again. Pushing against my forced indolence, past my reserve. It strikes at the core of who I am, who I had to become to survive. I'm back standing over a mass grave, a cooking pot. Lying on the ground as the rain washes over me. As I stand in a forest of crosses.

"Damn it."

I open my eyes to Peter then Katherine, seeing the pity in their gazes. Pity but no mercy. Katherine knows exactly what she is asking of me, and still, she asks.

"Fine."

I stand and walk away without a goodbye. I'm sure they'll send me the information. Send me the details of those who need killing. And then. Well, then I guess I do what I do.

Chapter 19

A week later, we're headed up the beanstalk again, leaving the city. A week. To train. To recuperate. To study and learn. To run the dungeons until Mikito could gain enough experience to Level up. At that thought, I turn my head and stare at my friend, taking in her new Class.

Mikito Sato, Spear of Humanity, Blood Warden, Junior Arena Champion of Irvina (Upper Samurai Level 1) (M)

*HP: 2311/2311**

*MP: 1681/1681**

Conditions: Isoide, Jin, Rei, Meiyo, Ishiki, Ryoyo, Feudal Bond

Galactic Reputation: 16

Galactic Fame: 6,998

My lips press together as I feel once more that weight of expectation and responsibility she has laid on me. I shake my head even as I call forth the Skill.

Feudal Bond (Level 1)

The Samurai is nothing without her master. The master is nothing without loyal servants. The Feudal Bond is a metaphysical representation of this relationship. This Skill provides strength to the Samurai derived from her master. However, this Skill is only in effect so long as the feudal status is in effect between the involved parties. Mana Regeneration reduced by 5 permanently.

Effect: User gains 5% of target master's attributes.

I sigh, shaking my head. I feel a bit of dread over exploring exactly what this new Skill means and what messed up view of samurai the System has. An alien entity, borrowing on public consciousness and viewpoint, creating an exclusive prestige Class. How could that go wrong?

"John?" Mikito says, alerting me to the fact that I've been staring at her.

I flush, shaking my head, and turn aside. That's a can of worms I'll deal with another time. For now, it's good enough to know that Mikito will be a much, much more powerful aide.

We're going to need it.

For a moment, I glance at my own Status. The fight had not produced much in terms of loot as the other attackers had taken everything. But the experience gain from fighting and defeating three Master Classers, even shared, was significant. Enough so that I've gone up another Level and a bit, putting me at Level 28 and giving me another Skill point. I'm holding off on using it as I consider my best options. Aspects of that battle made me deeply unhappy, so I want to run through my options a few more times before I commit.

We've spent a week training, healing, and waiting. Waiting for Harry to get back. To get the right ship. A week, and now we're off. As we stand on the platform, heading up the beanstalk, the three of us stare at the disappearing city, its massive size soon lost in the clouds. No more Galactic center, no more quiet reading. I have books downloaded, along with a better idea of what to study by myself. Information has been saved, some questions answered. New ones formed. But the world we are in has little time or space for a scholarly Paladin. Not yet.

I'll be back. There is more to learn, more to understand.

For now, there are rights to wrong. Killers who have run. People in power who think they are untouchable. Groups that think because they're so big, they cannot fall.

For now, it's time to get back to work. I look up, watching as we breach the cloud cover, and spot the station that looms above and the stars behind it. The numerous ships that wait, one of which is ready to take us away.

To the people waiting to be killed.

For now, it's time to go.

###

The End

John and friends will return in

Rebel Star (Book 8 of the System Apocalypse)

Author's Note

Stars Awoken is the first book in the new Galactic arc. This book was a bit of a struggle to write as my patrons know, mostly because I kept vacillating on how I was going to write this. In the end, I ended up deleting over forty five thousand words and rewriting entire arcs before I was happy with this book. Some of that material will end up in book eight, Rebel Star, which might make the third arc four books long instead of three. This is also the penultimate arc, one that will contextualize and explore Galactic space more before we approach the end game.

As always, I'm grateful for everyone who has followed me on this long, long journey. I hope you have enjoyed John's journey and the ever-expanding world. If you enjoyed reading the book, please do leave a review and rating.

Follow John's continuing quest in:

-   Rebel Star (Book 8 of the System Apocalypse)
    https://readerlinks.com/l/960891

In addition, please check out my other series, Adventures on Brad (a more traditional LitRPG fantasy), Hidden Wishes (an urban fantasy GameLit series), and A Thousand Li (a cultivation series inspired by Chinese wuxia and xianxia novels).

To support me directly, please go to my Patreon account:

-   https://www.patreon.com/taowong

For more great information about LitRPG series, check out the Facebook groups:

- LitRPG Society

  https://www.facebook.com/groups/LitRPGsociety/
- LitRPG Books

  https://www.facebook.com/groups/LitRPG.books/

About the Author

Tao Wong is an avid fantasy and sci-fi reader who spends his time working and writing in the North of Canada. He's spent way too many years doing martial arts of many forms, and having broken himself too often, he now spends his time writing about fantasy worlds.

For updates on the series and other books written by Tao Wong (and special one-shot stories), please visit the author's website:
    http://www.mylifemytao.com

Subscribers to Tao's mailing list will receive exclusive access to short stories in the Thousand Li and System Apocalypse universes:
    https://www.subscribepage.com/taowong

Or visit his Facebook Page: https://www.facebook.com/taowongauthor/

About the Publisher

Starlit Publishing is wholly owned and operated by Tao Wong. It is a science fiction and fantasy publisher focused on the LitRPG & cultivation genres. Their focus is on promoting new, upcoming authors in the genre whose writing challenges the existing stereotypes while giving a rip-roaring good read.

For more information on Starlit Publishing, visit their website: https://www.starlitpublishing.com/

You can also join Starlit Publishing's mailing list to learn of new, exciting authors and book releases.
https://starlitpublishing.com/newsletter-signup/

Glossary

Erethran Honor Guard Skill Tree

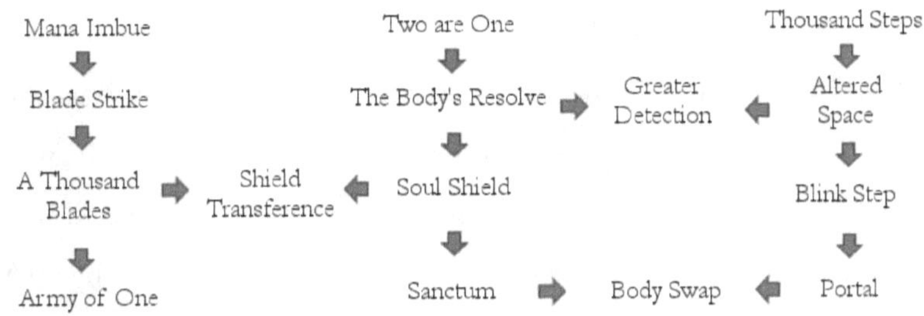

John's Erethran Honor Guard Skills

Mana Imbue (Level 3)

Soulbound weapon now permanently imbued with mana to deal more damage on each hit. +20 Base Damage (Mana). Will ignore armor and resistances. Mana regeneration reduced by 15 Mana per minute permanently.

Blade Strike (Level 3)

By projecting additional Mana and stamina into a strike, the Erethran Honor Guard's Soulbound weapon may project a strike up to 30 feet away.

Cost: 30 Stamina + 30 Mana

Thousand Steps (Level 1)

Movement speed for the Honor Guard and allies are increased by 5% while skill is active. This ability is stackable with other movement-related skills.

Cost: 20 Stamina + 20 Mana per minute

Altered Space (Level 2)

The Honor Guard now has access to an extra-dimensional storage location of 30 cubic meters. Items stored must be touched to be willed in and may not include living creatures or items currently affected by auras that are not the Honor Guard's. Mana regeneration reduced by 10 Mana per minute permanently.

Two are One (Level 1)

Effect: Transfer 10% of all damage from Target to Self

Cost: 5 Mana per second

The Body's Resolve (Level 3)

Effect: Increase natural health regeneration by 35%. On-going health status effects reduced by 33%. Honor Guard may now regenerate lost limbs. Mana regeneration reduced by 15 Mana per minute permanently.

Greater Detection (Level 1)

Effect: User may now detect System creatures up to 1 kilometer away. General information about strength level is provided on detection. Stealth skills, Class skills, and ambient mana density will influence the effectiveness of this skill. Mana regeneration reduced by 5 Mana per minute permanently.

A Thousand Blades (Level 3)

Creates four duplicate copies of the user's designated weapon. Duplicate copies deal base damage of copied items. May be combined with Mana Imbue and Shield Transference. Mana Cost: 3 Mana per second

Soul Shield (Level 2)

Effect: Creates a manipulable shield to cover the caster's or target's body. Shield has 1,000 Hit Points.

Cost: 250 Mana

Blink Step (Level 2)

Effect: Instantaneous teleportation via line-of-sight. May include Spirit's line of sight. Maximum range—500 meters.

Cost: 100 Mana

Portal (Level 5)

Effect: Creates a 5-meter by 5-meter portal which can connect to a previously traveled location by user. May be used by others. Maximum distance range of portals is 10,000 kilometers.

Cost: 250 Mana + 100 Mana per minute (minimum cost 350 Mana)

Army of One (Level 2)

The Honor Guard's feared penultimate combat ability, Army of One builds upon previous Skills, allowing the user to unleash an awe-inspiring attack to deal with their enemies. Attack may now be guided around minor obstacles.

Effect: Army of One allows the projection of (Number of Thousand Blades conjured weapons * 3) Blade Strike attacks up to 300 meters away from user. Each attack deals 3 * Blade Strike Level damage (inclusive of Mana Imbue and Soulbound weapon bonus)

Cost: 750 Mana

Sanctum (Level 2)

An Erethran Honor Guard's ultimate trump card in safeguarding their target, Sanctum creates a flexible shield that blocks all incoming attacks, hostile teleportations and Skills. At this Level of Skill, the user must specify dimensions of the Sanctum upon use of the Skill. The Sanctum cannot be moved while the Skill is activated.

Dimensions: Maximum 15 cubic meters.

Cost: 1,000 Mana

Duration: 2 minute and 7 seconds

Paladin of Erethra Skill Tree

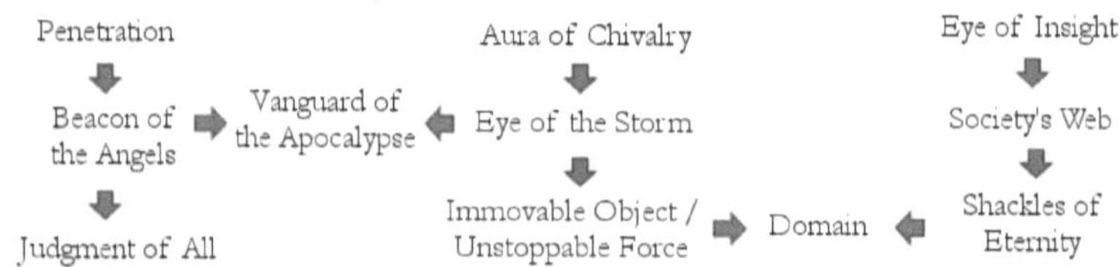

John's Paladin of Erethra Skills

Class Skill: Penetration (Level 3)

Few can face the judgment of a Paladin in direct combat, their ability to bypass even the toughest of defenses a frightening prospect. Reduces Mana Regeneration by 10 permanently.

Effect: Ignore all armor and defensive spells by 60%. Increases damage done to shields by 120%.

Class Skill: Aura of Chivalry (Level 1)

A Paladin's very presence can quail weak-hearted enemies and bolster the confidence of allies, whether on the battlefield or in court. The Aura of Chivalry is a double-edged sword however, focusing attention on the Paladin—potentially to their detriment. Increases success rate of Perception checks against Paladin by 10% and reduces stealth and related skills by 10% while active. Reduces Mana Regeneration by 5 Permanently.

Effect: All enemies must make a Willpower check against intimidation against user's Charisma. Failure to pass the check will cow enemies. All allies gain a 50% boost in morale for all Willpower checks and a 10% boost in confidence and probability of succeeding in relevant actions.

Note: Aura may be activated or left-off at will.

Beacon of the Angels (Level 2)

User calls down an atmospheric strike from the heavens, dealing damage over a wide area to all enemies within the beacon. The attack takes time to form, but once activated need not be concentrated upon for completion.

Effect: 1000 Mana Damage done to all enemies, structures and vehicles within the maximum 25 meter column of attack

Mana Cost: 500 Mana

Eyes of Insight (Level 1)

Under the eyes of a Paladin, all untruth and deceptions fall away. Only when the Paladin can see with clarity may he be able to judge effectively.

Reduces Mana Regeneration by 5.

Effect: All Skills, Spells and abilities of a lower grade that obfuscate, hinder or deceive the Paladin are reduced in effectiveness. Level of reduction proportionate to degree of difference in grade and Skill Level.

Eye of the Storm (Level 1)

In the middle of the battlefield, the Paladin stands, seeking justice and offering judgment on all enemies. The winds of war will seek to draw both enemies and allies to you, their cruel flurries robbing enemies of their lives and bolstering the health and Mana of allies.

Effect: Eye of the Storm is an area effect buff and taunt. Psychic winds taunt enemies, forcing a Mental Resistance check to avoid attacking user. Enemies also receive 5 points of damage per second while within the influence of the Skill, with damage decreasing from the epicenter of the Skill. Allies receive a 5% increase in Mana and Health regeneration, decrease in effectiveness from Skill center. Eye of the Storm affects an area of 50 meters around the user.

Cost: 500 Mana + 20 Mana per second

Vanguard of the Apocalypse (Level 2)

Where others flee, the Paladin strides forward. Where the brave dare not advance, the Paladin charges. While the world burns, the Paladin still fights. The Paladin with this Skill is the vanguard of any fight, leading the charge against all of Erethra's enemies.

Effect: +45 to all Physical attributes, increases speed by 55% and recovery rates by 35%. This Skill is stackable on top of other attribute and speed boosting Skills or spells.

Cost: 500 Mana + 10 Stamina per second

Society's Web (Level 1)

Where the Eye of Insight provides the Paladin an understanding of the lies and mistruths told, Society's Web shows the Paladin the intricate webs that tie individuals to one another. No alliance, no betrayal, no tangled web of lies will be hidden as each interaction weaves one another closer. While the Skill provides no detailed information, a skilled Paladin can infer much from the Web.

Effect: Upon activation, the Paladin will see all threads that tie each individual to one another and automatically understand the details of each thread when focused upon.

Cost: 400 Mana + 200 Mana per minute

Other Class Skills

Frenzy (Level 1)

Effect: When activated, pain is reduced by 80%, damage increased by 30%, stamina regeneration rate increased by 20%. Mana regeneration rate decreased by 10%

Frenzy will not deactivate until all enemies have been slain. User may not retreat while Frenzy is active.

Cleave (Level 2)

Effect: Physical attacks deal 60% more base damage. Effect may be combined with other Class Skills.

Cost: 25 Mana

Elemental Strike (Level 1 - Ice)

Effect: Used to imbue a weapon with freezing damage. Adds +5 Base Damage to attacks and a 10% chance of reducing speed by 5% upon contact. Lasts for 30 seconds.

Cost: 50 Mana

Instantaneous Inventory (Maxed)

Allows user to place or remove any System-recognized item from Inventory if space allows. Includes the automatic arrangement of space in the inventory. User must be touching item.

Cost: 5 Mana per item

Shrunken Footsteps (Level 1)

Reduces System presence of user, increasing the chance of the user evading detection of System-assisted sensing Skills and equipment. Also increases cost of information purchased about user. Reduces Mana Regeneration by 5 permanently.

Tech Link (Level 2)

Effect: Tech Link allows user to increase their skill level in using a technological item, increasing input and versatility in usage of said items. Effects vary depending on item. General increase in efficiency of 10%. Mana regeneration rate decreased by 10%

Designated Technological Items: Neural Link, Sabre

Analyze (Level 2)

Allows user to scan individuals, monsters, and System-registered objects to gather information registered with the System. Detail and level of accuracy of information is dependent on Level and any Skills or Spells in conflict with the ability. Reduces Mana regeneration by 10 permanently.

Harden (Level 2)

This Skill reinforces targeted defenses and actively weakens incoming attacks to reduce their penetrating power. A staple Skill of the Turtle Knights of Kiumma, the Harden Skill has frustrated opponents for millennia.

Effect: Reduces penetrative effects of attacks by 30% on targeted defense.

Cost: 3 Mana per second

Quantum Lock (Level 3)

A staple Skill of the M453-X Mecani-assistants, Quantum Lock blocks stealth attacks and decreases the tactical options of their enemies. While active, the Quantum Lock of the Mecani-assistants excites quantum strings in the affected area for all individuals and Skills.

Effect: All teleportation, portal, and dimensional Skills and Spells are disrupted while Quantum Lock is in effect. Forceable use of Skills and Spells while Skill is in effect will result in (Used Skill Mana Cost * 4) health in damage. Users may pay a variable amount of additional Mana when activating the Skill to decrease effect of Quantum Lock and decrease damage taken.

Requirements: 200 Willpower, 200 Intelligence

Area of Effect: 100 meter radius around user

Cost: 250 + 50 Mana per Minute

Elastic Skin (Level 3)

Elastic Skin is a permanent alteration, allowing the user to receive and absorb a small portion of damage. Damage taken reduced by 7% with 7% of damage absorbed converted to Mana. Mana Regeneration reduced by 15 permanently.

Spells

Improved Minor Healing (IV)

Effect: Heals 40 Health per casting. Target must be in contact during healing. Cooldown 60 seconds.

Cost: 20 Mana

Improved Mana Missile (IV)

Effect: Creates four missiles out of pure Mana, which can be directed to damage a target. Each dart does 30 damage. Cooldown 10 seconds

Cost: 35 Mana

Enhanced Lightning Strike

Effect: Call forth the power of the gods, casting lightning. Lightning strike may affect additional targets depending on proximity, charge and other conductive materials on-hand. Does 100 points of electrical damage. Lightning Strike may be continuously channeled to increase damage for 10 additional damage per second.

Cost: 75 Mana.

Continuous cast cost: 5 Mana / second

Lightning Strike may be enhanced by using the Elemental Affinity of Electromagnetic Force. Damage increased by 20% per level of affinity

Greater Regeneration (II)

Effect: Increases natural health regeneration of target by 6%. Only single use of spell effective on a target at a time.

Duration: 10 minutes

Cost: 100 Mana

Firestorm

Effect: Create a firestorm with a radius of 5 meters. Deals 250 points of fire damage to those caught within. Cooldown 60 seconds.

Cost: 200 Mana

Polar Zone

Effect: Create a thirty meter diameter blizzard that freezes all targets within one. Does 10 points of freezing damage per minute plus reduces effected individuals speed by 5%. Cooldown 60 seconds.

Cost: 200 Mana

Greater Healing (II)

Effect: Heals 100 Health per casting. Target does not require contact during healing. Cooldown 60 seconds per target.

Cost: 75 Mana

Mana Drip (II)

Effect: Increases natural health regeneration of target by 6%. Only single use of spell effective on a target at a time.

Duration: 10 minutes

Cost: 100 Mana

Freezing Blade

Effect: Enchants weapon with a slowing effect. A 5% slowing effect is applied on a successful strike. This effect is cumulative and lasts for 1 minute. Cooldown 3 minutes

Spell Duration: 1 minute.

Cost: 150 Mana

Improved Inferno Strike (II)

A beam of heat raised to the levels of an inferno, able to melt steel and earth on contact! The perfect spell for those looking to do a lot of damage in a short period of time.

Effect: Does 200 Points of Heat Damage

Cost: 150 Mana

Mud Walls

Unlike its more common counterpart Earthen Walls, Mud Walls focus is more on dealing slow, suffocating damage and restricting movement on the battlefield.

Effect: Does 20 Points of Suffocating Damage. -30% Movement Speed

Duration: 2 Minutes

Cost: 75 Mana

Create Water

Pulls water from the elemental plane of water. Water is pure and the highest form of water available. Conjures 1 liter of water. Cooldown: 1 minute

Cost: 50 Mana

Scry

Allows caster to view a location up to 1.7 kilometers away. Range may be extended through use of additional Mana. Caster will be stationary during this period. It is recommended caster focuses on the scry unless caster has a high level of Intelligence and Perception so as to avoid accidents. Scry may be blocked by equivalent or higher tier spells and Skills. Individuals with high perception in region of Scry may be alerted that the Skill is in use. Cooldown: 1 hour.

Cost: 25 Mana per minute.

Scrying Ward

Blocks scrying spells and their equivalent within 5 meters of caster. Higher level spells may not be blocked, but caster may be alerted about scrying attempts. Cooldown: 10 minutes

Cost: 50 Mana per minute

Improved Invisibility

Hides target's System information, aura, scent, and visual appearance. Effectiveness of spell is dependent upon Intelligence of caster and any Skills or Spells in conflict with the target.

Cost: 100 + 50 Mana per minute

Improved Mana Cage

While physically weaker than other elemental-based capture spells, Mana Cage has the advantage of being able to restrict all creatures, including semi-solid Spirits, conjured elementals, shadow beasts, and Skill users. Cooldown: 1 minute

Cost: 200 Mana + 75 Mana per minute

Improved Flight

(Fly birdie, fly! - Ali) This spell allows the user to defy gravity, using controlled bursts of Mana to combat gravity and allow the user to fly in even the most challenging of situations. The improved version of this spell allows flight even in zero gravity situations and a higher level of maneuverability. Cooldown: 1 minute

Cost: 250 Mana + 100 Mana per minute

Equipment

Silversmith Jeupa VII Anti-Personnel Cannon (Modified & Upgraded)

This quad-barrelled anti-personnel weapon has been handcrafted by Advanced Weaponsmiths to provide the highest integration possible for an energy weapon. This particular weapon has been modified to include additional range-finding and sighting options and upgraded to increase short-term damage output at the cost of long-term durability. Barrels may be fired individually or linked.

Base Damage: 787 per barrel

Battery Capacity: 4 per barrel (16 total)

Recharge Rate: 0.25 per hour per GMU

Ares Platinum Class Tier II Armored Jumpsuit

Ares's signature Platinum Class line of armored daily wear combines the company's latest technological advancement in nanotech fiber design and the pinnacle work of an Advanced Craftsman's Skill to provide unrivalled protection for the discerning Adventurer.

Effect: +218 Defense, +14% Resistance to Kinetic and Energy Attacks. +19% Resistance against Temperature changes. Self-Cleanse, Self-Mend, Autofit Enchantments also included.

Silversmith Mark II Beam Pistol (Upgradeable)

Base Damage: 18

Battery Capacity: 24/24

Recharge Rate: 2 per hour per GMU

Tier IV Neural Link

Neural link may support up to 5 connections.

Current connections: Omnitron III Class II Personal Assault Vehicle

Software Installed: Rich'lki Firewall Class IV, Omnitron III Class IV Controller

Ferlix Type II Twinned-Beam Rifle (Modified)

Base Damage: 57

Battery Capacity: 17/17

Recharge rate: 1 per hour per GMU (currently 12)

Tier II Sword (Soulbound Personal Weapon of an Erethran Honor Guard)

Base Damage: 307

Durability: N/A (Personal Weapon)

Special Abilities: +20 Mana Damage, Blade Strike

Kryl Ring of Regeneration

Often used as betrothal bands, Kyrl rings are highly sought after and must be ordered months in advance.

Health Regeneration: +30

Stamina Regeneration: +15

Mana Regeneration: +5

Tier III Bracer of Mana Storage

A custom work by an unknown maker, this bracer acts a storage battery for personal Mana. Useful for Mages and other Classes that rely on Mana. Mana storage ratio is 50 to 1.

Mana Capacity: 350/350

Fey-steel Dagger

Fey-steel is not actual steel but an unknown alloy. Normally reserved only for the Sidhe nobility, a small—by Galactic standards—amount of Fey-steel is released for sale each year. Fey-steel takes enchantments extremely well.

Base Damage: 28

Durability: 110/100

Special Abilities: None

Enchanted, Reinforced Toothy Throwing Knives (5)

First handcrafted from the rare drop of a Level 140 Awakened Beast by the Redeemer of the Dead, John Lee, these knives have been further processed by the Master Craftsmen I-24-988L and reinforced with orichalcum and fey-steel. The final blades have been further enchanted with Mana and piercing damage as well as a return enchantment.

Base Damage: 238

Enchantments: Return, Mana Blade (+28 Damage), Pierce (-7% defense)

Brumwell Necklace of Shadow Intent

The Brumwell necklace of shadow intent is the hallmark item of the Brumwell Clan. Enchanted by a Master Crafter, this necklace layers shadowy intents over your actions, ensuring that information about your actions are more difficult to ascertain. Ownership of such an item is both a necessity and a mark of prestige among settlement owners and other individuals of power.

Effect: Persistent effect of Shadow Intent (Level 4) results in significantly increased cost of purchasing information from the System about wearer. Effect is persistent for all actions taken while necklace is worn.

Ring of Greater Shielding

Creates a greater shield that will absorb approximately 1000 points of damage. This shield will ignore all damage that does not exceed its threshold amount of 50 points of damage while still functioning.

Max Duration: 7 Minutes

Charges: 1

Simalax Hover Boots (Tier II)

A combination of hand-crafted materials and mass produced components, the Simalax Hover Boots are the journeyman work of Magi-Technician Lok of Irvina. Enchantments and technology mesh together in the Simalax Hover Boots, offering its wearer the ability to tread on air briefly and defy gravity and sense.

Effects: User reduces gravitational effects by 0.218 SIG. User may, on activation, hover and skate during normal and mildly turbulent atmospheric conditions. User may also use the Simalax Hover Boots to triple jump in the air, engaging the anti-gravity and hover aspects at the same time.

Duration: 1.98 SI Hours.

F'Merc Nanoswarm Mana Grenades (Tier II)

The F'Merc Nanoswarm Grenades are guaranteed to disrupt the collection of Mana in a battlefield, reducing Mana Regeneration rates for those caught in the swarm. Recommended by the I'um military, the Torra Special Forces and the No.1 Most Popular Mana Grenade as voted by the public on Boom, Boom, Boom! Magazine.

Effect: Reduces Mana Regeneration rates and spell formation in affected area by 37% ((higher effects in enclosed areas)

Radius: 10m x 10m